Some Lucky Day

Some Lucky Day is Ellie Dean's seventh novel. She lives in a tiny hamlet set deep in the heart of the South Downs in Sussex, which has been h̶e̶r̶ ̶h̶o̶m̶e̶ for many years and where she raised her three children. To find out more visit www.ellie-dean.co.uk

Some Lucky Day

Ellie Dean

arrow books

Published by Arrow Books 2014

2 4 6 8 10 9 7 5 3 1

First published in Great Britain in 2014 by
Arrow Books
Random House, 20 Vauxhall Bridge Road,
London SW1V 2SA

www.randomhouse.co.uk

Addresses for companies within The Random House Group Limited can be found at:
www.randomhouse.co.uk/offices.htm

The Random House Group Limited Reg. No. 954009

A CIP catalogue record for this book
is available from the British Library

ISBN 9780099585299 (Paperback)
ISBN 9781448165261 (eBook)

The Random House Group Limited supports the Forest Stewardship Council® (FSC®),
the leading international forest-certification organisation. Our books carrying the FSC
label are printed on FSC®-certified paper. FSC is the only forest-certification scheme
supported by the leading environmental organisations, including Greenpeace. Our paper
procurement policy can be found at www.randomhouse.co.uk/environment

Typeset in Palatino by Palimpsest Book Production Limited,
Falkirk, Stirlingshire

Printed and bound by CPI Group (UK) Ltd, Croydon, CR0 4YY

There were 166 women pilots in the ATA (Air Transport Auxiliary). This book is dedicated to all of them, but especially to the fifteen who gave their lives in the service of this country. They were extraordinary women who rose to the challenges of an extraordinary time and proved they were more than worthy of being called heroes.

Acknowledgements

During my research into the background history of the ATA (Air Transport Auxiliary), I was delighted to discover the Maidenhead Heritage Centre which proved to be a treasure trove of uniforms, log books, charts, diaries, letters and photographs. I spent a lovely day delving through all these delights, and probably could have stayed a whole week without getting even mid-way through this lovingly amassed collection.

But the really fun experience was climbing into the Spitfire simulator and charting a flight from Maidenhead to Hastings, and then executing two victory rolls and looping the loop before following the coastline and landing safely – if a bit erratically – on the grassy runway of Shoreham airfield. I now have a certificate to say that this Granny flew a Spitfire!

My thanks go to Ian Runnalls who was my flight instructor, and to David Horton who shared some of his vast knowledge of the ATA with me and never tired of answering my questions. Thank you too to Richard who was manning the reception desk, and to my husband Ollie, who drove me there through the teeming rain without getting lost. My research could not have been completed without the help of these unpaid volunteers – although I did buy Ollie some lunch in the lovely little café in Maidenhead library.

I also want to thank Jean Relf for entrusting me with the precious letters, aerographs and diaries that her father, Pte Ken Fowler, wrote during his time in REME (Royal Electrical and Mechanical Engineers) when he was posted to the Far East. They have provided me with a great sense of the time and the attitudes of the people during the war, and have been an enormous help.

Background to the ATA

Churchill realised that only a vast superiority in the air could win the war. To this end, he sent a note to Sir Charles Craven, Secretary of State for Air, under the command, 'Action this day', demanding the creation of an Air Force twice the strength of the Germans' Luftwaffe.

Following this order, a gigantic chain of production was set in motion. The initial cost of producing this enormous number of aircraft was met by the Lend Lease loans signed by President Roosevelt, and this continued until the attack on Pearl Harbor rendered the question of payment secondary and brought an end to America's neutrality. Combat pilots were now queuing up to join the RAF, but there was a severe shortage of ferry pilots to deliver planes and men to where they were needed.

Gerard 'Pop' d'Erlanger was a merchant banker, private pilot and director of BOAC (now British Airways), who had been concerned at the start of hostilities with Germany that this shortage would happen if flyers like himself could not be used. Having informed Balfour of his concerns back in May 1938, he'd suggested forming a reservist Air

Force, made up of holders of private licences with at least two hundred and fifty hours in the air, but who were ineligible to join the RAF. He envisaged that this civilian Air Transport Auxiliary unit would be an aerial courier service for VIPs, medicines and the wounded, and thereby release the combat pilots to continue their defence of the country. It soon became clear that the ferrying of aircraft between factories, maintenance units and front-line squadrons was to be the unit's main task.

Permission was given and a thousand private licence holders were contacted. One hundred replied and in September 1939, thirty were selected to join the elite ATA unit after interviews and flight tests held at the British Airways wartime base at Whitchurch outside Bristol. This first intake jokingly called themselves the 'Ancient and Tattered Airmen', for they were made up of oddballs, intellectuals, artists, bank managers, civil servants, wounded veterans – some with missing limbs or poor eyesight – publicans, a motorcycle racing champion and even a retired admiral.

Some other recruits enlisted at the same time provoked consternation in the top brass in the RAF. Numbering eight, and including the famous aviatrix Amy Johnson, a group of women pilots was marshalled by Pauline Gower, the ambitious daughter of Sir Robert Gower MP, and led into the air by the imperious Lettice Curtis against great resistance from the RAF. Having learned to fly before the war made them an elite within an elite, but like the men in the ATA, they were never formally attached to RAF units and were based in their own all-civilian pools and funded by BOAC for the first few war years. As their numbers swelled, their nickname soon became the 'Always Terrified Airwomen', but they were to prove they were far more formidable than their 'Ancient and Tattered' male counterparts.

The RAF considered women to be temperamentally or physically unworthy of the privilege of flying operational aircraft, and would allow them only to fly the open cockpit de Havilland Moths, and later, Miles Magisters. It took two years of determined canvassing by these women and their supporters before they were permitted to fly fighter planes – and five before they were allowed to fly them to Europe.

These pioneering women pilots came mostly from titled or wealthy families and knew each other, not only through school and high society debutante circles, but from Stag Lane, Heston and Brooklands, which were London's most famous pre-war flying clubs.

They were a tight-knit, exclusive group, with cut-glass accents and rather autocratic attitudes that later women recruits from America, Poland, Chile, Argentina and Australia were to find daunting. The society editors of the *Daily Sketch* and the *Picture Post* loved these 'It Girls' who were doing their bit, but there was nothing superficial about their courage or motivation, for they were possessors of inner steel and a fierce, unspoken patriotism.

During the war, the men and women of the ATA ferried a total of 309,000 aircraft of 147 types, without radios, with no instrument flying instruction, no weapons, and at the mercy of not only barrage balloons, ack-ack fire and enemy attack, but the awful British weather.

In 1943 the women pilots were granted the unprecedented privilege of equal pay with the men of equal rank, but official British government recognition didn't come until September 2008, when all surviving veterans were awarded a special Veterans Badge in a ceremony at 10 Downing Street.

Chapter One

Pilot Officer Kitty Pargeter was just twenty-one,
but at the moment she felt like a small schoolgirl
up before her headmistress. The humiliation
burned in her face as she stood to attention next
to her best friend Charlotte Bingham and withstood
the angry tirade from Marion Wilberforce, the
Commanding Officer of Cosford Ferry Pool. There
was nothing she or Charlotte could possibly say
in their defence, for they were guilty as charged.
As this was not the first time they'd been carpeted
over their high jinks, she knew that a wrong word
now could easily bring the wrath of God on both
their heads.

Marion Wilberforce eyed them coldly. 'This is the
third time in the last eleven months that you've been
caught flying dangerously,' she said in tones that
could freeze the ears off a polar bear. 'You are *not*
part of a barnstorming air display team – neither
are you here for your own entertainment. The
aircraft entrusted to your care is vital to the war

1

effort, and performing barrel rolls and looping the loop is not only putting your aircraft at risk, but is damaging to the unit's reputation.'

Kitty's nape tingled from her icy glare, and she hardly dared to breathe as the older woman continued her tirade.

'It simply isn't good enough,' Marion snapped. 'We had enough difficulty in persuading the RAF top brass to let us fly their fighter planes in the first place. This sort of thing only gives them an excuse to expound on their theory that hare-brained women shouldn't be allowed anywhere near their precious aircraft. And at this very moment, I have to say that I'm inclined to agree with them.'

Kitty flinched at this. She was very well aware of the Air Force's misogynist view on female pilots, and was horrified that any woman should ever agree with it. Marion Wilberforce must be very angry indeed to say such a thing, for she had been one of the first eight pioneering women who had set up the women's unit of the ATA in the face of huge opposition from the RAF.

Kitty had been accepted into the ATA on her nineteenth birthday in the spring of 1940 and had been part of that same struggle to be recognised as capable and worthy of flying RAF fighter planes as well as the smaller trainer and communication planes. The battle to be permitted to fly the four-engine, heavy bombers was still ongoing, and the thought that her brief moments of grandstanding might damage everything they had strived for was shaming. Now she deeply regretted showing off.

If only she could learn to rein in the natural exuberance and competitiveness that always got her into trouble, she might actually save herself – and others – a lot of bother. But it was a failing she'd had since childhood, spurred on by her hero worship of her older brother Freddy and the determination to match – or better him – in everything. It was why she'd learned to fly in the first place.

The silence in the room was heavy, and Kitty could hear the drum of her pulse as those cold eyes settled on her again.

'Well? What do you have to say for yourselves?'

'I am sorry,' Kitty replied, echoing Charlotte's heartfelt apology. 'It was my fault entirely, so please don't blame Charlotte. And I promise I've learned my lesson and won't do it again,' she added in a rush.

Marion's lips twisted in disbelief. 'You seem to have made that promise before, Pargeter, and then you flew a Spitfire under the Severn Bridge. Twice.'

Kitty flushed scarlet and couldn't meet her gaze.

'It's time both of you took things seriously,' Marion continued sternly. 'Your boisterous behaviour is unacceptable, Pargeter. And Bingham – you should know better than to follow her lead.'

Both girls remained silent as the CO took a sharp,

impatient breath and then clasped her hands together on the open folders in front of her. 'You, Pargeter, were fortunate enough to be awarded a full scholarship to one of England's finest girls' schools, where the bywords are discipline, duty and decorum. I'm sure your parents would be most distressed to hear that those cornerstone lessons have gone unheeded.'

Kitty felt the colour drain from her face. 'Please don't write and tell my parents, ma'am,' she begged. 'I'm ashamed enough already, and I couldn't bear it if my behaviour caused them any upset.'

Marion closed the folders and rapped them forcefully on the desk to get the papers aligned with the cardboard covers. 'Perhaps you should have thought of that before you risked life, limb and Mosquito in an attempt to show off to the Americans,' she said briskly. 'These reports will be sent to your Commanding Officer, Margot Gore, at Hamble Pool, and entered into your service records. Rest assured, you are both treading a very fine line, and one more incident like this will mean instant dismissal.'

Kitty swallowed the lump in her throat as she heard the gasp of horror from Charlotte. Flying was their passion, and the chance to be a part of this elite, pioneering unit was something they'd both dreamed of since hearing about its formation in 1939. To lose their hard-won places now would be to lose everything.

Marion stood and tugged at the hem of her Savile Row tailored Air Force blue uniform jacket, making the gold braid epaulettes gleam in the lamplight. 'You're both good, naturally instinctive flyers, and despite your youth and woeful lack of restraint, you have the ability to become great pilots. Don't risk everything with your madcap tomboy ways. It would be a tragedy to lose either of you.'

Kitty felt the blush deepen, not with humiliation now, but with pleasure at such high praise coming from this most respected of women. 'Thank you,' she replied. 'And I'm sorry I keep letting the side down.'

'Then buck up your ideas, Pargeter. Rules are made for a reason, not on a whim, and it's time you knuckled down and accepted that they apply to you as well as everyone else.'

Kitty nodded and, daring to look the other woman in the eye, felt a modicum of relief. The stern expression had softened a little, and there was the hint of a smile tweaking her lips. It had been a narrow squeak, but it was going to be all right.

'Go and find some supper and then get an early night,' said Marion. 'The weather forecast is good for tomorrow, and I'm sure Central Ferry Control will have plenty of work to keep you out of mischief before you return to your pool at Hamble.'

'And the letters to our parents?' asked Charlotte fearfully.

'I hope they won't be necessary and that you can prove yourselves worthy of my trust by doing your job efficiently within the guidelines of the ATA from now on. Dismissed.'

They both snapped off a smart salute and quickly left the office, but they didn't speak until they were safely outside the building. The night was warm and they could hear music drifting across the airfield from the accommodation block, but the only light came from the twinkling stars and bright moon, for the blackout was strictly enforced.

'Whew,' breathed Charlotte as she swept off her neat cap, loosened her tie and undid the button on her shirt collar. 'I thought we were really in for it this time.'

'So did I,' admitted Kitty as she unfastened her uniform jacket, stuffed her cap in the pocket and ruffled her short blonde hair before lighting their cigarettes. She blew smoke, watching it curl away on the light evening breeze. 'And the thought of a letter being sent home is just too awful.'

'I know,' Charlotte agreed. 'Daddy probably wouldn't say much, but poor Mother would be frightfully upset. She's always despaired at my complete lack of respect for stuffy rules and regulations.'

Kitty smiled in sympathy at Charlotte, who'd been her friend and co-conspirator in some kind of mischief or other since the day Kitty had arrived as a scholarship student at the Sussex boarding school. Thirteen years old and fresh off the ship from Argentina where her father managed a polo pony stud, Kitty had been bewildered and already homesick when she'd arrived at this daunting place, but Charlotte had somehow recognised a kindred spirit and had immediately taken her under her wing.

Kitty had survived the ignominy of being a scholarship student, which was on a par with being a poor relation, the minefield of unspoken rules and the incomprehensible importance of family ties and social links, all thanks to Charlotte. And although she'd never perfected the plummy accent or adopted the superior attitude of so many of the other girls, her sunny personality and sporting prowess had made her popular, and she and Charlotte had become inseparable.

'Charlotte,' Kitty murmured, 'I'm really sorry for getting you into trouble. I shouldn't have started messing about like that.'

Charlotte shrugged almost nonchalantly as she tucked a few wayward strands of her dark hair back into the neat bun at her nape. 'I didn't have to follow you into that barrel roll or loop the loop, but I did, and I'm old enough to take full responsibility for my actions.'

'That's as maybe, but now you'll have a black mark on your records, and it's all down to me.'

Charlotte's brown eyes gleamed with humour as she placed a reassuring hand on Kitty's arm. 'Honestly, Kitts, we're both at fault, so don't blame yourself.' Her smile broadened into a mischievous grin. 'It was fun though, wasn't it? Quite like old times when we first got our wings and used to fly low over the school playing fields and interrupt the hockey matches.'

Kitty grinned back. 'We ended up in the head-mistress's office then as well, I remember. Gosh,' she sighed. 'We thought she was a dragon, but she's certainly no match for Marion Wilberforce. I've never seen anyone quite so furious before.'

Charlotte nodded. 'I suppose we deserved it, but I bet those American fly boys were impressed when we flew upside down over their baseball game.'

Kitty laughed. 'Their commanding officer clearly wasn't. He must have been straight on the blower to Marion the moment he saw us.' She took a last puff of the cigarette and ground it out beneath the heel of her black laced-up shoe. 'Come on, let's see what they've left for us to eat. I'm starving.'

Charlotte finished her cigarette and linked arms with Kitty, who was a good three inches shorter and as wiry and slender as a young boy. 'You're always starving,' she said without rancour as they strolled towards the canteen building, 'and I don't know where you put all that food you manage to stuff down. There's nothing of you.'

'You're not exactly fat yourself,' Kitty replied mildly, taking in her friend's neat figure. 'I just happen to have a very good appetite. Mother always reckoned I stayed short and skinny because I use it all up in nervous energy.' She giggled. 'All the best things come in small packages, Charley. I can't help it if I'm little, but you have to admit, I *am* perfectly made.'

Charlotte made a rude noise in her throat. 'No one could accuse you of modesty, that's for certain, Katherine Pargeter – but then you've had your head turned by all those drooling chaps trying to flatter you into going out with them.'

Kitty playfully dug her elbow into her friend's ribs. 'Jealousy will get you nowhere, Miss Bingham – and besides, you've only ever had eyes for my brother, so you can't really complain.'

'I got a letter from Freddy the other day,' she replied dreamily. 'He's been posted somewhere further along the coast. The censor blacked out the name of the airfield, so I don't know exactly where, but he's promised to try and get to the Hamble pool before the end of the month so we can have a few hours together.'

'He's at Cliffe,' said Kitty. Seeing Charlotte's frown, she hurried on. 'I was going to tell you, really I was. But what with one thing and another it completely slipped my mind. I met Roger Makepeace in the canteen at Croydon this morning when I dropped that Magister off. He was waiting for a lift down in one of the Anson air taxis and we had lunch together, which was terrific fun as always. If I hadn't had to ferry that Spitfire up to Ringway and bring the Mosquito back here, I could have gone with him and spent a little time with Freddy.'

Charlotte sighed. 'It's been ages since we've seen one another. Freddy's flying ops night and day and I'm working thirteen days out of every fourteen.

Even if we do get a day off, we can rarely co-ordinate them.'

'That's why I've decided to have lots of fun and not get bogged down in a hopeless romance,' said Kitty lightly. 'Freddy is living on the edge every day – as are we – and that's quite enough to cope with without having to fret over some boyfriend.'

They crossed the cobbled quadrangle arm in arm and then pushed through the door into the dimly lit canteen. It was late and the large room was echoing and deserted, so they helped themselves to the rather dried-out food left in the chafing dishes and sat down at one of the tables.

Kitty dug her fork into the almost meatless shepherd's pie and had a sudden longing for the tender steaks, crisp salads and heaped bowls of lovely fruit that were served regularly back home in Argentina. Her family had moved there from England before her second birthday, so life on the pampas was all that she'd known before she'd been sent back to England to finish her education. It was an outdoor existence except in the rainy season, with meals taken at a long table beneath a vine-covered trellis that ran the length of the sprawling wooden bungalow and overlooked the enormous swimming pool and the dusty red clearing that led to the numerous stables and lush, tree-shaded paddocks.

The talk of Freddy and the thought of those long, lazy meals and sun-drenched days brought back memories of the life she'd left so far behind. Sitting here in the deserted, silent canteen she could almost hear the melodic Spanish voices of the gauchos, the calls of the exotic birds in the drowsy heat and the sawing of the cicadas as dusk fell and the fireflies began to glow in the shrubbery.

She could see once again the glorious wide stretches of empty, shimmering pampas that she and Freddy used to explore on horseback; and the parties that had been held around the pool when all their friends would come and stay for the weekend. She could see the mares with their foals in the paddocks, tails swishing as they cropped the grass, their beautiful coats gleaming richly in the sun, and could remember the rush of excitement as she competed against the skilled and determined Freddy and his friends in fast and furious games of polo. It all seemed so far away suddenly, and tears pricked as the homesickness weighed heavy around her heart.

'Kitty? Whatever's the matter?'

She blinked back the tears and tried to quell the awful yearning for her mother and home. 'I was thinking about how long it's been since I saw my parents,' she admitted. 'There are times when I wish I hadn't come back to start university. We all knew there would be a war, and once it was declared my parents refused to let me risk the journey home, so I was stuck here.'

'But surely you don't regret joining the ATA? You couldn't have done that if you were in Argentina.'

Kitty shook her head as she put down her fork

and abandoned the barely touched food. 'Not for a single minute,' she replied firmly. 'But I miss my home and family, Charlotte, and if anything should happen to Freddy, then I don't know what I'd do.'

'You mustn't talk like that, Kitts. It's defeatist.' Charlotte also abandoned the tasteless food and pushed her plate aside before reaching across the table for Kitty's hand. 'I do understand how home-sick you must be, and I share your concern over Freddy – of course I do, I love him too. But we have to stay positive and believe we'll all come through this. If we don't, then Hitler will have won.'

Kitty shot her a watery smile and squeezed her fingers. 'Of course we do, and I'm sorry I'm being such a drip.'

'Think nothing of it,' replied Charlotte with a warm smile. 'We're all entitled to feel a bit sorry for ourselves after the stresses and strains of trying to fly planes we've never flown before, or battling to land in a force nine gale.'

She pushed back from the table. 'Come on, I've got a quarter bottle of brandy in my overnight bag, and I think we've earned it.'

Kitty cleared the table and they swiftly washed the plates and left them to dry on the wooden draining board before venturing back out into the night. It was cooler now, the breeze still holding a reminder of winter despite the fact it was the end of May, and they hurried across the quad, eager to reach the relative warmth of the very basic barracks accommodation.

The lines of parked planes glimmered beneath the swaying silver blobs of the giant barrage balloons and all was still. Yet it was an ominous stillness, as if the land itself was holding its breath, waiting for the enemy raid that would surely come with the bright bomber's moon.

Kitty felt the cold slither of dread trace her spine and determinedly ignored it. She and Freddy, Roger and Charlotte might be tiny cogs in the vast war machine that was fighting to defend this country from Hitler's tyranny, but as long as they held their nerve and stayed strong, then homesickness was a small price to pay for freedom.

There had been no enemy raid after all, and with the aid of Charlotte's brandy, Kitty's sleep was undisturbed. She woke before dawn, and like the other women who'd stayed at the ferry pool overnight, she was washed, dressed, breakfasted and ready for duty by first light. The promise of clear skies two days running after being grounded for weeks of rain and low cloud was enough to enthuse all of them.

Dressed in regulation shirt, tie, uniform jacket and trousers, she'd dragged on the blue overalls known as a Sidcot suit over everything and added the fleece-lined leather jacket for extra warmth. Fur-lined boots, leather flying helmet, goggles, gloves and a cumbersome parachute and harness completed her outfit, and with her overnight bag at her feet, she stood in the cool pearly dawn with the others outside the Ops room smoking a cigarette, waiting to find out what jobs they'd been allocated.

Depending on their qualifications and experience, the day's work could involve several flights in different types of plane, not all of them familiar to the pilots, which meant they had to use the thin volume of Ferry Pilots' Notes. This was a pocket-sized flip pad of instructions that covered the basics for every aircraft in service. The Avro Anson or the Fairchild Argus would provide an air taxi service to get them to their first job, and if possible, collect them at the end of the day. If not, they would stay overnight at an airfield or in a hotel, or even take a night train back to base if that was feasible, which was why each of them had packed a small overnight bag.

Kitty's contained the usual washbag and make-up as well as her uniform skirt and clean underwear, but she also made sure she'd packed her cream silk evening dress, for there was nearly always a party to go to. This dress wasn't as eye-catching as the 'Gone with the Wind dress' the American Dorothy Furey always packed, but it served its purpose and Kitty always felt very feminine when she wore it.

Kitty and Charlotte were now qualified to fly Classes one, two and three aircraft which included the trainers and communication planes as well as

14

the Moths, Spitfires and the Hawker Hurricanes. No woman had yet been allowed to fly the massive four-engine bombers, but there were growing rumours that it would happen very soon, and there was keen competition between them all to be the first.

The shutters on the Ops room window were flung back and the women crowded round to collect their order chits for the day. Kitty glanced down at her chit and hurried over to join Charlotte, who was already heading for the nearby Anson taxi.

'I've got to pick up a Spit from the factory airfield outside Castle Bromwich and ferry it to Peterborough before I pick up a Typhoon to take south to Wayfaring Down. That's only a few miles from Cliffe, so if I can cadge a lift with someone I might even be able to see Freddy.'

'Lucky you,' Charlotte replied gloomily. 'I've got to take a trainer to White Waltham, then a Moth over to Croydon for repairs before I can get my hands on a Hurricane which has to be delivered to Salisbury.' She gave a deep sigh. 'I won't get back to base tonight, that's for sure.'

'Never mind,' Kitty soothed. 'We'll catch up soon enough. Take care, Charlotte.'

'And you, Kitty. Give my love to Freddy if you see him, and tell him I miss him.'

As they would be going in different air taxis, they hugged swiftly and went their separate ways. Kitty clambered into the broad belly of the Fairchild that would take her up to Castle Bromwich, and as soon as every seat was filled, they were taxiing down the runway and lifting into the clear skies. The forecast was good with no mention of the heavy cloud cover that had frequently kept them grounded over the past two years and was the enemy of all pilots, so the atmosphere was jolly despite the early hour.

The Spitfire factory's output was three hundred and twenty machines a month, and because both the factory and its airfield were priority targets for the Luftwaffe, the planes were ferried away as soon as they left the production line. Kitty handed in her chit to the CO, and within minutes she was checking the Spitfire over before she climbed into the close-fitting cockpit and strapped herself in.

On the ground the Spitfire was nose heavy and would tip forward if the pilot braked harshly, but it was perfectly balanced in flight and Kitty loved it. From the cockpit she could see only the big, black, semicircular panel with the same six instruments as on any operational plane, a dome of sky around it, and a rear-view mirror. It was unarmed and without a radio to keep her in contact with anyone, but she felt comfortable and snug in what she regarded as the most perfect of machines, and she was eager to take off.

As the beautifully proportioned aircraft raced along the runway and lifted into the air at great speed, Kitty experienced the familiar surge of joy.

There was nothing to compare with how it felt to fly a Spitfire. First there was the massive power of the Rolls-Royce Merlin engine that kicked her in the back when she released the brakes. Then came the lift generated by a wing with a slower stalling speed at its tips than closer to the fuselage. This meant that just before it fell out of the sky in a vertically banked turn, or on a misjudged final approach, a Spitfire would give a shudder as a uniquely generous final warning which saved many lives.

Kitty barely had to touch the joystick that pivoted from a fulcrum on the floor to adjust the height and begin the turn towards Peterborough, and she was reminded once again of the old cliché that you didn't fly a Spitfire at all, you wore it.

As the powerful engines throbbed and the sun glinted on the aluminium wings, Kitty felt at her happiest. To be flying on a clear May morning above the patchwork quilt of English fields was utter bliss, and she revelled in the solitude as she followed rivers and railway lines and concentrated on the gauges and the weather. The newspapers might be full of praise for the brave women of the ATA, but Kitty shared the same selfish delight as all the other women pilots and didn't think of herself as heroic at all – just extremely lucky to be doing what she loved best, even though the death toll in the ranks was rising every month.

As she kept an eye on her instruments and checked beneath her for the landmarks that would lead her to Peterborough, her thoughts turned to her brother. Freddy was five years older, and in her and Charlotte's opinion he was the handsomest, most dashing Spitfire pilot the RAF had ever had.

Kitty had adored him for as long as she could remember, and as soon as she had learned to walk, she'd trotted around behind him and tried to join in his boyish games. He'd never really been cross or impatient with her, and as she learned to ride and play polo and conquered her fear of the powerful motorbikes he and his friends rode about on, he even started to admire her in a grudging, brotherly sort of way.

Kitty's passion for speed had begun when her father's wealthy Argentinian employer had insisted upon every child on the stud learning to drive, so that if there was an emergency someone could go for help, no matter how young. Kitty had been six years old when she'd first taken the wheel, propped on cushions and sitting on the very edge of the seat so she could reach the pedals. It had also been Señor Fernandez who'd encouraged Freddy and his own son to learn to fly the Gypsy Moth which he'd bought so he could travel the vast distances quickly and conduct his business far from the stud. The moment Kitty had seen him take off in that little Moth she'd known this was something she'd been born to do.

Señor Fernandez and her parents were not at all keen on the idea, but Kitty was determined to show them that girls of fourteen were just as capable of flying as boys of nineteen, and used a mild form of blackmail to convince the boys she wouldn't tell their fathers what she'd seen them doing with those girls in the hay barn if they taught her how to fly the Moth.

Kitty smiled as she checked her altitude and followed the long, straight railway line beneath her. It had taken almost two years of subterfuge, but in the long school holiday of 1937, and much to her father's surprised delight, sixteen-year-old Kitty was awarded her pilot's licence. Not wanting to be left grounded, Charlotte had wheedled flying lessons out of her indulgent and very rich father, who was inordinately proud of his tomboy daughter, and she got her licence a few months later.

Kitty had no such financial back-up and realised that any flying she wanted to do in England could not be paid for from the allowance her parents were able to provide. Having cajoled Charlotte's father to put in a good word to the headmistress so they got permission to leave school after lessons and on Sundays, she managed to persuade the owners of the small airfield nearby to let her give evening classes in navigation to novice pilots in exchange for three hours of flying every Sunday.

Kitty gave a deep sigh of pleasure as the Merlin engines rumbled reassuringly and the sun continued to shine from a clear sky. Those weekends had lightened up their lives and they'd hurried away from school on their bicycles, log books firmly tucked in the baskets, and not returned until the sun was sinking over the Channel. When Charlotte finally qualified, her doting father bought her a de Havilland Dragonfly and the girls shared this wonderful machine, rapidly building up their air miles in their log books.

It was during those halcyon days before the war that they learned to fly purely on their instruments, which was something the new recruits of the ATA were not taught. No one really knew the reason, but they assumed it was to deter the more daring pilots against flying in thick cloud or going above it. But Kitty and Charlotte were immensely grateful for their lessons from a retired pilot at Shoreham, for they had saved their bacon more than once when they'd been caught by a sudden bank of cloud and had to fly blind.

Her landing at Peterborough was smooth and uneventful, and she climbed stiffly out of the Spitfire, overnight bag in hand, parachute and harness slung over her shoulder. She was chilled to the bone despite the thick leather jacket and boots, and desperate for a hot cup of tea and something to eat, so she quickly made her way to the office with her chit and log book, made her report, and then found the canteen.

Having eaten a large plate of what purported to be boiled mutton, onions and potato, she washed it all down with an enormous mug of tea and lit a cigarette. There was a fair amount of chatter going on in the canteen and she spent a short time catching up on the gossip with a couple of girls she knew from the ATA headquarters at White Waltham before she gathered up her belongings and headed back out to the runway.

It was still early afternoon, and now the days were longer, there would be plenty of time to ferry the Typhoon south to Wayfaring Down. As long as she didn't have to take another aircraft somewhere else, she might indeed get the chance to cadge a lift to Cliffe to see Freddy. This detour would probably mean having to catch the night train all the way to Hampshire and the Hamble Pool if she was to get back in time for duty the following day, but she could sleep on the train and any inconvenience would be worth it if she spent some time with him – if he wasn't on ops, of course, which unfortunately was quite likely.

The Typhoon or 'Tiffy', as it was affectionately called, was a small, single prop interceptor with a 2,000 horsepower Rolls-Royce Vulture engine and a top speed of 400 miles per hour at maximum boost, making it one of the RAF's fastest piston-powered aircraft, capable of catching the Luftwaffe's Focke-Wulf 190. But the gull-shaped wings caused a drag which hampered its speed when in a dive or sharp turn, and most pilots had found it quite tricky to fly.

Kitty climbed into the single cockpit, buckled

herself into the seat and closed the canopy. Within minutes she was roaring down the runway and soaring into the clear blue sky. There was no sign of the drizzle and low cloud that were forecast further south, and she hoped it would clear by the time she got closer to Wayfaring Down.

Flying the Typhoon was very nearly as exciting as being in a Spitfire, and with the sun shining and their shadow falling on the fields and villages beneath, it was a very pleasant way to spend an afternoon.

Kitty had been flying for about twenty minutes when there was suddenly an enormous surge of power and the airspeed indicator shot up to 400 mph. Her stomach clenched and fear made her heart thud, for she knew she couldn't lower her landing gear at this rate and that she'd arrive at Wayfaring Down in less than five minutes, with absolutely no hope of surviving a landing.

She tried to throttle back and cut the boost setting, but they were stuck at maximum and wouldn't budge.

The sweat was stinging her eyes behind her goggles and her breathing was shallow as she forced herself to keep calm, turning the Tiffy into a wide climbing circle in an attempt to lose speed. It didn't work, for when she began to descend again the speed shot back up to 400 mph.

She could now see Wayfaring Down and the distant coastline with its sprawl of towns and villages, and knew she couldn't bale out and risk killing not only herself but the people living down below. She hurtled over the airfield at full power and within minutes was approaching the smaller and more remote Cliffe, desperately looking for somewhere she might be able to land without causing too much damage.

Cliffe's crash wagon was already racing across the grass as she put the plane into another long turn over the airport buildings, opened the canopy and cut the engine and fuel supply. She was rapidly losing height but still travelling at almost maximum speed in an aircraft designed to land at 100 mph, so she unbuckled her seat belt and put the plane into a series of floundering rises and falls in a last-ditch attempt to slow it down as she made her final approach.

The runway was a blur beneath her as she shot low across the airfield buildings and headed straight for a church spire. Pulling with all her strength on the joystick, she managed to miss it by inches, and then she was going full tilt across fields of stampeding, terrified cows.

She wrestled to keep the plane on an even keel, but the nose was too low and the propeller caught the soft mud and sent her spinning towards two huge oak trees. Her survival instinct kicked in and she scrambled frantically out of the cockpit, fell awkwardly for several feet, and landed with a bone-jarring thud into the mud.

Disorientated, and almost paralysed with fear, she lay there winded and numb with shock as she watched a section of the wing being ripped off by the low branch of one of the oak trees.

But the Typhoon was still travelling at speed and it bounced over a ditch and into a small copse of trees, scattering branches and leaves like confetti and trampling everything in its path until it came to rest with an almighty crash against the trunk of another great oak.

Kitty dragged off her helmet and goggles and waited to see if the Typhoon would burst into flames despite her having shut off the fuel line. But it sat there like a wounded metal beast, the engine ticking as it cooled. Her legs were trembling so badly she could barely stand, and her fingers were clumsy as she unfastened the parachute harness and let it drop to the ground. Taking long, deep breaths to regain some vestige of calm, she staggered across the muddy field past the bewildered and skittish cows towards what remained of her Typhoon.

It had lost both wings, the propeller and its tail, the canopy was shattered, and the fuselage had been battered to the point where she doubted it could ever be fixed again. Leaning into the cockpit, she retrieved her overnight bag then went to sit on a distant log to smoke a well-earned cigarette before she began the long walk back across the fields to Cliffe airfield.

It's a good thing I don't mind cows, she thought

wryly as they slowly came to inspect her with bovine curiosity. *But I do wish they wouldn't try and lick me.* 'Go away,' she said firmly as she dodged the long black tongue and unpleasantly wet nose.

The cows stayed where they were, so she finished her cigarette and was just gathering up her belongings when she heard a shout and saw people running across the far field towards her. Not wanting them to think the worst, she stood on the log and waved her arms about, then began to trudge towards them.

A figure broke away from the group and began to race towards her.

Kitty would have known him anywhere, and she broke into a lumbering run to meet him. 'Freddy!' she yelled. 'It's all right. I'm not hurt.'

His handsome face was lined with concern as she dropped everything on the ground and threw herself into his open arms. 'I didn't know it was you,' he breathed, his voice cracking with emotion as he held her tightly. 'We saw the Tiffy disappear and heard the crash, and we all feared the worst.'

She clung to him, glad of his solidity and strength as her legs once again threatened to give way. 'Honestly, Freddy, I thought I was a goner,' she managed through chattering teeth. 'I've never been so scared.'

He seemed to realise how wobbly she was for he kept a tight hold of her as he drew back and looked down into her face. He was ashen, his blue eyes dark with an unspoken fear. 'What the bloody hell did you think you were doing?' he barked. 'Don't you realise you could have damned well killed yourself by pulling a stunt like that?'

She was immediately on the defensive and shoved him away. 'It wasn't me,' she retorted hotly. 'Something went wrong with the mechanics and I couldn't slow the bally thing down.'

He grabbed her to him again and held her tight. 'I'm sorry I shouted,' he said gruffly. 'But you gave me a scare.'

'Nothing like the scare I gave myself,' she replied with a catch in her voice.

Roger Makepeace came running up to them, his face pale and anxious. 'Are you hurt, Kitty?' he asked.

She forced a smile for Freddy's wingman and best friend. 'There's nothing wrong with me that won't be cured by a very large gin and a long soak in a hot bath,' she replied with more than a touch of bravado.

He grinned down at her as he grabbed her parachute harness and overnight bag. 'You really are the limit, Kitty,' he said with fond exasperation. 'There're not many girls that can prang a kite quite so spectacularly and come out of it without a scratch. You've certainly earned both the bath and the gin.'

Kitty walked between them as they headed across the field, but despite her bravado, she discovered that she needed to hold their arms, for her legs felt like jelly.

Chapter Two

In accordance with the Standing Orders for Delivery Pilots, which was posted at all ferry pools in case of emergency, Kitty had gone straight to the administration office to ring in her report to Mayfair 120 and get her ongoing orders. She'd then sat down to carefully write the same report for her commanding officer at Central Dispatch Pool. This report had to be signed and sent immediately, for the loss of a plane was serious, and schedules would have to be changed.

Glad that the paperwork was done, Kitty had a quick word with the billeting officer and then dumped her things on a spare bed in the female accommodation hut. Deciding she needed a bath rather more than the large gin, she found the ablutions block, stripped off her clothes and sank with a sigh of pleasure into the permitted few inches of hot water. She ached in places she hadn't known she had, and there was a lump on her temple the size of a small egg, but the hot water soon eased the sore muscles, and by the time the water had cooled she was feeling much calmer and ready for that gin.

Dressing quickly in clean underwear and a fresh

shirt, she pulled on the navy blue uniform skirt and jacket and straightened her tie. The gold flashes on the shoulders and round the cuffs of her jacket, the standard issue black silk stockings, the gold badge on her cap, and the wings sewn above her breast pocket made the outfit very glamorous – though that was not a word that sat easily with the women pilots, for most didn't consider what they did as glamorous at all. But they agreed that it turned heads, secured the best hotel rooms and restaurant tables and represented a certain exciting and daring image of which they were very proud.

Kitty fluffed out her thick, wavy fair hair which had been trimmed to regulation length just above her collar, and carefully placed the cap so the front point was directly over her right brow. A dash of lipstick and a dab of powder over the swelling on her temple, and she was ready.

It was like being struck by a wall of sound as she stepped into the smoky atmosphere of the Officers' Mess. There was a game of pirates going on, and she stood by the door with some of the other girls from the ATA and watched the fun as grown men tried to get around the vast room without touching the floor.

Freddy, of course, was in the thick of it, his fair hair flopping over his eyes, his tie askew, shirtsleeves rolled up as he swung from a rafter, landed delicately onto a chair, which he balanced on two legs, before hopping off onto a narrow windowsill and running along it to another rafter.

He was being pursued with great gusto by the rather burly Roger Makepeace, who was about as delicate and nimble as a rugby prop forward, but to give him his due, he was doing rather well until he tried to copy Freddy's trick with the chair and landed with a great thud in the middle of a table.

Great shouts of laughter boomed out as the table collapsed and Roger was covered in the contents of bottles, glasses and ashtrays. More shouts rang out as Freddy reached the bar which was the end of the circuit, slid along it and landed on the piano stool, where he began to thump out Chopsticks on the out-of-tune keys.

Kitty exchanged a knowing glance with the ATA girl standing beside her as Roger was helped to his feet, dusted down and handed a pint of beer. They'd seen it all before in just about every RAF mess they'd been in. These brave boys lived on a knife-edge every day, and the long roll call of those who hadn't returned was merely a reminder that life had to be lived to the very last breath, for no one knew what tomorrow would bring.

Sobered by the thought of how close she'd come today to being numbered amongst the lost, Kitty went to the bar and asked for a drink. There was no gin, only beer, but as it wasn't the watered-down stuff served in civilian pubs, it was worth drinking.

Freddy and Roger saw her at the same time, and

within minutes she was surrounded by them and their colleagues, and being good-naturedly teased about the mess she'd made of the Tiffy, and that she'd probably put those cows off giving milk for a week with her antics. There were jocular remarks about how women should stick to knitting and cooking and not try to compete in boys' games, and Kitty tried to take it all in good part, but she was still feeling quite fragile after the crash and the jokes were beginning to wear a bit thin.

'If I wasn't wearing this skirt I'd challenge you to a game of pirates,' she shouted above the noise to Freddy. 'You know I always win.'

Freddy grinned and put his arm round her shoulders. 'Now there's a challenge,' he shouted back. 'When are you due to leave Cliffe?'

'Late tomorrow afternoon. Why?'

His smile broadened as he looked across at Roger. 'Hear that, Roger? What do you reckon? Think she's up to it?'

Roger's eyes twinkled as he smoothed his moustache and studied Kitty from head to toe. 'I think by the gleam in her eye she's more than up to it, Freddy, old son. But I'd be careful if I were you – she might get the better of you in that one.'

Kitty looked from one to the other, noted their silly grins and burst out laughing. 'Go on, then. What is it?'

'There's a motorcycle event tomorrow at the circuit just outside Cliffehaven,' shouted Freddy.

'Roger and I have got a twelve-hour pass, so we thought we'd put it to good use. I've got my Ariel NG, and Roger's got his old Montgomery Greyhound. I'm sure he won't mind you borrowing it for the morning.'

'I say, old chap,' protested Roger. 'Kitty might be a competent rider, but that's a classic bike. I'm not sure . . .'

'I won't prang it if that's what you're worried about, Roger,' she hurried to assure him. 'I learned how to ride bikes when I was still in junior school.'

Roger still didn't look convinced, but was then distracted by the rather attractive little ATA pilot who'd been admiring him for the past half hour.

'Don't worry, Kitts,' Freddy said with a knowing smile. 'I'll get you something to race on. That's if you really are up to the challenge?'

She folded her arms and regarded him sternly. 'When have you ever known me not to take up one of your challenges? What's the prize?'

'The glory of watching me win – yet again,' he said with a wink.

'In your dreams,' she countered sweetly, and went to get another beer which she put on his mess bill.

Kitty was still feeling the effects of the crash, so after an hour she left Freddy and Roger to their raucous games and beer, grabbed a bite to eat in the canteen and then went to bed. There were five other girls staying overnight in the women's accommodation block, but there was no sign of them when Kitty set her small travelling alarm clock and turned off the light, and she didn't hear them come tiptoeing in much later.

When she woke at first light she felt refreshed and was looking forward to spending the day with Freddy and Roger, and to getting onto the back of a motorbike again. The other girls were fast asleep, so she quietly washed and dressed in her trousers and shirt, packed her bag and went in search of breakfast.

The canteen was packed and, to her amazement, Freddy and Roger were bright-eyed and full of themselves despite the amount of beer they'd consumed the night before and were already tucking into enormous plates of bacon and eggs. 'Where did you manage to get food like that?' she gasped in awe.

'The RAF like to feed their pilots,' said Freddy as he mopped up his egg with a slice of golden fried bread. 'I'm sure we can spare a rasher or two for you, even if you did wipe out one of our Typhoons.'

Kitty went to the counter and returned with a loaded plate and a big mug of tea. Her mouth was watering and she tucked in, not saying a word until she'd wiped the plate clean with the last of the bread. As she pushed the plate away and reached for the mug of tea, she caught Freddy and Roger staring at her. 'What's the matter?'

'I still can't believe that someone your size can eat that much food,' Roger said with a hint of admiration.

'Pranging Typhoons makes me hungry.' She shot him a cheeky grin and drank her tea. 'So, what bike have you managed to get me?' she asked Freddy.

'Roger rather set his heart on taking part in the races today, so I've managed to persuade one of our American pilots to lend you his 1000cc Ariel Square 4. He bust his leg a few weeks ago and is flying a desk at the moment, so he won't be needing it.'

'He does know you've borrowed it for me, doesn't he?' she asked suspiciously.

Freddy nodded. 'It's cost me a bottle of whisky and a carton of cigarettes, so you'd better not prang that too.' His blue eyes sparkled as he grinned. 'It's a powerful bike for a skinny girl. Are you sure you can handle it?'

Kitty pushed back her chair. 'There's only one way to find out,' she said. 'Lead me to it, Freddy.'

The motorbike was sheltered beneath a tarpaulin in the back of a hangar, and when she uncovered it she felt a great surge of excitement. It gleamed with chrome, the four cylinders in a square, the two crank-shafts geared together, the tyres black and fat. But Freddy had been right in one aspect, she conceded silently as she struggled to wheel it outside, for it was a heavy bike and she'd have the devil's own job of keeping it upright if she lost it on a corner. Not that she'd ever let him know, of course.

She swung her leg over the broad leather seat and had to use all her strength to keep the bike up and her other foot on the ground. Once she got going, she realised, she'd have to lean right across the smooth curve of the tank to be able to reach the low-slung handlebars.

Kitty listened as Freddy gave her a rundown on all the bike's functions and explained about the four-speed gearbox, but the toe of her boot was all that was keeping her upright and her arms were beginning to tremble from the effort. Deciding she couldn't lose face by toppling off the thing, she turned the key and kicked the starter.

The clatter of the powerful engine echoed all across the airfield, so she tweaked the throttle, took her foot off the ground and set off down the runway. It was smooth, powerful and very, very fast – and by the time she came back to the hangar, she knew she was glowing with pleasure.

'I can see Roger and I are going to have to look to our laurels,' said Freddy thoughtfully, 'but I'm confident my Ariel NG can match the speed.'

Kitty put the kickstand in place and climbed off the Ariel Square, rather alarmed at how badly her arms were trembling from the effort of keeping the thing under control. 'It's not the speed that counts, Freddy,' she teased. 'It's the skill of the rider.' She chuckled at his po-faced look. 'What time do these races start, and what do they cost?'

He looked at his watch. 'In an hour, so we'd better leave in the next ten minutes. And they cost a couple of bob a race, all proceeds going to the Cliffehaven

Spitfire Fund. It would be a good idea to bring your flying helmet and goggles,' he advised. 'It's a dirt and cinder track, and after all the rain we've had lately it will be sticky.'

Kitty hurried off to fetch her flying kit and Sidcot suit. Getting mud all over her uniform would not be a good idea, as she wouldn't have time to clean it before she had to catch the Anson taxi back to Hamble Pool.

The motorbike ride from Cliffe airfield to the track in the hills behind Cliffehaven was very pleasant in the clear early morning, and Kitty happily ambled along behind the men as she got used to the borrowed machine.

The racing circuit was already well attended, and there was an expectant buzz in the air as bunting flapped in the breeze and families settled on the grass with their picnic baskets and deckchairs. It was hard to believe there was a war on, and the atmosphere reminded Kitty of the country fairs she'd attended while staying with Charlotte during the half-term holidays and Easter breaks.

The girls were all in their Sunday best, and the older women were wearing pretty hats and summery dresses beneath their warm coats as they set out the picnics and enjoyed a good gossip. There were stalls selling tea, sandwiches, beer, motorbike spares and second-hand leather jackets, boots and helmets – and gaggles of girls gave the glad eye to the Americans who were showing off on their flash motorbikes.

The uniforms were of just about every allied service, and the men who were not competing were examining the motorcycles with undisguised envy.

'This is Rita,' said Freddy as he introduced a pretty, dark-haired girl in trousers and an old WWI flying jacket. 'She's responsible for all this.' He put his arm about the girl's shoulder. 'How much have you got for the fund, Rita?'

'We're nearly there,' she said, easing away from his tethering arm. 'Another fifty quid and we can get our town's name printed on one of your Spitfires.' She shot Kitty a grin. 'It's good to see another girl competing,' she said. 'I'm usually the only one.'

'What bike have you got?'

'A Triumph,' she said proudly. 'But it won't match that beast, so we'll be in different heats until the last race when it's a free-for-all scramble.'

'That sounds like fun,' said Kitty. 'I can't wait to get stuck in.'

Rita grinned. 'I look forward to seeing how you do.' She took their money and handed them a neatly typed list of the races. 'See you on the track,' she said cheerfully, then walked away and was soon lost in the crowd.

'She seems like a nice girl,' said Kitty. 'And what a marvellous thing to do.'

Freddy nodded. 'She's a lodger at Commander Black's mother-in-law's, that's how we got to know about these race meetings in the first place.' He pointed towards a small, dark-haired woman of about forty who was helping to serve the teas. 'That's Peggy Reilly,' he said. 'She's Rita's landlady and a jolly good sort.'

Kitty watched as the little woman bustled about dispensing tea and laughing and chatting with everyone. She didn't know much about landladies except for what the comedians and postcards made of them, but Peggy Reilly certainly didn't seem to fit that mould at all.

'The Commander took some of us round to her boarding house for tea last Sunday,' Freddy added with a grin. 'It was great fun, and Roger and I got to meet the four other girls who lodge there.' He leaned closer. 'I think Roger was rather taken with the little red-haired nurse,' he murmured.

Kitty wasn't surprised, for Roger enjoyed playing the field, and he always had some giggling female in tow.

All conversation came to an end as the first race was announced and everyone drew closer to the wooden barriers that surrounded the twisting course. There were huge piles of old tyres at every corner to protect the cyclists should they skid off, and there was even a small stand by the winning post where it cost a bit more to sit on the hard wooden benches.

Kitty waited breathlessly as the first competitors rode their bikes to the starting line and waited with engines revving for Rita to drop the flag. Silence fell and the tension grew – then the flag went down and the crowd erupted into bellows of encouragement as the less powerful bikes took off and roared around the first bend.

There were great groans as the leader took the dog-leg too fast and smashed straight into the heap of tyres, and a round of applause as he got to his feet and shamefacedly collected his bike. Mud and cinders flew beneath the wheels, showering the spectators and smearing the riders' goggles, and when the winner went through the chequered flag there was a roar of approval which made the dogs bark with all the excitement.

As the races continued and her own class approached, Kitty began to feel quite nervous. She hadn't raced for years, and the bike was on loan and still felt unfamiliar. There were some very skilled riders here today, and it would be humiliating to lose to Freddy after all her boasting the previous night. Her doubts burgeoned as she pulled the Sidcot overalls over her trousers and tied the sleeves around her waist under her sheepskin-lined flying jacket.

'Not having second thoughts, are you?' Freddy asked as they wheeled the bikes through the crowd to reach the starting line.

'Not at all,' she lied as she rested the bike on its kickstand, strapped the flying helmet firmly under her chin and pulled on the goggles and gloves. 'I'll be waiting for you on the other side of the winning line.'

Despite her challenge, her mouth was dry and

her heart was banging against her ribs with fear and excitement as she straddled the Ariel and started the engine. There were eight riders competing in this race and all of them were men, hell-bent on reaching the winning post first. She eyed the track which stretched in front of her and disappeared into the wickedly sharp bend which had caused so many spills already. Failure was not an option – she had to hold her nerve.

She dug the toe of her boot into the ground, struggling to keep the bike upright as the roar of the surrounding engines drowned out the noise from the crowd and the flag was raised to flutter in the breeze.

The flag went down and she shot off the starting line so fast the rear wheel skidded and she had to fight to keep control and not stall the engine. The others were edging ahead in those precious few lost seconds, so she changed gears, leaned across the tank and gauged the line she should take for the optimum advantage without risking going into another skid or causing a crash.

It was clearly every man for himself, with no concessions given because of her sex, and as she managed to get back into the melee, she saw Freddy nudging to the front. She negotiated the sharp bend by whipping through on the inside as the bike in front swerved and opened up a gap.

She was closer to Freddy now, and could see Roger tucking in behind him. She upped the gears and her speed on the long straight then smoothly took the long, sweeping bend which led into a dip. The Ariel roared down it and raced up the hill, taking to the air over the brow and landing with a firm thud that would have thrown her off if she hadn't been such a skilled and experienced horseback rider. She'd overtaken two riders by using that little stunt, and was now edging up on Roger.

Exhilaration banished fear as well as caution, and she kept her speed high as she took the next long bend at such an angle her knee was almost touching the track. She could barely see through the splattered goggles now, but she didn't dare clear them, for the course twisted away again and the second dog-leg was coming up.

Freddy was still in the lead with Roger edging up to his rear wheel and Kitty closing the gap on the third rider. But Freddy was going too fast into the dog-leg and his back wheel skidded, making the bike yaw right and left. Roger almost crashed into him because he was so close, and the third rider took advantage of the situation and shot past them both. Kitty didn't have time to worry about Freddy as she negotiated the wickedly sharp bends and tried to catch Roger.

The winning post was up ahead and Roger was across it in second place. Freddy had caught up with her and was right alongside as they both opened up their throttles and hurtled for the line. It was anyone's guess as to who had taken that third place.

Kitty's heart was racing, the adrenalin pumping as she cut the speed to an amble and slowly turned back to the finishing line. This was on a par with flying a Spitfire, and she'd never felt quite so alive. 'Who won?' she asked the moment she brought the Ariel to a halt.

'Billy Smith,' said Rita, nodding to the big chap on a powerful Triumph. 'But only by a whisker from Roger.' She grinned at Kitty. 'I'm sorry, but I couldn't split you and Freddy, so you're both in third place.'

Kitty laughed as she pulled off the goggles. 'Well done to Billy and hard luck Roger. As for you, Freddy Pargeter, perhaps now you'll agree that I'm just as good as you.'

'There are three more races,' he replied. 'So don't start crowing just yet.'

Kitty wasn't placed in any of the other races, but she didn't mind at all. She'd had the best day she could remember in a long time, and spending these few precious hours with Freddy had been just what she'd needed to banish the homesickness.

They said goodbye to Rita, who made her promise to come back and race again when time and geography allowed, and made their leisurely way back to Cliffe airfield. The motorcycles were cleaned and stowed back in the hangar under tarpaulins, and then their riders headed for their separate ablutions blocks.

One look in the full-length mirror hanging from the door in the female accommodation hut had her in tears of laughter, for like Freddy and Roger, she was splattered from head to foot in mud and cinders, and the only clean patches were where her goggles had been. She looked like a demented panda after a mud bath.

Having soaked away the muck and the aches and pains, Kitty dressed once more in her uniform and stowed her filthy clothes in a side pocket of her overnight bag. She would wash them when she got back to Hamble.

It was still a lovely bright day, and after getting a sandwich from the canteen and a glass of beer from the mess bar, she and Freddy sat in deckchairs outside and talked of Charlotte and family and the life they'd left behind in Argentina as they waited for the Ansen to arrive to take Kitty back to her ferry pool.

The Ansen duly arrived and they reluctantly went to meet it. Freddy gathered her into his arms and held her tightly for a long moment before kissing the top of her head and releasing her. 'Give my love to Charlotte and tell her I'll see her next weekend, all being well. And you take care of yourself, Kitty,' he said solemnly. 'I don't want another scare like yesterday.'

She gave him a brave little smile and gathered up her things. 'Neither do I,' she said ruefully. 'Look after yourself, Freddy,' she managed as the tears pricked. 'Fly safe.'

Without waiting for his reply, she turned away

and climbed aboard the air taxi. Having stowed her gear, she found a seat by the window and looked out, hoping to exchange a wave and a smile. But Freddy already had his back turned and was walking away, soon to be lost in the deep shadows of a nearby hangar. He hated goodbyes as much as she did.

Chapter Three

Cliffehaven

It had been two weeks since Peggy Reilly had helped Rita at the race meeting, and although she'd enjoyed the experience, she'd been very tired at the end of it. Now she was feeling the effects of the long walk to and from Cliffehaven station and was glad to have the pram to lean on. She still tired quickly, although the operation had been several weeks ago, and now there was a dull ache around her hysterectomy scar and she knew that by the time she reached home she'd be wrung out and in need of a cuppa and a bit of a sit down.

As she reached the end of Camden Road and waited for a convoy of army trucks to rumble up the hill from the seafront, she dabbed her hot face with a handkerchief, wondering if she'd been wise to make that long trek on this surprisingly warm June day. But really, she'd had no choice, for Ruby and her mother had arrived from London this morning, and of course she'd had to be there to hand over the numerous letters that had come for Ruby during her absence and welcome them both to Cliffehaven.

Peggy gave a soft smile as she crossed the main road and trudged further up the hill to the twitten that ran between the backs of the Victorian terraces. The letters had clearly come from the lovely Canadian soldier who'd taken such a shine to Ruby, and she rather hoped their fledgling romance would blossom once he'd returned from his training course.

It had been a very small welcoming party, with just herself, baby Daisy and Rita, and, of course, Stan the stationmaster. Stan was a widower in his early sixties who would have retired from the railways if it hadn't been for the war. He'd had a soft spot for little Ruby from the moment she'd first stepped off the train from London in the middle of a freezing winter's night, carrying the marks of her husband's fists on her face, and with no coat and nowhere to go. Stan had soon taken on the role of guardian and surrogate grandfather, and had been the driving force behind saving her from the clutches of a predatory landlord, and seeing that she was safely billeted with Peggy.

Ruby had obviously been delighted to see them all again, for she and Rita had got on like a house on fire. But there was added warmth in her greeting to Stan, and Peggy could have sworn there had been tears in his eyes as he bashfully succumbed to her enthusiastic hug.

Peggy stopped by the back gate to catch her breath. Beach View Boarding House had survived quite well so far, she thought as she regarded the four-storey Victorian terraced house. The damage caused to the basement by the bomb blast that had nearly been the death of her, Daisy and Cordelia had been beautifully repaired by their friends and neighbours in an overwhelming act of kindness, and she counted herself very blessed.

She stood and admired the fresh brickwork and sturdy new guttering. There was a new frosted window beside the donated stone sink in her scullery, and a freshly painted second-hand back door. The flint wall at the bottom of the garden had been expertly repaired and the gate no longer hung from a single hinge. The shattered windows had been reglazed and heavily taped against further bomb blasts, loose tiles fixed or replaced, and the chimney made safe.

She gave a deep sigh of thankfulness that she hadn't suffered the same fate as her less fortunate neighbours on the other side of the twitten. The damage had been so severe to two of the houses that they'd had to be demolished, and the poor residents were now in emergency lodgings on the far side of town. Even the third house still had scaffolding up and a tarpaulin covering the huge hole in the roof, and Peggy knew just how close she and her loved ones had come to being killed on that fateful night.

She opened the gate and wheeled the big pram along the slab path that ran past the ugly Anderson shelter and her father-in-law's vegetable garden to the heavily laden washing line and the back door. Ron had repaired the hen house and coop, and the chickens didn't seem at all upset, for they still provided lots of eggs and the rooster continued to be full of himself and very vocal. But Ron had yet to build another outside lav – and that was a big inconvenience.

Smiling at her unintended joke, she opened the back door and wheeled the pram into the basement which provided a scullery and two bedrooms. Ron slept down here with his dog Harvey and his two ferrets – hence the pong of damp dog, old socks and straw bedding. Before the war her two young sons had slept in the second bedroom, and every time she came down here she half expected to see Bob and Charlie come rushing out, demanding to be fed.

The thought of how far away Somerset was and how long they'd been away was depressing, and made her feel more tired than ever. At least her eldest daughter Anne was safely with them now she had a daughter of her own, but that didn't make the separation any easier to bear, or ease the worry of knowing that her husband Jim and his brother Frank were somewhere up north with the army and unlikely to be home on leave any time soon.

Ignoring the jumble of Ron's boots, coats and general rubbish piled everywhere, Peggy unfastened the rain cover on the old pram and drew back the blankets that covered an awakening Daisy. This blasted war had scattered her family to the four winds, and if she let herself think about it too much, she'd just curl under a blanket into a ball of misery and not come out until it was all over.

But, she reasoned as she carried the squirming baby up the stone steps, giving in to things was not her way, and she would battle through until the war was won. She could be thankful that her daughter Cissy, and Anne's husband, RAF Commander Martin Black, were stationed at Cliffe airfield, which was less than an hour's drive away, so they could make the occasional visit.

The kitchen was deserted for once, with no sign of Ron or his oversized and boisterous lurcher Harvey, and Peggy was rather relieved. With so many people living at Beach View it was often quite noisy, and at this moment she just wanted to see to Daisy and then put her feet up for a quiet moment with a cup of tea and a fag.

She changed Daisy's nappy, gave her some sweetened water to drink and a rusk to chew then placed her in the playpen which had been jammed into the corner of the kitchen. Now six months old, Daisy had just learned to crawl and could travel surprisingly fast. It had got to the stage where there had to be a sturdy fireguard fixed in front of the Kitchener range, and anything of value placed out of her reach.

With Daisy drooling happily on her rusk, Peggy placed the kettle on the hob and went out to fetch the washing off the line. Returning to the kitchen, she flung open the window and left the doors open to garner some relief from the heat of the range, which had to be lit all year round to provide hot water and cooking facilities. Folding the nappies and bed linen into a neat pile on the kitchen table, she made a pot of tea from the used leaves that had been left to dry in a saucer. Adding a drop of milk and a few grains of precious sugar, she sat down with a long sigh of relief and lit a well-earned cigarette.

Beach View Boarding House had been in her family now for two generations. Peggy had moved back in after she married Jim, and then they'd taken over from her parents when they'd retired to a bungalow further along the coast. They had died some years ago, and in the few quiet moments Peggy had, she still mourned them.

Once war had been declared the holidaymakers no longer came to Cliffehaven, and although the elderly, bird-like Cordelia Finch was a long-term boarder, and the two nurses Suzy and Fran had moved in, Ron's pension didn't go far and Peggy had found it hard to make ends meet on Jim's meagre wages as a projectionist at the local cinema. She had gone to the billeting office and put her name down, and soon every room had been filled.

Peggy sighed. That had been back in the winter of 1939 when it seemed as if all the talk of war was hot air, and the threats of bombing raids and invasion were merely the wild predictions of the pessimists. It felt like a lifetime ago, and now the country was almost on its knees from the battering of the Luftwaffe and the day-to-day struggle to feed and clothe a family while keeping a roof over their heads and a fire in the hearth. The cinema had been flattened, Jim had been called up, and the lovely seaside holiday town was now barely recognisable.

But some things never changed, she thought contentedly. The kitchen was still shabby, the furniture had definitely seen better days, and the colourful pattern on the oilcloth covering the battered table had faded to a mellow blur. But the pale yellow lino on the floor was new, and the blue and white gingham curtains at the window and beneath the stone sink brought notes of cheerfulness. This was the heart of her home, and no matter what ailed her or made her fret, she could always find peace in this room.

Peggy let her gaze trawl over the battered shelves in the chimney alcove which groaned beneath the weight of mismatched china and cooking pots; and over the crowded mantelpiece lined with ration books, photographs, old letters, cheap ornaments and a plethora of hastily written reminders and shopping lists that no one ever read.

She eyed the wireless that brought them all entertainment as well as the news from the outside world, and smiled at a giggling Daisy before glancing disconsolately at the corner larder. There was very little in it now, for the Atlantic convoys were finding it harder than ever to get through with supplies and therefore rationing was necessarily even tighter. Finding a tin of anything was like unearthing gold dust, and the queues at the shops were endless, and very often disheartening.

She leaned back in her chair and smoked her Park Drive cigarette, too tired to think about what to cook for tea. It was a never-ending trial to feed so many people and try to be creative about it – and if it hadn't been for Ron's poaching and his vegetable garden, and the eggs from the chickens, she suspected they would all go hungrier than ever.

Despite her weariness and the challenges she was forced to face every day, Peggy remained optimistic. Ron might be a scruffy old Irish scoundrel who carried ferrets about in his poacher's coat and let his dog sleep on his bed, but he'd been a tower of strength even before Jim had been called up. He'd since proved to be an absolute rock on which everyone in this house of women had leaned upon at one time or another.

As for Cordelia, she had become the grandmother they had all been missing, and her gentle wit and sense of fun endeared her to all of them – especially when her hearing aid was on the blink and conversations became convoluted and almost surreal.

Peggy smiled as she thought of her other lodgers. The girls all came from very different backgrounds, and yet they had formed a close bond as they battled the day-to-day inconveniences and strove to find humour in the darkest of situations, and Peggy couldn't imagine life without them. Elegant Suzy and flame-haired Irish Fran worked long hours as nurses at the nearby hospital, and Suzy was now courting Peggy's nephew, the lovely, rather shy Anthony. Cordelia's great-nieces, Sarah and Jane, had escaped the fall of Singapore by a whisker and had fitted into life at Beach View extremely well, despite their rather exotic upbringing in Malaya. Now Sarah worked as a lumberjill on the Cliffe estate, and Jane divided her time between delivering the morning milk and doing the accounts for a nearby uniform factory.

And then there was dear little Rita, who was a local girl and a childhood friend of Cissy's. She'd lost her mother while still at school and now her father was away with the army. Rita had had the misfortune to be bombed out twice before Peggy found her and brought her into the fold, and as she was a bit of a tomboy, and preferred dashing about on her motorbike to going to dances, she was perfectly suited to her job as a fire engine driver.

Peggy stubbed out her cigarette and was about to pick up Daisy and take her into the garden away from the heat of the range when she heard the slam of the front door.

'Only me,' called Cordelia from the hall. 'Is anyone at home?'

'I've been back for a while,' Peggy replied as she went to greet her at the kitchen door. 'Did you enjoy your bridge party?'

Cordelia nodded and smiled as she took off her hat and carefully placed it on the table, well away from Daisy's searching fingers. 'I certainly did.' She hooked her walking stick over a chair and patted Daisy's dark curls. 'It's been a while since I last played, but I've lost none of my skills, and thankfully Albert Marsh was a worthy partner and didn't let the side down.'

Her smile broadened into a wide grin as she dug into her capacious handbag. 'Look what I won,' she declared.

Peggy gasped at the wondrous sight of the perfect orange. 'I haven't seen one of those since the summer of 1939,' she breathed.

'Albert got one as well, so we don't have to feel guilty about eating all of it,' said Cordelia as she handed it reverently to Peggy.

Peggy closed her eyes and breathed in the long-forgotten scent of the fruit, her mouth watering at the thought of sinking her teeth into the soft flesh and letting the sweet juices run into her mouth. 'But where on earth did it come from?'

'Mrs Fullerton.'

Peggy's eyes widened. 'Not the old dragon that lives in the manor house behind the rhododendron hedge on the main road?'

Cordelia nodded. 'One and the same. Ghastly old trout and horribly snooty about everyone – but she evidently has an orangery at the back of her posh house, and very graciously decided to provide two of her oranges as first prize.'

Peggy shook her head in awe as she carefully placed the orange in the centre of her kitchen table like an art exhibit. 'She and my sister Doris know each other well, and share the same unfortunate belief that they're better than the rest of us,' she murmured.

She looked across the table at Cordelia and shot her a mischievous grin. 'They're always trying to outdo each other – but I do believe Agatha Fullerton has come up trumps this time. Doris can't hope to compete with something as grand as an orangery.'

Cordelia sniffed delicate disapproval of the pair of them and poured herself a cup of the very weak tea. She and Doris had never seen eye to eye, and things had become heated between them when Doris had moved, uninvited, into Beach View to look after things while Peggy was in hospital recovering from her operation. Thankfully Doris was back in her own home and rarely ventured to this side of Cliffehaven – which she deemed to be the less salubrious part of the town – so Peggy and Cordelia no longer had to put up with her.

'Did Ruby and her mother get here on time?' Cordelia asked as she sat at the table with her cup of tea and gazed at the orange.

Peggy couldn't take her eyes off it either as she nodded. 'Ruby looked very well and was clearly delighted to be back here again. Stan was just as pleased. He'd pressed his stationmaster's uniform, had a shave and polished his shoes for the occasion, and was quite bashful when Ruby introduced him to her mother.'

The little face was bright, the blue eyes twinkling with curiosity. 'What's Ethel like?'

Peggy forced herself to look away from the orange. 'She's short and far too thin, with dark curly hair and brown eyes just like Ruby. Some decent food, good fresh air and proper living conditions will put some meat on her bones and bring colour to her face, that's for sure.' Peggy chuckled. 'She doesn't say much, but when she does it comes out at the speed of machine-gun fire, and is almost impossible to understand.'

'I expect she was feeling a bit daunted by having to meet you and Rita and Stan all at once,' said Cordelia.

'Maybe, but I'm sure Ruby would have warned her that we'd be there to meet them off the train.' Peggy's gaze returned to the orange. 'Ethel's younger than I expected,' she continued. 'Probably not much more than thirty-eight or nine, and although life has clearly ground her down, she still seems to possess the indomitable spirit of a true survivor.' She smiled. 'She was clearly nervous about starting a new life down here, but her determination to make the best of things showed in her choice of hat. It was quite magnificent, with blowsy silk roses all over the crown that matched her defiant red earrings and lipstick.'

'She sounds a bit too much like dear little Sally's

ghastly mother,' said Cordelia. 'That one was a complete floozy.'

Peggy had a sharp vision of her first evacuee's mother and quickly shook her head. 'Oh, no. Ethel might be a rough diamond, but she's fearsomely protective of Ruby and is nothing like the awful Florrie.' She chuckled at the memory of Stan's rather awed expression. 'I got the feeling Stan was quite taken with her.'

Cordelia pulled a face. 'He's far too old for all that nonsense,' she said firmly.

'Oh, I don't know,' said Peggy. 'Ron's about the same age, and he's doing all right with Rosie Braithwaite.' She frowned. 'Where is Ron, by the way? I thought he was supposed to be building our outside lav?'

'He was, but Harvey's gone missing again and he's out looking for him,' said Cordelia with a hint of asperity.

'It's not like Harvey to keep running off,' said Peggy.

Cordelia went pink. 'Ron thinks he's gone courting,' she said in a fluster.

'Ah,' said Peggy and tried not to smile. 'It sounds as if he and Ron have got their second wind and are searching for their lost youth. Good luck to the pair of them, I say. I wouldn't mind a bit of romance to liven things up, and that's a fact.'

Cordelia was not amused. 'Returning to a rather more wholesome subject,' she said primly, 'do you think Ethel will settle down to life in Amelia's bungalow? It's awfully quiet here in Cliffehaven, and she sounds as if she's the sort of woman who might miss the bright lights and excitement of London.'

Peggy shook her head. 'The only bright lights in London are the fires consuming the East End and the searchlights following the pom-pom bursts. Ethel strikes me as a down-to-earth, no-nonsense sort of woman and far from flighty, despite the over-blown hat. I think she's shrewd enough to realise what a wonderful chance she's being offered, and I'm sure she'll settle down to her new life in your sister's bungalow with great gusto.' She grinned at Cordelia. 'That's if the pair of them survive the ride up to Mafeking Terrace in Rita's borrowed motor-cycle and sidecar.'

Cordelia chuckled. 'They're braver than me, and that's a fact. You wouldn't catch me gadding about in such a thing.'

'I bet you would if you got the chance,' Peggy teased fondly. 'We all know you enjoy a challenge.'

'That's as maybe,' she replied with a naughty twinkle in her eye, 'but there are limits.' She sipped her tea and changed the subject. 'We performed miracles with Amelia's bungalow, didn't we?'

'We certainly did,' agreed Peggy as she thought of the hours of work they had all put in to help Ruby get the bungalow ready before she went to London to persuade her mother to leave the tenement in Bow for a new life in Cliffehaven.

Ethel had clearly been reluctant to leave all she

knew, for it had taken over two weeks of steady, determined persuasion by Ruby to get her down here. In that time, Ron and Stan had mended guttering and loose tiles, cleared the garden of the mounds of rubbish, clipped the hedge at the bottom, repaired the outside lav, and dug and planted a generous vegetable plot.

The neglected bungalow had been cleared of mice droppings, rubbish and rotting food, the walls freshly distempered and the floors scrubbed and revarnished. Now the windows sparkled, the net curtains were snowy and the bedrooms smelled of fresh linen and furniture polish. The kitchen was spotless, and although the furniture in the sitting room was shabby, the wireless was in good working order, the chimney had been swept, and the sun was now able to shine through the cleaned windows.

'Amelia must have been ill for a long time to let things go so badly,' murmured Cordelia. 'She was usually so fastidious about everything.'

'Your sister was a very sick woman,' Peggy said softly. 'It was just such a shame she shut herself away from her neighbours so no one realised what was happening to her until she started wandering the streets in her nightclothes.'

'I still feel guilty about not keeping in touch with her,' fretted Cordelia. 'She was alone and struggling with dementia all the while I was happy and snug with you here at Beach View.'

'You're not to think like that, Cordelia,' Peggy

said as she reached to gently take her hand. 'Amelia was the one who snubbed you and would have nothing to do with the family. Look at the way she refused to help Sarah and Jane when they arrived from Singapore.'

'I know, but she was my older sister, and although we didn't get on and I didn't much like her, I should have made the effort to stay in touch.'

Peggy looked at her old friend evenly. 'Cordelia,' she said firmly, 'life is always full of regrets, but there's no profit in wishing things were different. Amelia was her own worst enemy by the sound of it, and you have nothing to be ashamed of.'

'I suppose so,' Cordelia conceded sadly. 'Poor Amelia. I'm glad I'm not all alone.' There were tears glistening in her eyes as she squeezed Peggy's fingers. 'You have no idea how much I appreciate all you've done for me, Peggy,' she said with a catch in her voice. 'You're so very generous with your care and your time. We're all so lucky to have you.'

Peggy was horribly embarrassed by this effusive praise. 'Actually,' she admitted, 'I feel rather mean at the moment.'

Cordelia's eyes widened in surprise. 'Why on earth is that?'

'Well, it would have been lovely to ask Ruby and Ethel to share our meal on their first night here, but things are so tight, there simply isn't enough to go round. I do hope they won't think me rude for not asking them.'

'Good heavens, dear, of course they won't.' Cordelia's little face tightened into a fierce expression. 'You're a good woman, Peggy, and Ruby knows how lucky she was that you took her in after that horrid, beastly man tried to . . .' She dithered and blushed. 'Well, you know what he tried to do,' she said hastily. 'Anyway, my point is, you've done enough, and if you try to do any more they might see it as over-generous, and be embarrassed that they can't reciprocate.'

'You mean they might think I'm playing Lady Bountiful like my sister Doris,' Peggy said on a sigh. 'I suppose you're right. I am inclined to get carried away sometimes, but I just want them to settle in and be happy here in Cliffehaven. It must be grim up in London, and from what Ruby told me, poor Ethel hasn't had much of a life.'

'They'll settle in and get used to things without you fussing around them like a mother hen,' replied Cordelia with a gentle smile.

Peggy realised she was fretting needlessly, so she gathered up their dirty cups and took them to the sink. 'There's still no sign of Ron or Harvey,' she murmured as she glanced out of the window to the back garden. 'Why don't we follow suit and take some time off too? It won't matter if tea's a bit late this evening, and it's far too hot in this kitchen to sit in here any longer.'

'I think that's a splendid idea,' said Cordelia as she carefully placed the precious orange in the larder, eyeing the bottles of milk stout that sat on the marble shelf. She fetched her walking stick and bag of knitting. 'And perhaps we could even have a glass of that milk stout you refused to drink when you were supposed to. It's lovely and cold and just the thing for a hot day.'

Peggy raised an eyebrow. She hated milk stout, and Cordelia knew it.

'Humour me,' said the old lady dryly. 'You need building up, and milk stout won't kill you.'

Peggy looked at her with deep affection and went to fetch the milk stout and the baby. It was too hot, and she simply didn't have the energy to argue.

Ron had quickly realised why his lurcher had been disappearing on a regular basis. After asking around, he soon discovered that the object of Harvey's desire was a pedigree whippet that belonged to the snooty old battleaxe who lived in the large house set back from the main road into Cliffehaven.

Sprawling behind high rhododendron hedges that encircled at least two acres of garden, a sizeable lake and woodland, this grand edifice had been built over a century ago for a wealthy merchant who valued his privacy. To this end, only the tall chimneys and ornate ridge of the roof could be seen from the road, and the nearest neighbour – a large mansion which had been turned into a Forces hospital – was over a mile away.

And yet Ron knew the place rather well, for he'd

long since discovered that the woodlands provided a fair number of rabbits, the odd roving deer and even game birds that had escaped from Lord Cliffe's estate. The lake was a good source of ducks and their eggs as well as the sizeable eels that had become trapped after swimming down through the many streams that cross-crossed the woodlands. As there was no trigger-happy gamekeeper here like the one up at the Cliffe estate, Ron had been a fairly frequent visitor these past few years.

In his younger days he'd been employed by the owner to do a bit of gardening and some odd jobs when the weather had made it impossible to take out his fishing boats, so he knew his way around both the house and the grounds. Mr Fullerton had been alive then, traipsing back and forth to London on the train with his bowler hat, umbrella and briefcase to his office, where he was something big in banking.

Ron had come to quite like him, for he'd always had time for a pipe and a chat, and knew a fair bit about gardens. But he'd been henpecked, that was for sure, and as often as not their pleasant few minutes would be interrupted by the foghorn voice of his awful wife demanding his immediate presence.

Ron was not in the best of moods as he clumped up the hill in his wellington boots, for he'd missed lunch, and there were a thousand and one things he should be doing instead of coming up here looking for his lovesick, heathen dog. Rosie had asked him to change the barrels before she opened the Anchor tonight, Peggy was expecting to have her outside lav in full working order by the end of the day, and his ferrets Flora and Dora were getting fat through lack of exercise.

He finally reached the high hedge that fronted the property, and stood there for a moment to admire the view of Cliffehaven spread out below him. The town followed the line of the horseshoe bay and sprawled northward into the surrounding hills. There were chalk cliffs to the east and rolling hills tumbling almost to the promenade to the west, and from here, Ron could see the gun emplacements that dotted those hills, and the enemy plane which had been shot down and was now rusting into the remains of the pier.

It was still an attractive place if you didn't look too closely, but it had grown during the war, with ugly factories and emergency prefab houses springing up where there had once been green fields. Now the sun shone on glinting barrage balloons and emphasised the stark reality of the bomb sites that scarred the once orderly lines of Victorian terraces.

He gave a deep sigh and returned to the problem of finding Harvey. There was no guarantee that he was even here, and if he wasn't, then this whole enterprise was a waste of time. Ron eyed the hedge and considered the more prudent approach might be to go the long way round and enter the estate from the woodland at the back where he was less likely to be seen by Agatha Fullerton – but he dismissed the idea almost immediately. It was yet another long trek and he was in no mood for going much further on an empty stomach.

Hitching up his baggy corduroy trousers, he looked up and down the deserted road and then, satisfied no one could see him, eased his way through a narrow gap in the rhododendrons. It was cool and deeply shadowed amongst the tangled branches, and he knew he was well camouflaged in his dusty brown clothes, so he squatted down, regarded the terrain in front of him and thought about a plan of action.

If his information had been correct and Harvey was here, then no doubt he'd be circling the house trying to find a way in. And if Agatha Fullerton caught him, there would be ructions and no mistake. Harvey was well known in this town and instantly recognisable. One glimpse of him would have Agatha on the doorstep of Beach View Boarding House causing untold trouble for him and his dog – and upsetting Peggy into the bargain.

Ron chewed on the stem of his unlit pipe as he eyed the large lake between him and the house. If Harvey did appear, then Ron didn't have a hope in hell of getting round that lake and grabbing him before he ran off – and he certainly wouldn't come to a whistle, not with all the distractions of that whippet bitch. He would have to find another hiding place nearer to the house, and just hope Agatha wasn't looking out of one of her many windows.

He crouched lower and studied the ornamental lake. There was a clump of pampas grass and another of bulrushes and irises which might provide cover, and if he made it across the gravel path to the house, there was the jut of the porch he could hide behind. Though he'd have to be quick to catch the old bugger as he shot past, for Harvey could run like the wind, and was an expert in evasion tactics.

His gaze trawled the tranquil water, noting that the small flock of quacking ducks was huddled together at one end and looking very put out about something. This was odd behaviour and Ron frowned as he looked more carefully to see if he could spot what had disturbed the birds. If it was a big eel, then maybe he'd come back tonight and see if he could net it for the dinner table – it had been a long while since he'd had jellied eel and the thought made his mouth water.

Then something stirred beneath the lily pads in the middle of the lake, and a brindled head and two ears emerged, swiftly followed by a pair of eyes and the top of a long, pointed nose.

Ron had to bite his lip to smother his laughter. Harvey was using commando tactics to win his prize. God love him, the old lothario must be desperate.

The ears and head didn't move beneath the lily

pads as the eyes darted back and forth, the brows wriggled, and the water stirred gently around the nose at every breath. Harvey was perfectly camouflaged and poised for action.

Ron stayed absolutely still, fascinated to see how long Harvey would remain there and what would happen next.

He didn't have very long to wait, for minutes later the front door opened and the redoubtable figure of Agatha Fullerton strode out onto the gravel path, her sleek grey whippet in her arms. She looked around her warily, and deciding that the coast was clear, set the whippet down. 'Run along, Princess, there's a good girl,' she ordered.

Princess was a very obedient animal and she ran off quite happily to the far side of the lake, where she sniffed the grass intently as her owner smiled benignly from the doorway.

Ron glanced quickly at the lake. Harvey hadn't moved a muscle, but his gaze flew between the woman in the doorway and the grey whippet which was now moving fairly swiftly towards the closely fenced woodland.

Agatha Fullerton must have come to the conclusion that her precious pedigree pet was safe from marauding vagabond dogs, for she went back inside.

Harvey was out of the lake in a flash and haring across the lawn at lightning speed, dirty water and mud flying off his coat. Hell-bent on claiming his prize, he hurtled into the trees and was lost from sight.

Ron heard the welcoming yips of the whippet and eased back through the hedge. Emerging into the bright sunlight, he took a moment to light his pipe. There was absolutely nothing he could do now but wait for Harvey to return to Beach View.

He grinned round the stem of his pipe as he clumped back down the hill towards home. The old so-and-so clearly still had some life left in him, but he was punching well above his weight with that expensive whippet, and Ron just hoped to God Agatha never discovered the identity of the old rogue who had so enthusiastically deflowered her precious Princess.

He was still smiling and shaking his head in amusement at the memory of Harvey in that lake. There was no doubt about it, he thought, Harvey was a highly intelligent and resourceful dog, even if he was a ruddy nuisance. But there would be ructions, and from now on Harvey would have to be kept on a lead every time he went outside.

Quite how he was going to achieve this, Ron had no idea – but he was sure he could come up with some solution by the time Harvey returned home.

Chapter Four

Hamble Ferry Pool was placed between the Solent and the Hamble River, and its airfield made it the obvious jumping off point for the hundreds of Spitfires that were being built at the Vickers works in Southampton. The day-to-day routine of flying these new planes to country airfields like the nearby Chattis Hill and High Post on the edge of Salisbury Plain, where they were tested and armed, was never straightforward, for Southampton was constantly under attack.

The all-women pool loved flying the perfect lady's plane, but when the sirens went off to warn of an incoming raid, the barrage balloons went up to protect the Spitfires that were lined up like sitting ducks beside the grass runway. This manoeuvre left only a narrow corridor for friendly incoming aircraft, and as the alignment of that corridor changed each day, it often meant the women had to employ aerobatics to avoid them. This sometimes led to accidents, for not all were as experienced as Kitty and Charlotte in this particular skill, and the RAF certainly didn't make it part of their training.

Three weeks had passed since she'd last seen

Freddy, and Kitty had returned to Hamble after a long day of delivering a Spitfire to High Post, a Mosquito to Aston Down and a damaged Mitchell to the Dunfold Maintenance Unit in Surrey, where it was to be broken up. The tiny cottage she and Charlotte had been allocated right next to the runway felt rather empty with Charlotte away, and as she hadn't felt like playing another endless game of bridge in the mess, or listening to the wireless, Kitty had decided to stretch her legs and get some fresh air before going to bed.

It was a pleasant evening, but still cool enough to warrant an overcoat, and she dug her hands in her pockets as she walked down the narrow lane that ran through the village to the water's edge. The stench of the refineries and the ugly sight of the factory roofs in Southampton couldn't diminish the charm of this place. She looked out over the Solent, listening to the ever-present cries of the gulls. It was quintessentially English, and despite everything, she doubted it had changed in decades.

There were still reminders of peace-time in the ancient trellised verandas that offered a shady spot to sit on a hot day, and in the tiny shops nestled between the five pubs which became favourite bolt-holes during a raid. The Bugle, which faced the water next to the yacht club, was the most famous, for people had flocked there before the war to eat the lobsters that were regarded as second to none.

On a quiet, early summer evening like this, she

could imagine how it must once have been, with bright sailing boats and the sound of laughter coming from the yacht club and the pubs, as the armchair seadogs shared their opinions on weekend sailors with anyone who would listen, and children played in the shallows with their buckets and spades.

She stood there watching the seabirds dabbling at the water's edge as the wind ruffled her hair and the sun dipped low behind the factory chimneys, leaving the sky streaked with pink and orange – perhaps a harbinger of good weather for the next day. Realising her face was cold and that it would soon be too dark to find her way back safely, Kitty turned away from the peaceful scene and trudged up the steep lane to the wider road that would lead her back to the cottage.

Despite the lovely little cottages they were billeted in, Hamble Pool was run a bit like boarding school, with a strict timetable, little cliques and a definite hierarchy. Yet the ATA was a civilian organisation and the many rules were largely ignored. Only the most serious of infringements could be punished by instant dismissal, and everyone knew this was rarely enforced, for ferry pilots were essential to the war effort.

As she walked, Kitty thought of Freddy and Charlotte, who had finally managed to wangle an entire weekend together. Charlotte wouldn't be returning to Hamble Pool until the early train came in the next morning, and Kitty could only hope that she'd manage to snatch some sleep before she had to start work again, for tiredness led to carelessness, which caused accidents.

Although Kitty treasured her independence and shied clear of romantic involvements that might interfere with her work and her emotions, she rather envied them. They were so clearly suited, and if it wasn't for this war, she was sure Freddy would have popped the question by now. It was what Charlotte was hoping for, but Kitty knew Freddy was hanging fire because making that sort of commitment at a time like this was not to be taken lightly. They'd all heard of someone who'd lost a husband or fiancé, and Freddy had confided that he was too much in love with Charlotte to let her go through such pain should anything happen to him.

'Foolish boy,' she murmured as she approached her cottage. 'Doesn't he realise she'd be devastated with or without an engagement ring on her finger?'

'Talking to yourself, Pargeter?'

Kitty nearly jumped out of her skin. She hadn't seen the Ops Officer, Alison King, standing in the dark open doorway of the next-door cottage. 'It's the first sign of madness, I know,' she said with a wry smile. 'But at least that way no one can give me an argument.'

Alison smiled back. 'I know exactly what you mean. But I suggest an early night, Pargeter. The forecast is good for tomorrow and it will be another busy day.'

Kitty wished her goodnight and went into her cottage. Within the hour, she was fast asleep and dreaming of flying a Spitfire over the Argentine pampas.

Charlotte arrived in a rush just as Kitty was handed her orders for the day. 'Gosh,' she breathed, 'I so nearly didn't make it on time. The train was delayed.'

Kitty noted the sparkling eyes and radiant face and grinned. 'I can see the break was worth all the trouble,' she said. 'Hurry up and get your chits. We've only got a couple of minutes to catch up before we're off.'

Charlotte collected her orders and they hurried away from the queue. 'I'm doing Spitfires all day,' she said breathlessly. 'What about you?'

'I'm picking up a Mosquito from Whitchurch to deliver to Leeds, and then taking a Tiffy to Blackpool. From there I've got an Oxford to deliver to Kidlington.' They regarded one another in frustration. 'So, quick, what happened, Charlotte? Where did you go – what did you do?'

Charlotte blushed and giggled, her face alight with happiness. 'Freddy borrowed Roger's car and we went for a lovely drive in the country, followed by lunch in a sweet little pub that overlooks a tiny river. Then we went for a long walk by the river before he drove me to a very smart hotel for a candlelit dinner and some dancing. On Sunday, we did much the same.'

Her blush deepened as she pulled off the glove from her left hand. 'He proposed, Kitty,' she breathed as the diamond flashed on her finger.

'Oh, Charlotte, that's the best news ever.' Kitty grabbed her friend in an awkward hug, both of them hampered by parachute harnesses and bulky clothing.

'It is, isn't it?' laughed Charlotte. 'Now we really will be sisters.'

'Poor old Freddy.' Kitty giggled. 'He won't know what's hit him with two of us to keep him on his toes.'

There were tears in Charlotte's eyes as she squeezed Kitty's hand. 'I'm so happy, Kitts,' she murmured. 'So very, very happy.'

'And so you should be,' replied Kitty as she examined the beautiful ring. 'My brother is quite a catch – and so are you. You were made for one another.' She grinned in delight. 'Oh, Charlotte, I'm so pleased for you both.'

'Pargeter and Bingham, stop gossiping and see to your duties.'

They both turned to face Margot Gore's steely glare. 'Sorry,' stammered Charlotte, 'but I've just become engaged to Kitty's brother, and we were celebrating.'

'Congratulations,' she said dryly. 'Unfortunately the war doesn't stand still for such things, and the day is wasting. Now get on.'

Kitty gave Charlotte another swift hug and they

hurried their separate ways. 'I'll see you tonight,' shouted Kitty over her shoulder. 'And the first drink is on me.'

'I'll hold you to that,' Charlotte shouted back as she headed for the long line of Spitfires.

Warmed by Charlotte's happiness, Kitty was still smiling as she climbed into the air taxi Anson and stowed her kit.

The orange they'd all shared a week ago was now a distant memory, and although they'd each had only a tiny section of this wondrous gift, it had been savoured right to the last drop, and the peel shaved to flavour Daisy's sugar water. They had licked their fingers and sat quietly at the table for some minutes afterwards, not wanting to break the spell as the scent of the fruit drifted in the room.

It was a totally different atmosphere at the breakfast table this morning, for it was proving to be a very uncomfortable experience for everyone. They could all hear Harvey howling piteously from the basement bedroom, and now Daisy began to yell in sympathy.

'For goodness' sake, Ron,' sighed Peggy in exasperation. 'Isn't there something you can do to shut him up? We've had to put up with this all week, and he's worse than any air raid siren. Now he's set Daisy off as well.'

Ron waggled his wayward eyebrows as he filled his pipe. 'Ah, to be sure, Peggy, there's nothing I can do. He's pining, so he is.'

'You should have had him seen to when he was a pup,' Peggy retorted. She plucked the screaming Daisy out of her high chair and tried to placate her with a sliver of toast.

Ron shrugged. ''Tis too late now to be thinking like that, Peggy girl. I'm sorry for the noise he's making, but if I don't lock him in down there he'll just be off and getting into terrible trouble with Agatha Fullerton, so he will. And you'll not be wanting that harridan on your doorstep.'

'I agree that I don't want that woman coming here,' replied Peggy over Daisy's yells and Harvey's howls, 'but surely there's something you can do to stop him making that racket?'

Ron chewed on the stem of his pipe. 'Well,' he drawled, 'I'm thinking the whippet will be coming out of season any minute now, and then Harvey will quieten down, so he will.'

'Oh, I think the cricket season has already started,' said Cordelia with a frown. 'I didn't know you liked cricket, Ron. Are you thinking of playing this season?'

Fran and Rita collapsed into a fit of giggles, and even Peggy had to smile at this, but none of them encouraged Cordelia to turn up her hearing aid as she was the only person in the kitchen not being deafened by the baby and the dog.

'Lord bless you, Cordelia,' Ron shouted above the noise. 'I've not held a cricket bat in me life.'

Cordelia frowned again and looked at the others

in helpless confusion. 'What's his wife got to do with it?' she asked. 'She's been dead for years.'

Ron gave up trying to explain and shrugged his shoulders as the girls continued to giggle.

Sarah pushed back her chair and gathered up the gabardine raincoat which was part of her Women's Timber Corps uniform. 'It's such a lovely day I think I'll leave now and take my time getting to work,' she said with great diplomacy. 'The walk over the hills to the estate will help to clear my head ready for this morning's stock-take.'

'I'm sorry it hasn't been exactly restful around here just lately, dear,' said Peggy, retrieving her daughter's discarded bit of soggy toast from the front of her apron. 'Let's hope he'll be quieter by tonight and then we can all get some peace.'

Sarah gave her a wan smile before kissing her great aunt Cordelia on the cheek. 'I'll see you all later.' She headed for the front door, which was the only exit from the house now that Ron had made the garden door out of bounds in an effort to keep Harvey in.

Suzy poured a second cup of stewed tea from the pot. 'Do you think he might make less noise if you let him come into the kitchen, Ron? It might be that he just hates being shut away after having the run of the house all his life.'

'I tried that, so I did,' replied a gloomy Ron. 'But the kitchen window was open and he took a swallow dive straight out of it and was off.' He gave a deep sigh. 'To be sure he was lucky not to break his neck from that height, but I'm sorry he's such an inconvenience.'

Peggy's expression was grim as she jiggled Daisy up and down on her lap in an effort to quieten her. 'Your blessed dog is not the only inconvenience to be borne in this house, Ronan Reilly,' she retorted. 'The outside lav still isn't finished, and you've been promising to see to it for weeks.'

'Ach, well, I've been awful busy.' He squirmed in the kitchen chair, refusing to meet her gaze. 'There's all the work we had to do after the bomb blast, and the cleaning up. And then I've had to look after me ferrets and rush about after Harvey, and do me duty with the Home Guard and . . .'

'All right, all right,' interrupted Peggy wearily. 'I should have known better than to ask. You and Harvey are as bad as each other – one whiff of a distraction and you're gone.'

'Will ye be listening to yourself, Peggy? Don't be fretting, girl. I'll be doing the lav today, so I will. Straight away after I've helped Rosie to change the beer barrels and bottle up, and taken me ferrets and Harvey for their exercise.'

Peggy rolled her eyes and tried to stem the surge of impatience that shot through her. It was always the same when it came to the jobs she needed doing here, and the fact that Ron had painted Rosie Braithwaite's living quarters above the pub only served to irritate her further. 'If it's not done by the end of the week then I'll get out a hammer and nails and do it myself,' she threatened.

'Now then, Peggy, there's no need to be putting yourself out like that,' he soothed. 'You'll only injure yourself, and then you'll have something else to moan about.'

'You'll have something to moan about if you patronise me like that again,' she snapped with a glare. 'Just see to it, Ron, or I'll use some of your pension to pay a man to do it for you.'

His blue eyes widened in horror beneath the bushy brows. 'You'll not be spending me pension on such a thing,' he gasped.

'Then fix the lav,' she said flatly.

Rita pushed back from the table and picked up the WWI leather flying helmet and sheepskin-lined jacket she always wore over her fire brigade uniform to ride her motorbike. 'You've lost the argument, Uncle Ron,' she said, 'so you might as well give in gracefully and get on with it. You can't expect Grandma Finch to go up and down the stairs all day, and Peggy has enough to do without you making life more difficult.'

'I agree,' said Fran as she tossed back her mane of russet hair and reached for her nurse's cloak. 'And to be sure, Uncle Ron, I'm thinking perhaps the job is too difficult for you, which is why you keep putting it off.'

'And to be sure you're a cheeky wee girl,' he countered with the ghost of a smile. He gave a great sigh as if the world was lying heavily on his sturdy shoulders. 'All right, I give in. 'Tis punished I am for me sins to be living in a house of bossy, demanding women.'

'And 'tis punished we are to have to listen to that dog,' murmured Fran. 'Come on, Suzy, let's get to the hospital.'

'But it's still early,' protested Suzy, 'and I really don't want to face Matron with my hair in such a mess.'

'Facing Matron is the lesser of two evils if you're asking me,' said Fran as she swept the cloak over her striped dress and starched apron. 'If I have to listen to that racket for one more minute, I'll be going demented.'

'Hang about, I'm coming with you,' said Rita as she gave Peggy and Cordelia a quick peck on the cheek and clumped after them in her heavy boots.

Peggy glared at Ron, who was now contentedly lighting his smelly pipe and leaning back in his chair like a lord, and wondered how he had the nerve to lounge about when there were so many things to see to today.

'Oh, dear,' sighed Cordelia, seemingly oblivious to the noise and the atmosphere as she read her morning copy of the *Telegraph*. 'Rommel and his army have reached El Alamein. I suppose now there will be another long drawn-out, horrible battle to take it back. Thank goodness Jim and Frank are still safe in England.'

Peggy smiled fondly at the elderly woman and

hoped with all her heart that her husband and brother-in-law stayed where they were for the duration. The thought of either of them having to fight again after what they'd gone through in the first war was unbearable.

It was like a physical pain squeezing her heart as she thought of her scattered family. Jim hadn't been home since he was called up, and the boys were growing up without her down on that farm in Somerset. Bob was already fifteen – on the cusp of manhood – and in less than three years would be considered old enough to fight.

Please God this war doesn't last that long, she prayed silently as the sorrows and frustrations of life seemed to multiply and lie heavy in her heart. She heard the howling dog and held the screaming, squirming baby and longed desperately for peace and order, and the certainties of the time before this awful war had started. They'd never been rich, but they'd been happy, and there was always food on the table and the freedom to go dancing on the pier where the coloured lights blazed through the night.

Unable to bear her thoughts any more, Peggy pushed away from the table and carried Daisy out into the hall. Having buckled her wriggling little body into the pram, she ignored her screams and went to fetch clean nappies and a bottle from the kitchen. There was no sign of Ron and no sound from Harvey, which could only mean that Harvey was on a tight leash and being taken for a walk.

Taking off her wrap-round apron, Peggy folded it into the string shopping bag alongside her purse, the nappies and bottle, and the list of things she needed to buy. With a headscarf over her dark hair and a thick cardigan to keep off the chill of this early June morning, she bent to kiss Cordelia goodbye.

'I'm going for a walk,' she said clearly so she was understood. 'Then I'm due at the Town Hall. I'll be back at lunchtime.'

'Are you all right, dear?' Cordelia asked with a concerned frown.

'I'm fine,' she lied. 'I just need some fresh air before I'm stuck in that crowded hall for three hours.'

'You do too much,' grumbled Cordelia. 'The doctor said you should be resting.'

Peggy just nodded. There would be time enough to rest when she was in her box and six feet under. She had far too much to do to be sitting about with her feet up. 'Just promise me you'll use the commode in my bedroom and not go up and down the stairs when you're alone in the house,' she said firmly.

'Yes, dear, of course.'

Peggy knew that look of wide-eyed innocence and didn't believe her for one minute – but then Cordelia hated using that commode, and if Ron had fixed . . .

Impatient with her thoughts, Peggy went back into the hall, opened the front door and bumped the pram down the steps. She was almost two hours early for her stint at the WVS centre in the Town Hall but she had to escape for a while, for the inner peace and fortitude she'd once possessed had deserted her, and she needed to find it again.

It was a lovely bright morning despite the chill breeze coming off the sea. The gulls and terns were making their usual racket on the rooftops, but it was a sound Peggy had lived with all her life and she found it strangely soothing in its familiarity as she headed purposefully for the promenade.

Daisy's screams slowly faded as the movement of the pram rocked her to sleep, and Peggy breathed in the salt air and felt refreshed. She would take a long walk along the prom, she decided, and perhaps treat herself to a cup of tea in the café if it was open. By then she would be more able to face whatever dramas awaited her in the Town Hall.

The morning had progressed smoothly, and after a rather bland lunch of corned beef and mashed potato in the canteen at Blackpool, Kitty had avoided the ever-present journalists with their intrusive cameras and picked up the Airspeed Oxford – or Ox Box, as it was affectionately known. She took off in bright sunshine for Kidlington, which lay five miles north of Oxford. There was a report of low cloud further south, but this was thought to be temporary and therefore shouldn't pose a problem.

The Ox Box was a lumbering, slow plane compared

to the smaller fighters she'd already delivered today, but as she sat at the controls and followed the flight path she'd plotted on her map, she knew that this plane was the work-horse of the RAF fleet, and therefore hugely important. It served as a trainer for air gunners, pilots, navigators and cameramen, and was frequently used as an air taxi or put into service as an air ambulance.

Kitty always felt small and rather alone in this particular plane, for there was an empty co-pilot's seat beside her and another for a navigator behind her. When used for transporting personnel, there was room for six passengers as well. She kept an eye on her instruments and the railway lines beneath her as the twin engines rumbled reassuringly and the skies remained clear.

At this rate, she thought, *I'll be back in Hamble with plenty of time to spare to have a bath before Charlotte and I go for that drink – and if I'm very lucky, I might even be able speak to Freddy on the telephone to congrat-ulate him too.* With these pleasant thoughts, Kitty continued the flight towards Kidlington.

She had been flying for over an hour when, without warning, she was faced with a great curtain of rain. She adjusted her speed and took the Ox Box down to just a few hundred feet above the ground, where the visibility was only slightly better. She now had two choices. To turn back and land at the nearest airfield, or to carry on and hope this downpour was just a passing quirk of the weather. It was certainly much further north than had been forecast, so she decided to risk it and keep going.

But the rain slowly became heavier and Kitty found herself engulfed in a thick blanket of cloud, which blotted out the land beneath her with alarming swiftness and forced her to fly blind.

She rammed open the throttles, pulled the control column back and went into a steep climb. Trying to keep the angle of the climb constant and watching her instruments keenly, she saw the altimeter needle pass the two thousand-feet mark and then the three.

It was just touching four thousand feet when the clouds splintered into bright sunlight, and she was able to level off. Looking beneath her she could see only the cotton wool clouds stretching to every horizon, and the shadow of the Airspeed Oxford as the sun lit it from above.

Kitty felt suddenly horribly vulnerable, for she'd never been in this situation before and had now broken the ATA's strictest rule of all by 'going over the top'. She just had to pray that she'd find a hole in the cloud to get back down again. But as she checked her instruments she felt a sharp surge of dread. The fuel gauges were showing that both tanks were suddenly, and inexplicably, half empty. They must have sprung a leak somehow during that sharp climb, and now she had no choice but to go down through the cloud and hope she didn't crash into something.

Experience of flying on instruments alone told

her she was still an hour away from Kidlington, but having flown there before, she knew there was high ground to cross, as well as the sprawl of numerous towns and villages, which she had to avoid at all costs if civilian lives were to be spared.

She licked her lips and tried not to grip the control column too tightly as she desperately searched for a hole, no matter how small, in the cloud. The fuel gauge needles were dropping at a terrifying rate and soon she'd be running on fumes. But there was no hole in the cloud and she was all out of options. She had to land.

Her pulse was racing and the sweat was stinging her eyes behind the goggles as she throttled back and eased the nose down. The clouds clung to the Oxford as it slowly descended and the altimeter ticked off the altitude like a demonic clock. Three thousand feet. Two thousand feet. Fifteen hundred – one thousand – six hundred.

Every cell in her body was screaming at her to stop this madness and go back up. But the fuel gauges were hovering dangerously close to empty now, so she gathered all her courage and tentatively eased the Oxford even lower through the cloud. If she'd calculated correctly, then she should be clear of the hills and high ground and approaching the Vale of Evesham and the River Stour. But if she hadn't then she could be dead within the next few seconds.

There were now less than ten minutes of fuel left

and Kitty was sweating beneath her goggles and leather flying helmet. The cloud was as thick as ever and she was flying less than four hundred feet above ground. A church steeple on a hill would be enough to send her crashing into oblivion.

And then the cloud suddenly broke, revealing the great hills and valleys of the Cotswolds right in front of her. She yanked back on the control column and opened the throttle as she went into a steep climb to avoid them.

The engines screamed and the Oxford began to judder as she was once more engulfed in cloud. It was clear the plane didn't like this heavy handling, so when she reached a thousand feet she levelled out again and slowly turned the Oxford further east.

Unable to see anything in the white-out that surrounded her, she checked her instruments and did some rapid calculations. She now had less than five minutes of fuel left. She had to land immediately – regardless of the dangers.

She took a deep, shuddering breath, blinked away the stinging sweat from her eyes, and forced herself to stay calm as she slowly eased the joystick down again so the Oxford's nose tipped towards earth.

Breaking through the cloud she gave a sob of relief. The Cotswold Hills were no longer in sight and there was an airfield in the distance. It wasn't Kidlington, but she didn't care – any runway was welcome. But another glance at the fuel gauges and the deep tremor of the stuttering engines told her she wouldn't make that runway. The tanks had run dry and she was flying too low to bail out.

Kitty saw the fallow field, and from three hundred feet up, it appeared to be clean of any anti-aircraft traps. She had to risk it.

The Oxford gave another shudder as she unbuckled herself and opened the canopy above her head to provide a quick escape route. Then, with a muttered prayer, she eased the juddering plane into a shallow turn and reached for the hand-crank to lower the landing gear.

She was a hundred feet above ground, the field dead ahead of her, when the engines died and the propeller stopped turning. The plane lurched, dipped its nose and gave her a bird's eye-view of the deadly anti-aircraft stakes and coils of barbed wire lying in wait beneath her. Landing gear could catch on the traps and flip her over, so she swiftly cranked it back up and battled to keep the plane level as it glided with ominous determination towards the field.

Her mind was racing with swift calculations as they hurtled towards the ground. If she could stay up long enough to clear this field and hop over that nearby hedge, she just might have a chance. The field there had been ploughed and was clear of traps. She hauled on the control column, using every ounce of strength to try and keep the great, wallowing plane afloat.

But gravity won and the heavy Oxford belly-flopped into the field with a bone-jarring thud and ploughed a deep furrow in the mud before it crashed into the stakes and barbed wire.

Kitty had been thrown clear but was already unconscious by the time it flipped over and broke its back across the remains of an old flint wall that lay hidden by the hedge.

Chapter Five

Peggy had managed to get most of the things on her shopping list, including a large helping of minced meat, before she had to begin at the Town Hall. The walk had cleared her head and made her feel very much better, and she'd happily spent the morning helping people to sift through the piles of donated clothing to find a new coat, dress, nightwear or shoes to replace what had been lost in the latest air raid. With so many families made homeless, it was vital to make sure they were provided with the essentials.

The Town Hall in Cliffehaven's High Street was a hive of industry, for it had become the centre for the WVS and the Women's Institute, and their volunteers worked hard to collect and sort through the very generous donations of clothes, kitchen equipment, toys, books and bedding.

Nothing was wasted, for old sweaters were unpicked, the wool wound into crinkly balls to be used again, and dresses, skirts and shirts that were too worn to pass on were cut up for cleaning rags, or scraps to be sewn into quilts. A retired cobbler did his best to repair some of the battered shoes, and the owner of the toy shop that had been fire-bombed came in regularly to collect broken toys so he could mend them in the workshop he'd set up in his allotment shed.

And then there was the busy little café to run, the comfort boxes to be filled with treats and warm socks for the troops fighting abroad – and the sandwiches and tea to be made to take to the station to feed the men on their way to their various postings. An almoner gave practical advice to those seeking help with their children, accommodation or work, and at night the mattresses were laid out on the floor of the main hall to provide the homeless with somewhere temporary to sleep while they waited to be rehoused.

Peggy enjoyed working there, for Daisy's pram could be parked in a corner while she got on with things, there was always someone to gossip with, and the tea and biscuits were cheap. The only fly in the ointment was Peggy's sister, Doris, who was on the WVS board and considered herself far too important to actually do anything that might dirty her hands.

She swanned in late that morning showing no sign of embarrassment at the scandal her husband had caused by leaving her for a much younger, rather brash woman who worked behind the counter in the Home and Colonial store. Dressed in the tailored dark green uniform of the WVS and looking immaculate as always, she headed straight for

Peggy, who was trying to find a suitable skirt for a fat woman who refused to believe she wasn't a size ten.

'Margaret,' she said imperiously. 'I need to talk to you.' She shot the fat woman a withering glare. 'In private.'

Peggy hated being called Margaret and Doris knew it, so she gritted her teeth, smiled at the woman and handed her a skirt the width of a barrage balloon. 'Why don't you just try that on, dear,' she said. 'And if it's too big, then you can always take it in at the seams.'

The skirt was snatched with bad grace and a glower and Peggy gave a sigh as she turned to her sister. 'What's the matter?'

Doris hooked her hand into the crook of Peggy's elbow and drew her away from the crowded table. 'Edward and I had a long talk last night,' she said quietly. 'He has left that floozy and moved into one of the apartments above the Home and Colonial.'

Peggy was delighted to hear it for her sister's sake. The shock of Ted's infidelity had rocked Doris to the core, and the following scandal had proved all too clearly that her inclusion in what passed as the high society set in Cliffehaven was no longer encouraged. To Peggy's mind, this was no bad thing: they were a bunch of rich snobs, and probably laughed at the social-climbing Doris behind her back as they got her to do the more onerous tasks for their charities and then took the glory.

'At least Ted won't have far to go to work,' she said lightly.

'*Edward* is the area manager of the Home and Colonial, not one of the counter staff,' Doris said snootily.

Peggy let this pass. 'What about her, the floozy? She's not still working there, is she?'

Doris's lips thinned. 'I believe she's found employment at the dairy, where she'll feel much more at home among the other cows.'

Peggy snorted with laughter. 'Careful, Doris,' she warned with a giggle, 'your lowly upbringing is starting to show.'

'Well,' she replied with a huff, 'there are times when one's feelings have to be given vent.' She hitched the strap of her expensive brown leather handbag over her shoulder and regained her composure. 'Anyway, Edward will not be coming back to live in Havelock Road just yet. He has to prove he is genuinely sorry for causing me so much shame and suffering. But I have agreed that he may come to supper twice a week and for lunch on Sundays. Anthony is delighted, of course. It has been very hard for the dear boy to see his mother laid so low.'

'That's marvellous, Doris,' sighed Peggy. 'I'm so glad you two are talking again.' She smiled. 'How is Anthony? We don't see much of him these days.'

'Neither do I,' she replied with a steely glint in her eye. 'He's got his very important work with the MOD, of course, which keeps him terribly busy, but he seems to prefer Susan's company to mine when he's off duty. I might as well be living alone for all the time he spends with me,' she added with a sniff of disapproval.

'He's young and in love and there's a war on,' said Peggy. 'He and Suzy are a delightful couple, and you should be glad that he's happy.'

Doris eyed her coldly. 'Well, I've said all I'm going to say on the matter,' she said abruptly, pulling on her expensive leather gloves. 'I just wanted you to know how things are panning out between me and Edward.'

Peggy was about to ask if she'd like her to come and keep her company one evening, but Doris had already turned away and was striding towards the front door. 'It's always all about you, isn't it, Doris?' she murmured. 'No thought for how I'm doing, or if Daisy and the family are well.'

She could hear Daisy yelling again and looked at the clock. Her shift had ended two hours ago and she'd missed lunch. No wonder Daisy was beginning to complain.

She took off her wrap-round apron and headscarf, stuffed them in her bag along with her shopping and wheeled the pram down the steps, between the high walls of sandbags to the pavement. She was looking forward to washing the smell of musty old clothes off her hands, and tucking into a spam and tomato sauce sandwich.

*   *   *

When she arrived back at Beach View, Cordelia was sitting in a deckchair in the sunlit back garden, peacefully dozing beneath the brim of her straw hat as Ron finished oiling the hinges on the door of the lovely new outside lav.

Harvey was lying, nose on paws, tethered firmly by a rope that had been lashed tightly through a sturdy ring embedded into the back wall of the house. He eyed Peggy mournfully, his ears drooping and his eyebrows twitching in distress as he crawled on his belly towards her and lifted his nose in a pitiful attempt to gain her sympathy and be freed from this terrible imprisonment.

'You're an old rogue,' Peggy soothed as she stroked the soft head. 'But you don't get round me like that. I'll fetch you a biscuit when I've made a pot of tea.'

'And would you be thanking me for the craftsmanship of this fine edifice, Peggy?' said Ron as he tested the hinges for squeaks.

'It's quite magnificent,' she said, and laughed. 'Let's hope it actually works.'

'To be sure it does,' he protested, his blue eyes beady beneath the wayward brows. 'Cordelia was my first customer, and she said she felt quite regal sitting there.' He opened the door to reveal a shining white porcelain lavatory and matching cast iron cistern with a chain and decorated china handle. 'As you can see, Peggy, me darlin', only the best will do for this family,' he said proudly.

Peggy eyed it all and was immediately suspicious. 'Where did you get it?'

Ron took off his cap and ran his fingers through his thatch of wiry, greying hair, his gaze drifting away from her. 'Well now, Peggy, you'll not be needing to know that.'

'Oh, but I do,' she said, leaving the pram beside the dog and going into the shed to inspect the lav more closely. 'If this lot has been stolen, then you'll not only have the police to deal with, but me as well – and believe me, Ron, you wouldn't like that at all.'

'Ach, Peggy, you're a hard woman so y'are. I've built you the new convenience you've been badgering me for, and all you can do is complain.'

Peggy ignored him and regarded the fancy lettering etched into the cistern and the prettily decorated china handle on the flush chain that bore the same legend. 'The Imperial Hotel,' she read aloud.

'Well now, I can explain all that,' he said quickly. 'When the hotel got bombed, me and Fred the Fish went down there to see what we could find. And there were dozens of these just lying about without a scratch on them. It seemed a shame not to make use of them. Fred's wife's delighted with hers, and Alf has put one in his house too.'

Peggy was trying very hard to keep a straight face as she turned to look at her father-in-law. 'It's called looting, Ron,' she said rather unevenly. 'You should all be ashamed of yourselves.'

'There's no shame in making use of things that were no longer needed,' he replied, 'and there will be no trouble from the police, because the sergeant and two of the constables have got some of these as well, and they asked the hotel owner if it was all right to take them,' he said all in one breath. 'So there,' he finished triumphantly.

Peggy couldn't be cross with him for very long and she burst out laughing and gave him a hug. 'I do love you, Ronan Reilly,' she said fondly.

'Ach,' he said bashfully, 'don't be talking so soft. Go and make that tea.'

Kitty was vaguely aware of hearing voices close by. At first they were muffled as though coming from the depths of the sea, and she wondered fleetingly why that should be. But then she seemed to be floating in a warm womb of darkness and didn't have the strength or will to open her eyes and try to solve the puzzle.

She drifted in this comfortable place, uncaring and unaware of anything very much, until the unmistakable sound of Charlotte's voice penetrated her solitude.

'She looks so small and fragile,' sobbed Charlotte. 'Oh, God, she's going to die, isn't she?'

The darkness was holding Kitty hostage, making her limbs too heavy to move and deadening her ability to speak. But the protest was roaring in her head as she fought the debilitating dumbness to convince

Charlotte that she was mistaken. 'No, Charlotte,' she screamed silently. 'I'm not dying. I can hear you – I'm all right.'

And then suddenly it didn't seem to matter, and she sank gratefully back into the soft, enveloping oblivion. Time lost all meaning, and although she drifted on the cusp of light and dark and caught snatches of conversation and the impression of people around her, she had no will to move further into the light which she knew was just beyond the horizon of this grey, silent, pain-free world where she felt safe.

'Kitty, wake up. Come on, Sis. It's time to open your eyes and come back to the land of the living.'

Freddy's voice penetrated this comfortable cocoon in which she floated and his words seem to draw her from the darkness and softly carry her towards the dawn she could see glimmering in the distance. She wanted to see him, to reach out and reassure him that she knew he was there and that she was all right. But she simply didn't have the strength to open her eyes, not even for her beloved brother.

'Kitty, come on,' he implored softly. 'I know you can hear me, and I'm sure it's really hard to open your eyes, but you have to stop messing about and wake up now.'

She felt as if she was hovering on the very edge of that secure and sheltering darkness, and for a moment she was afraid of leaving it for the unknown beyond – but Freddy was waiting for her there, calling her into the light, and she knew she must go to him.

Slowly and inexorably, she found she was being drawn from that soft twilight into a glaring glow that hurt her eyes and sent shock-waves of pain right through her. She closed her eyes and turned away, trying to curl into the pain – but that made it worse, and she yearned to return to the soothing nothingness of that darker plain.

'Hello, Kitty Cat,' he murmured. 'I know you can hear me. Welcome back.'

The pain stirred like a waking monster, burning through every part of her, its claws digging into her stomach and legs as if threatening to devour them. 'Freddy?' she rasped, her voice sounding strangely vulnerable and unfamiliar.

'Yes, I'm here, Kitty.' She felt the soft touch of his fingers on her cheek. 'It's all right. You're quite safe, and I've moved the bedside light so it won't blind you now.'

She dared to slowly open her eyes, confused by the pain and the unfamiliarity of her surroundings. She seemed to be strapped into a bed and there was a floral curtain surrounding her, closing her off from the darkened room beyond. And then he leaned over her and she could see his regular, handsome features and blue eyes. But his face appeared to be lined with fatigue, his eyes shadowed by some indefinable sorrow, and she felt a stab of alarm. 'Has something happened to Charlotte?' she rasped.

'Charlotte's on duty in Manchester,' he said quickly. 'She's absolutely fine.'

Kitty closed her eyes as the relief rushed through her. 'But she was here just a minute ago,' she murmured with a frown. 'I heard her voice.'

'That was some time ago,' he replied softly.

She tried to accept this, but was certain Freddy had made a mistake. Charlotte had been here, and she'd been talking to someone. But the puzzle was too taxing to deal with now, for the monster of pain was flexing its steely fingers through every inch of her body. 'Sleep,' she muttered. 'I want to sleep.'

'I know, Kitty,' he replied, 'but the doctor says you must wake up now so he can talk to you.'

She didn't want to talk to anyone, but to be left alone to sink back into oblivion and banish this awful pain.

'Kitty.' His fingers lightly brushed her cheek again. 'Kitty, he's on his way, and it's important you wake up and listen to what he has to say. Come on, Sis.'

She opened her eyes again and looked up into his concerned face. 'What happened, Freddy? The pain is . . . almost unbearable.'

'The doctor will give you something to stop the pain after he's spoken to you,' he said gently. He leaned forward, the gold buttons and epaulettes of his Air Force uniform glinting in the pool of lamplight which illuminated the bed and the surrounding curtain like an oasis in the darkened room.

'As for what happened; you pranged the Oxford and got banged up pretty badly,' he said, his soft voice rough with controlled emotion. 'Luckily you came down close to a factory airfield, so the rescue crew got to you quickly, which undoubtedly saved your life. Now you're in the special hospital for service personnel just outside the town of Cliffehaven.'

The fog of confusion and disorientation cleared enough for her to have sudden total recall of those last few terrifying seconds when she'd thought she was about to die. But Cliffehaven was nowhere near the crash site – so what on earth was she doing here? None of this made any sense at all, and as she tried to sit up to remonstrate with Freddy, she was immediately poleaxed by a stab of fire which knifed through her chest and took her breath away.

'Try not to move, Kitty,' her brother said anxiously. 'You'll only hurt yourself again.'

Kitty blearily lay against the pillows and tried to take stock of her injuries. It slowly registered that beneath the crisp white sheet she was almost naked but for the tight bandaging that seemed to cover her from neck to hip. Both arms were in plaster casts and there were needles and tubes stuck into the back of her hands.

She stared down at her fingers which peeked from the plaster and noted the broken nails and the ragged scars of many cuts. Then she looked towards the foot of the bed where one heavily plastered leg was suspended by a series of pulleys, and the other was beneath some sort of cage that held up the sheet. A cautious wriggle of her toes sent a shot of pain up her legs and into her groin. She was clearly lucky to be alive.

And then, as she cautiously touched her face and traced the bandage that seemed to cover her head and part of her face, she was filled with a new kind of crippling horror. 'Was I burned?' she breathed.

'No,' he replied quickly. 'You must have been thrown clear before the kite went up in flames.'

She felt weak with relief and managed a wan smile.

Freddy shot her an affectionate grin. 'The old visog has been bashed about a bit, but you didn't break your nose or cheekbones. The bruising and swelling have mostly gone down, so you don't look quite as frightful as you did when you were first brought in,' he said in that over-cheerful, gung-ho manner of all RAF fighter pilots which set her teeth on edge.

'Don't worry, old thing,' he continued. 'You'll soon be as ugly as always, never fear.'

'Thanks,' she muttered. 'I knew I could rely on you for sympathy.'

His answering grin was a little forced. 'It's what big brothers are for,' he replied. 'You were lucky, actually,' he went on. 'The crash crew found you several feet away, tangled up in barbed wire and anti-aircraft stakes. It took them quite a long time to get you free of that, but they had you in the local cottage hospital within an hour of the crash.'

Kitty regarded him evenly and knew he was uneasy with this conversation, and clearly not telling her everything. 'So why aren't I still there?'

Before Freddy could answer, the curtain parted and a tall, grey-haired man wearing a long white coat over his khaki uniform stepped into the circle of light surrounding the bed. He nodded to Freddy, refused the chair and perched on the very end of Kitty's bed, his kindly face creasing into a gentle smile.

'I'm Surgeon General Thorne. It's good to have you back with us, Pilot Officer Pargeter.'

Kitty felt instantly at ease with him, for he was about the same age as her father and had the same trustworthy smile and deep voice. 'Please, call me Kitty. I don't feel much like a Pilot Officer right this minute – more like a broken bag of bones.'

'That's hardly surprising,' he said in his mellow tones. 'You have indeed broken most of them.'

'But why am I here and not in the cottage hospital near Kidlington?'

'The cottage hospital didn't have the right facilities to treat you, Kitty,' he replied. 'So they put you in an air ambulance and brought you here to us.' He gave her a reassuring smile. 'We have the most up-to-date facilities, and our surgeons and nursing staff are the best in England, so you've been in safe hands ever since you arrived.'

Kitty was still trying desperately to remember anything that happened after the crash, but simply couldn't. 'How long have I been here?'

'You've been with us for two weeks,' he replied. 'I know this will come as a bit of a shock, but you've been heavily sedated, so of course you won't remember any of it.'

Kitty stared at him in disbelief. 'Two weeks?'

The army surgeon nodded. 'You had to have a series of operations, Kitty,' he said solemnly, 'and I thought it would be best to keep you heavily sedated for a while so that your body had time to begin to heal.'

He glanced across at Freddy, and Kitty thought she saw a silent message pass between them. She knew then that something was terribly wrong, and she shivered with dread.

'I began to lessen the dose of morphine to wake you up again,' the surgeon continued. 'You see, I need to discuss with you the procedures I've had to perform, and I had to be sure you were able to understand fully what I'm about to tell you.'

Kitty's heart began to thud painfully against her ribs, and the worm of fear curled more tightly in the pit of her stomach as she looked to her brother. 'Freddy? Freddy, what's happened to me?'

He immediately moved closer to the bed and laid a gentle hand over her fingers, but there were tears in his eyes and he couldn't seem to talk – which only served to stoke the rising terror.

'Kitty, I want you to remember that you're a very brave, tough girl, who can fly Spitfires and survive crashes in Typhoons and Oxfords,' said the army surgeon.

'Just tell me,' demanded Kitty, now on the very edge of hysteria.

'Kitty, you were brought in with just about every bone broken. The ribs and collarbone will heal on their own beneath those tight bandages. The fractures in your arms and right leg are expected to heal perfectly within the usual six weeks, and the scarring on your skull, cheek and ear should fade to nothing by the time you are ready to be released from here. I have had to do some repairs to your spleen, and some of the tendons in your hips, but they too are mending well.'

Kitty regarded him, wide-eyed and hardly daring to breathe as he paused in the long litany of her injuries. She didn't want to hear any more – but knew there was to be no escape. 'There's something else, isn't there?' she whispered. 'Something you're afraid to tell me.'

'Kitty, my dear, the damage to your left leg was extremely severe,' he continued softly, his kind grey eyes filled with sympathy. 'The two bones in your lower leg were badly crushed, and your foot . . . Well, it was found some way away from where you landed.'

She stared at him as the full horror of his words trickled coldly into her brain. 'My foot?' she whispered. 'It's gone?'

He slowly nodded. 'I would have attempted to attach it back on, but the damage to it and the limb was too severe for such pioneering surgery.' He edged nearer to her on the bed and gently took her fingers in his warm hand. 'Kitty, I'm sorry, but infection set in and I was forced to amputate your left leg to just under the knee.'

She couldn't move as she stared back at him, his awful words ringing in her head like a death knell. The tears were hot as they rolled down her face, but she was frozen inside as the full horror of her situation sank in. 'No,' she breathed. 'No, no, no.'

'Oh, Kitty,' said Freddy as he tried to brush away her tears. 'I'm so sorry this has happened to you, but you're strong, you'll get better and . . .'

'But I'll be a cripple,' she sobbed. 'A useless, bloody cripple.'

'I won't allow you to be useless, Kitty,' said the doctor firmly. 'I know it's the most appalling thing for you to take in right at this moment, but you will learn to accept what has happened to you, and with the fortitude and strength of character I know you possess, you will come through this.'

'To do what?' she rasped through the tears and the pain. 'I'm a pilot, and a polo player. I'm barely twenty-one and enjoy riding motorcycles and going swimming and dancing.' She collapsed back against the pillow as the agonising truth tore through her. 'You should have let me die instead of leaving me like this,' she sobbed.

'Don't talk like that, Sis,' Freddy implored. 'I know it must feel like the end of the world now, but you're strong and stubborn, and you'll find a way to battle through this.' He leaned closer. 'You've always had a fighting spirit, Kitty, and now is the time to use it.'

Kitty had no strength to fight anything, for her spirit had withered and died in the full horror of her situation. She couldn't bear to see the stark distress in Freddy's face, or to face the cold, cruel future that stretched endlessly before her, so she closed her eyes and turned deep within herself in search of solace and release from this awful reality.

And then, as if in answer to her prayer, she felt the cool slide of a needle in her arm and the welcome clouds of oblivion claimed her once more.

Chapter Six

It was a beautiful early July morning and Peggy had decided that she and Daisy should have a stroll along the promenade. Now she was making her slow way back up the hill to Beach View as Daisy wriggled about in her pram to watch the mewling seagulls hovering and gliding against the blue sky.

Despite the lovely day and the welcome heat of the sun, Peggy was mourning the loss of those glorious days before the war when she'd taken her other children down to the beach. She'd always packed sandwiches in her large bag, and enough money to buy a bottle of pop or an ice cream for everyone, and they had stayed there nearly all day, digging in the dark wet sand, hunting for treasures in the rock pools, or splashing about in the water. And then, sandy and sun-kissed, they'd trudged for home with their buckets, spades and towels, for a hot bath and a filling tea.

It was all so very different now, even though the sun had sparkled so prettily on the water, for the beach was mined and closed off with great coils of barbed wire. There were ugly shipping traps that marched in a grim concrete line across the bay, manned gun emplacements dotted along the promenade, and even the salty air was permeated by the stink of the oil that rolled in with every wave and lay in clumps on the pebbles. They were a black and terrible reminder of the ships and aircraft that had been lost, and the ever-growing number of men who would never come home again.

Peggy determinedly plodded up the hill. There was no ice cream to be had, and few bottles of pop, and Daisy had yet to know what it felt like to have sand between her toes, or to dip her feet in the shallows. But life went on, and no good came from being miserable and moaning about things – she just had to get on and do her best like everyone else.

She pushed her rather scratched sunglasses back up her nose and then steered the old coach-built pram along the twitten to the back gate, and past the Anderson shelter where they'd had to spend the previous night. She was sweating after that trudge home, and in need of a nice cup of tea.

Cordelia was in the back garden, sitting in the shade of a large umbrella that Peggy suspected Ron had also liberated from the Imperial Hotel, for she seemed to remember seeing some just like it on the hotel terrace the summer before. It was quite a surprise that he hadn't filched one of the wrought-iron tables and a couple of chairs while he was at it, she thought with a wry smile. The old deckchairs were definitely past their best, and a three-legged stool served as a garden table.

'Hello, dear,' said Cordelia as she set aside her knitting. 'Did you have a nice walk?'

Peggy lifted a gurgling Daisy out of the pram, adjusted her cotton bonnet and sat her on the blanket in the playpen, which had been brought outside now the weather was fine. 'The sea looked very inviting,' she said as she shifted the umbrella so it also shaded the baby. 'But on the whole it was a bit depressing having to look at the barbed wire and all the damage to the seafront hotels.'

She sat down in the other rickety deckchair and untied the laces on her scruffy sandshoes. They had seen better days too, for the canvas was shredding and the rubber soles were worn thin.

'There's damage everywhere one looks,' said Cordelia, nodding towards the tarpaulin that still covered the roof of the house opposite. 'But we can't let that spoil such a beautiful day. This heat is so very kind to my old bones, and I haven't had a twinge of arthritis for weeks.'

They both looked up as several squadrons of bombers and fighter planes came roaring overhead to shatter the peaceful morning. Daisy clapped her hands and laughed as she watched them, for it was now a familiar sight and the noise didn't frighten her one bit.

'It looks as if our boys are on their way to give Germany another hammering,' said Cordelia once they'd disappeared over the Channel. 'It amazes me that Hitler hasn't surrendered after all these weeks of day and night bombing raids.'

'Poor Martin must be exhausted,' sighed Peggy as she reached for the teapot which sat on the little stool between them. 'The responsibility for all those men, the constant ops and the endless list of missing or dead has to be wearing him down.'

'I suspect that when you're in the thick of it, you don't notice,' said Cordelia. She smiled at Peggy. 'Your son-in-law is tougher than you think,' she said firmly. 'He's a born leader and his men adore him. He'll be all right, you'll see.'

Peggy hoped with all her heart that he would be, for she loved him very much and her daughter's happiness was at stake. She drank some of the horrid stewed tea and grimaced. 'I think I'll make a fresh pot and then do some spam sandwiches for lunch.'

She suddenly realised it was very quiet, and that was as unusual as all the girls having the same day off work. 'Where is everyone?'

'Rita's gone to pick up Ruby on that infernal machine of hers. I think they're meeting up with that nice little Lucy Kingston and going for a picnic in Havelock Park.'

'Oh, that's lovely,' said Peggy contentedly. 'I'm so glad Ruby has settled in so well and made such good friends. She's earned some happiness and youthful fun after all she's been through.'

Cordelia chuckled. 'It seems Ethel is settling in very well too. She's working in the same factory as Ruby and has already made lots of friends with the other girls from the East End, so she's feeling quite at home now.'

'Yes, I know,' said Peggy. 'I bumped into her the other day as she was coming out of the station and almost didn't recognise her. She's filled out a bit and looks so much younger and happier now she's lost that London pallor, and she's thrilled with the bungalow.'

Cordelia frowned. 'What was she doing at the station? Surely she's not going back and forth to London?'

Peggy shook her head. 'It seems she and Stan have hit it off. She told me she's doing a bit of cleaning and cooking for him, as a man on his own couldn't be expected to feed himself properly, and Stan needed building up.'

'Goodness me,' gasped Cordelia. 'Stan's not exactly fading away, and he's always seemed very capable of looking after himself.'

Peggy shrugged. 'Perhaps he just likes having a woman about the place again to fuss over him,' she murmured. 'He's been a widower for a long time.'

Cordelia eyed her over the half-moon spectacles and clucked like a fussy hen. 'For goodness' sake, Peggy,' she said on a sigh, 'you must stop this match-making. She's almost half his age.'

Peggy smiled. 'That she might be, but I suspect she wants to fuss over Stan because of how good he was to her Ruby. From what Ruby has told me, her mother was a lonely woman trapped in an unhappy and violent marriage just as she had been, so I'm glad Ethel's found some companionship in Stan.'

'It was all very different in my day,' said Cordelia with a sniff. 'Married women had a bit of decorum and wouldn't dream of carrying on like that.'

Peggy understood how bewildering this modern way of life must be for Cordelia, but there was little point in trying to make her see things differently, so she turned the conversation back to the whereabouts of her lodgers. 'So, where are the others? Are they expected home for lunch?'

'I shouldn't think so. Suzy is spending the day with Anthony. Sarah and Jane have packed sandwiches and are going for a walk in the hills, and Ron has taken Harvey to the Anchor now he's calmed down and is back to his old self. I think Ron was planning to take Rosie for afternoon tea in the café at the end of the promenade before the pub opens again at six.'

'And Fran? Where's she got to?'

Cordelia frowned with disapproval. 'An enormous car pulled up five minutes after you'd gone for your walk, and an American army officer with a swagger and far too many white teeth whisked her away. She shot out of the door so fast I didn't have time to ask who he was and where she was going.'

Cordelia pursed her lips. 'I got the distinct impression she didn't want me to know anything about him – which is highly suspicious, if you ask me.'

Peggy silently agreed. She would have a quiet word with Fran tonight just to make sure she wasn't doing anything silly, for the American glamour boys could easily turn a girl's head, especially if she'd been as strictly raised as Fran.

Daisy had been fed and stripped of her clothes so she could splash about with her plastic ducks in the old tin bath that had been consigned to the shed once the bathroom had been installed. Peggy had decided that it was much too nice a day to spend doing housework, and so, after a sandwich lunch, she fetched her basket of mending and sat beneath the umbrella with Cordelia.

She was just sewing yet another button on one of Ron's much faded shirts when she heard the click of the back garden gate. 'Martin,' she called in delight. 'What a lovely surprise, we were only talking about you earlier.'

He was tall, broad shouldered and very dashing in the RAF uniform, and his luxuriant moustache tickled her as he planted a resounding kiss on her cheek. 'Nothing too bad, I hope,' he teased. 'A chap has got his reputation to worry about, you know.'

'No, nothing bad,' she said around the sudden lump in her throat.

'And how is my very best girl today?' he boomed at Cordelia.

Cordelia blushed scarlet and twittered like an overexcited little bird as he gallantly kissed the back of her hand. 'All the better for seeing you, you cheeky boy,' she replied coquettishly.

'That's splendid,' he said with a broad smile. 'And I must say, you look very chipper on this lovely day.'

He took off his hat, placed it carefully on the stool and turned back to Daisy, who was laughing up at him from her makeshift pool. 'Hello, sweet pea,' he said softly. 'My goodness, haven't you grown?'

He put down his sturdy-looking document case and lifted the delighted baby into his arms, taking absolutely no notice of the water that was now dripping down his pristine uniform and dulling the brass buttons. 'You remind me so much of Rose,' he murmured as he let her tug his moustache and pat his face with her tiny wet hands.

There were tears in Peggy's eyes as she watched this little scene, for she could see the longing for his own daughter in his face, and hear the wistfulness in his voice. 'You'll ruin your uniform,' she said gruffly.

'It doesn't matter a jot,' he replied as he tickled Daisy's tummy and made her giggle. 'Uniforms can be cleaned, but a cuddle with a baby is a rare pleasure that cannot be missed for anything.'

He kissed the chubby little face and carefully dipped her toes in and out of the water, which made her kick and gurgle in delight. Then he finally sat her down in the tub and handed her one of the rubber toys. 'We'll play again later when we've both dried off,' he promised.

Peggy laughed as she got out of the deckchair. 'I'll get you another towel. Daisy's is a bit small.'

'No, wait, Peggy.' He picked up the document case. 'I have something here that is perfect for such a lovely day.' Unfastening the locks, he pulled out a large bottle of gin and three more of Indian tonic water. 'I thought we could enjoy these in the sun while we catch up on all the news,' he said.

He placed the bottles on the ground and dug back into the case. 'I also managed to get a couple of these,' he added with a broad grin.

'Good heavens,' breathed Cordelia.

Peggy reached for one of the lemons and breathed in the long-forgotten scent. 'But where on earth did you manage to find them?'

'Ah, well, I probably shouldn't tell you that,' he said as he twirled one end of his dampened moustache. 'Let's just say they fell off the back of an American transporter plane.'

Peggy and Cordelia burst out laughing. 'You're beginning to sound like Ron,' Peggy spluttered.

He winked and chuckled. 'Well, I'll take that as a compliment, Peggy. Ron is a fine man, so he is, and his skills as the provider of the little luxuries in life are quite legendary. So they are.'

Peggy giggled at Martin's gentle mimicry. 'You'll have to work on that Irish accent a bit more, Martin,' she teased. 'Eton and Oxford plum doesn't quite do it.'

'I say,' he drawled with a comical show of hurt pride. 'Steady on. I'll have you know I was quite something in the Oxford drama group.'

Peggy was smiling as he went off to inspect Ron's vegetable plot, and she lifted Daisy out of the tub and began to dry her. Once her nappy and thin vest were on, and the bonnet tethered under her chin, she put her in the pram with her bottle of weak cordial, and pulled up the hood to keep off the sun.

'Are we going to have that gin and tonic? Only I'm getting a bit parched with all this sun,' Cordelia piped up rather querulously.

'I'll get the glasses and slice up this lemon now Daisy's organised,' said Peggy. 'Martin, there's another deckchair in the basement. Make yourself at home.'

She hurried indoors and found some mismatched glasses in the dining-room cupboard. They hadn't been used since the wonderful send-off Martin and Ron had arranged before Jim and Frank had to leave for their training camp barracks.

She stood in the neglected and cluttered dining room, deep in her memories. It had been a marvellous day, for Martin had arranged to bring Anne, Rose and both her young sons for a short visit as a special surprise. But, of course, the merriment had withered away as they'd all eventually had to say goodbye, not knowing when they would be together again.

Not wanting to dwell on these poignant memories, she gave the glasses a quick rinse under the tap, sliced the lemon as thinly as she could, grabbed a towel from the pile on the table, and then returned to the garden.

Martin had been busy during her short absence, she noted. He'd stripped off his uniform jacket, rolled up his shirtsleeves and taken off his tie. There were now five deckchairs placed within the shadow of the vast umbrella, and he'd managed to unearth the old bedside table from Ron's tip of a room, and had covered it with a large square of bright blue silk.

When Peggy looked at him questioningly, he grinned. 'I thought the others might come back, hence the extra chairs,' he explained. 'And I brought the scarf with me for just this purpose. Thought it might liven things up a bit and make tiffin special.'

'It's far too good to be used as a tablecloth,' Peggy protested as she handed him the towel. 'I'll fetch one of mine.' Before he could give her an argument, she'd shot back indoors, fetched one of her mother's hand-embroidered linen cloths she used for best and returned to the garden.

Cordelia was in raptures over the scarf. 'Oh, you naughty boy,' she twittered. 'It's lovely. But you shouldn't have.'

'It was made for you,' he said affectionately. 'The colour matches your eyes.'

'You really do talk a lot of nonsense, Martin,'

chuckled Peggy as she smoothed the cloth over the table and laid out the bottles, glasses and saucer of lemon slices. 'Cordelia is quite beside herself, and you're beginning to sound like my Jim. He's always full of the blarney.'

Martin grinned and poured out the drinks, adding a sliver of lemon, before he raised his glass. 'Here's to a pleasant afternoon in the sun. Chin chin.'

Peggy took a sip and sighed with pleasure. There was nothing like a gin and tonic in the garden on a hot summer's day.

An hour later Cordelia had fallen asleep with her chin dipped to her chest, her straw hat tilted askew as she gently snored. Peggy carefully adjusted the hat and took the empty glass out of her hand before it could fall and smash on the paving.

'I think you were a bit heavy-handed with the gin, Martin. Poor Cordelia's not used to such large measures,' she scolded softly as she returned to her deckchair. 'I'm feeling decidedly tiddly too, if the truth be known, but it was a lovely treat. Thank you.'

'It was my pleasure.' He stretched his long legs, leaned back and closed his eyes against the sun. 'I get so little time to relax and really unwind, and with Anne and Rose down in Somerset, it's wonderful to come here and feel at home.'

Peggy's heart was warmed by this sweet sentiment. 'You know you're always very welcome, Martin.'

She lit a cigarette, checked on the still sleeping Daisy and returned to her chair. 'Have you been to your cottage lately?'

'It's near enough to Cliffe aerodrome to pop over on a fairly regular basis to make sure there aren't any burst pipes or unwanted visitors. I feel rather mean not renting it out, but I keep hoping this war will be over soon and Anne and I can move back in with Rose and make it a home again.'

'Do you think things are beginning to turn in our favour now we have the Americans on our side? The news on the wireless doesn't really tell us much, and it's a bit frustrating at times not to have a complete picture.'

Martin shifted in the deckchair. 'The news is censored, of course, because so much of what we're doing has to be kept secret from the enemy. As you've probably guessed by the number of planes going over here, we've been on blanket bombing ops night and day for several weeks. The RAF has carried out night attacks on a thousand-mile front from Norway to France, but our main targets have been Bremen, Essen and Bremerhaven. Northern France is another target, and the German factories in Lille.'

He squinted into the sun and put on a pair of dark glasses. 'A new offensive on the Eastern Front has begun, for the Russians have lost control of Crimea, and the Germans are beginning to drive towards Stalingrad.'

He lit a cigarette and then gave a deep sigh. 'There have been retaliations because of our bombing campaigns, with a nasty raid over Southampton the other day, and some in the West as well as here and in the Midlands. And we're paying a heavy price, Peggy. I lost eight excellent young men the other night.'

Peggy saw the anguish in his face and heard the break in his voice, and felt a heart-wrenching ache for all those young lives cut brutally short. She put her hand on his arm. 'How are *you* coping, Martin?'

He sat forward in the deckchair, his elbows on his knees as he stared into space and puffed on his cigarette. 'The top brass has ordered me to do fewer ops, so I fly a desk more often than not, and try to keep a patriarchal eye on my young men.'

Peggy didn't speak as he paused, for she could see he was struggling with some very strong emotions.

His voice was unsteady as he continued. 'Some of them are barely out of school, Peggy, with only a few hours of flying solo under their belts. I've seen them white with terror and trembling like a leaf as they head out to climb into their kites. But their chins are up, and not one of them would ever admit their fear or chicken out of an op. They are so fiercely determined to do their bit that it breaks my heart when they don't come back.'

'I don't know how you can bear it,' she murmured.

He ground the cigarette beneath his shoe and sat

straighter. 'It's my job, Peggy. They're my boys, and they look to me to stay strong and always be there for them when things go wrong.'

As Martin fell silent, Peggy could see that he wanted to talk, to perhaps give vent to some of the fears and stresses he'd been under for the past three years. For Martin had taken part in the Battle of Britain, had flown on endless missions over France and Germany, and had had the unenviable task of having to write letters to the parents of the boys who hadn't made it home again. And yet she could understand his reluctance to talk, for once he started, she suspected he wouldn't be able to stop.

She sat quietly in the sunny suburban back garden with her baby asleep in the pram, and Cordelia gently snoring beside her as the birds sang joyfully in the nearby trees. All was calm on this summer's day, and a world away from the horrors Martin must have had to face, and she could only guess at the turmoil in her son-in-law's thoughts.

'My chaps are under increasing pressure these days, so when they are free to play, they play hard. They can get a bit carried away at times, but it's good for them to let off steam, and I thoroughly approve as long as it doesn't affect their judgement during operations. And yet I'm all too aware that the heartiness and gung-ho spirit are employed to hide the underlying stresses and fears we've all experienced. Even the bravest and best suffer from terrors, though they'd never in a million years admit to it.'

Peggy realised he was speaking not only about his men, but about himself and the fears he'd had to hide, and she wondered how long it would be before he reached breaking point. For no one was invincible – not even Martin – and that thought made her very anxious. And yet she said nothing, knowing he had yet to finish talking.

'They live for the moment,' he continued softly, 'and rarely talk about their private lives and the families they've left behind in the world beyond the aerodromes. But I can always tell when they've had bad news from home, or they've been dumped by some silly girl. It shows in their eyes, and in the sudden and uncharacteristic loss of concentration.'

He offered his cigarette case to Peggy, and when their cigarettes were lit, sat back in his chair again and stared at Ron's vegetable patch. 'There's one young pilot in my squadron at the moment who is barely twenty-six, but he's one of the best flyers I've had the privilege to know. He's hugely experienced, having flown in air shows before the war, and although he's more than earned the right to fly a desk or train new pilots, he's just begun his second tour of ops.'

'How many ops is that?' asked Peggy quietly.

'Thirty in a tour, so thirty-four,' he replied, 'which is quite miraculous considering the odds against him.' His smile was wan. 'The others have begun to regard him as their lucky mascot, for his squadron has had the least amount of fatalities so far – but it's an added responsibility that he really doesn't need.'

Martin smoked his cigarette, his expression solemn. 'Squadron Leader Pargeter has always been level-headed and dependable, but within the past two weeks I've noticed his mind isn't on his work, and although his wingman Roger Makepeace is a steadying and reliable influence, there have been some serious lapses in Freddy's concentration. He had a very close shave the other day, and I could see that it had shaken him up badly, but he shrugged off my concern with his usual devil-may-care grin, and went off with Roger to get roaring drunk.'

'He was probably exhausted,' said Peggy, 'and no wonder after such a gruelling schedule.'

'I knew it was more than that, so when he'd sobered up, I hauled him into my office for a man-to-man chat. After a great deal of cajoling he finally admitted that he was worried sick about his young sister, Kitty.'

He took a long drink of the gin and tonic. 'Kitty's a ferry pilot with the ATA and had a very nasty prang in an Oxford she was taking down to Kidlington. The surgeon saved her life but he couldn't save her leg, and she's only just twenty-one.'

'No wonder he couldn't concentrate. How simply

awful for both of them – especially for that poor little girl.'

'Yes,' he sighed. 'She was evidently a real tomboy and extremely athletic.'

Peggy listened silently as he gave a short summary of the young Pargeters' upbringing in Argentina.

'So they only have each other over here, and that must be hard for both of them,' he finished. He gave a snort of amusement. 'She came third on a monster of a motorbike at one of Rita's races only a few weeks ago. I believe all her male competitors were most put out.'

'Oh, but I think I remember her,' gasped Peggy. 'She had a boyish figure and short curly blonde hair, and was wearing one of those blue overalls. Rita pointed her out because she was the only other girl competing.' Her spirits sank further. 'She looked so young, so full of life and energy – how will she cope without a leg?'

'Apparently she's not coping at all well,' he replied as he finished his drink and crushed out his cigarette. 'Freddy said she was extremely depressed and would hardly talk to him or Roger when they last visited her.'

'But it can't be long since the accident,' Peggy protested. 'Of course she's depressed – any young girl would be.'

She stubbed out her own cigarette and put her hand on Martin's arm. 'Girls set great store on how they look, and by the sound of it, she's used to being up and doing and in the thick of things. She probably thinks it's the end of the world at the moment – and who could blame her? She needs time to come to terms with things, Martin.'

'I agree,' he replied on a sigh. 'I've seen the same depression in some of my injured pilots. But they soon come to realise there is a future out there even if they have a limb missing, and although the ATA might not seem as glamorous after the RAF, they hardly turn anyone away, and the boys can still use their flying skills and do their bit.'

'Well, of course there's the famous Douglas Bader who has two false legs. He was flying with the RAF back in 1941.'

Martin smiled. 'He's unique, and although he's now a POW in Germany, I understand he's made himself a regular nuisance by constantly trying to escape. But returning to the subject of Kitty and her brother, I accept she will find it extremely hard to come to terms with what has happened to her. And Freddy will have to as well. I've kept him grounded since his close shave, but I can't do so for much longer. I need every man I have in the air – and I need them to fly with clear minds.'

'I'm sure there must be some way to get Kitty to see that there is a future for her other than sitting in a dull office every day. Let me have a think about it, and if I come up with any ideas I'll give you a ring.'

Martin patted her hand and then poured her another

gin and tonic. 'You'll come up with something, Peggy,' he said affectionately. 'You always do.'

Martin ended up staying for tea, which turned out to be quite a jolly occasion, for Jane, Sarah and Rita returned from their day out and fell with delight on the remains of the gin and tonic. As Peggy listened to the chatter going on around her, she wanted to feel as contented and happy as her girls, but the absence of Fran at the table made her fret.

And yet she didn't want to spoil the evening for the others, so she said nothing as she dished out the slices of spam and homegrown salad and placed the bottles of last year's pickles on the table. The last jar of preserved blackberries she'd been keeping for a special occasion had been dressed with the top of the milk to provide a pudding.

'That was quite a feast,' said Martin, as he sat back and lit cigarettes for both of them. 'Thank you, Peggy.'

'You're welcome,' she said lightly as the girls cleared the table and Rita tackled the washing-up. She glanced up at the clock on the mantelpiece. It was nearly seven o'clock and there was still no sign of Fran.

'Have you got plans for the evening, Peggy?' he asked worriedly. 'I'm not keeping you, am I?'

'Good heavens, no,' she hurried to reassure him. 'I don't go out much in the evenings since Jim was called up, and I'm enjoying having you here. It makes a lovely change.'

'Have you heard from Jim lately?'

Peggy smiled. 'He writes regularly, but the letters come in higgledy-piggledy order, so we've started to number them so we know if there's one missing.'

'How's he getting on with army life? It can't be easy for him after going through the last war.'

'Jim always lands on his feet,' she chuckled. 'He fixed a colonel's car and made such a good impression on the man that he's now his permanent driver, which gets him out of doing the dirty work in the maintenance sheds.'

Her smile was soft with affection. 'He's not lost his skill at keeping his eye on the main chance, because he's also done a couple of favours for the cook in charge of the Officers' Mess, so he often gets given choice tidbits to liven up the rather stodgy diet in the canteen. I think he's quite enjoying himself.'

'No sign of him being sent abroad then?'

'Not yet, but something's in the wind, because his last letter mentioned a training course they were all about to go on. Of course the censor blanked out most of what he'd written, but I got the distinct feeling Jim wasn't looking forward to it.'

Martin smoked his cigarette in silence and Peggy wondered suddenly if he knew more than he was letting on. 'I don't suppose you could guess what he might be training for?' she asked hopefully.

'It could be for anything,' he said. 'What the army is doing is a complete mystery to us in the RAF.' He smiled at Peggy. 'I shouldn't worry too much,' he said comfortably. 'Jim seems to be fairly settled and useful where he is, and I doubt that at his age he'll be sent anywhere abroad.'

'That's what I'm hoping,' she replied fervently. 'He did his bit in the first one – as did his brother, Frank.' She gave a sigh. 'At least Frank is of the age when he definitely won't be sent abroad. He'll be fifty early next year, so he'll get discharged and sent home.'

Martin nodded and then smiled up at Sarah as she put the teapot on the table. 'And how are you and Jane getting along? Still enjoying being a Lumberjill?'

Sarah laughed as she twisted her silky blonde hair back from her face and tethered it with several hairpins. 'It's great fun until I have to help load the lorries,' she replied. 'Even with thick gloves, I manage to break all my fingernails. But the girls are a great bunch, and the Americans certainly liven things up on the estate.'

'And I'm really enjoying working at the dairy,' piped up her younger sister Jane, whose fair hair lay across her shoulder in a thick plait. 'The horses are absolute darlings, and there are times when I wish I could stay with them all day. But of course the pay is really low, so I have the part-time bookkeeping job at the uniform factory now.'

'Mr Goldman, her boss, has asked her to do more hours,' said Sarah proudly.

Jane fidgeted with the hem of her cardigan. 'Yes, well, I'll see. I don't really want to give up my job at the dairy.'

Sarah rolled her eyes and gave a sigh. 'I have never understood the passion some people have for horses. It seems to rule their lives.'

Jane shrugged and grinned. 'That's because you've never tried to get to know them,' she said.

'Where has that girl got to?' said Cordelia as she placed the tray of teacups on the table and sat down. 'She went out very early this morning, and now it's almost eight o'clock.'

'I'm sure she'll be back soon,' soothed Peggy, trying to mask her own anxiety. 'She has an early shift tomorrow.'

'So have I,' said Rita, whose olive skin had darkened in the summer sun. 'John Hicks has ordered a complete audit of every last bit of equipment at the fire station, and I've also got a motor to fix on the winding gear of the big fire engine. I'd better get to bed.'

She kissed Peggy and Cordelia and was halfway out the door when she turned back. 'Oh, I almost forgot. Ruby's had more letters from her handsome Canadian. He's still very keen on their getting together after he's finished his training course, and I think she's quite taken with the idea too.'

'Oh, I'm so glad,' said Peggy in delight. 'He was such a nice young man.'

'There you go, matchmaking again,' muttered Cordelia with a glint of humour in her eyes. 'Honestly, Peggy, will you never learn?'

Peggy grinned. 'Probably not,' she admitted contentedly.

'Well, as pleasant as this is, I have to get back to Cliffe,' said Martin, and he stood and reached for his jacket.

He fastened the buttons and picked up his hat, then bent to kiss the back of Cordelia's hand. 'Keep smiling through,' he murmured, 'and I'll see you again as soon as I can.'

Peggy followed him out into the hall after he'd said goodbye to everyone else, and watched from her bedroom doorway as he bent to softly feather his finger over the sleeping baby's hair. His yearning for his own baby was etched in his face, and Peggy felt again the squeeze on her heart.

'Keep in mind what I told you about young Freddy and his sister,' he said quietly as they stood on the doorstep. 'And if you have any suggestions, I'll be glad to hear them, for Freddy needs to be clear of his worries the next time he climbs into that Spitfire.'

Peggy nodded and stepped into his embrace, the top of her head barely reaching the winged badge above his breast pocket. She held him tightly, hoping that he understood how much he meant to them all, and then let him go with a silent prayer that he stay safe.

She stood on the doorstep to wave as he drove the borrowed car down the cul-de-sac and around the corner. Her heart was heavy despite the pleasant day they'd spent, for there were no certainties any more.

Chapter Seven

Kitty wanted her mother with such longing that it hurt, and as the nurse gently removed the bandages from her head, she could feel the tears gather in a great lump in her throat. She felt so weak and alone, more helpless than she could ever have imagined, and simply didn't have the will to do anything about it.

'Now, I'm just going to take out the rest of your stitches, Kitty,' murmured the doctor. 'Everything seems to have healed beautifully, and once your hair grows back, you won't see the scarring at all.'

Kitty kept her eyes closed. The fact that her hair had been shaved off was simply another item in the long catalogue of horrors she'd been presented with since waking up from her induced sleep, and she wanted to be left alone to curl into her misery.

'That's very good,' he continued as he leaned over her and snipped away the stitches. 'Now, let's have a look at your cheek. It was a minor laceration, and I used the finest needle and thread, so I'm hoping the scarring has been kept to a minimum.'

She felt the padded dressing being eased away from her cheek, and his gentle fingers probing the flesh before once again she heard the clip of the scissors and felt the slight sting of the stitches being drawn out. 'It doesn't matter one way or the other,' she said almost wearily. 'No one's going to look at me now, anyway.'

'That's defeatist talk, Kitty, and I won't stand for it,' he said firmly. 'Even though I say so myself, that is an excellent piece of sewing. Open your eyes, Kitty, and take a look.'

She shook her head. 'I don't want to look. What's the point?'

'The point, my dear, is that you are still the pretty girl you were before the accident.' He paused. 'All the bruising and swelling has gone down, and although you don't have a lot of hair left, it is starting to grow back, and I wouldn't mind betting that in another few days you'll be asking for a brush and comb.'

Kitty kept her eyes closed as she rolled her head away from him. She didn't want to see herself – didn't want to see the doctor, or the world outside the surrounding curtain. She simply wanted her mother – to hear her voice and feel her arms about her – and to go back to sleep so she didn't have to face the cruel reality of her situation.

'All right,' the doctor said on a sigh. 'I'll let it go today, but sooner or later you are going to have to start fighting back, Kitty. I know you feel very down at the moment, but you're young and strong, and despite the dark thoughts going round in your head, you are a very lucky young woman.'

She opened her eyes and glared at him. 'Lucky?' she rasped.

He smiled down at her. 'You survived a crash that should have killed you. I'd call that lucky, wouldn't you?'

'Survived for what?' she asked bitterly. 'To live the rest of my life as a useless cripple?'

'You'll certainly have to adapt to using a prosthesis,' he replied quietly. 'But that doesn't mean your life can't be fulfilling.' He perched on the side of the bed, the brass buttons on his uniform jacket glinting in the shaft of sunlight that came through the ward window. 'You can still fall in love and have children – still do a great many of the things you used to do before the accident. You just have to adapt, Kitty. And from what your brother tells me, you've never been one to turn down a challenge, so why change the habits of a lifetime now?'

She closed her eyes as the tears welled. 'That was before,' she whispered. 'I can't do it now.'

He took her fingers in his warm hand. 'Oh, I think you can,' he replied softly. 'You're a fighter, Kitty Pargeter, and although the battle ahead seems daunting, I have no doubt you'll find the strength to win it.'

Kitty looked at him through her tears, saw that he genuinely believed she had the strength to fight this awful thing, and felt a spark of something she'd thought was lost. 'A challenge?' she murmured.

'A challenge,' he said firmly. 'And I'm laying

down the gauntlet, Kitty. Don't disappoint me,' he added with a gentle smile. 'I like a good fight.'

Kitty slowly smiled back as the spark inside her blossomed. 'So do I,' she breathed. Then the spark flickered as the doubts crept in. 'But I'm scared,' she admitted softly.

'Of course you are,' he replied in his deep, gentle voice. 'Anyone standing at the top of a mountain and preparing to ski down it has that moment of doubt, that adrenalin rush of fear. But fear doesn't have to weaken you; it can be used in a positive way.'

She looked back at him through the haze of tears, remembering how frightened she'd been when she'd crashed the Typhoon. Her fear had sharpened her mind and stoked her determination to survive then – perhaps it *was* possible to do it again?

'I can see you're thinking about it,' said the surgeon. 'In your line of work you must have had many a scare, but you came through them, didn't you?'

She nodded, and her gaze fell on the small hand-mirror that lay on the bed. Perhaps it was time to trust in him and begin to face things. She licked her dry lips as her pulse began to race. 'Let me see just how good you are at sewing,' she murmured.

He held onto the little mirror as he placed it in her fingers. 'Are you sure?'

She nodded and he released the mirror. With a shallow, trembling breath, she lifted it and stared at her reflection.

A great wave of relief swept through her, for the scar on her cheek was just a thin red line, and she could see it would fade with time. Her hair looked as if someone had hacked at it with a pair of garden shears, and the short style made her look like a young boy, but it would grow as he'd said. Yet it was her eyes that told the story of what she'd been through, for they were dull and lifeless in her thin, wan little face.

'What do you think?' he asked.

'I think someone around here needs to learn how to cut hair properly,' she said with a shaky smile. 'It's truly awful.'

He took the mirror and placed it on the bedside cabinet. 'It'll grow back soon enough, and then we can get the visiting hairdresser to do something with it.'

Kitty looked down at the cage beneath her blankets. Her hair would grow, certainly, but the leg was gone forever, and the knowledge made her sink back into despair.

'I think that's enough revelation for one day,' he said as he got to his feet. 'We'll leave you to rest now it's almost supper time. Do you want the curtain drawn back, so you can finally get to meet the other girls?'

She'd heard them talking, and they sounded a nice bunch, but the thought of having to face strangers, of seeing pity in their eyes, was just too much. 'Not now,' she murmured. 'Perhaps tomorrow.'

The army surgeon nodded his understanding and followed the nurse out, carefully drawing the curtain so she was once again cocooned against the outside world.

Kitty lay there listening to the women on the other side of that curtain. They sounded quite cheerful as they discussed articles in magazines, their love lives and the latest matinee idols that made them swoon. It was obvious that none of them could have suffered such devastating injuries as she had, and she rather resented their cheerfulness.

She shifted on the mound of pillows she was propped against. Both her arms were still in plaster, but at least the tight bandaging around her chest had been removed now her ribs had mended, and she could wear a nightdress – though it did get rucked beneath her and it was the devil's own job to get it straight again.

Her gaze once again settled on the cage beneath the blanket. Her right leg was still suspended from a pulley and encased in plaster of Paris, but she had yet to see the left – or what there was of it. She'd always closed her eyes and turned away when the doctor came to examine it, or when one of the nurses changed the dressings or attended to her other needs.

Kitty plucked at the corner of the blanket and sheet, feeling an urgent need to scratch her ankle. They had explained that this itching was something to do with memory and nerve endings, but it seemed real enough now. Without giving herself time to think about it and change her mind, she gripped the sheet and blanket and drew them back until her left leg was exposed.

It was tightly bandaged from her groin to the rounded end at her knee. She stared at it, still feeling the phantom itch in the phantom ankle, her emotions in turmoil, the tears streaming down her face as she collapsed back against the pillows. This was one challenge she had no hope of winning, and the sobs came from deep within her as she buried her face in the pillow.

'It's a bugger, ain't it?' said a cheerful voice beside her. 'Fair knocked me sideways when I first saw what they done to mine.'

Through the blur of her tears, Kitty saw a short, curvy girl with a freckled face, a big smile and lots of red lipstick that clashed horribly with her lurid red dressing gown and bright ginger hair. 'Get out,' she rasped. 'Go away.'

'It's all right, love,' the little Cockney said as she pushed through the curtain on crutches, and made herself comfortable in the chair beside Kitty's bed. 'I knows just how you feel, so you cry and shout all yer like. I don't mind. Dun it meself, if the truth be known. Howled like a baby, I did. Fair put the wind up the other girls, and that's the truth.'

'I don't want you in here,' Kitty snarled. 'Go away.'

Impervious to Kitty's anger, she shook her head.

'Nah, I ain't going nowhere.' She adjusted the folds in her dressing gown and ran her fingers over the embroidered gold dragons that breathed orange fire all over it. 'You been shut in 'ere over three weeks now, and that ain't no good for yer, believe me.' She shot Kitty a smile. 'The name's Doreen Larkin, by the way. You're Kitty Pargeter, ain't you?'

Kitty was so astonished by the sheer audacity of this brash girl that the tears stopped flowing.

Doreen took a handkerchief out of her dressing-gown pocket. 'Don't worry, it's a clean one,' she said, before she dried Kitty's face and held it to her nose. 'Blow,' she ordered as if Kitty was three years old.

Kitty was still so stunned by this force of energy, colour and noise that she did as she was told.

'There, that's better, ain't it?' Doreen reached into the pocket again and drew out a packet of cigarettes. 'Fag?'

Kitty could only stare at her and shake her head.

'I don't blame you,' said Doreen with a grimace. 'These are them Pashas. Taste like . . .' She grinned. 'They taste foul, but it's all I could get off the tea lady, so beggars can't be choosers.'

Her green eyes narrowed against the smoke as she coolly regarded what was left of Kitty's leg. 'So you've 'ad a look then,' she said casually. 'Wotcha think? Bit of a bugger, ain't it?'

Kitty felt the laughter bubbling just under the surface. It was impossible to stay sorry for herself in the light of this persistent, irritating yet delightful barrage of cheerfulness. 'It certainly is,' she managed with a smile.

'Yeah, they took mine off in the same bleedin' place.' She swept back her dressing gown to reveal a sheer black nightdress and what was left of her right leg. 'I thought I'd liven it up a bit with this,' she said, twanging the scarlet and black lacy garter. 'Wotcha think, eh? Looks pretty swanky, don't it?' She gave a naughty grin. 'It don't 'alf cheer up the blokes on the men's ward, I can tell you.'

Kitty eyed the garter and was in awe of Doreen's devil-may-care attitude to what had happened to her. Never in a million years could she have done something as flippant and eye-catching as putting a garter around her butchered leg – let alone flaunt it in front of the male patients. 'How can you be so cheerful?' she asked quietly.

Doreen shrugged as she blew smoke. 'Well, there ain't no point in being miserable, is there? It ain't gunna bring me leg back.' She twanged the garter again, then smoothed the silky bright dressing gown over her neat bosom and waist. 'At least I've still got all me other working bits, and once I've got the 'ang of the false leg, there won't be no stopping me.'

'You're very brave,' Kitty murmured.

'No I ain't,' she said firmly. 'I just decided to make the best of things, that's all. When you've been born in the East End you learn to sort yerself out, 'cos no other bugger can do it for yer, and that's a fact.' She smoked her cigarette while Kitty absorbed this bit of philosophy.

'How did . . .? I mean what happened to . . .?'

Doreen grinned. 'I were on me motorbike delivering dispatches between Cliffe and Wayfaring Down when I got caught out in the open by a Messerschmitt 109 on a solo raid. The pilot obviously thought it would be fun to use me as flaming target practice. I dodged and weaved and went hell for leather, but 'e shot out me tyres and I went flying. I ended up with a leg full of holes from his bleedin' bullets, and concussion where I 'it me 'ead on some hard rocks hidden in the grass.'

She stubbed the butt of her cigarette out in the ashtray on the bedside table. 'Luckily the blokes from a nearby gun emplacement saw what happened, and after they'd shot Jerry out of the sky for his flaming cheek, they came to rescue me.'

Kitty just nodded, for she could imagine the scene, with this feisty girl trying to avoid the enemy fighter plane.

'What about you, then? What brought you to this house of fun?'

Kitty smiled. 'I pranged an Airspeed Oxford in the middle of a field covered in anti-aircraft stakes and barbed wire. It was my own fault,' she admitted. 'I should have turned back when the weather closed in.' She eyed the pathetic remains of her left leg. It had been a hefty price to pay for breaking the rules.

Doreen's green eyes widened. 'Blimey, you're one

of them famous ATA glamour girls,' she breathed. 'I thought I recognised you. You've 'ad yer picture in the *Picture Post* and the magazines, ain't yer?'

Kitty squirmed against the pillows. She'd always been uncomfortable with the press exposure and the photographs. 'The reporters follow us about,' she muttered. 'None of us likes being singled out, and we all find the pictures embarrassing.'

'Cor,' Doreen breathed. 'I wouldn't have minded a bit of that – always fancied 'aving me picture in the paper.' There was deep respect in her eyes as she regarded Kitty. 'You call me brave,' she said solemnly, 'but you're much braver than I'll ever be, what with flying them fast planes.'

She sat forward in her chair, her face alight with curiosity. 'So, what's it like to fly a Spitfire, then?'

Kitty smiled. 'It's the best, most thrilling thing I've ever done.'

Doreen leaned closer. 'I 'eard tell it's better than sex,' she whispered.

Kitty thought of the single, hugely disappointing occasion when she'd allowed herself to be persuaded into bed by a man. 'It certainly is,' she replied, 'and it lasts a good deal longer too.'

They both collapsed into giggles and it was some time before they were able to talk again.

'So, Doreen, what's it like here?' Kitty asked after she'd borrowed her new friend's handkerchief and dried her eyes again.

'It ain't bad. The nurses are lovely, and General

Thorne is a diamond geezer for sure. But Matron's a right old battleaxe who came out of retirement because of this flamin' war.' Doreen leaned her elbow on the bed and rested her chin on her hand. 'She's built like a tank, has a heart of stone and is as friendly as a grizzly bear with piles.'

Kitty giggled. Doreen certainly had a way with words.

'Gawd knows why she became a nurse,' continued Doreen. 'She'd have made a better prison warden.'

'She sounds horrid,' said Kitty with a shudder.

'She is, so try not to cross her.' Doreen leaned back in the chair and grinned. 'It's ever so nice to have someone new to chat to,' she said. 'It can get a bit boring in here now I've 'eard all the gossip from the other girls. But there's a lovely garden, and once you've got your leg out of that pulley thing you'll 'ave to have a butchers for yerself. The weather's ever so warm at the moment, and me tan's coming along a treat.' She rolled up the wide sleeves of her dressing gown to show Kitty her brown arms.

The curtain was suddenly whipped back to reveal a large square woman with beefy arms and a furious expression. An enormous bosom heaved beneath the starched white bib of her apron as the ribbons from her fancy white cap trembled like some small trapped bird on her big head. 'What is going on in here?' she boomed.

'Gawd help us, Matron,' spluttered Doreen. 'You nearly give me an 'eart attack, coming in like that.'

143

'You shouldn't be in here, Larkin,' Matron ordered. 'Remove yourself immediately.'

Kitty realised that Doreen's description of a bear with piles was all too accurate and she began to giggle – which set Doreen off as well.

'I can't,' spluttered Doreen. 'Me leg 'as gorn all to jelly.'

Kitty's sides and stomach were hurting from her laughter as Doreen waved the stump of her leg and twanged the elasticated garter.

'Pull yourselves together,' stormed Matron. 'As for you, Larkin, you will leave this cubicle immediately.'

'I can't,' Doreen howled through her laughter. 'Really I can't.'

Matron grasped Doreen's arm and hauled her none too gently out of the chair. 'Do not defy me, Larkin,' she said ominously as she rammed the crutches beneath Doreen's armpits, 'or you will find that I am not as easy-going as you think.'

Doreen was no longer laughing. 'Gerroff me, you old cow,' she snarled, pulling her arm out of Matron's grip.

Kitty had sobered too, and didn't like the way Matron was manhandling her new friend. 'Doreen was just keeping me company,' she protested. 'And I do think you're being rather unnecessarily rough with her.'

Matron's gimlet gaze fell on Kitty with such force that she felt as if she'd been pinned against the pillows. 'Your opinion is neither sought nor warranted,' the big woman said coldly, 'and I would remind you that I am in charge here and you will both do as I say.'

She gripped Doreen's arm and began to forcibly steer her down the long ward.

Doreen turned her head and made a face behind the old gorgon's back, and Kitty had to bite quite hard on her lip to stop the giggles from bubbling up again.

She watched in horrified fascination as Matron settled Doreen in a bedside chair and confiscated her crutches – and noticed that the nurses skittered away and found something to do rather than catch Matron's all-encompassing glare.

There were twelve beds in the ward, but only the patients trapped by pulleys and plaster casts could be seen, and Kitty guessed the others had made themselves scarce the moment the awful woman entered the ward. She rather wished she could escape too, for Matron had turned on her sturdy heel and was lumbering back towards her, the vast bosom heaving like a stormy sea beneath the apron bib.

Before Kitty could say anything there was a thermometer in her mouth and a cold finger on the pulse in her neck. She looked at the meaty hand that was cradling the watch pinned to the vast bosom, and then at the suspicion of a moustache above the narrow line of the woman's lips. She really was the ugliest woman she'd ever had the misfortune to meet, with a personality to match, but surely she had to possess some saving grace?

If she did, then it wasn't evident in the stony silence as the thermometer was inspected, shaken and returned to the glass phial of antiseptic solution that had been placed on the wall behind the bed. The silence continued as the results were noted down on the chart that hung from the end of the bed, the pillows were pummelled, and the blanket and sheet were straightened and tucked in so tightly that Kitty found she could barely move.

'Do you think I could have some water, please?' she dared ask.

The water was wordlessly supplied and then the glass returned to the top of the bedside cabinet where it was out of Kitty's reach. 'Mr Fortescue will be coming to see you before supper,' she said as she tidied the curtain away.

'Who's Mr Fortescue?' Kitty asked.

'Mr Fortescue is an extremely famous and gifted consultant,' retorted Matron with the gleam of the devotional in her eyes. 'It is a great honour to welcome him here, so I expect everyone to behave themselves.' She glared meaningfully at Kitty and then stomped off.

Kitty managed to keep a straight face until the woman was out of earshot and then collapsed once more into a fit of giggles. The healing process might take time and she had little doubt that there would be a great deal of pain to cope with, but Doreen had given her something priceless today – for the gift of laughter was better than any medicine, and she suddenly felt strong enough to begin the long battle that lay ahead of her.

Chapter Eight

Now the curtain had been pulled back, Kitty was able to see the other women on her ward for the first time and to put faces to the voices she'd been listening to. It was a sobering sight and Kitty felt a sharp pang of guilt, for she'd been very wrong in her estimation of the other women's injuries. She and Doreen weren't the only amputees.

There was one woman who had a missing foot, another had half an arm, and a third had lost an entire leg. There was someone with her head and eyes bandaged who had to be led everywhere as she hobbled along on crutches, another with two broken legs, and one poor girl had her jaw wired and a brace round her neck. Broken or missing limbs seemed to be the order of things on this ward, but the human spirit was an extraordinary thing, and Kitty felt ashamed of how sorry she'd felt for herself in the light of such life-changing injuries being so bravely borne.

She was cheerfully greeted and welcomed to the ward by the other women, but although she would have liked to chat to them, she found she simply didn't have the energy to join in any long conversation after Doreen's exhausting visit.

She closed her eyes wearily as Doreen enthusiastically told everyone that they had a famous ATA pilot in their midst. No doubt the story would be heavily embroidered, and by the end of the evening she'd be a flying ace, glamour girl and the darling of the press. But Doreen was clearly enjoying herself, and if it kept everyone amused, then what harm did it do?

Matron's booming voice rudely jarred her from her doze, and Kitty blearily acknowledged the rather pompous Mr Fortescue who now stood at her bedside. Not wanting to upset the old battleaxe further, she didn't resist as he silently examined her from head to foot as if she was a choice bit of meat on a butcher's slab. She kept her eyes closed most of the time, especially when he removed the bandages on her leg. Seeing it covered up was one thing, but she wasn't yet brave or curious enough to see it out in the open.

After he'd gone she fell asleep again, only to be woken by the rattle, clang and clatter of the metal food trolley as it was wheeled into the ward by one of the NAAFI girls. She didn't feel the least bit hungry, and the sight of pale fish and boiled potatoes floating in a thin white sauce was far from appetising. One of the nurses came to help her as she couldn't yet use a knife and fork, and she was again forcibly reminded of just how helpless she was.

The food was as tasteless as it looked, and after

a few mouthfuls Kitty had had enough. She lay back against the pillows and sleepily watched the NAAFI girls clear away the plates as the nurses rushed about tidying up the ward in preparation for visiting time.

It was doubtful Freddy or Roger would be able to make it, for she'd heard wave after wave of bombers and fighters overhead on yet another raid over the Channel. But it would be lovely to see either of them now she was feeling more positive about things, for they'd looked so very down and worried the last time they'd come.

The chatter among the other women patients grew louder as they helped each other to brush their hair, apply lipstick and powder and don pretty bed-jackets over their bandages and utility nightwear. Expectation was high as they watched the clock and counted the minutes before the door opened on the first visitor. There was a lot of giggling going on, Kitty noticed, but it stopped dead as Matron pushed through the swing doors and began her inspection.

Kitty watched as the ghastly woman barked out orders and complained about the slightest thing, which made the nurses clumsy as they hurried to do her bidding. And then she was gone and everyone gave a deep sigh of relief.

'Oi, Kitty,' called Doreen from the other end of the ward. 'You expecting that brother of yours tonight?'

'He's probably on ops,' Kitty called back.

'Proper 'andsome, he is,' sighed Doreen. 'I wouldn't mind 'anging on his arm, I can tell you.'

Kitty smiled. 'He's engaged, Doreen.'

'I might 'ave known,' she groaned dramatically. 'All the best ones are always taken.'

'But surely you've got a chap of your own?' said Kitty.

'Not one like your Freddy,' she replied as the sentiment was echoed throughout the room.

Kitty raised an eyebrow. Her brother had obviously got to know the other girls on the ward during the first two weeks when she'd been dead to the world.

'You don't want to take any notice of Doreen,' said the girl in the next bed with a hint of asperity. 'She's got men flocking around her all the time, and I wouldn't mind betting she'll have at least four come to visit her tonight.'

'I'm not surprised,' said Kitty lightly. 'She's a lively, attractive girl.'

'I suppose some might think so,' the girl replied with a sniff. 'But you have to agree, she's frightfully common.'

Kitty was familiar with this attitude – she'd lived with it at boarding school – and certainly didn't agree with this snooty girl in the next bed. 'She's a lovely, jolly girl who made me see things in a better light,' she replied coolly. 'I think we should all be grateful to her for bringing some fun into the ward.'

The pale blue eyes regarded her for a long appraisal, and then the moment was broken by the clatter of the swing doors and the entrance of the first visitor.

Kitty watched enviously as mothers, sisters, husbands and children came pouring in with their gifts of flowers and food parcels. The yearning for home and her parents deepened and she wished with all her might that it could have been possible for them to come and visit. She so longed to hear their voices, to feel their arms about her and glean something of their strength.

The doors clattered again and a group of American soldiers made a beeline for Doreen. There were six of them, all very handsome and clean-looking with their severe haircuts and flashing teeth. Doreen was blushing prettily as she accepted their gifts of chocolates, nylons and cigarettes, and ordered them to find more chairs.

The laughter around her bed soon had heads turning and the girl next to Kitty tutted with disapproval. *Good for Doreen*, thought Kitty, as she noticed the other girl's visitor was a sour-faced woman in an expensive navy two-piece costume and silly hat. The immaculate make-up and hair and the diamonds on her fingers spoke of money, but the po-faced looks of both of them shouted snobbery.

Kitty was about to try and read the magazine one of the other girls had left her when the doors squeaked again and Freddy strode in. Tall and handsome in his RAF uniform, he grinned at Doreen's shout of greeting in the swashbuckling manner that never failed to make women blush. Smiling at each woman in turn as he passed, his progress down the ward was followed with wide-eyed admiration and many a giggle.

Kitty witnessed this display with the affectionate, weary acceptance of one who'd seen it many times before. He simply couldn't help himself. According to their mother, it had begun when he'd first smiled up from his pram and discovered he could enchant every female into doing his bidding. Poor Charlotte had a job on her hands if she was to keep him on the straight and narrow and get him up the aisle.

'I see you haven't lost your ability to make an entrance,' she said wryly as he sat down in the chair at her bedside.

'And I can see that you're feeling very much better,' he retorted as he placed a small box of sweets on the bed. He shot her a grin. 'These are from Roger, who sends his regards.' He gave a deep sigh of pleasure. 'It's marvellous to have you back again, Sis. You've no idea how worried we've been about you.'

'Then you mustn't fret any longer,' she said firmly. 'I'm coming to terms with things, really I am, and before you know it, I'll be out of this bed and rushing about again.'

'Promise me you won't try and do too much too soon,' he pleaded. 'I know you when you get the bit between your teeth; you go rushing off like a bull in a china shop.'

Kitty chuckled. 'Don't worry. I'll be the model patient.' Then she had a sudden, terrible thought. 'Have you told Mum and Dad what's happened?'

'I didn't have any choice, Kitts,' he said solemnly. 'We weren't terribly sure that you'd pull through when you were first brought in, and I wanted to prepare them in case . . .' He took a deep breath. 'I've since written them a long letter explaining exactly what you've been through and reassuring them that you are at last on the mend. But of course the mail is erratic, so I'm still waiting for a reply.'

Kitty knew her brother was a very good letter writer and she was sure he'd couched the news in careful terms, with a hefty dollop of optimism. Still, no matter how carefully he'd worded his letter, it would have come as a terrible blow to their parents, and she could only imagine the distress it must have caused.

'Oh, Freddy,' she said as tears pricked. 'They'll be so worried. What a fool I was to disobey orders and go over the top. I should have turned back and not thought I was invincible. Then none of this would have happened.'

'Accidents in our line of work are part and parcel of everyday life,' he said as he shifted to sit beside her on the edge of the bed and put his arm round her shoulders. 'We all break the rules at one time or another, so you've got to stop blaming yourself and just thank God you're still alive.'

Kitty rested her head against him, glad of his solidity and comfort. 'I do realise how lucky I am,' she said as she blinked away her tears. 'Your little friend Doreen has made me see that there is a future after . . .' She stumbled on the word. 'After amputation,' she managed.

'She's quite a card, isn't she?' he chuckled.

Kitty drew back from his embrace and gave him a watery smile. 'She's a force to be reckoned with – and so is Matron. Don't let her catch you sitting on the bed or she'll be down on you like a ton of bricks.'

'I'd like to see her try,' he countered. 'We've had a couple of run-ins already, and she hasn't won one yet!'

'No, I don't suppose she has,' she said with a soft smile full of affection. 'It seems no woman is impervious to your wicked charms.'

'Talking of which,' he replied. 'Charlotte sends her love and is trying to wangle a bit of time off to come and visit you again. She came to see you shortly after the accident, but of course you were out cold and so I told her to wait until you were awake.'

'That would be lovely. How is she?'

He shrugged. 'Rushing about delivering planes

as usual. She had to fly to Scotland the other day and got chased by a Jerry fighter.' He grinned. 'She managed to lose him in a bank of cloud and then was lucky enough to find a hole in it to land safely.'

There was a teasing light in his eyes as he continued. 'So, you see, Kitty, you aren't the only one to go over the top – you just need to learn how to land a plane properly and not prang the bally thing.'

She dug him in the ribs with the side of her plaster cast. 'I seem to remember someone not too far from this bed who almost wiped out half a squadron by coming in to land too fast,' she teased.

'But I didn't, did I? I managed to swerve at the last minute and take her up again for another shot at the runway.' He hugged her against him. 'You've absolutely no idea how wonderful it is to see you back to your usual irritating self,' he said gruffly. 'I honestly thought I was going to lose you during that first couple of weeks.'

'You don't get rid of me that easily,' she replied through the lump in her throat. She looked up at him, feeling safe in the crook of his arm. 'So, how come you aren't on duty?'

He looked away from her to the other people on the ward. 'I've got some leave owing, so Commander Black gave me permission to take it now you're awake and with us again,' he said casually.

Kitty eyed him suspiciously. 'You've been grounded, haven't you? What happened, Freddy?'

He removed his arm and returned to the bedside chair, digging in his pocket for his cigarettes. As if playing for time, he lit the cigarette and made a show of shifting the ashtray about on the bedside cabinet.

'Freddy?'

'All right,' he replied on a sigh. 'Commander Black grounded me for a couple of days after a bit of an incident. But it was nothing for you to worry about, and I'll be back on ops tomorrow, so there's no harm done.'

'What incident?'

He refused to meet her gaze, playing with his cigarette. 'We were coming back from a raid on the German factories in Lille. I was dog-tired and lost my concentration for a minute. There was a bit of a sea-mist and the Dover cliffs . . .' He shot her one of his boyish grins. 'I pulled up in time, and here I am. It was nothing to make a fuss about.'

Kitty's heart was thudding painfully against her ribs as she realised she'd nearly lost him. 'It's time you stopped flying, Freddy,' she said sternly. 'You've done more ops than anyone could ever expect of you – and you're getting careless.'

'Can't do it, old thing,' he replied airily. 'My chaps depend on me, and I'm not going to let them down because my little sister is dishing out orders.'

'Of all the pig-headed, stubborn idiots,' she breathed crossly.

He patted her fingers peeking out from the plaster

cast. 'Don't worry about me, Kitty. You just concentrate on getting better, and leave me to get on with what I'm good at.'

Kitty was about to give him a good piece of her mind when they were interrupted by one of the NAAFI girls, who was carrying two cups of tea.

Young and rather plain, she blushed scarlet as Freddy hurried to relieve her of the cups and shot her a beaming smile. 'You must be delighted to see your sister looking so well, Wing Commander Pargeter,' she simpered.

'That I am, Maureen, and I appreciate your concern as well as your scrummy tea and biscuits.' His smile was just for her, his very blue eyes looking deeply into her grey ones.

'Ooh,' she breathed as she went a deeper scarlet. 'You are a one, Wing Commander.' With a giggle and an added sway of her hips, she reluctantly went to serve the rest of the patients and their visitors.

Kitty eyed him with fond exasperation. 'Scrummy tea and biscuits? Honestly, Freddy, you really are the limit.'

'But I made her smile, and that's the important thing,' he said as he dunked the stale biscuit into the very weak tea. 'It doesn't hurt to brighten someone's day.'

'I don't know how Charlotte can stand it when you flirt with every woman in the room,' she said on a sigh.

'She knows I like women, but that I love her – and

only her,' he replied. 'By the way,' he added casually as he finished the biscuit. 'You'd better hurry up and get out of that bed. We're getting married in December, and you're to be the bridesmaid.'

'Really? Oh, Freddy, that's wonderful!'

He grinned. 'Yes, it is rather, isn't it? I'm a very lucky man.'

He put down the cup and saucer as the ward sister rang her little bell to warn that visiting time was over. 'I'll come and see you again as soon as I can,' he said as he tucked his peaked hat beneath his arm. 'But it will depend on what ops I'm on. Charlotte should be in within the next few days, so you'll be able to chatter on about wedding dresses, or whatever it is you women find to talk about.'

'Promise you won't worry about me, Freddy. I'm well, as you can see, and will get better every day from now on.'

'Take care, Kitty Cat,' he said as he softly kissed her brow. 'You might be a pain in the neck and a ruddy nuisance most of the time, but you're the only sister I've got and I want you at my wedding.'

Kitty could have sworn she saw a glimmer of tears in his blue eyes as he donned his hat and turned to leave. 'Fly safe, Freddy,' she said through a tight throat. 'And don't be a ruddy hero.'

He looked over his shoulder, shot her a wink and a grin and then was gone.

Kitty lay there for some time after his footsteps

had faded, the warm tears rolling down her battered face to soak the pillow. She had no idea why she was crying and could only put it down to the strong medicine she was on, and the fact that she was exhausted after what had turned out to be quite a day.

Chapter Nine

It was now almost ten o'clock and everyone had gone upstairs, including Suzy who'd come home bright-eyed and radiant after her day with Anthony. Peggy had seen that Cordelia was settled in her bed with her book and reading glasses, and had gone back downstairs to check on Daisy, who was still fast asleep in her cot, her thumb plugged into her mouth.

Peggy kissed the warm cheek and breathed in the wonderful scent of new skin and baby powder before adjusting the sheet over her little shoulders. Leaving the door ajar, she went back into the kitchen and settled down at the table to write another long letter to Jim.

Half an hour later she was disturbed by a soft voice. 'Peggy?'

She looked up to see Sarah standing in the doorway in her dressing gown with her lovely hair tumbling to her shoulders, her eyes bright with unshed tears. 'What is it, love?' she asked as she rushed to her side. 'Aren't you feeling well?'

'Oh, Peggy, I can't sleep,' she said as she dabbed her eyes with a handkerchief and sat down at the table. 'I keep thinking about Philip and Pops, and remembering that last time I saw them on the docks in Singapore as we were about to sail. I lie there with the thoughts going round and round in my head, worrying about what's happened to them.'

Peggy grasped her hands. 'I can't begin to imagine what you must be going through,' she said softly, 'and there's so little I can do to help, I feel absolutely useless.'

'I try to keep my worries from Jane, but poor Mother's frantic,' Sarah said as more tears slid down her face. 'We've heard the most awful rumours, but nothing we can really rely on as any kind of truth – nothing that might at least give us a bit of hope that they're both still alive.' She looked up at Peggy, her anguish clear in her tear-streaked face. 'Why will no one tell us anything?'

Peggy had long suspected that the old adage of 'no news was good news' was far off the mark when it came to the Japanese invasion of the Far East, but that was not something Sarah needed to hear right now.

'I've talked to the people at the Red Cross, and Martin and I discussed your situation only this afternoon,' she said carefully. 'Sarah, darling, the Japanese are refusing to let the Red Cross have any access to their POW records. And as the whole of that area is now in enemy hands, it's impossible for anyone to find out what has been happening.'

'Then how will we ever know? Why are they being so secretive? Surely they have to abide by the Geneva conventions like everyone else?'

'I don't know,' said Peggy helplessly. 'One would have thought so, but it seems they're a law unto themselves. Martin reckons that as time goes on news will start to filter out in letters smuggled by local fishermen, or through the Chinese merchants, who have numerous lines of outside contact through their businesses.'

'But the Japanese hate the Chinese,' Sarah replied. 'And they've probably put them all into prison by now.' She blew her nose and dried her eyes. 'Oh, Peggy, I just can't see an end to it,' she sighed. 'I worry and worry, and try to believe that I'll see Pops and Philip again, but the waiting for news is unbearable.'

'You've done very well up to now,' said Peggy as she lit their cigarettes. 'I know what a strain it's been for you to keep hopeful for Jane, and your mother would be very proud of you. But there will be times, like now, when you need to have a jolly good cry and get it all out of your system.' She lovingly tucked the girl's hair behind her ear. 'So don't be ashamed of those tears, or think you're being weak. We all have our fears, and we all cry – even strong, brave men like Martin.'

Sarah looked at her in surprise.

Peggy nodded. 'This war isn't just being fought on the battlefields and in the air, Sarah, but in our hearts and minds. And we must shed our tears and swallow our terrors, and grow strong in the knowledge that we are not alone.'

'Oh, Peggy,' Sarah sighed. 'You're so wise.'

Peggy laughed. 'No, I'm not. I've just been listening to too many of Mr Churchill's wonderful speeches.' She left the table and put the big tin kettle on the hob. 'Now, why don't I make us a nice cup of tea before you go back up to bed?'

Sarah gave a watery smile and nodded. 'Thanks, Peggy. I don't know how any of us would manage without having you to turn to.'

Peggy's smile faltered as she busied herself with cups and saucers. There were times when she cried into her pillow until she thought her heart would break. Times when the fear for her family became so strong she was weakened by it – but as long as she had breath in her body, nobody would ever know.

It was now past eleven o'clock and there was still no sign of Fran. Peggy sat in the light of the range fire, her eyelids drooping with weariness. At least Sarah had gone back to bed feeling a bit more able to cope with the stresses and strains of trying to shield her younger sister from her fears, but Peggy no longer had the energy to continue writing her long letter to Jim tonight. She would do it sometime tomorrow.

'What the divil are ye doing sitting here in the

dark?' exclaimed Ron as he tramped up the cellar steps half an hour later and switched on the light.

She was about to reply when Harvey shot past Ron and hurtled across the kitchen towards her. 'Get off,' she spluttered as he trampled his great paws in her lap and tried to lick her face.

'Harvey, sit, you heathen beast,' ordered Ron. 'To be sure, you're too big to be sitting in Peggy's lap.'

Harvey slumped to the floor where he lay with his nose on his paws and gave the impression that his feelings had been mortally wounded by Peggy's rejection.

Peggy repented and stroked his soft head. 'You're a lovely boy, and I appreciate the warm welcome.' She reached across to the tin of digestives and he sat up, ears pricked, alert and waiting for the treat he knew was coming.

The stale biscuit went down without touching the sides and Peggy laughed. 'There are no more, you greedy old thing. Now lie down and behave.'

'So,' said Ron, as he took off his one decent jacket and hung it on the back of a chair. 'Why were you sitting in the dark?'

'I'm waiting for Fran to come home. She went out with some Yank in a big flash car this morning and hasn't been seen since.'

'Oh, aye? Her mother will be having something to say to that, so she will. Fran was raised in a strict Catholic household.'

'I'm rather hoping her mother won't get to hear about it at all,' Peggy said flatly. 'Fran's obviously had her head turned, and if I don't nip it in the bud now . . . Well, you know where these things can lead.'

'Aye, I do,' he sighed. 'But to give the wee girl her due, she's never done something like this before. She has a good head on her shoulders, Peggy. Don't go jumping to conclusions just because she's a bit late for once.'

'It's after eleven and she has an early shift starting at seven tomorrow morning,' she said crossly. 'It's irresponsible, and I don't appreciate her making me worry like this.'

'Ach, to be sure, Peggy, you worry about everything – and I'm suspecting you quite enjoy it.' He must have noted her glare, for he dipped his chin. 'Well, I'll be off to me bed then,' he muttered. 'Come on, Harvey.'

Peggy watched them leave the kitchen. As Ron closed the door behind them, she got up to turn the light off again. Returning to her chair she glanced at the clock and decided it wouldn't hurt to have a little doze while she waited for Fran to come home.

The soft click of the front door closing woke her instantly, and before Fran had time to get past the second stair, Peggy was in the hall. 'And what time do you call this?' she snapped.

'Well now, I'm thinking it's a wee bit late,' she giggled as she clung to the newel post in an effort to keep her balance. 'I'm sorry, Peggy, but I was having such a wonderful time that I forgot to look at my watch.'

'In the kitchen. Now.'

'Ach, Peggy, I'm needing me bed. I've an early shift in less than seven hours.'

Peggy grabbed her arm, dragged her off the stairs and across the hall into the kitchen where she plonked her down into a chair. 'You're drunk,' she said crossly.

Fran rubbed her arm and pouted. 'To be sure I've had a wee drop or two, but there's no need to be so rough,' she protested.

Peggy turned on the kitchen light, and as Fran blinked in the sudden brightness, Peggy knew there had been rather more than drinking going on tonight. Fran's copper curls were in disarray, the top two buttons on her dress were fastened in the wrong order, and her mascara was as smudged as her lipstick.

Without a word, Peggy put the kettle back on. She'd get no sense out of the girl until she'd sobered up. Once the old tea leaves had been stirred back into frail life, she poured two cups and went to sit at the table. 'Drink that,' she ordered.

'I don't want it,' muttered Fran.

'You will drink it, whether you want it or not,' she said quietly. 'And then you are going to tell me where you've been, who that American was, and what you've been doing until gone midnight.'

'Will you be listening to yourself, Peggy? Ach, bejesus, you're sounding just like me mam.'

'Good, because that's exactly what I am all the time you live in this house, and I'll thank you to give me the same respect.'

Fran drank the tea and then sulkily clattered the empty cup in the saucer. 'Satisfied? Can I go to bed now?'

Peggy poured another cup and pushed it towards her. 'When you've finished that and answered my questions,' she said sternly.

'I don't know what all the fuss is about,' Fran complained. 'To be sure, I'm not a little girl any more. I'm over twenty-one and perfectly entitled to see who I want, when I want.'

'That you are,' replied Peggy, 'but as you're living under my roof, I expect the courtesy of knowing who you're with, and what time you plan on coming home.'

She watched as Fran sipped the tea, then went to dampen one of Daisy's flannels. 'Here,' she said, 'use this to wash your face. You look like a clown with all that mascara and lipstick smeared over your cheeks.'

Fran slowly ran the warm flannel over her face, looked at the mess of make-up she'd left on it and slumped in her chair. 'To be sure, I'm sorry, Peggy,' she said softly. 'I didn't mean to stay out so late, but he took me to a dance, and I forgot the time.'

'Why don't you tell me about him?' Peggy encouraged.

Her green eyes sparkled and her face became animated. 'His name's Charles Hoskins, but everyone calls him Chuck. He's twenty-eight and has just been promoted to Captain. He comes from New Jersey and went to Yale. His father is a surgeon and Chuck was studying medicine when he was called up. After the war he plans to finish his studies and join his father's private practice. He's an absolute dream on the dance floor,' she finished with a sigh.

Peggy thought he sounded far too good to be true, but she let it pass. 'You must invite him in the next time he comes to pick you up,' she said. 'I'd like to meet him.'

Fran grinned. 'You'll like him, Aunty Peg, really you will. He's tall and handsome, with beautiful teeth and the sort of smile that makes you go weak at the knees. He has lovely manners, too, and he makes me feel like a princess when we're together.'

The alarm bells were ringing and Peggy couldn't ignore them. 'Then he must definitely come to tea,' she said. 'How about this weekend? Saturday's clear.'

Fran squirmed in her chair. 'Well, it will depend on his duties, Aunty Peg.'

'I'm sure it will,' said Peggy, 'but before you go out with him again, I'm afraid I'm going to have to insist we are introduced. It's what your mother would want, and if this young man is everything you say he is then I can't see why you're reluctant for me to meet him.'

'I'm not at all,' Fran said with wide, innocent eyes. 'It's just that it's early days, and I don't want him to think I'm trying to push him into anything by bringing him home to meet the family.'

'Just how long is it since you started seeing one another?'

'I met him at one of the dances up at the Cliffe estate,' she said defensively. 'We've been walking out for about two months.'

'Then it's definitely time I met him,' said Peggy. 'Tea on Saturday. Four o'clock sharp – and no excuses. Now go to bed.'

'I'm sorry if I've upset you, Peggy,' Fran said mournfully.

Peggy took her into her arms and gave her a reassuring cuddle. 'Just for pity's sake be careful, Fran,' she murmured into the halo of autumnal curls. 'Those American boys are far too sure of themselves, and most of them have wives or sweethearts waiting for them back home.'

Fran drew back from the embrace. 'Chuck's not married,' she said with a shy smile. 'And I'm not doing anything silly, I promise.'

Peggy shooed her out of the room and then sank back into the kitchen chair. She hoped for Fran's sake that Chuck was all he said he was, for despite her Irish charm and cheeky enthusiasm, Fran was far from sophisticated, and clearly madly infatuated. She could only hope it wouldn't all end in tears.

Chapter Ten

Daisy was in her playpen in the back garden, taking great interest in what her grandfather Ron was up to as Harvey sat as close as he could to her, keeping guard. It was still early morning, but it promised to be another hot July day.

Ron finished picking the juicy raspberries off his canes and carefully draped the fine netting back over them to keep off the marauding birds. He popped a raspberry into Daisy's mouth as a treat, then took them in to show Peggy.

'There are plenty more where these came from,' he said proudly. 'So I'm thinking they will make a lovely summer pudding for tea tonight.'

Peggy admired the plump red fruit. 'What a treat!' She was standing at the sink in the scullery, the steam rising from the hot water as she washed the nappies and baby clothes. 'I've got plenty of stale bread left over, as long as you don't use it for the chickens' mash or the ferrets' breakfast.'

'Ach, to be sure, there's enough bread to go round, and I've asked Mr Timmons at the bakery to put another two loaves aside for you to pick up later.'

He stood and watched her for a moment, noting the damp curls sticking to her forehead, the weary set of her narrow shoulders, and her reddened hands. Peggy worked so hard, and there was little let-up with a baby in the house. 'But maybe I'll be fetching the bread before I go fer me walk,' he said. 'Ye've enough to be doing here.'

Peggy began to thread the sodden nappies through the mangle rollers. 'That would be helpful,' she replied. 'I've got the WVS this afternoon, and Cordelia and I plan to bake a cake later this morning.'

She dropped the flattened nappies into the washing basket at her feet and pulled out more from the hot rinsing water which had been coloured by the blue-bag she always used to get things white. 'Cordelia found a lovely recipe for scones, so we're going to try and eke everything out to make a batch as a special treat. She's in the kitchen now, washing out the baking tins.'

Ron's mouth watered at the thought of cake and scones. It had been a long time since Peggy had done any baking and he loved her sponges. 'Where on earth did you manage to get hold of flour, butter and sugar?' he asked.

Peggy went rather red and refused to look at him as she fed the nappies through the wringer and turned the handle. 'I stood in a queue for an hour yesterday and got the sugar, and Jane brought butter home from the dairy.'

'And the flour?' he asked suspiciously.

Her blush deepened. 'I managed to get hold of some from one of Jim's old friends.' She stopped turning the mangle and wagged a finger at him. 'Don't look at me like that, Ron,' she said defensively. 'It's not as if you're whiter than white.'

'I'm cut to the quick at your insinuations,' he protested with a hand on his heart and a twinkle in his eyes.

'Well,' Peggy said. 'I just happened to mention I had no flour and he just happened to have some, and I've got some strawberry jam left over from last year's crop, and the chickens are laying well, so I'm planning on doing a Victoria sponge,' she finished in a rush.

Ron laughed. Peggy was a dear, and obviously feeling very guilty about buying flour on the black market, so he decided not to tease her. 'That would be a real treat, so it would,' he murmured appreciatively. 'Me mouth's watering at the thought already.'

'It's for tomorrow, so I don't want you helping yourself and cutting great chunks out of it,' she said sternly.

'As if I would,' he protested with wide-eyed innocence. 'Anyway, what's so important about tomorrow?'

'Fran's American GI is coming to tea,' she replied.

Ron frowned. 'I thought you didn't approve of her seeing him?'

'I don't,' she said flatly. 'But I want to meet him

and see what he's made of before things go any further. It's important he realises she's a respectable girl, living with a respectable family, and that I will not tolerate any nonsense.'

Ron could understand her reasoning, but he didn't quite see how feeding the Yank with Victoria sponge was going to be any sort of help. With a sigh of puzzlement, he picked up the heavy laundry basket and carried it outside, past the baby in her playpen to the washing line. What went on in women's heads was a mystery to him.

'I'll be getting the bread then,' he muttered. 'And when I get back, I'll be taking Daisy for a bit of fresh air while I exercise Harvey and the ferrets.'

'That will certainly help me get through the morning more easily,' Peggy replied as she began to peg out the nappies. 'She's been a bit grizzly since she woke, and I think she's teething again.'

Ron looked down at the playpen where Daisy was chewing frantically on a brightly coloured plastic ring. There was high colour in her little cheeks, and he could tell that she was feeling miserable. 'Poor wee wain,' he muttered. 'I know just how she feels when me shrapnel's on the move and there's no comfort.'

'Your shrapnel only seems to be on the move when there's something unpleasant to be done around the house,' retorted Peggy dryly.

'Ach, to be sure, you're a hard woman, so you are, Peggy Reilly,' he grumbled without rancour.

'Me shrapnel's no laughing matter, and a man should be shown a bit of sympathy after what he went through in those heathen trenches.'

'Go and get the bread, Ron,' she said with the hint of a smile.

Ron grabbed the string bag from the back of the door and stuffed it into his trouser pocket. He rolled up the sleeves of his faded shirt and hitched up his sagging trousers, wishing he could find the belt that had disappeared in his bedroom several weeks ago. But the room was in a bit of a jumble and it would take a month of Sundays to find anything, so he got a bit of garden twine from the shed and used that instead.

'Come on Harvey,' he said. 'To be sure, it's no sympathy we'll be getting around here, and no cake either if Peggy gets her way.' He shot his beloved daughter-in-law a cheeky grin and stomped off down the garden path, his dog at his heels.

It was a pretty day and despite his grumbling, all was right with his world. Ron paused at the end of the twitten to light his pipe and take an appreciative look at the glittering sea at the bottom of the hill and the clear sky above him. The gulls were hovering and gliding, and the sun was warm on his face. One could hardly believe there was a war on such a lovely day – but for the reminders in the wrecked house on the corner and the huge bomb crater halfway down the hill that still hadn't been filled.

Content and at peace with himself, he crossed the street and headed down Camden Road towards Timmons' Bakery. He paused again as he reached the Anchor, and after a momentary hesitation, went down the alley and through the side door into the gloom of the ancient pub.

'Rosie, me darlin',' he called up the narrow wooden stairs. 'Are ye decent?'

She appeared at the top of the stairs, gloriously tousled and eminently desirable in a cream silk dressing gown. 'About as decent as a girl can be at this unearthly time of the morning,' she replied with a soft smile.

Ron felt stirrings as he imagined what was beneath that dressing gown. For a woman nudging fifty, Rosie was a glorious temptress. 'It's nearly nine o'clock,' he said.

'But I didn't get to bed last night until gone midnight, as you very well know,' she replied.

He grinned foolishly as he remembered the kisses he'd stolen as they'd cleaned the bar and restocked the shelves after everyone had been turfed out and the pub door was bolted. 'Are you not going to ask me up for a cup of tea?' he asked hopefully. 'To be sure, I'm parched, so I am.'

Rosie laughed and flicked back the platinum hair from her heart-shaped face. 'And to be sure you're not coming one step further, Ronan Reilly. There's a gleam in your eyes that I know all too well, and if it's tea you're after then I'm a Dutchman.'

He chuckled. 'Would you be after coming with me for a walk in the hills then, Rosie? 'Tis a beautiful day, and I'm taking me grand-daughter for a breath of air after I've done Peggy's shopping.'

She shook her head and tightened the belt on her dressing gown, which only served to emphasise her tempting curves. 'I can't, Ron,' she said regretfully. 'The other girls are off today, so I'll be running the bar on my own this lunchtime.'

'Ach, well, it was just a thought,' he sighed as his gaze drifted longingly over the swell of her breasts and hips beneath that cream silk.

'If you're back before I have to open again at six, why don't you call in for a cup of tea?' She smiled broadly. 'I've got cake.'

It wasn't cake he was after – and Rosie knew it – but she also knew that cake was a temptation he couldn't resist, even if it was a poor substitute. 'You're a wee tease, Rosie Braithwaite,' he replied with a wink. 'I'll see you this afternoon.'

She blew him a kiss, then, with a giggle, she flitted away into her living quarters.

Ron left the Anchor, warmed by her lovely smile and feeling very chipper. He strolled down Camden Road, his thoughts in a jumble as Harvey watered every lamp-post and sniffed up walls. To be sure he didn't want to wish a man dead, but Rosie's sick husband was all that kept them apart. The ridiculous laws barring people from divorcing their insane partners meant they would have to wait until he was dead, which rather overshadowed what he and Rosie felt for one another.

He stopped to relight his pipe, and then continued on towards the bakery. Rosie was a good, honest woman who took her marriage vows very seriously, and she'd kept him at arm's-length ever since their relationship had begun to blossom. It was a sadness and a frustration that he bore because he loved her, but he did wish he hadn't seen her in that alluring dressing gown.

'Sit there and don't move,' he ordered Harvey as he reached the bakery. Stepping into the shop, he found he'd walked straight into a furious argument.

'This isn't proper bread,' said one woman crossly.

'You can't palm us off with this,' said another. 'It weighs a ton, looks dirty and is nothing like a proper loaf of bread.'

Mr Timmons was usually a mild-tempered, patient man, but he'd clearly had enough this morning. 'Ladies, ladies, please just listen,' he pleaded, his face reddening. 'It's the new government ruling because of the shortage of white flour.'

'I don't care what the government says, my Bert won't eat that,' said a large woman in a flowery wrap-round apron and matching headscarf. She slammed the loaf back down on the counter and folded her meaty arms. 'I want my usual two white loaves,' she demanded.

'I'm sorry, Mrs Pike, but as you very well know, there's a war on,' he retorted rather crossly. 'Most of our flour has to come from abroad, and it takes up space on the convoys for more important things. So the government has ordered all the bakers to use only the home-grown wheat flour, to ensure that all the crops we grow are used to the full.'

'What's more important than putting decent bread into our family's stomachs? This has got bits in it,' snapped someone else.

'Winning the war,' he barked, the colour in his face rising to quite an alarming hue. 'This is the new National Wholemeal Loaf. It is healthy and nutritious and it is all I can sell you today, tomorrow and until the end of the war.' He folded his arms over his white apron and glared, daring them to argue further.

'I'd rather go without than eat that,' muttered Mrs Pike as she stomped out of the bakery.

Ron eyed the loaves of bread Mr Timmons had on his shelves. They certainly didn't look appetising, but if there was nothing else then he supposed he had no choice but to buy them. Bread wasn't rationed, and it had become a staple part of their diet at Beach View and filled the gaps left by the tight rationing. To go without bread was unthinkable.

There was a lot of muttering as the women reluctantly bought this new bread, and Mr Timmons, usually so cheerful and polite, remained grimly determined not to take the blame for this latest government decree.

'Hello, Ron,' he said as he handed over the two loaves he'd put by under the counter. 'Sorry about this, but there's nothing I can do about it.'

'Well, they're sturdy enough, I'll say that,' he replied as he felt their weight. 'To be sure, they'll stick to the sides of the stomach so they will.' He pulled Peggy's string bag out of his trouser pocket and placed them inside.

Mr Timmons reached under the counter and handed over a fairly large brown paper bag. 'There will be more tomorrow,' he said quietly.

'What's that?' said the woman behind Ron sharply. 'Are you selling something else that we don't know about?'

'It's the breadcrumbs swept off the floor at the end of every day,' said Mr Timmons with a sigh. 'It's not fit for human consumption, Mrs Brown, but it ensures that nothing goes to waste.'

Ron opened the bag to prove there was nothing of any value in it and was immediately surrounded. 'I use them to feed me chickens and ferrets,' he explained to the women. 'They don't mind a bit of dust and dead spider mixed in with their food.'

There were some sniffs of disapproval and a few glares, and Mr Timmons had clearly taken umbrage at the mention of dust and spiders being anywhere near his shop, so Ron decided that retreat was the better part of valour and made a hasty exit.

On his return to Beach View, he regaled Peggy

and Cordelia with what had happened at the bakery, and then placed the dingy-beige loaves on the table. Taking the breadknife from the dresser drawer, he carefully cut off the crust and shaved a thin slice for them all to sample.

'Urgh, that's awful,' grimaced Peggy. 'It's got hard bits in it that get into your teeth, and when you start to chew it goes soggy and sticks to the roof of your mouth.'

As Cordelia echoed this sentiment, Ron examined the wafer of bread and came to the conclusion that they'd certainly used every part of the crop, for he could see bits of husk in it. He put it in his mouth and discovered it bore little relation to any bread he'd ever tasted before. 'I'm thinking we won't be eating as much bread from now on,' he muttered. 'But I suppose we'll get used to it.'

'Thank goodness I've got enough stale white bread to make that summer pudding,' said Peggy. 'This wouldn't do at all.'

''Tis a good thing you got that white flour,' said Ron. 'Does Jim's friend have any more, do you think? Only once word gets round, it'll be as expensive as gold dust.'

'He said he did, but I didn't have enough money on me at the time to buy more,' murmured Peggy. She reached for her purse. 'It's Johnny Carter down in Green Street.'

Ron knew Johnny very well from back in the days when they used to go night fishing off the coast of France. He was as sharp as a tack and as wily as a bag of ferrets, but friendship and shared experience meant that Ron knew how to get round him.

'Keep your money in your purse, Peggy,' he said. 'I'll go there now.'

The curtain was closed around Kitty's bed as Nurse Hopkins finished rubbing the icy surgical spirit into her back and buttocks. 'There we are,' she said cheerfully. 'That will keep the nasty old bed sores at bay.'

Kitty's smile was wan, for although the girl meant well, she was getting a bit fed up with all this heartiness. She felt low today, and was utterly sick and tired of being imprisoned in this damned bed with her one decent leg strung up towards the ceiling.

She lay there, unable to help, as the nurse struggled to get her dressed in the hospital nightgown and do up the buttons down the front. 'It'll be much easier once the plaster's off my arms,' she said. 'I'm sorry to be such a nuisance.'

'Good heavens,' the girl replied, her brown eyes widening. 'You're not a nuisance at all. I just haven't got the hang of the bally thing properly, that's all, and with Matron on the warpath this morning, I'm all fingers and thumbs.'

Kitty had long since realised that Nurse Hopkins had probably gone to boarding school and been very good at games. 'I feel sorry for you nurses,' she said. 'She really is the limit, isn't she?'

'Frightful woman,' Nurse Hopkins replied with a roll of her eyes. 'Honestly, she's far worse than any headmistress I had the misfortune to cross – and I can tell you, there were one or two old dragons.'

'Yes, I know exactly what you mean,' replied Kitty as she thought of the times she'd been hauled in to face the wrath of her own headmistress.

Nurse Hopkins beamed her lovely smile. 'I can see you're a bit down in the dumps this morning,' she said. 'But we have a special treat for you, which I guarantee will cheer you up no end.'

Kitty perked up immediately. 'Freddy's here?'

The nurse shook her head. 'Unfortunately not, although I have to say, he does liven things up around here when he visits.' She must have seen the disappointment in Kitty's face, for she hurried on. 'General Thorne has said you can get out of bed today.'

'Really? That's marvellous, but what about that?' She eyed the pulley contraption which had been lowered so the nurse could attend to her.

'Oh, you won't need that once you're up and about,' said the nurse as she eased Kitty's leg out of the harness. 'So, what do you think? Would you like to go and see the garden? It's a beautiful day.'

'Yes,' Kitty replied firmly. 'I'm fed up with lying here.'

'Jolly good show,' said the nurse. 'I'll just go and

fetch Nurse Gardner to help me get you into the chair.'

She dashed off through the curtain and Kitty wriggled her bottom up the bed until she was bolstered by her pillows. With her leg out of the pulley it was so much easier to move around. Yet she didn't dare try to do any more, for she was still hampered by the plaster casts on her arms, and all the wriggling had pulled at the scar in her abdomen where her spleen had been repaired.

With a sigh of frustration, she leaned against the pillows, sadly remembering the times she'd swung her legs out of bed in the morning without a moment's thought. Now she had to wait to be helped with the slightest thing.

'Here we are,' Nurse Hopkins said brightly. 'Now, I know you're impatient, but you need to take things slowly and carefully. You'll feel a bit odd for a while, but that's only natural after lying in bed for so long.'

Kitty found she couldn't help at all as the two nurses sat her up and lifted her to the edge of the bed. They joined hands beneath her thighs and behind her back, and with one orchestrated heave, had her in the bedside chair.

'There, that was easy, wasn't it? Light as a feather, you are. How does it feel to have disembarked the bed?'

'Odd,' admitted Kitty, 'but in a very nice way,' she added hurriedly.

Nurse Gardner straightened Kitty's nightdress and in several efficient moves had the hospital dressing gown on and tied round Kitty's narrow waist. 'We don't want you getting a chill, even if it is lovely and sunny out there.'

'Your chariot awaits,' said Nurse Hopkins as she brought in the wheelchair. 'Let's pop you in and get you a good dose of lovely sunshine.'

Kitty was lifted from one chair to the other. A blanket was tucked over her lap, and a leg-rest was drawn out from underneath so her plastered leg was fully supported. 'Let's go,' she said impatiently.

The curtain was drawn back and there was a chorus of congratulations from the girls who were still confined to their beds as Kitty was wheeled down the ward.

Kitty grinned with delight as Nurse Hopkins steered her through the swing doors and out into the corridor. This had clearly once been a rather grand house, for there was a magnificent oak staircase leading to the floor above, dark wood panelling halfway up the walls, and a highly decorated ceiling with plaster angels, roses, unicorns and heraldic shields dancing across it.

'What was this place?' she asked.

'It used to belong to an old lady,' Nurse Hopkins replied. 'She was the last in line of a very grand, wealthy family. Her son and grandson were both killed on the Somme in the last war, so she decided to leave it in their memory to the services as a hospital. Between the wars it was used as a nursing home for the elderly veterans with long-term health problems, and now it's proving to be a wonderful place to treat the injured from this war. Every service is accounted for here, including the Women's Timber Corps, the Land Army, the NAAFI and dozens of others. You're in the east wing, and the larger west wing has been allocated for the men.'

Kitty was eager to see more of this lovely house, but for now she was happy just to be out of bed and on the move.

Nurse Hopkins brought the wheelchair to a halt at the open French windows. 'There,' she breathed. 'Isn't it lovely?'

Kitty gazed out at the sweeping lawns where a game of croquet was being played with great enthusiasm and little skill by a group of men on crutches. There were dense trees forming a barrier at the end of the garden, and the neat flowerbeds being tended by some of the more able patients were alive with colour. She could hear birdsong and smell the roses that clambered over the stone parapet of the broad terrace where people were gathered in groups in their wheelchairs, or sitting at tables beneath vast umbrellas.

'It's beautiful,' she sighed. 'But . . .' She suddenly felt afraid to go out there and be stared at by all those strangers – especially the men. 'I don't think . . .'

Nurse Hopkins knelt beside her and softly placed her hand on Kitty's bandaged thigh. 'You're no different to everyone else out there,' she said quietly. 'They've all been injured one way or another, and the majority of them have lost limbs too. Don't imagine that they'll stare or make comments, for each and every one of them knows how hard that is to bear.'

Kitty watched as the group playing croquet laughed uproariously at something one of them had said. Then she regarded the men and women in wheelchairs who were chatting in groups as they drank tea and smoked cigarettes – and the quiet few who were reading, or strolling on their crutches across the lawn.

'Oi, Kitty!' yelled Doreen from the terrace. 'What you doing there? Come out here. I saved yer a place.'

Nurse Hopkins laughed. 'A foghorn would have a job making itself heard when Doreen's about.' She tilted her head. 'So, why don't I take you over there to join in the fun?'

Kitty realised Doreen had drawn unwanted attention to her, and she knew that if she chickened out now she'd be thought of as terribly feeble and a bit of a wet blanket. 'All right, but just for a little while,' she replied reluctantly.

Nurse Hopkins patted the stump of Kitty's thigh, and with a rather knowing smile, pushed her wheelchair through the French windows and onto the terrace.

Kitty returned the various greetings with some bravura, despite feeling horribly exposed.

'Blimey, it took you long enough,' said Doreen, who was sitting at a big wooden table with five other people. 'I thought you'd changed your mind.'

Nurse Hopkins brought Kitty's wheelchair to a halt and set the brake before striding off.

Kitty felt abandoned and quite vulnerable, but Doreen was having none of it. 'You know Beth, Joan and Sybil from the ward, of course, and this 'ere's James – he's RAF – and this is Edward who's a Marine,' she said as she made the introductions.

Kitty smiled shyly at the two men opposite her as they just as shyly welcomed her to the group.

'Doreen's frightfully bossy, isn't she?' said the young airman with an empty left sleeve in his dressing gown. 'But she's jolly good fun and cheers us up no end.'

'Yes, she's quite a girl, is our Doreen,' agreed Ed, who had heavy bandaging over his head and right eye.

'I bet you say that to all the girls,' said Doreen flirtatiously. 'I've heard about you Marines.'

'It's sailors who have a girl in every port,' he replied with a smile. 'Marines are much more selective.'

Kitty began to relax as the banter went back and forth in the dappled shade of the nearby trees. It was a beautiful day, she was alive and amongst people who understood exactly what she was going through. Everything would be all right.

Doreen lit a cigarette and picked up the pack of rather grubby cards from the table. 'Right,' she said. 'We was about to 'ave a few 'ands of five card brag.' She squinted at Kitty through her cigarette smoke. 'You up for it, gel?'

'Only if you're prepared to lose,' smiled Kitty.

'Now that's what I call fighting talk,' laughed Doreen. 'Yer on, gel.'

Ron strode across the hills with Daisy happily ensconced against his broad chest in the old army satchel he'd adapted for just this purpose. Harvey was galloping about trying to catch flies, wasps and butterflies as they hummed and flitted above the long grass, and the air was scented with warm earth and the salt from the sea.

These hills had become his second home, and he loved the sense of youthful freedom they gave him, for he was at one with the elements, and he could turn his back on all his responsibilities and just be.

After giving the ferrets a bit of a run through the maze of rabbit warrens that lay beneath the chalk and grass, he'd put their catches in one of the pockets of his long poacher's coat, and with Dora and Flora now asleep in another, he'd set off again. He'd decided to take a different route today, and instead of heading down into the valley which eventually led to Cliffe aerodrome and the tiny village where Anne and Martin had a house, he turned north-west.

Lord Cliffe's vast estate encompassed not only an ancient forest and several lakes, but a salmon farm, a mansion, gate-lodge and dower house, pheasant pens, stables and farms. Outside the high wire fences that the Land Army had put up, there were numerous cottages and acres of fields, which were served by a pub and a church and formed a close-knit village community over which Lord Cliffe held sway.

Ron tramped past the electrified fence, mourning the days when he'd used the estate as his private larder. The new gamekeeper was far too keen-eyed and efficient for his liking, and after a couple of run-ins with him and his vicious dog, Ron had admitted defeat. And yet there were other places to go poaching that weren't guarded at all, and that was where he was heading now – although he'd have to face Peggy's wrath for taking Daisy with him on such an enterprise.

Daisy wriggled and blew raspberries as she kicked against him, and Ron grinned down at her, chucking her under the chin. She was getting a wee bit too big for the old satchel, so he'd had to cut holes in the bottom to accommodate her chubby little legs, but as long as he could carry her out here into his special kingdom, he was happy to do it. Daisy was a Reilly and this was her birthright – and the silent, majestic sweep of the hills, valleys, fields and forests held the essence of what those brave youngsters were fighting to protect.

He stopped for a moment on the brow of a hill and took in the scene. Bright yellow gorse blazed in vast, untidy clumps and gnarled trees grew bent from the years of being battered by the wind. The sea glittered beneath the Mediterranean blue of the cloudless sky, and he could hear the skylarks' beautiful songs as they soared way above him.

'Look at that, Daisy,' he said as he lifted her out of her makeshift pouch and adjusted her cotton bonnet. 'Can you see the sea – and hear the skylarks? They won't change, no matter if there's a war or not.'

Daisy burbled and grabbed his eyebrow, giving it a sharp tug.

'Ach, to be sure, you've a fair grip on you, so you have.'

He gently prised her fist from his brow and held her in the crook of his arm so she could get a clear view of everything. 'See that road, Daisy – and the big wooded hills beyond it? That's where we're heading, so we are. There's eels to be had there, and you'll taste nothing better, I can promise you that.'

Daisy wasn't listening. She was far too interested in what Harvey was up to, and Ron almost dropped her as she threw herself forward to reach him as he rushed towards her.

Ron hastily put her back in the satchel, though it

was a bit of a struggle as Daisy didn't want to go in it. She kicked and wriggled and screamed, and it took a divil of time to get her safely inside.

'Get down, you heathen beast,' he growled at Harvey, who was trying to jump up to lick the baby's face. 'To be sure, you've far too much energy. Go and do something useful for a change.'

Harvey shot off, tail like a flag as his tongue lolled and his ears flapped.

'Daft auld t'ing,' Ron muttered affectionately. He hitched the bawling baby to a more comfortable position against his chest and tramped on, knowing Harvey wouldn't let him out of his sight no matter how occupied he was.

The main road into Cliffehaven ran past the Cliffe estate, through the quiet hamlets and over the quaint stone bridges that arched over the gravel bed of the fast-flowing river. This river made its way through farmland villages from its source some miles away where reed beds flourished.

As Ron reached the road, the peace was shattered by the roar of aircraft. Daisy didn't even flinch as the fighters and bombers took off from Cliffe aerodrome and thundered overhead towards the Channel. 'God speed,' murmured Ron as he watched them until they were out of sight.

Harvey trotted alongside him as he turned off the road and headed up the steep lane which passed Rita's motorcycle racing track and would take him to the woods behind Agatha Fullerton's house. These woods stretched for five or six miles and were divided by a boundary fence that ran between Agatha's property and the large manor house estate that had once belonged to the Finlay-White family.

As Ron plodded up the hill with the sleeping baby's head now resting beneath his chin, he thought about the tragedies that had befallen the wealthy Finlay-Whites. He'd known their grandson, for they'd both joined the same regiment at the start of the last war, and like so many men, neither he nor his father had survived.

Mrs Finlay-White had lived on in that great rambling house, alone but for the servants – and perhaps the ghosts of her loved ones – and Ron had done a bit of gardening and maintenance for her when his fishing allowed. She'd worn black until her death, he remembered; rather like Queen Victoria after Albert had died. But her fierce glare and authoritarian manner hid a kind heart, for she'd always asked after his family and given him a plump turkey every Christmas, and the gift of a crisp white pound note on his birthday.

Ron reached the top of the lane and looked down on Holmwood House. It was now the Finlay-White Memorial Hospital For Injured Servicemen, and apart from a new addition to the west wing, it didn't look that different from when he'd once worked there. The brick walls were mellow ochre in the sunlight, the many windows glinting as they looked out from beneath the fancy gabled roofs to the spread of the lawns and formal flowerbeds. He could just make out the movement of people on the sunlit terrace, and wondered if the girl Peggy had told him about was with them.

With a sigh of sadness for the many lives that had been lost or changed forever because of war, he turned away and headed for the gap he'd made in the boundary fence which would give him access to Agatha Fullerton's land.

He'd disguised it with tree branches, but he knew exactly where it was, and he wriggled through with Harvey at his heels, and the baby clasped to his chest. He tramped through the trees, looking forward to sitting in the shade by the deep pool where the eels swam, for it was a hot day, and his heavy poacher's coat was making him sweat.

All was silent but for the birdsong and the crackle of leaves beneath his boots, and as Ron reached the spot where the streams fed a deep, shadowed pool, he took off his coat and placed it on the ground. Daisy was still asleep, so he gently removed the satchel and laid it on his coat.

Harvey took a long drink from the pool and then sat down beside the cocooned baby and rested his nose on his paws, eyebrows twitching as he waited to see what Ron was doing.

Ron rolled up his shirtsleeves and regarded his quiet surroundings with pleasure. Agatha rarely came this far into the trees, and as there was no gamekeeper to bother him, he knew he had plenty of time to wait for the eels to come sliding into the net he had in his pocket.

Chapter Eleven

It was very hot in the kitchen, so they'd thrown open the window and back door to try and garner some fresh air. But the delicious aroma of baking cakes and scones more than made up for the discomfort, and Peggy and Cordelia were happily washing up in anticipation of getting out into the garden with a cup of tea once everything had cooked.

A batch of scones was already cooling on a wire tray on the table, and there were a dozen fairy cakes just about ready to get out of the oven. There was no icing sugar or cream, but Peggy had decided a spot of jam would do instead.

'I hope this American is worth all the trouble,' said Cordelia with a sniff as she hung the damp tea towel above the range to dry.

'Whether he is or not, we'll get to eat cake.' Peggy dried her hands and carefully drew the bun tin out of the oven. 'There, don't they look lovely?'

Cordelia eyed the small golden buns and licked her lips. 'I don't suppose we could have one with our cup of tea?' she asked hopefully.

Peggy laughed as she pushed the damp tendrils

of her dark hair from her forehead. 'I don't see why not. We've earned a treat, and that's a fact.' She placed the kettle on the hob and put out cups and saucers. 'Why don't you go into the garden and get settled? I'll be out with the tea in a minute.'

'It's a good thing Ron and the girls aren't here,' said Cordelia with a twinkle in her eyes. 'They'd fall on this lot like a horde of locusts.'

She grabbed her walking stick and battered straw hat then slowly went down the cellar steps and out into the garden, where the purloined umbrella cast a pleasant shade over the old deckchairs.

Peggy made the tea, and although it was as pale as straw, there was a bit of sugar to give it some flavour, which was a blessing. She checked on the two round tins of sponge and carefully slipped a long darning needle into each of them to check they were cooked through. They'd risen wonderfully and the smell was quite heavenly, making her mouth water as she carefully drew them out and left them to rest on another wire tray.

Leaving them to cool a bit before she took them out of the tins, she quickly sliced off the top of two fairy cakes, added jam and replaced the top in two halves so they looked like wings. Setting them on a plate, she put the teacups, teapot and plate of little cakes on a tray and took them out into the garden. 'Don't eat it too quickly,' she advised Cordelia. 'There's only one each.'

'What about the rest?'

'I thought Ruby and Ethel might appreciate them. They've invited Stan for tea tomorrow.' She poured the tea. 'Rita's going up there this evening to pick up Ruby and they're going to the pictures, so she can take them with her.'

Peggy returned to the kitchen to see to her sponge, and had just settled in the deckchair to drink her tea and enjoy her cake when the telephone rang. 'Blessed thing,' she muttered. 'Honestly, Cordelia, there are times . . .'

She hurried back indoors and into the hall where she snatched up the receiver. 'Beach View Boarding House,' she said automatically.

'Margaret, I've had the most awful news,' said Doris, her voice high and anxious.

Peggy sank onto the hall chair, her heart thudding with alarm. 'What's happened? It's not Anthony, is it?'

'Of course not,' she retorted. 'If anything happened to my Anthony, I wouldn't be able to speak, let alone telephone you.'

'Then what is it?' Peggy's tone was sharp with fear and impatience.

'I've been ordered – ordered, mind you – to take in some ghastly evacuees.'

Peggy sagged with relief. 'For goodness' sake, Doris,' she hissed. 'I thought something serious had happened.'

'This is serious,' Doris snapped. 'I can't possibly be expected to take in strangers when I have so many other concerns. But the billeting woman came round, took one look at my two spare bedrooms and insisted that I accommodate these people.'

Peggy had to force herself not to giggle at her sister's ridiculous carrying on. 'But Doris, surely you can see that two spare rooms are an absolute godsend to the billeting office with so many homeless to house?'

'I've told her I refuse to have men, or anyone with children – and that I insist upon interviewing them before they put one grubby foot over my doorstep,' said Doris. 'But it seems I have no say in the matter.'

'Oh, Doris,' sighed Peggy. 'You really are the limit. Can't you see that this is your chance to do your bit? Those poor people at the Town Hall have so little, and here you are begrudging them a bit of comfort.'

'Some of us have standards, Margaret. You may throw open your doors to all and sundry, but I refuse to let my home become a dosshouse.'

Peggy's eyebrows shot up. 'I hardly think there's any call for that sort of talk. Haven't you got even the slightest bit of charity in your soul, Doris?'

'I might have known you wouldn't understand,' Doris said bitterly. 'You always were too soft for your own good, and look where it's got you.'

Peggy went very still. 'And where is that, exactly?' she asked with quiet fury.

'Not only do you have a disgusting dog and

stinking ferrets running about the place, but you're married to an Irish layabout whose father is little more than a tramp. Your house is home to a dotty old woman who should be put away; a common guttersnipe who has the grace and manners of a hoyden; and a flibbertigibbet Irish nurse who's no better than she should be. I saw her with that American, so I know exactly what she's up to.' Doris seemed to have run out of breath.

Peggy was so angry she could hardly speak. 'You weren't so fussy when you moved in after Ted ran off with his floozy,' she snapped bitterly. 'Which, I have to say, is hardly surprising if this is how you carry on. Put your own house in order before you start criticising mine, Doris.'

'How *dare* you speak to me like that?' Doris gasped.

'I'll speak to you any way I want,' Peggy fired back. 'And for once in your life think of someone else. People need rooms, you have two – so stop complaining and make the best of things, like we all have to.'

'But they're ghastly, common women who work at the munitions factory,' Doris wailed. 'I can't possibly . . .'

Peggy slammed the receiver down and stomped back through the kitchen and down to the garden. Plumping into the deckchair, she lit a cigarette and puffed furiously on it until she became quite light-headed.

'Good heavens,' said a rather startled Cordelia. 'You look as if you're about to explode. What on earth has happened?'

'Doris is the rudest, most selfish, arrogant person I have the misfortune to know,' snarled Peggy. 'And to think that I'm related to her only makes it worse. She winds me up to the point where I want to bust my springs.'

Cordelia giggled. 'Oh, dear. What's she done this time?'

Peggy was about to reply when there was a ripping sound, and before she could do anything about it, the canvas parted company with the deck-chair frame and she was deposited abruptly onto the ground.

After the momentary shock, she burst out laughing. She knew she looked ridiculous, with her dress rucked up to her knickers and her bare legs stuck up in the air, but at least she'd been brought down to earth with a bump, in more than one sense, and her sister's nastiness was easily dismissed.

Kitty had been surprised by how much she'd enjoyed the morning, but by the time Nurse Hopkins had returned to wheel her back indoors she was feeling utterly exhausted. The added difficulty of using a proper lavatory for the first time since she'd been brought here merely served to tire her further, and she was very happy to return to her bed for a sleep.

When she woke to the sound of the food trolley being wheeled in, she discovered that she was hungry for once, and could only hope it wasn't fish again. As the NAAFI girl put the plate on the bed-table, she eyed the slivers of chicken and crisp salad with pleasure and anticipation, and wished the nurse would hurry up and help her to eat it.

The nurse came eventually, and after Kitty had managed to eat every last morsel, she tucked into the jelly. 'Aaah,' she sighed as she rested back against the pillows. 'That's better. Thanks, Nurse.'

'It's good to see you've got your appetite back,' she replied with a smile. She dug into the pocket of her apron. 'These should perk you up no end as well,' she said as she pulled out two letters and a couple of postcards. 'I'll just open the letters for you and then leave you to enjoy them.'

Kitty waited impatiently and then greedily reached for the first of the thin blue airmails that had come all the way from Argentina. Her mother's familiar looped writing blurred as Kitty read the single page.

Darling girl,

My heart aches with longing to be with you, to hold and reassure you, and to chase away the terrors which I know must beset you at this terrible time. We can only imagine what you are going through, but your father and I know our dearest girl, and we draw some comfort in the knowledge that you possess a formidable inner strength which will help you to overcome the injuries you have suffered, and find a way ahead.

My brave, brave girl, I'm so proud of you that my heart is full to bursting, and I think of you in my every waking moment, and pray that we can soon all be together again. I feel so helpless being so far away from you, and the house seems so empty and lifeless without you and Freddy here. And yet the memories linger in every corner, and sometimes I think I can hear you and your friends laughing and playing in the pool, and although it saddens me, it is a memory to cling to while we're all apart.

Freddy wrote a beautiful letter to tell me what had happened, and although your father and I wept at the news, and were tormented by the fact that we couldn't rush to your side, we knew you would not be alone. Freddy might seem to be devil-may-care, but when it comes to his little sister, he takes his responsibilities very seriously – and I am certain that dear Roger and Charlotte will also be stalwart in their comfort, for they are good, loyal friends who have only your best interest at heart.

We were delighted to hear that Freddy and Charlotte are planning a Christmas wedding, but once again we mourn the fact that we cannot be there. It seems that all the while this terrible war persists, your father and I will be forced to follow your lives through letters, but our thoughts and prayers are with you every step of the way.

Señor Fernandez and everyone here send their love, and their very best wishes. Your ponies are being exercised a bit more after putting on winter condition, and Juan Carlos told me to tell you that he will look after Sabre for you until you return.

I kiss you, darling, and hold you tight, just as I did when you were a tiny little girl. Never forget that you're loved and that even in the darkest of days I will be with you in spirit.

Mother

Kitty let the thin blue paper drift to the bed and sniffed back her tears. Her mother's gentle voice could be heard in every word of that letter, and the longing to be with her deepened.

She thought of the house and the beautiful landscape of the pampas, of seeing her father relaxing in his chair with a glass of good red wine after a hard day in the stables, and of her mother happily planning yet another luncheon party. Juan Carlos, Señor Fernandez' son, would certainly look after Sabre, but she felt a stab of jealousy when she thought of him racing about the polo field on her pony – for she doubted she'd ever get on a horse again.

Determined not to let these depressing thoughts get her down, she swiftly read the second letter, which was lighter in tone, but just as loving. Her mother had clearly decided she needed cheering up, for there were snippets of gossip and a few light-hearted descriptions of various happenings around the stud and scattered neighbourhood.

Kitty felt a little more cheered, and so turned to the postcards. They were both from Charlotte, and were the naughty seaside variety, with very fat women in swimsuits being ogled by small, bumptious men. She gave a giggle and read the short message on the back.

'I'm glad to see they made you smile.'

Kitty looked up with surprise and pleasure. 'Charlotte,' she yelped. 'Oh, Charlotte. How lovely to see you.'

Charlotte grinned as she dumped several brown paper packages on the bedside chair and carefully gave Kitty a hug. 'Freddy said you were feeling a lot better,' she said, drawing back from the embrace and stuffing her uniform cap in her jacket pocket. 'It's so good to see you awake and cheerful. I was terribly worried about you the last time I came.'

Kitty noticed how her friend studiously kept her gaze from the stump of bandaged thigh that rested on top of the sheet. 'Well, you've no need to worry about me,' she said firmly. 'I got out of bed today for the first time *and* won thirty Swan Vestas at five-card brag. Which rather proves I haven't lost my mind as well as half my leg.'

'Oh, Kitty.' Charlotte's brown eyes glistened with

tears. 'I can't believe this has happened to you. I do so wish . . .'

'Please don't get sentimental on me, Charley,' she broke in. 'I've just read a letter from home, and I'm already feeling soppy enough.' She looked down at her stump. 'There are people in this place who are far worse off than me, so I've decided to follow Doreen's example and make the best of it.'

'Doreen?'

Kitty explained about Doreen and the garter. 'I don't think I'd go as far as that,' she said hastily as Charlotte frowned, 'but I'm not cut out to be a shrinking violet, so I'd like a really pretty dress to wear at your wedding – preferably scarlet, with a matching hat.'

Charlotte giggled. 'That's a bit of a tall order, and I was thinking of pink for my bridesmaid, but I'll do what I can. Mummy's got hat boxes and trunks full of clothes from when she and Daddy used to go to Ascot. When I go home next I'll have a look in the attic, but I doubt there'll be anything in scarlet – Mummy's more a cream and pastel sort of woman.'

'As long as it's something bright and eye-catching,' said Kitty. 'I don't look good in pink, neither do I plan on wearing beige or navy blue, like some maiden aunt.' She smiled as her friend dared to shoot an anxious glance at her thigh. 'Don't worry,' she said. 'I'll have a new leg by then, so I'll be able to carry your train and do my bridesmaid's duties without showing you up or falling over.'

'I never for one minute thought anything of the sort,' said Charlotte, who'd visibly relaxed now the thorny subject of amputation was done and dusted. 'By the way, Mummy and Daddy send their love and asked me to tell you that Granny's lift has been serviced and your bedroom is all ready for you when you're released from this place. Mummy says that as you spent so much time there during school breaks, you'll feel much more at home than in some rehabilitation hospital.'

Charlotte's parents were endlessly kind and their home had been a haven during her school holidays when time didn't allow her to make the long journey back to Argentina. It was the only private home she'd ever been in that had a lift, but the idea of burdening them with the sort of problems she no doubt faced in the future was unthinkable.

'That's very sweet of them,' Kitty murmured, 'and I do appreciate their kindness, but I'm better off here, Charlotte, really I am.'

'Well, don't worry about it now,' said Charlotte. 'You may feel differently once you've been here a while.'

She picked up the little packages. 'Mummy and I thought you might appreciate a few treats,' she said. 'This one's from Freddy, though where on earth he managed to get them I daren't ask.'

'You've seen him? How is he?'

'I wangled it so I delivered a Spitfire to Cliffe early this morning, and we managed to have breakfast together before he went on ops. He's looking very much more cheerful now he knows you're on the mend.' Charlotte gave a deep sigh. 'The poor man was beside himself with worry, you know, and Commander Black had to ground him for a while after he nearly went into the side of the cliffs.'

'Yes, Freddy told me. His Commander seems to be a very understanding man. Freddy's lucky to have him.' She looked down at the packages that were now strewn across the bed. 'You'll have to open these for me, Charley. It's a bit tricky with all this blasted plaster on my arms.'

Charlotte undid the string and folded back the paper on each little gift. There was a heart-shaped box of chocolates with a fancy pink ribbon round it from Freddy; a lovely bar of scented soap from Roger, and a pretty nightdress with lace at the neck and hem from Charlotte's parents; the latest Agatha Christie novel; two packets of Players' cigarettes and the latest copy of the *Picture Post*.

'Oh, Charlotte, you must thank your mother for me. The nightdress is gorgeous, so do tell her I'll write when I've had the plaster casts off.' She eyed the box of chocolates. 'As for this, where on earth did Freddy manage to find such a luxurious thing?'

Charlotte grinned. 'He *said* he won it in an

arm-wrestling contest with one of the American pilots, though where he *really* got them is anyone's guess.' She shrugged as she sat down next to Kitty's bed. 'As long as they taste as good as that fancy box promises, it doesn't really matter, does it?'

'Open the box,' said Kitty eagerly. 'Let's try them and see.'

Charlotte opened the box to reveal two layers of glistening heart-shaped chocolates, and they both fell silent as they closed their eyes and let the sweetness slowly melt in their mouths.

'I'd forgotten how wonderful strawberry creams taste,' breathed Kitty after the last morsel was gone. 'Put the lid back on before I devour the lot, and then you've got to tell me what plans you've made for the wedding.'

With the box closed and tucked away in the bedside cupboard, Charlotte drew the chair closer to Kitty's bed. 'We decided we'd get married in our local church back in Berkshire where I was christened. Mummy's already in a complete lather over the reception, which will be held at home, and is absolutely furious that it isn't to be a summer wedding because her garden is now in full bloom and will be as dead as a dodo by Christmas.'

'I'm sure your mother will make the house look beautiful, regardless of the lack of flowers,' said Kitty, who'd always admired Charlotte's mother's flair for decoration. 'Have you found your dress?

Or will you do what most girls do these days and wear your uniform?'

'Not likely,' replied Charlotte. 'Mummy's lending me her beautiful wedding gown that she had made in Paris before the last war, and Grandma Elizabeth has promised I can use her lace veil and diamond tiara.' She gave a rueful smile. 'I'll have to watch what I eat from now on, because the dress only just fits round my waist.'

As Charlotte happily went on to chatter about the guests, the flowers and the champagne her father had stored in the vast cellar beneath the lovely old Georgian house, Kitty began to have serious doubts about attending. Her presence might put a damper on things – after all, who wanted a cripple on a tin leg clumping about amid all the fine silks and lace of the county set?

And then there was the horror of having to face old school friends and the local girls she'd befriended during the holidays. It was one thing to feel at ease here among the others who were going through the same experience, and quite another to mingle with people who couldn't possibly have the first inkling of what it was like to be in her situation.

For all her fine words and cheerful bravado, she just knew she couldn't do it. And yet, as she tuned back into what Charlotte was saying, she also knew she couldn't say anything today. Charlotte was happy and excited with her plans, and she wasn't about to spoil it for her.

*   *   *

Peggy was just finishing her two-hour stint at the Town Hall when she saw her friend Dorothy from the billeting office come in. Slim and neat in a blouse and skirt, Dorothy was a bundle of energy, and, with her creamy complexion and rich brown hair, she looked at least ten years younger than her forty-three years.

'Hello, Dotty,' she said in delight. 'I haven't seen you in ages. How are things?'

'Chaotic as usual,' she replied. 'With Tom away at sea and the kids down in Devon, you'd think I'd have time on my hands, but there are never enough hours in the day.'

'I know exactly how that feels,' said Peggy, 'and I don't have the added responsibility of trying to find homes for everyone.'

'Speaking of which,' said Dorothy with the hint of a smile, 'we've finally caught up with your sister and her two spare bedrooms.'

Peggy chuckled as she took off her apron and headscarf and tucked them into her capacious handbag. 'She's not happy about it, I can tell you.'

'She should be thankful I didn't inform the police about her,' said Dorothy. 'It was in my rights to do so, you know,' she said defensively. 'And she could have been given a police record and very heavily fined if I had.'

'I am grateful,' said Peggy. 'I know my sister can be awful, but she's going through rather a lot at the moment, and that would have been the final straw.'

Dorothy folded her arms. 'It's only because you and I have been friends since we were in junior school that I didn't inform on her,' she said. 'And I'm all too aware that you get the flak if something upsets her comfortable little life.'

'That's kind of you, Dot,' murmured Peggy. She could see that Dotty was struggling to keep her anger with Doris under control. There was clearly a lot more she needed to say. 'I don't know how Doris managed to evade having evacuees before this,' she prompted.

Dorothy's lips thinned. 'She's been lying through her teeth about those rooms ever since the war began, you know. First, she said she had her maid living in; then she said a maiden aunt was staying – then her son needed one of the rooms as a study as he was involved in important work for the MOD, which meant that putting an evacuee in the other spare room would break the official secrets act. We didn't push it, because she does a lot of charity work in the town and has quite influential friends.'

Peggy was intrigued. 'So what made you go round there this morning?'

Dorothy leaned closer so they couldn't be overheard. 'We had a telephone call accusing us of turning a blind eye to Doris's spare rooms and treating her differently to everyone else. The caller threatened to make a formal complaint if something wasn't done about it, so I had no option but to go to Havelock Gardens and find out what was going on there.'

'Did you answer the call? Could you recognise the voice?'

'It was a woman, certainly, but her voice was muffled, probably by a handkerchief. The call came from a telephone box, because I heard the pips as the money went in.'

Peggy suspected it was Ted's discarded mistress – there was certainly nothing more dangerous and vengeful than a woman scorned. But she didn't mention this to Dotty. 'Well, whoever it was certainly wanted to cause trouble. But then Doris upsets so many people with her uppity ways, it's hardly surprising.'

'Anyway, I've found four nice friendly girls to share the two rooms. They had to leave their billet when the house next door was demolished and took half of the hostel with it. I've just come back from taking them round to Doris, and although she was very po-faced about it, she was polite enough. I warned her of the consequences should the rooms become vacant again, so hopefully things will work out all right.'

Peggy smiled. 'Poor old Doris, she's her own worst enemy, isn't she?'

Dorothy grinned. 'She is indeed. Have you got time for a cuppa before you go home? It's been ages since we managed to have a proper gossip.'

'I've always got time for a cuppa and a sit down,'

said Peggy. 'Let me check on Daisy, and I'll be right with you.'

Peggy arrived back at Beach View almost two hours later, but as she pushed the pram into the basement, she was met by the reek of boiled eel. Lifting Daisy out of the pram, she carried her up the concrete steps into the kitchen.

'Ron's been boiling eels and vinegar,' said Cordelia the moment Peggy stepped through the open door. 'The stink is nearly as unpleasant as the sight of them sitting there in their jelly.' She shuddered delicately. 'I've had to open all the doors and windows, but the smell is still lingering.'

Peggy eyed the thick rings of jellied eels that lay in a grey mess in a bowl on the table. She put Daisy in her high chair and gave her a rusk to chew on. 'Where's Ron?' she asked.

'Said he had some things to do for Rosie,' Cordelia replied with a knowing smile. 'Shot out of here like a scalded cat when it was time for you to come home.'

'I just bet he did,' Peggy said fiercely. 'He said nothing about eels when he brought Daisy home. Just slapped a couple of rabbits on the draining board and began to gut them.'

Cordelia giggled. 'He waited until you'd gone to the Town Hall to cook the eels,' she said. 'He knew you wouldn't approve, you see.'

'He was certainly right about that,' snapped Peggy

as she picked up the bowl of eels and deposited it on the marble slab in her larder then shut the door. 'I'll be having a word with Mr Ronan Reilly about taking my daughter poaching,' she said ominously.

'Oh, dear,' Cordelia twittered. 'Don't be too cross with him, Peggy. He only meant well, and Daisy didn't come to any harm.'

Peggy patted her softly on the shoulder and set about cutting up the rabbits for a stew. If Ron dared to show his face any time soon, he was likely to get a piece of her mind, and no mistake.

The stew was simmering with barley, onions and potatoes in the slow oven, and Peggy had taken Daisy out into the garden to join Cordelia in the last of the sun. Cordelia was dozing in the newest, sturdiest deckchair, but after what had happened this morning, Peggy was unwilling to put any of the others to the test, so she kicked off her sandals and sat on the sun-warmed doorstep.

She had just lit a cigarette when the latch clicked on the back gate. Expecting to see Ron, she stiffened, ready for a set-to, but it was Sarah who came down the path towards her, looking far too hot in her WTC uniform of thick shirt, heavy plus-fours and sturdy boots.

'Hello, dear. You're home nice and early.' Her welcoming smile faded as she noted the fretful expression on the girl's face. 'Is something wrong, Sarah? You're not ill, are you?'

'No, nothing like that,' she replied as she flicked back her fair hair from her damp face. 'I just asked for permission to leave early today. Is Fran back from the hospital yet?'

Peggy shook her head. 'She's not due home for another hour. Why?'

Sarah twisted her hands together and shuffled her feet, darting an anxious glance at the sleeping Cordelia. 'It's a bit awkward, actually,' she confessed. 'I don't want to cause trouble, but . . .'

Peggy shifted on the doorstep. 'Come and sit down. Now,' she said when the girl had settled beside her, 'what is it that might cause trouble?'

'The Americans were having a bit of a celebration up at the big house today,' Sarah began hesitantly. 'It got rather noisy and boisterous and they must have been drinking quite heavily, because they were soon racing along the woodland tracks in their jeeps, yelling like a tribe of marauding red Indians on the warpath. It was a miracle no one got hurt, but someone reported them to their commanding officer and he soon put a stop to it.'

'Youthful high spirits,' said Peggy. 'But if nobody was hurt, why has it bothered you so much, Sarah? And what has all this to do with Fran?'

'It didn't bother me, not really. Like you, I'd put it down to high spirits, but I was concerned for the safety of the girls who work down those tracks. Once it had quietened down, I thought no more of it.'

Peggy waited while Sarah lit a cigarette. 'But something else happened after that, which did bother you?'

Sarah nodded, and delicately picked a thread of tobacco from her lip. 'Their commanding officer came to my office to apologise for the noise and the bad behaviour. He said they'd all been confined to quarters and were on kitchen duty for the next week.'

'So what were they celebrating to get them into such trouble?' Peggy still couldn't see where this was leading, or how it could possibly have anything to do with Fran.

'One of the young officers had just learned he'd become a father to a bouncing baby boy weighing seven pounds nine ounces,' said Sarah. 'He and his wife already have two daughters, so he was thrilled to have a son at last.' Sarah paused and looked directly at Peggy. 'The officer's name was Chuck Hoskins.'

'Oh, no,' breathed Peggy. 'Are you sure?'

Sarah nodded. 'Positive. I've seen him round the estate, and I was at the party where he and Fran met for the first time.' She finished her cigarette and squashed it out beneath her heavy WTC boot.

'Poor little Fran,' murmured Peggy. 'I hope you told his commanding officer what a rat that man is,' she said crossly.

'I didn't think it was appropriate,' Sarah confessed. 'After all, it wasn't me that Chuck had been lying to, and I doubt the American army could do anything. But the General seemed happy to discuss the new father and his family when I asked about him over a cup of tea.'

Sarah gave a deep sigh. 'It turns out Chuck's from Milwaukee and used to work on a production line in a biscuit factory. His mother cleans office blocks, his father disappeared while he was still a baby and Chuck left school at fourteen. He's been married to Loretta for five years, and she works evenings in a local bar.'

Peggy's anger rose as she remembered Fran's face lighting up when she'd talked about him. 'So the whole thing was a filthy, rotten lie,' she said flatly. 'What a mean trick to play on our poor little Fran. If he walked through that gate at this moment I'd kill him, and that's a fact.'

'I don't know what to do for the best,' said Sarah. 'Fran's fallen hard for that lying toerag and she'll be terribly hurt. Perhaps I could just tell her he's been posted to another camp?'

Peggy took Sarah's hand in her own. 'You leave Fran to me. I've dealt with broken hearts before with my two girls – and although it's not easy to break such news, it's amazing how quick the recovery can be. But Fran must know the truth, Sarah. It wouldn't be fair to add another lie to all the others she's been told.'

'Yes,' said Sarah. 'You're right, as always, Peggy.' She put her arm around her and rested her head on

Peggy's shoulder. 'We do put you through the wringer with all our troubles, don't we?'

Peggy smiled and smoothed the silky fair hair back from the girl's face. 'That's what I'm here for,' she said softly.

Chapter Twelve

Peggy had been watching the clock anxiously since Sarah's revelation, and she managed to waylay Fran as she came through the front door, steering her immediately into the cluttered dining room so they could talk in private.

'Whatever's the matter?' the girl asked with a frown.

'I need to tell you something,' said Peggy as she closed the door. 'Don't worry, it's nothing to do with your family in Ireland,' she said hastily as she saw the sudden fear flicker in the girl's green eyes. 'It's about Chuck Hoskins.'

'He's not coming tomorrow, is he?' Fran said with heavy disappointment.

Peggy sat down and patted the chair beside her. 'No, dear, he won't be coming to tea tomorrow – or any other day, for that matter.'

'Has he been posted somewhere else? Did he leave me a note or anything so I can stay in touch?'

Peggy saw the hope in her expression and her heart ached for the girl as she shook her head. 'He's still at Cliffe, dear.' She took Fran's hand. 'But it seems he isn't quite what you thought,' she said carefully.

She looked into the sweet face, saw the colour drain from her cheeks and knew that bad news had to be told clearly and without any possibility of being misunderstood. 'I'm so sorry, Fran, but he's a married man, and today he was celebrating the birth of his third child.'

'No,' Fran breathed as her lovely green eyes filled with tears. 'That can't be true. He swore he wasn't married, and I've seen photographs of his home and his parents.'

Peggy realised this was going to be as hard as she'd expected, for Chuck Hoskins was clearly a consummate liar who'd carefully prepared his story to get his way with the starry-eyed girls over here. She continued to hold Fran's hand as she repeated what Sarah had told her and made sure there could be no room for doubt.

There was a long silence after Peggy had finished speaking, and Fran's tears glistened on her eyelashes and slowly rolled down her pale face. 'To be sure, Auntie Peg, he's a lying rat, so he is,' she said tremulously. 'How could I have been such a fool to believe him?'

'Because he made you think he felt the same way as you, Fran. He's a smooth-talking liar and knew just the right way to make you fall for him.'

'But I loved him,' she sobbed. 'And he promised that when the war was over we'd get married and I'd go back to America with him.'

'You didn't let things go too far, did you?' asked

Peggy softly. 'It's easy to get carried away when you're in love.'

'No,' Fran breathed. 'He begged me to take things further, but all of me mam's warnings were ringing in my head, so they were, and I didn't dare.' She covered her face with her hands and collapsed into a storm of tears. 'But I wanted to, Auntie Peg,' she wailed.

'I know, darling,' Peggy soothed as she put her arm round the girl's shoulders and held her close. The shattered dreams and broken promises were falling around Fran like splinters of glass, and she could hear the heartbreak in her sobs. It was the end of something Fran had believed was real, but Peggy knew that, like all deaths, the time for mourning would pass, and then the anger would come. This would be followed by acceptance, and with harsh lessons learned, the courage to face a different future.

The tears finally eased and Fran moved out of Peggy's embrace to blow her nose and regain some composure. She wrung the sodden handkerchief between her fingers. 'I must look a fright,' she said with a shaky smile that didn't reach her eyes. 'Do the other girls know?'

'Sarah will say nothing,' said Peggy as she dipped in her apron pocket for a clean handkerchief. 'She was very upset for you, Fran, and hated having to bring such horrid news home. But she's a good friend, and you can trust her to keep things to herself if you need to confide in someone.'

The tears shone in Fran's eyes once again, but she sniffed them back almost impatiently. 'There's no point in keeping it a secret,' she said bitterly. 'And to be sure, they'll guess soon enough when he doesn't turn up tomorrow. I'll tell them when they come home for tea.'

She got to her feet, brushed the creases from her starched apron and pulled off her white cap. 'But first, I'll have a wash and get out of my uniform.' She bent and softly kissed Peggy's cheek. 'Thanks, Peggy,' she murmured. 'To be sure, we're all very lucky to have you look after us so well.'

Peggy remained in the cluttered dining room for some time after Fran had run upstairs. The five girls in her care had become like daughters, and Peggy had willingly taken on the role of mother to them all. She'd comforted Sarah and Jane through their homesickness and worry over what was happening in Singapore; had helped Rita through the trauma of being made homeless twice after her father had been called up; and supported Suzy as her romance blossomed with Doris's lovely son Anthony and she had to run the gauntlet of Doris's disapproval and possessive jealousy.

She regarded the almost forgotten room which had become a storage space and general dumping ground for unwanted furniture and odds and ends. It was a large room, with an ornate fireplace and mantel, a high ceiling and big windows behind the plywood that had been nailed over them.

This had been the guest dining room in the old days, and the scene of many a riotous family gathering, the echoes of which still lingered. But now it needed a good spring clean and a thorough tidy up, and she knew she should really do something more useful with it after deriding her sister over her lack of charity. It would make a lovely big bed-sitting room for some poor homeless family.

But that wasn't really uppermost in her mind at the moment, for in a sudden burst of clarity, she'd realised that the youngsters in her care were not the only ones who needed a mother to soothe and cuddle them through the dark times.

Without stopping to think it through, Peggy went into the hall and picked up the telephone receiver to ring Martin at Cliffe aerodrome.

'Hello, Peggy,' said Martin rather distractedly. 'You've only just caught me. We've got a bit of a flap on, so I can't talk for long.'

'Do you think Kitty Pargeter might like me to visit her at the hospital?' she asked breathlessly. 'Only I've realised she's all alone up there, and far from home and her mother, and I thought . . . Well, I thought she might like someone older to lean on and help see her through things,' she finished lamely.

'That's a super idea, Peggy. I knew you'd come up with something.'

'You don't think she might resent having some strange woman butting in?'

'Not if you take your time to get to know her

before you try mothering her,' said Martin with a smile in his voice. 'Freddy won't be able to visit for a while, we're fully stretched at the moment, so I'm sure she'll be delighted to have you visit.'

Peggy was about to ask him how he was and if he'd heard from Anne lately, when she heard a confusion of loud noises on the other end of the line.

'Sorry, Peggy. I've got to go. I'll ring you tomorrow, if I can.'

The line went dead and Peggy replaced the receiver. She wasn't at all sure if she was taking on rather more than she could chew by befriending Kitty Pargeter, but deep in her heart she knew it was the right thing to do – for there was always room for one more chick to be tucked safely under her wing.

Daisy was bashing a spoon against the tray of her high chair, but there was still no sign of Ron or Harvey as Peggy returned to the kitchen. She exchanged the spoon for one of Daisy's soft toys to lessen the racket, for the stresses and strains of the day were beginning to take their toll. Ron might be making himself scarce, but he'd have to come home sooner or later, and Peggy was determined to have her say before the long day was ended.

As the first squadron of fighters and bombers roared overhead on their way across the Channel, Rita came running up the cellar steps, dark curls bobbing as she ripped off her leather flying helmet and goggles.

'I'm late,' she declared as she wriggled out of her heavy boots and pulled off her thick socks. 'The picture starts in less than an hour and I can't go like this. I'm covered in engine oil after servicing the fire station vans.'

'Make sure you come and see me before you go out again,' called Peggy after her as she ran into the hall. 'I've got something for you to give to Ethel.'

'Righto,' shouted Rita, who was now halfway up the stairs.

Peggy went to the larder and opened the tin where she'd stored the buns. Taking three out, she wrapped them in greaseproof paper. As she turned to place them on the table her gaze fell on the big cake tin. It wasn't where she'd left it.

With a prickle of dark suspicion, she opened the tin. She could have wept with frustration, for her beautiful Victoria sponge had a great wedge cut out of it. Peggy's patience finally ran out and she carried the tin over to Cordelia. 'Is this Ron's doing?' she snapped.

'Oh, dear,' Cordelia sighed. 'He must have done that while I was in the garden hanging out my washing.' She giggled. 'Sly old devil. I thought there was a naughty twinkle in his eye as he went off whistling with a spring to his step.'

'I'll give him whistle,' said Peggy crossly.

'What was that about thistles, dear?' Cordelia

fiddled with her hearing aid. 'I hope you're not planning on making thistle soup again. It really was quite horrid.'

Peggy shook her head, dumped the scavenged cake tin back in the larder and went to stir the stew. 'What with eels and cake, and taking my daughter on one of his poaching expeditions, that man has pushed me too far,' she muttered furiously. 'He's going to get what for when he dares to show his face in my kitchen again.'

'Space in this kitchen for a car and water exhibition?' Cordelia clucked and shook her head. 'You do talk nonsense sometimes, Peggy dear. It must be the heat and all the work you've done today. I'd sit down and put your feet up if I were you.'

Peggy dredged up a weary smile. There were times when conversations with Cordelia could veer off into very strange territory, and she simply didn't have the energy to explain what she'd really said.

When Rita came dashing back into the kitchen in a smart pair of dark linen slacks and a lightweight oyster-pink sweater that matched the ribbon in her hair, Peggy noticed the mascara and dash of pale pink lipstick and hoped to goodness Rita hadn't stumbled into the same trap as Fran. 'It is just a girls' outing to the pictures, isn't it?' she asked as she handed over the little cakes for Ethel.

Rita grinned. 'Fran told me about Chuck. It's just me, Ruby and Lucy – and not a lying Yank in sight.

And don't worry if I'm a bit late, we're having fish and chips after.'

'What shift are you working tomorrow?' Peggy asked.

'Early morning.' Rita slipped on her shoes and reached for her sheepskin-lined WWI flying jacket. 'Why, did you want me to do something?'

Peggy nodded. 'I'd like you to take me up to the Memorial hospital in the afternoon to visit Kitty Pargeter.'

'That's a brilliant idea,' Rita said. 'But I must rush now.' She kissed Cordelia and Peggy, picked up the greaseproof packet and ran down the steps. Minutes later they heard the roar of the motorbike as she drove it down the twitten and out onto the main road.

'That girl will kill herself one day,' muttered Cordelia. 'Why can't she wear a dress and be like other girls her age? Trousers and motorbikes are so unbecoming.'

'Unbecoming they might be,' said Peggy, 'but they get her from A to B, and I'm quite looking forward to having a ride on that bike tomorrow.'

'What? Do speak up, dear. You're muttering,' said Cordelia crossly.

Peggy realised that the heat in the kitchen and her bad mood was also affecting Cordelia, for she was rarely sharp with anyone. She took a deep breath and made winding signals by her ear so that Cordelia knew to turn up the volume on her hearing aid. 'Can you hear me now?' she asked.

Cordelia bridled. 'There's no need to shout, dear. I'm not that deaf, you know.'

'I need to warn you about the tea party tomorrow,' said Peggy as she came to squat by Cordelia's chair. 'Fran's young man won't be coming, and she's very upset, so I don't want you to mention it when she comes down.'

Cordelia regarded her thoughtfully. 'Does that mean they're no longer walking out together?' At Peggy's nod, Cordelia sniffed. 'I've always been of the opinion that men with that many shiny teeth shouldn't be trusted,' she said darkly, 'but then he was an American, and one can never be too sure about them either.'

'I think that's a bit harsh, Cordelia,' said Peggy with a wry smile.

'Maybe so, but if he's not coming and Fran's lovesick and off her food, it means there'll be more cake for us,' she replied with a chuckle.

Peggy laughed and kissed her cheek. 'Bless your heart, Cordelia. I can always rely on you to cheer me up.' She went back to the stew and then helped Cordelia to lay the table.

Fran came downstairs with Sarah and Jane, and although her eyelids were swollen from her tears, she'd put on her make-up and a pretty dress to bravely face the world. 'Suzy will be down in a minute,' she said. 'She's just getting washed and changed.' She ruffled Daisy's dark curls, dodged tiny, sticky fingers and planted a soft kiss on her head. 'I told Rita about Chuck when she came in earlier, so everyone knows now,' she said sadly.

'You sit down and tuck into that,' said Peggy as she placed a bowl of stew in front of Fran. 'A broken heart is soon mended with good food inside you and close friends to keep you company.'

'It seems that men these days have no stamina,' said Cordelia as she sat down at the table. 'You're better off without him, dear, believe me.'

Fran dipped her chin so her russet curls hid her brimming eyes. 'I know,' she muttered, 'but it doesn't make it hurt any less.'

'The stew is not a mess,' protested Cordelia. 'Ron's eels are a mess, and you should be grateful you don't have to eat them.'

Fran looked at her and giggled. 'To be sure, Grandma Finch, I'll not be eating any eels today. This stew is lovely.'

'Well, get on and eat it then. Ron's ferrets worked hard to catch those rabbits and it would be an awful shame to waste them.'

Peggy smiled as the chatter went on round the table and Daisy began to droop with sleep over her food. Things were getting back to normal and, with the family's support, Fran would soon get over her heartache.

The meal was over, the dishes washed and put away, and a fresh pot of tea placed on the table. Peggy gave Daisy and each of the girls one of the fairy cakes, and cut Ron's into two for herself and Cordelia. Rita could have hers with her cocoa when she got in. Ron had had more than his share already and could damned well go without.

After every crumb of fairy cake had been devoured, the four girls put cardigans over their cotton dresses and went arm-in-arm for a stroll to the Anchor. A glass of beer and a bit of a sing-song would cheer Fran up no end, and if it got too hot inside there was always the garden to sit in, for it was a balmy night.

Peggy put Daisy to bed and then joined Cordelia in the back garden. The night was soft and so still they could hear the sharp cry of a distant vixen, the returning bark of a dog fox, and the hooting owls that lived in the trees at the top of the hill. The moon sailed above the house, casting blue shadows across Ron's vegetable patch and fruit canes as the stars twinkled benevolently in the indigo velvet sky.

'I wouldn't mind betting Ron doesn't come home until well after closing,' said Peggy as she smoked a cigarette. 'He knows I'll be cross with him and no doubt thinks I'll have forgotten his sins if he leaves it long enough.'

'I shouldn't let it niggle you, Peggy,' said Cordelia as she looked up at the sky. 'Ron is a rogue and he's far too old to change his habits now. No matter how cross you get, he'll never . . .' She was interrupted by the mournful first whine of the air-raid siren.

Peggy was on her feet instantly and helping

Cordelia to struggle out of her low-slung deckchair. 'Go straight to the Anderson shelter while I fetch Daisy,' she shouted as the first wave of fighter planes from Cliffe flew overhead.

She checked that Cordelia was safely making her way down the path, then turned and ran into the house to her hall-floor bedroom. Daisy was fast asleep, so she gently gathered her up in a blanket, grabbed some pillows on the way through the kitchen, and hurried back to the shelter.

Cordelia had already pulled the collapsible canvas cot out from beneath the wooden bench, and Peggy settled the sleeping baby inside it. Daisy's special Mickey Mouse gas mask was placed beside it and wouldn't be used unless absolutely necessary, for Peggy distrusted it and Daisy hated being cocooned inside it.

Yet more planes were taking off from Cliffe and the surrounding aerodromes, and the sirens were now wailing at full pitch all through the town as the searchlights spluttered into life and began to sweep their beams across the skies. Peggy knew she didn't have very long and certainly had no intention of getting caught in the house during a raid – not after what had happened last time.

She raced back into the house, grabbed the two gas masks, both their overcoats and the box of things she always had packed for just such an emergency. Dumping two blankets on top, she turned off the light and fumbled her way down the cellar steps to the back door. Heavily laden, she struggled to pull the door shut but finally managed it, just as she heard the furious whine and roaring engines of a distant dogfight.

In her rush, Peggy almost fell down the steps into the Anderson shelter, but she managed to stay on her feet long enough to dump the things she was carrying on the bench and then slam the door behind her. The first of the enemy bombers were already thundering overhead, the ack-ack guns were firing and the big guns down on the seafront and along the hills were booming.

'Whew,' she said as she sat down with a thump on the hard bench to catch her breath. 'That was close. I wonder why the warning was so late?'

'I don't know, dear, but could you light the tilley lamp? It's awfully dark in here, and I need to keep an eye out for the spiders.'

Peggy smiled as she fumbled in the box she'd brought from the kitchen and found the matches. Cordelia hated spiders, and she didn't blame her – nasty scuttling things. Once the lamp was lit, the warm glow made the smelly, damp shelter seem infinitely more homely.

'Right, Cordelia, let's get you settled, and then I'll make us a nice cup of Bovril.'

Because Cordelia couldn't possibly be expected to sit through bombing raids on a hard bench, Ron had refurbished a deckchair especially for her. With new canvas and all the screws and nails firmly applied, there was no danger of it collapsing. This deckchair stayed wedged in the corner of the shelter and therefore had to be brushed down to rid it of the spiders and small bugs that persisted in living in it. There wasn't much anyone could do to stop the damp turning it a bit green, but then everything was mouldy in here and they'd all become inured to it.

Once Peggy had made sure it was as clean as she could get it, she helped Cordelia into her overcoat and waited for her to settle in the chair, then propped her firmly on both sides with pillows so that when she fell asleep, she wouldn't slide out of it.

'There,' said Peggy as she placed a soft blanket over her knees. 'Is that comfortable?'

Cordelia smiled up at her. 'Yes, dear, I'm as snug as a bug.'

Peggy lit the primus stove and poured fresh water from a flask into the small tin kettle. A good slug of gin and tonic would have gone down nicely, and no mistake, she thought wistfully as she spooned Bovril into the mugs and listened to the earth-shattering noise of the dogfights going on and felt the boom of the big guns reverberate beneath her feet. But the gin had long gone, and there wasn't a drop of alcohol in the house but for two bottles of the horrid milk stout she'd determinedly put to the back of her larder.

They drank the beefy drink as bombers thundered overhead and the ack-ack spat their tracer bullets into the sky. The big guns shook the ground and made the corrugated iron around them shudder, and through the cracks in the door they could see the flashes of the pom-poms briefly light up the night.

The roar of the fighter planes rose and fell as they crossed the skies in deadly battle, and Peggy could now distinguish between the sound of a Spitfire or Typhoon from a Messerschmitt 109, or a Focke-Wulf. And yet that was hardly something to be proud of, she thought wearily – even small children could do it after so many raids on their little town.

Cordelia finished her drink, took out her hearing aid and wished Peggy goodnight. Closing her eyes, she was soon asleep, untroubled by the terrible booms, bangs and whines that were going on.

Peggy tucked the blanket over her hands and up to her chin, for it could get very cold in this damp shelter as the night progressed. She then checked on Daisy before she settled down to wait out the raid.

Ron and the girls would be all right, for he'd converted the pub cellar into a shelter, and the walls of the ancient pub were sturdy enough so deep underground. Rita, Ruby and Lucy were only a few steps away from the shelter behind the hall which now served as a cinema, so she didn't have to worry too much about them either.

She eyed her dreary surroundings with little pleasure. As long as this bit of corrugated iron kept off bullets, bombs and shrapnel then she'd be fine too, but she didn't have much faith in it – not after experiencing the damage that could be done to bricks and mortar from a bomb that had fallen two streets away.

Determined not to dwell on these morbid thoughts, she reached into the box of necessities that was constantly restocked from her kitchen and pulled out the *Radio Times* magazine that had been delivered that morning. Settling down to read it by the flickering lamplight, she tried to ignore the awful noise going on overhead by concentrating on the review of a play that was to be broadcast early next week.

Chapter Thirteen

Kitty realised that the air-raid precautions were well rehearsed, for within seconds of the siren going off, every single member of the hospital personnel came running. Within minutes she was lifted into a wheelchair, covered with a blanket and taken out of the ward along with the beds of those who couldn't be moved.

The tide of beds, wheelchairs and walking wounded was moved efficiently down the long corridors to the sturdy ramps that led to the vast underground shelter beneath the house. And orchestrating it all was Matron, her booming voice rising above the siren and the roar of RAF fighters.

Kitty was amazed by the enormous cellar, for it was even bigger than the one beneath Charlotte's home in Berkshire. But if there had ever been wine stored down here, there was no sign of it now, for the floor had been concreted, the walls painted army issue beige, and the lights protected by wire cages. The NAAFI had set up a makeshift canteen at one end, and there were canvas screens to give privacy for those who needed to use the commodes or bedpans.

The beds were pushed against the wall in a neat line, leaving a large central space where a collection of chairs and couches had been placed to accommodate those who were mobile. There was a gramophone and a pile of scratched records on a low table, and lots of rather tattered magazines and newspapers to help while away the time until the all-clear sounded.

Kitty watched the nurses and doctors move among the patients with quiet efficiency as the orderlies tidied blankets and pillows and the canteen staff bustled about preparing tea in the vast urn and making piles of spam sandwiches.

Doreen flopped into the chair beside her. 'It's a blooming cheek, that's what,' she said crossly. 'Why can't flaming Jerry stay on his own side of the Channel for once? I was really enjoying the film.'

Kitty hadn't fancied going into the big common room to watch a Laurel and Hardy film, preferring to read a magazine in bed. She giggled at Doreen's crossness. 'I don't think Jerry picked you out to annoy you personally, Doreen. He's not fussy who he drops his bombs on.'

'Yeah, well. It's a flaming nuisance, that's what.' She folded her arms around her waist and pouted. 'You're not even allowed to 'ave a fag down 'ere, either,' she continued. 'It's a right bugger, and I'm just about fed up with it.'

'Never mind, Doreen,' Kitty soothed. 'It's better

to be down here without a fag than up there with all the bombs.'

She grinned. 'Yeah, I suppose yer right.' She tightened the belt on her garish dressing gown and smoothed it over her thighs, then regarded Kitty thoughtfully. 'I see you 'ad a visit from one of yer mates in the ATA,' she said. 'I recognised her from the *Picture Post* an' all. She's the society deb, Charlotte Bingham, ain't she?'

Kitty nodded. 'We were at school together and joined the ATA at the same time.'

'Cor, were you a deb as well? Did ya get to meet the King and Queen?'

She smiled. 'No, I wasn't presented at court. The debutante season is for the daughters of the very rich and well connected, and although Charlotte's parents offered to sponsor me, I didn't want to go through all that dreadful rigmarole of being mauled about by chinless wonders with two left feet. The whole thing is little more than a cattle market for pushy parents to get their daughters married off to someone even richer.'

Doreen roared with laughter. 'You are a scream, Kitty. Blimey, gel, you should be on the stage.'

Kitty couldn't really see what Doreen was finding so funny, but let it pass. 'I'm surprised *you* never went on the stage,' she said. 'You've got enough personality to fill a theatre.'

Doreen shrugged. 'I'd've loved it, if the truth be known,' she admitted with a sigh of longing. 'I always fancied being a dancer like in the Busby Berkeley films where the girls get to wear gorgeous frocks and feathers, but I 'ad to earn a proper living to help out me mum. I'm the oldest of nine, you see.'

Kitty couldn't begin to imagine being one of nine, or how it must be to live in one of the awful hovels or tenements of the East End that she'd seen on the Pathé News, and her admiration grew for this cheerful girl who seemed to meet every disaster with a curse and a grin. 'Have your mother and the younger ones moved down here too?' she asked.

Doreen shook her head, her fiery curls bouncing on her shoulders. 'The three eldest boys are in the army. Me sister's got a sprog now, so she lends an 'and with the WVS, and the other one's joined the Wrens. The littler ones were evacuated to Somerset for a bit, but Mum didn't like the thought of them being farmed out with strangers who might not look after them proper, so she brought 'em home again.' She gave a wan smile. 'Turns out she were right, 'cos they come home with horrible great boils on their bums through being fed beetroot and not much else.'

'But that's awful,' gasped Kitty. 'I hope she complained to the authorities.'

'Gawd bless you, Kitty,' chuckled Doreen. 'People like us don't complain to them what's in charge. There was no real 'arm done, and they're right as rain now.'

They both fell silent as they listened to the distant thunder of the bombers and Kitty wondered if Freddy and Roger were up there in their Spitfires, fighting for their lives. She closed her eyes and silently prayed that they'd come through.

'He'll be all right,' soothed Doreen, who'd obviously read her thoughts. 'Blokes like your Freddy have charmed lives.'

'I hope you're right,' murmured Kitty. 'But it only takes a second of lost concentration, or a stray bullet . . .'

'It's a bugger, all right,' Doreen said cheerfully, 'but there ain't no point in getting down about it and thinking the worst. What you need is another game of five card brag.' She pulled the pack of greasy cards from her dressing gown pocket and waggled it under Kitty's nose. 'Up for it?'

Kitty smiled and nodded. 'As long as you've got the matches to lose, I'm up for it.'

The all-clear sounded just after eleven, and once Peggy had settled Daisy back in her cot and Cordelia in her bed, she went downstairs to put the kettle on the hob. There was just about enough cocoa to go round, and with the extra ration of milk she got because of the baby it would be nice and creamy.

Sarah, Jane, Suzy and Fran came in giggling. 'Honest to God, Auntie Peg,' said Fran as she plumped into a kitchen chair. 'Ron's got a complete home from home down in the cellar. There's a bar and a kettle for tea, a gramophone and records, and even a couple of old couches and chairs. It was quite a party.'

Peggy realised that all four girls were slightly tipsy but she said nothing, for it was good to see Fran almost back to her old self. 'And where is Ron?' she asked casually as she doled out the cups of cocoa.

'He's helping Rosie tidy the bar and clean the glasses,' said Suzy as she blew on the hot cocoa. 'There's little doubt he knows you're cross with him, and I think he's rather hoping that you'll be in bed by the time he gets back.'

Peggy didn't reply, for the anger had dwindled into mild annoyance and she was far too tired to start a row at this time of night. She glanced at the clock. 'Rita should be back by now.'

'We saw her taking Ruby home, so she shouldn't be long,' said Sarah. 'There was no damage to Cliffehaven tonight, so she won't have to go back on duty until her shift tomorrow.' She finished her cocoa and washed out the mug. 'Come on, Jane, we've both got a very early start in the morning. It's time for bed.'

One by one the girls finished their drinks, washed out their mugs and kissed Peggy goodnight before trooping up the stairs to their rooms.

Peggy refilled the flasks with water and washed out the tin mugs and the kettle before putting them back into the air-raid box alongside the packet of biscuits, the matches, candles and first-aid kit. She folded the blankets and stacked them in a corner with the pillows, hung up the overcoats and dampened down the fire in the range. Turning out the light, she wearily crossed the hall in the darkness and went into her bedroom.

Sinking onto the bed, she flopped against the pillows and closed her eyes. It had been a very long, trying day – the sort of day when she'd felt Jim's absence most strongly. She curled her knees up and hugged the pillow, missing him so much it was an ache weighing heavy in her heart. Where he was and what he was doing was a mystery, and all she could do was pray that he'd soon get some leave.

Peggy woke to the sound of Daisy's furious yells, and for a moment she wondered what on earth she was doing lying on top of the bedcovers fully dressed and shivering with cold. Then she remembered how tired she'd been last night, and realised that while she was thinking of Jim she must have nodded off.

Daisy was standing in her cot and clutching at the rails as she bawled with fury, and Peggy groggily left the bed to see to her. 'It's all right,' she soothed as she quickly peeled off the sodden nappy and wrapped her in a blanket. 'Mummy will soon have you all clean and dry. Just please stop yelling. You're giving me a headache.'

She carried her into the kitchen where she found that Rita and Jane had already left for their early shifts, and the other girls had prepared the breakfast porridge and were also on the point of leaving. There was still no sign of Ron or Harvey, but Fran looked much better this morning, Peggy noted as she filled the sink with warm water and tried to placate the screaming Daisy with a brightly coloured teething ring.

The ring was angrily thrown to the floor and Peggy took a deep breath. It was going to be another one of those days.

'I'm seeing Anthony this evening,' said Suzy. She fastened her nursing cloak round her neck and then picked up a small case. 'I'll change my clothes at the hospital. Anthony's picking me up from there and taking me out to dinner, so don't keep me any tea. I shouldn't be too late; we've both got early starts in the morning.'

'I'll be back for me tea,' said Fran. 'I've some darning to do on me stockings, and Matron says I'm not to have any more until there's more darn than stocking.' She rolled her eyes. 'To be sure, that woman's mean.'

'Well, there is a war on and stockings aren't easy to come by,' said Peggy as she struggled to wash a squirming, kicking Daisy in the sink and not get soaked herself.

'Don't I just know it,' muttered Fran.

The three girls left together, and moments later

Cordelia came into the kitchen. 'Good morning, dear,' she said brightly. 'The papers have come. Isn't it a marvel that, despite everything, we still get milk and papers delivered every morning without fail – even on a Sunday?'

'It certainly is,' said Peggy as she lifted Daisy out of the sink and wrapped her in a towel. 'And it's girls like little Jane that we have to thank for that. She's up before the birds every morning to bring the milk, and is always cheerful.'

Sitting down at the table, she began to dry Daisy, and then had to wrestle her into a clean nappy, rubber pants and a cotton dress. At least she wasn't yelling any more, Peggy thought thankfully, but she was clearly full of energy this morning and would no doubt prove to be a handful for the rest of the day.

With Daisy finally ensconced in the high chair, she drank the tea Cordelia had poured for her, and then spoon-fed Daisy some milky porridge. 'So, what's in the papers this morning?' she asked Cordelia in the blessed silence.

'Nothing to cheer about, as usual,' the elderly woman replied sadly. 'The Germans lost thirty-three fighters in the raid yesterday, but in the process, we lost fifteen bombers. There's fierce fighting on the Russian Front, and the destroyer *Fearless* was lost defending a convoy in the Mediterranean. There was a bad raid on London the other night, and a vast number of Japanese troops are pouring into

Indo-China. The only good news is that some German air-ace has committed suicide,' she finished with a sniff.

Peggy was about to reply when Ron came stumping up the cellar steps, followed swiftly by Harvey, who delightedly began to lick the remains of Daisy's porridge from her face.

'Don't do that,' she scolded as she pushed his great head away and swiftly cleaned the laughing baby with a damp flannel. 'Honestly, Ron,' she said in exasperation, 'can't you *ever* keep him under control?'

He eyed her warily from beneath his bushy brows as he shooed the dog out into the garden. 'I'm thinking you're still a wee bit put out that I took Daisy on me fishing trip,' he said.

'And you'd be right,' she retorted. 'I've told you before, I will *not* have my baby put in danger like that. What if a gamekeeper shot at you – or you got arrested?'

'Agatha Fullerton doesn't have a gamekeeper,' he said as he calmly poured himself a cup of tea and added three sugars. 'And to be sure, I always check there are never any coppers about.'

Peggy removed the sugar bowl before he could take any more. 'You really know how to wind me up, don't you, Ronan Reilly?' she said crossly. 'First you take my daughter poaching, then you eat my cake – and now you're helping yourself to double your ration of sugar.'

His blue eyes were twinkling as he tickled Daisy's tummy and made her giggle. 'To be sure, someone's mammy got out of bed the wrong side this morning,' he said to her.

Daisy burbled and slapped her hands on the highchair tray, and Peggy wondered how she'd suddenly gone from a miserable, screaming baby to this angelic little girl. But then she shouldn't be surprised – Daisy was a Reilly, after all, and imbued with the same charm and contrary temperament as her father and grandfather.

'Wrong side or not,' Peggy snapped, 'you will never do that again. My cooking and the safety of my baby are the two things I will not compromise on. There will be no more defying me, Ron. Is that clear?'

'Aye,' he replied, his mouth twitching with humour. 'I'm thinking 'tis clear enough, and I'm sure the neighbours would agree, for they must be hearing you on this quiet Sunday morning.'

Peggy couldn't continue to be cross with him – not when his eyes twinkled like that, and his brows wiggled. 'You really *do* have an answer for everything, don't you?' she said in weary defeat.

'Aye,' he replied with a wink. 'I've not kissed the Blarney Stone for nothing, wee Peggy. You should know that by now.'

'Oh, I do, Ron,' she giggled. 'You and Jim certainly share a gift for the gab, and no mistake.'

They were interrupted by the persistent banging of the front door knocker. 'Who the divil is calling here at this time of a Sunday morning?' muttered Ron as Harvey shot past him into the hall and started barking furiously.

'That's not like Harvey,' said Peggy with a stab of alarm. 'What on earth is going on?'

'Whoever it is, it sounds like trouble,' said Cordelia.

Ron grabbed Harvey and held tightly to his collar as he reached for the door handle. 'Will ye be patient,' he yelled, 'and stop banging on me door like a . . .'

Agatha Fullerton stood on the doorstep, resplendent in her Sunday best of feathered hat and matching coat and dress, the effect of which was rather spoiled by her furious expression. 'I've a good mind to sue you,' she stormed. 'Do you realise that that creature,' she jabbed a gloved finger at Harvey, 'has ruined any chance my Princess might have had to breed prize-winning puppies?'

Peggy knew all about Harvey's commando tactics to get to Princess and certainly was in no mood to face a volcanic Agatha, so she stayed in the shadows of the kitchen doorway to watch the fun. Agatha was clearly not a woman to be easily placated, and Peggy was most interested to see how Ron's blarney could get him out of this latest confrontation.

'Now then, Mrs Fullerton,' Ron soothed. 'There's no need to be coming round here with your accusations on such a beautiful morning. Will ye not come in for a wee cup of tea?'

'I don't want your tea,' she boomed. 'Neither do I wish to be anywhere near you or your unruly dog.'

'Ach to be sure, Harvey's a well-behaved dog, so he is, and is quite the hero at helping to rescue folk after the bombing raids, as I'm sure you've heard. I can assure you he wouldn't be dreaming of ruining your Princess.'

'And I can assure you, Ronan Reilly, that he has.' Agatha was now very red in the face and fairly pulsating with fury.

'To be sure, you've no proof, Mrs Fullerton,' he said with his most winning smile. 'Your wee bitch could have got out and been mated by any one of the dogs in this town.'

Peggy watched in amusement as Mrs Fullerton picked up a box from the step that neither she nor Ron had noticed until now.

The angry woman shoved it against Ron's chest, giving him no alternative but to let go of Harvey to grab it. 'The proof is in there,' she stormed, 'and if one word of this gets out to the Kennel Club, I will sue you and see your dog is not only impounded, but castrated.'

Harvey went stiff-legged and bristling as he barked at her, but before Ron could reply, she'd turned on her heel and was marching down Beach View Road.

'Well, your blarney certainly deserted you that time, Ron,' Peggy said wryly. 'Agatha ran circles round you.' She eyed the box. 'And I can guess what's in there, so you'd better open it.'

Harvey was dancing on his toes and sniffing the box eagerly, making small whining noises in his throat as his tail whipped back and forth.

Ron put the box on the floor, and as he drew back the folded cardboard, a narrow grey muzzle and small pink tongue was swiftly followed by two bright button eyes, a pair of brindled paws, a neat head and two tiny, floppy brindled ears.

Harvey was in raptures as he whined and licked the small head, before gently grasping the little creature's scruff in his soft mouth and lifting it out of the box to present it to Ron.

'To be sure, there's no doubt about it,' Ron muttered as he cradled the puppy and let it lick and nibble his chin. 'Harvey,' he said to the delighted dog that was whining at his feet, 'you're the proud father of a wee son. What about that then?'

Harvey barked, rested his paws against Ron's stomach and nuzzled his offspring.

Peggy cleared her throat. 'Before you both get carried away in your celebrations, don't you think I've got enough to cope with, without a puppy getting under my feet?'

'Ach, Peggy, I'll be looking after him, so I will. You can't be turning away a poor wee orphan pup just because you're busy.'

Before Peggy could reply, he'd placed the puppy in her arms where it nestled sweetly against her chest and promptly fell asleep. Peggy's heart melted as she stroked the tiny soft head, the silky ears and dear little paws that rested so trustingly in her hand. He was the spitting image of Harvey, but in miniature – of course she couldn't refuse to keep him.

'You'll have to get him house-trained quickly,' she said rather gruffly. 'And if there are any puddles left about the place, then you'll clean them up.'

Ron beamed at her, and Harvey ran round in circles as if he knew what had just happened. 'Ach, to be sure, Peggy me darlin', he'll not be a bother to you at all.'

She kissed the sleeping puppy's head and gave Ron a knowing glare. 'That's what you said about your blasted ferrets,' she reminded him before taking the puppy into the kitchen to show Cordelia.

Kitty was sitting in the shade of an umbrella on the terrace, happily dozing away the afternoon while Doreen and her friends played a raucous game of croquet that didn't seem to follow any of the rules, but looked great fun.

She watched idly through half-closed lids as a group of men on crutches attempted a game of football at the far end of the garden, and was about to drift off back to sleep when she felt a hand on her shoulder.

'Sorry to disturb you, Kitty, but you've got visitors,' said Nurse Hopkins.

Hoping it was Freddy, she looked beyond the

nurse and saw only a small, dark-haired woman in her early forties who looked a bit ruffled and unsure of herself, clasping a handbag and small tin to her chest.

Then she saw the girl standing next to her and recognised her instantly as the one who'd organised the motorcycle races. Feeling suddenly shy and defensive, Kitty checked that the blanket covered her stump.

'Hello, Kitty. Remember me? I'm Rita from the motorcycle track, and this is Auntie Peggy – Mrs Reilly. She's my landlady really, but I've always called her Auntie,' she said all in a rush. 'We heard from Commander Black that you were up here and thought you might like a visit.'

Kitty still felt very shy, but she remembered her manners and greeted them both, urging them to pull up chairs so they could sit down. 'It's nice to see you again, Rita,' she said with brittle brightness, 'though the circumstances are unfortunately rather different.'

Rita smiled. 'Yes, this place is utterly lovely, and a world away from the track.' She took off her coat and looked over the sweeping lawns and bright flower beds. 'It's so much prettier, and quieter too,' she added with a giggle. 'You can actually hear the birds all the way out here.'

Kitty liked this girl for her gentle tact and friendly smile. 'You can also hear Doreen trying to play croquet,' she said wryly, as a great screech of laughter drifted to them across the lawn. 'She can be louder than any motorbike, believe me.'

'She seems to be having fun, though,' said Peggy. She ran her fingers over her dishevelled hair and adjusted her cardigan over her blouse and slacks. 'You'll have to excuse me, dear, but Rita brought me up here on the back of her motorbike and I'm all at sixes and sevens.'

Kitty eyed her with surprise and admiration. 'That was brave,' she replied.

Peggy grinned. 'Well, I do have to confess I was very nervous to begin with. Rita does go very fast, and it's a bit scary round the bends. But once I got used to it, I rather enjoyed it – and it certainly beats sitting in my back garden with my knitting.'

Kitty laughed and began to relax. 'I'm glad you both came. It gets a bit boring not being able to read or get about until my plasters are taken off.'

'When will that happen?' asked Peggy.

'At the end of this coming week, thank goodness. I'm really looking forward to starting my new Agatha Christie, and to being able to feed myself. And once the plaster is off my leg, I'll be able to get about on crutches and join in a bit more.'

'Well, you be careful,' said Peggy. 'That leg will feel very weak for a bit, so you mustn't go rushing about like a mad thing.' She tutted and shook her head. 'There I go again. Telling people what to do and fussing.'

'But that's why we all love you, Auntie Peg,' said

Rita. 'It wouldn't be the same at Beach View without you fretting over one of us.' She turned to Kitty. 'Peggy's like a mum to all of us, and although we moan a bit, we like it really and couldn't do without her.'

'Tell me about Beach View,' said Kitty. 'How many of you are there?'

As Peggy and Rita took it in turns to tell her about the girls, Daisy, Grandma Finch, Ron and his dog Harvey, Kitty could just imagine the warmth and love that must flow in that house. She laughed at Ron and Harvey's antics with the eels and the cake, and the strange conversations they'd both had with the lovely little deaf lady, and was quite melted by Peggy's description of the sweet puppy that had been dumped on her.

'It all sounds such fun,' she said wistfully. 'You clearly run a very happy home, Mrs Reilly.'

'Good heavens,' said Peggy. 'I quite forgot to give you the cake.' She opened the tin to reveal a buttered scone and a large slice of Victoria sponge.

'It's been ages since I had cake and it looks absolutely scrummy,' breathed Kitty. 'But I'm afraid one of you is going to have to help me with it.'

'I'll do that,' said Peggy. 'Rita, go and see if you can round up a cup of tea for us all.'

Kitty smiled with pleasure as Peggy delicately popped a morsel of cake into her mouth. 'You can come again,' she said. 'This cake is delicious.'

'Thank you, dear. I'd like that.' Peggy gave her

some more cake. 'By the way, I telephoned my son-in-law Martin Black this morning at Cliffe. Everyone got back safely last night, and I managed to talk briefly to your brother.' Peggy grinned. 'He's quite the charmer, isn't he?'

'To a fault, I'm afraid,' Kitty replied with a rueful smile. 'He's got all the nurses in a lather, and most of the women patients too.'

Peggy put another bit of cake into Kitty's mouth and gently brushed away a loose crumb from her chin. 'Well, Freddy said to tell you he'll try and come next weekend. If not, he may send his friend Roger, or come up one evening when he's not on stand-by.'

'That would be nice,' Kitty murmured. 'I don't see him nearly enough, and it's very frustrating that he's so close by.'

'I feel the same about our Martin,' sighed Peggy as she fed Kitty the last of the cake. 'He's very good and telephones quite regularly, but he rarely has the time to come to Beach View.'

'Tell me about the rest of your family, Mrs Reilly.'

'Please call me Peggy,' she replied as she brushed away the last of the crumbs from Kitty's dressing gown. 'Everyone does, and it's nice to be a little less formal when amongst friends, isn't it?'

Kitty nodded, and then sat back to listen to her talk about her children and granddaughter. Peggy was friendly and kind and clearly the sort of woman who was a born mother with an endless supply of love to give. Her family and the rest of the girls at

Beach View were very lucky, and Kitty felt a sudden pang of longing for her own mother. As she hastily blinked back the tears, she felt a warm hand on her fingers.

'We are all separated by this war, Kitty,' said Peggy softly. 'My two sons and my daughter and granddaughter are down in Somerset, and my husband is God knows where with the army up north. With Cissy and Martin so busy at Cliffe aerodrome, I rarely see them either. So I can understand how isolated you must feel, being so far from home, especially now. So I thought I would give you this.'

She placed a folded slip of paper into the pocket of Kitty's dressing gown. 'It's my telephone number, and I want you to promise that if you're feeling down, or need a friend or a cuddle, or even a bit more cake, you will ring me.'

Peggy's sweet words brought the tears back. 'That's very kind, Peggy, but I don't want to be a bother – and besides, you hardly know me.'

'I know you better than you think,' she replied softly. 'I know you're fighting the biggest battle of your life, and I also know you must be missing your home and your mother terribly. You're brave, because you've been doing a job that only very few girls would dare to do.'

She leaned back and regarded Kitty with a smile. 'And you're certainly not a bother, my dear. Far from it, and if you'll let me, I'd like to be your supporter and comforter, and to share in your struggle so you won't feel quite so alone.'

Kitty looked into her face, saw the yearning to help and felt the barriers to resist begin to tumble. 'Oh, Peggy, would you? Do you mean it?'

Peggy's expression was earnest as she gently held Kitty's fingers. 'My word is my bond, Kitty, and together we'll get you through this.' She softly dabbed at Kitty's tears. 'It's far too nice a day for those old things,' she said, 'so give me a smile and then you'll feel much better.'

Kitty smiled, and indeed it did make her feel a lot better.

'I see Auntie Peg has been working her magic,' said Rita as she returned with a tray of teacups and a plate of biscuits. 'You'll be in safe hands with Peggy, I promise, Kitty. Now, how about I help you with this cup of tea?'

Kitty lay in bed long after the others in the ward had gone to sleep, her thoughts filled with the events of a surprising and eventful afternoon. Peggy Reilly's genuine offer of help and support had been almost overwhelming, and for a moment, Kitty had been slightly suspicious about why a stranger should care what happened to her.

But as they'd talked and got to know one another a bit better, she'd come to realise that Peggy Reilly was an extraordinary woman who possessed an enormous capacity for love and understanding.

Combined with a fierce determination to protect and nurture those in her care, Peggy had given Kitty's spirits a terrific boost, and she counted herself very fortunate to have been taken under her wing.

Kitty smiled in the darkness. She didn't feel quite so alone any more.

Chapter Fourteen

Ron had decided that the puppy should be called Monty, after General Montgomery had been put in command of the Commonwealth and British Eighth Army who were fighting in the West African desert. There hadn't been much debate over it, for everyone adored the puppy – especially Daisy. And it seemed Monty loved Daisy, for when she fell asleep in her playpen, he would crawl through the bars and snuggle next to her and doze off.

Peggy smiled as she glanced down. The little creature was curled up with Daisy in the shade of the umbrella, and Harvey – who revelled in the role of proud father and guardian – was keeping a watchful eye on the pair of them from outside the bars of the playpen.

Monty was a delightful addition to the family, although there had been a couple of puddles to clean up, and he seemed to really enjoy tearing up newspapers and creating havoc with Cordelia's knitting. Not that it really mattered, for Cordelia's attempts at knitting were chaotic at best, and Peggy had lost count of the times she'd had to unravel things and start again.

She glanced across at Cordelia, who was sitting beside the playpen under the umbrella with her newspaper, and with a smile of contentment, she returned to pegging out the washing. It was a beautiful early August morning, with the sun already quite hot and the birds twittering away in the trees, and Peggy was looking forward to taking the bus this afternoon to the Memorial hospital to visit Kitty.

She'd already been once this week, and she'd felt ridiculously proud at how resilient the girl was in the face of such a challenge. Today she would finally have those horrid old plasters removed, and as it was the first step on the long road to recovery for Kitty, it was important to Peggy to be there.

With the nappies and sheets gently flapping in the warm breeze, Peggy took the laundry basket back indoors and set about making a pot of tea. She was just about to pour the boiling water over the last of the tea leaves when the telephone rang. With a frown of concern, she went to answer it.

'Hello, Mum.'

'Anne. Oh, darling, what a wonderful surprise.' Peggy sat down on the hall chair and settled in for a bit of a chat with her eldest daughter. 'But how did you manage to get through?' I've been trying for a week with no luck.'

'Like you, I just kept on trying. How are things there? Have you heard from Dad?'

'I get several letters every week. He can't tell me much, of course, and the censor blacks out the important bits, so I don't know exactly where he is or what he's doing. But he seems his usual cheerful self and has managed to wangle a cushy job as a driver for some colonel or brigadier or something.'

'Trust him,' said Anne with a chuckle.

'How are the boys and Rose Margaret?' Peggy asked anxiously.

'Bob's grown tall and strong and is capable of doing a man's work around the farm. He's still talking about becoming a farmer next year after he's finished school. Charlie is nearly as tall and as cheeky as ever. He's become fascinated with the farm machinery and spends hours down at the sheds with the mechanic. I think he's going to take after Dad and Granddad, because he's showing a real flair for mending things.'

Peggy laughed. 'The only flair for mending things is in your father and grandfather's minds. They can talk a good tale but manage to evade the practical side.' She dug in her apron pocket and lit a cigarette. 'How are you and Rose Margaret?'

'Rose is blooming,' Anne said with a chuckle. 'She's spoiled rotten by the land girls and likes nothing better than getting covered in muck. She's also learning some unfortunate language – some of the girls are from very poor backgrounds and are rather careless around her, so I've had to ask them to tone things down a bit.'

Anne paused. 'As for me, well, I'm still teaching at the village school and I really love it – but in a few months' time I'm going to have to get someone else to take over. I'm pregnant again.'

Peggy beamed with delight. 'Oh, Anne, I thought you might be when you came home to see your father off to camp.'

'Nothing much gets past you, does it?' she giggled. 'I was only a couple of months gone.'

Peggy did some rapid calculations. 'But that means you're in your sixth month,' she breathed. 'Oh, Anne, why didn't you tell me sooner? I'd have started knitting a layette.'

'I didn't want you to worry. Not that there was anything to worry about,' Anne added hastily. 'I'm as fit as a fiddle, and get plenty of good butter, eggs, milk, meat and vegetables down here. You wouldn't think rationing existed while you live on a farm.' She laughed. 'We've all put on weight, even Sally's little Ernie.'

Ernie had been struck down by polio as a baby, and was the younger brother of Sally, Peggy's first evacuee from London. It was Sally's aunt who owned the farm in Somerset and who had so kindly offered to take in Peggy's family as well. Sally had stayed on in Cliffehaven and had married John Hicks, the local fire station boss.

'Sally will be delighted to hear it,' Peggy said. 'He was always far too skinny.'

'Has she told you about how well he's been doing without his calipers? He dashes about on walking sticks now, and his Auntie Violet massages his legs every morning and evening. He still has a bit of a limp, but the doctor is very pleased with his progress. I wouldn't mind betting he'll soon throw those walking sticks away.'

Peggy's soft heart went out to the little boy who'd briefly come to live with her from the London slums. He'd been so pale and thin, and dependent on his sister, but he'd possessed great spirit even then, and she had no doubt at all that those sticks would soon be abandoned.

'That's wonderful news,' she said. 'I don't often see Sally now she's got her baby to care for, and another on the way. I must make the effort to pay her a visit. But there are so many other things I have to do there's rarely time for anything else.'

Anne listened as Peggy told her about Harvey's puppy, her run-in with Ron over the cake and eels, and her new friendship with Kitty. When Peggy had finally run out of breath, Anne gave a sigh. 'Honestly, Mum, you're stretching yourself too thin. You can't possibly run the house, put up with Granddad's shenanigans, care for Daisy, go to the WVS and start making hospital visits. It's at least half an hour away on the bus.'

'I agree there don't seem to be enough hours in the day,' Peggy replied, 'but I promised, and I'm not about to let the poor girl down. You see, I regard myself as blessed to have a family and a comfortable home. Kitty is far from home and has only her brother, and because he's one of Martin's Spitfire pilots, he's rarely able to even visit her.'

Peggy's concentration was broken by the sight of the puppy skidding across the hall floor tiles and tumbling onto the mat, where he promptly cocked his leg against the door. 'Monty,' she scolded. 'Out. Out now.'

'Let me guess,' giggled Anne. 'The pup's done a wee on your floor.'

'It's an occupational hazard,' sighed Peggy as Monty scratched the mat dutifully, and then galloped back into the kitchen looking very pleased with himself. 'Now, where was I?'

They managed to talk for another five minutes before the woman at the Somerset telephone exchange cut them off. Peggy replaced the receiver, and with a happy sigh for Anne's lovely news, went to find a bit of paper and a damp cloth to clean up after Monty.

Kitty could no longer avoid looking at her stump, but it wasn't a pretty sight, and it still took a lot to get used to it. Her thigh looked pale and skinny, the bones of her knee sticking out sharply above the rounded end of what was left of her lower leg. She could see how the surgeon had folded the skin over, almost like an envelope, and although the stitches had long since been taken out, the site of the wound still looked red and swollen.

'I'm going to have to put a drain in, Kitty,' surgeon Thorne said as he examined his handiwork. 'This swelling is caused by excess fluid, and I don't want infection to set in.' He smiled at her benevolently. 'Don't worry, it won't hurt more than having an injection, and by draining the fluid it will relieve some of the pain you've been experiencing.'

'When will I be able to have a new leg?' she asked.

'Not for a while yet,' he murmured as he gently applied the tube and small drainage bag to her thigh. 'The muscles have to strengthen again, and the skin around the wound has to harden so it can take the pressure of your weight in the prosthesis and not be rubbed raw. That's why the nurses massage it every morning and evening to strengthen the muscles and stop blood clots forming.'

'That could take weeks,' said Kitty as she eyed the tender flesh at the end of her thigh. 'And how long will it be after I get my leg before I can get out of here?'

He applied sticking plaster to the drainage tube and bag to ensure it stayed in place and then pulled a long gauze sock over her entire stump. 'That will all depend on how well you get on with the new leg,' he said cheerfully.

'What's the average recovery time?' she persisted.

'There isn't one,' he said firmly. 'Every patient is different. It depends very much on their general fitness and strength – and of course their determination.' He smiled. 'I get the feeling you'll be one of my star patients. I've never known anyone so set on getting out of here.'

'It's not a reflection on you or this place,' she replied quickly. 'But I'm bored rigid and want to be up and doing again.'

'Then let's get these plasters off and start the process. Once you've got the hang of going about on crutches, you'll feel a lot better, I assure you.'

Kitty knew he was right, but it sounded as if she was facing a very long haul.

He eyed her thoughtfully. 'You know, Kitty, that once the swelling has gone down and there's no risk of infection, you could become an outpatient here. The fitting of the prosthesis and the ongoing help to learn how to use and maintain it can easily be done with you coming in to our physiotherapy centre every day.'

Kitty's spirits plummeted further. She couldn't imagine trying to struggle on her own in some dreary flat with a false leg and walking sticks, and Freddy wouldn't be able to help either. 'I've got nowhere else to go, so it looks like I'm stuck here, then,' she said miserably.

The army surgeon patted her shoulder. 'Never mind,' he soothed. 'It's not a bad place to live while you recuperate, and we aren't about to throw you out until we're completely satisfied that you're fit and have somewhere to go.'

He picked her up and placed her gently in the wheelchair. 'Come on, let's get those plasters off.'

The green and yellow charabanc had trundled up the hill from Cliffehaven town centre and followed the meandering road heading north-west. This road led past the factory estate and the new prefabs, then wound at leisure between high hedgerows and the rhododendron bushes that hid Agatha Fullerton's grand house. The glorious blooms had faded now, but the hedge was still a verdant screen.

Peggy had left Daisy with Ron on the strictest instructions not to take her further than the town, and she could only pray that for once he would do as he was told. As the conversations among the other passengers drifted around her she looked out at the vista of sweeping farmland and hills that lay beyond Cliffehaven.

She could see the distant glimmer of the sea, and despite the ugly dark humps of the many gun emplacements that dotted the landscape, she fully understood why Ron so loved it. Even though she rarely had time to explore these hills any more, it was enough to know they were there, an intrinsic part of what they were all fighting for.

She gave a rueful smile as she thought of him tramping over these hills with Daisy strapped in the old army satchel. He'd done the same for Jim and Frank when they were small, and had continued to do it when his grandchildren came along. The sun glinting on the window made her blink, and tears welled up at the thought that two of Frank's lovely three boys would never again come home.

Determined not to be gloomy on such a beautiful

August day, she forced back her tears and turned her thoughts to Kitty.

Her first visit to the hospital had been an eye-opener. There was no denying that she'd been shocked and deeply saddened to see so many youngsters battling with missing limbs, head wounds and blindness, but within moments of her arrival, she'd been forcibly reminded of how strong the human spirit was, for there was an almost tangible determination amongst them to survive – to overcome the worst a person could bear – and have the courage to face what could only be an uncertain and rather frightening future. Their fortitude and cheerfulness had made her feel ashamed of her pity, and although she suspected they hid their fears and sorrows behind those smiles, she knew they would never admit it.

Kitty's friend Doreen was a prime example. Loud she might be, but she was a force to be reckoned with, and seemed to face every tribulation with a fearsome determination not to be beaten by it. Her coarse cheerfulness gave others something to smile about, and it seemed her sunny nature, in the face of such adversity, encouraged those who might have been overwhelmed by their misfortune to be more positive.

Peggy checked in her capacious bag to make sure the little gift she'd brought for Doreen was safely stowed away with the things she'd brought for Kitty. Turning back to the window, she realised she was almost there, so she gathered up her bag and cardigan and waited for the wheezing old bus to grind to a halt.

With a cheerful 'ta ta for now' to the middle-aged clippy, she stepped down, and was almost engulfed by the exhaust fumes from the ancient bus as it jerked back into life with an almighty backfire.

She turned away as the bus groaned onwards, and walked between the majestic pillars which had once held a pair of fine wrought iron gates, her shoes crunching on the freshly raked gravel driveway. From what Ron had told her about the place, the grounds of Holmwood House extended for several acres and included a large wood – but she wasn't here on a sightseeing trip, however curious she might be, and Kitty would be waiting for her.

The long drive swept past rhododendron and azalea hedges, which were looking a little drab now the blooms were gone. Beyond the hedges lay formal lawns, flower beds and a weeping willow drooping gracefully over a small lake where a family of swans had taken up residence amongst the ducks and moorhens. It really was the most beautiful, peaceful place, thought Peggy as she hurried along, and so perfect for those who needed respite from this world at war.

She rounded the last bend and was met by the sight of the house itself, and once again she couldn't fail to be impressed. This grand old building had stood the test of time and now, under the care of the combined forces, it had been brought back to life again with a fresh coat of paint and repaired windows, chimneys and roofs.

She went in through the large, heavily studded oak door which led to a square hall and an elegant oak staircase which rose majestically up to the third floor. It was dark and cool after the brightness and heat outside, and she could hear the echo of voices and the distant sound of music. Knowing her way around by now, she hurried to the east wing.

The nurse smiled as Peggy came into Kitty's ward. 'Hello, Mrs Reilly. You've only just missed Kitty, she's having her plasters taken off.' She gave Peggy directions to the plaster room. 'Just go in,' she said, 'we don't stand on ceremony here.'

Peggy hoped she wasn't too late as she hurriedly followed the directions. She'd promised Kitty she'd be here when the plasters came off and didn't want to break her word. She found the room easily and, after a momentary hesitation, pushed through the door.

'Peggy!' cried Kitty in delight. 'Look, I've got a leg and an arm again. And in a minute this arm will be free too.' She was sitting on a chair while the doctor carefully manoeuvred the heavy cutters through the plaster on her left arm.

Peggy put down her bag and hurried over. She noted how pale and thin the girl's limbs were, but that was more than made up for by the bright grin across her face. She gently clasped her free hand. 'How does it feel?'

'Strange,' Kitty said with a giggle. 'But oh so light and free – my leg and arm feel as if they can just fly away.'

'There we are,' said the doctor as he carefully pulled back the two halves of the plaster and eased it from her arm and hand. 'Flex your arm and wriggle your fingers for me, Kitty.'

Kitty did as she was told and giggled again. 'As good as new,' she said in delight, 'but I'll need some time in the sun to get the colour back. My skin looks a bit like a suet pudding.'

The doctor smiled with understanding and began to gently massage her arms and fingers. 'You'll need to get the muscles working again in your limbs, so there will be plenty of physio for the next few weeks,' he said. 'But with your leg you must take extra care, Kitty, and not try to do too much at first. You'll find it's much weaker than before.'

'But I can have a pair of crutches?'

'You may. But you're to use them only when supervised for the first few days. We don't want you falling and hurting yourself again, do we?'

'Not likely,' she replied and grinned. 'Can I give them a go now?'

He shrugged. 'Why not?' Handing over the crutches, he glanced at Peggy. 'If you could hold onto her right arm, I'll take the left to steady her. She'll be a bit wobbly at first,' he warned.

Peggy gently took Kitty's arm, fretting that it was

all a bit too soon, and that if this didn't go well, the girl might get upset and lose heart.

Kitty put her foot to the floor, and with the help of the others, managed to get out of the chair and stand. 'Gosh,' she breathed. 'I didn't realise how much energy it takes just to stand up.'

'You'll soon find it isn't as much of a struggle.' The doctor placed the crutches in her armpits. 'Is that comfortable, Kitty? Do your arms feel strong enough to take your weight?'

Kitty nodded, but Peggy could see the sudden hesitancy in her. 'Just stand for a minute,' she said softly. 'Get the feel of the crutches before you try anything.'

'They feel quite comfortable, but . . . But I don't feel balanced at all,' she confessed, 'and my arms are trembling even before I try to put my weight on them. I don't know . . . I don't know if I can do this.'

'If you can fly a Spitfire, you can fly a pair of crutches,' said Peggy with an encouraging smile. 'Lean all your weight on the crutches and then take a step – just a small step – or even a bit of a shuffle. You'll see. You can do it.'

Kitty's expression became determined, and Peggy could see her knuckles whitening as she gripped the crutches and willed herself to take that first step. 'It's like being a baby learning to walk again,' she muttered. 'But I'll do it. Yes. I'll damned well do it.'

Kitty's first step was more of a tentative shuffle.

The second was slightly bolder, and the third was bolder still. 'See, I told you I could do it,' she panted in triumph.

'That's enough for now,' said the doctor as he pulled the wheelchair towards her and gently pressed her into it. 'You'll find you tire easily at first, but the physiotherapist will work on those weak muscles, and if you practise little and often, you'll soon be swinging along as well as Doreen.'

Peggy softly kissed the girl's damp brow, her heart swelling with pride. 'Well done,' she breathed. 'Now, if we've finished here, how about we go out onto the terrace and enjoy the sun while we have a cup of tea?'

Kitty had tears in her eyes as she grasped Peggy's hand. 'Thank you, Peggy. I couldn't have done it without you here.'

'Stuff and nonsense,' retorted Peggy gruffly. 'You'd've done it with or without me, because you're made of strong stuff. Now, let's find that cuppa. I don't know about you, but I'm parched after all that excitement.'

Once she'd wheeled Kitty outside and made sure she was in the shade and comfortable, Peggy asked one of the orderlies if it would be possible to have a pot of tea. As he went off, they were both startled by a shout from the French windows.

'Oi, wot you think then? Look, no crutches.'

Doreen came towards them with almost a piratical swagger, her pretty face alight with triumph as she leaned heavily on a walking stick.

'You've got your leg,' Kitty called back in delight.

'And you ain't got yer plaster,' she replied cheerfully. 'But you look as pale as a fish on a slab,' she added as she swung the leg out and forward, carefully placing it before making any further advance with her good leg. 'You wanna get out from that umbrella and in the sun, gel.'

'I'll catch up with you soon enough,' said Kitty with a chuckle.

Doreen plumped down into a nearby chair and blew a loud sigh of relief. 'Blimey,' she panted. 'It don't 'alf take it out of yer. I ain't never been this puffed after such a short walk.'

'But you're managing very well,' said Peggy with admiration. 'Is this your first time, Doreen?'

Doreen shook her head and then lit a cigarette. 'I've been practising with the physio in the gym. He reckoned I was ready enough to be let loose with it out 'ere. But by the cringe, Peg, it's a bugger. Look at the state of *that*.' She stuck her false leg out so they could examine it.

'It's no different to everyone else's,' said Kitty with a giggle. 'What did you expect, Doreen? Bells and tinsel with fairy lights?'

'Summink a bit more glamorous, that's what,' she grumbled. 'Well, I mean, look at that shoe for a start. Wouldn't have been seen dead wearing summink like that before. It's a right bugger, and that's a fact.'

Peggy understood Doreen's dislike of the shoe. For a pretty girl used to wearing dainty footwear, it was a huge let-down – black, clumpy and laced, it was like something an old woman would wear. 'Maybe, once you've got used to the leg, you could adapt another shoe to take its place,' she offered.

'Yeah, maybe,' said Doreen as she regarded the offending object rather dolefully. 'But I can't see me dancing the light fantastic in me lovely red high heels again, can you, Peg?'

'Knowing you, I wouldn't put it past you to try,' said Peggy as she dug in her bag. 'Anyway, I brought something that might cheer you up. It's only small, but the minute I saw it, I knew you had to have it.'

Doreen opened the small packet and her eyes widened as the glittering black and gold garter fell into her lap. 'Cor,' she breathed as she held it up admiringly. 'I ain't never seen one as lovely as this.'

'I found it among some stuff in a trunk under the stairs,' said Peggy. 'My younger daughter, Cissy, used to be on the stage, and this was part of a costume she once wore.'

'And she don't mind you giving this lovely thing to me?' Doreen asked in awe.

Peggy smiled. 'I doubt she'll even remember she had it. And now she's in the WAAF, she won't be needing it.'

'Thanks ever so, Peg. I'll take great care of it, I will.'

She wrestled to get the garter over her ugly shoe and then up the steel frame of the leg, over the fittings that cupped her knee, and settled it on her thigh. Keeping the folds of her vivid scarlet dressing gown drawn back, she admired how the gold sequins sparkled in the sunlight.

'This won't half cheer them poor buggers up in the men's ward,' she said with a naughty wink. 'I think I'll go and show it off right now before they all go to sleep.'

'Mind how you go, Doreen,' warned Kitty. 'I saw Matron earlier and she was heading that way.'

Doreen grinned and got to her feet. 'She ain't no match fer me,' she said. 'Not today.'

Peggy and Kitty watched with affectionate smiles as she swung away determinedly, showing off her new garter to all and sundry as she crossed the terrace.

'I like Doreen,' said Peggy after she'd gone indoors. 'She has such spirit.'

'I do too,' murmured Kitty. 'And I'll miss her dreadfully once she's discharged. But she's right about that shoe. It has to be the ugliest thing known to man.'

'But Doreen's walking about on it, so it serves a wonderful purpose.' Peggy reached for her pale, thin hand. 'Don't worry, Kitty,' she said softly. 'Once you're up and about, I'll see if we can find something a bit more attractive.'

Kitty didn't look too convinced, so Peggy dug into her bag again. 'And to congratulate you on losing all that horrid plaster, I've brought you some presents too.'

Kitty looked immediately apprehensive, and Peggy laughed. 'No, dear, there are no more garters. But I did find this lovely cardigan when I was sorting through stuff at the WVS centre. It's all washed and clean,' she added hastily, 'and I don't reckon it's been hardly worn at all. And here are some magazines and a couple of books which I enjoyed and thought you might find interesting.'

Kitty threw her arms round Peggy. 'Thank you so much for being here, Peggy,' she said tearfully. 'There are so many things that are frightening and new, and I'm so glad I have you to talk to and lean on.'

Peggy's tears blinded her as she held the slender girl to her heart. 'My shoulders are broad, Kitty,' she replied softly. 'You lean as heavily as you like, my dear.'

Chapter Fifteen

More than two weeks had passed since Kitty took possession of her crutches, and now she could get about at some speed. The physiotherapy was working wonders and her arms and leg felt very much stronger, so she continued with her exercises at every spare moment, determined to be in good shape when her new leg was fitted the following day.

She was feeling much more positive about things, for Freddy and Roger had managed to come and see her twice on their evenings off, and Peggy had been to visit every Sunday and Thursday, sometimes with Rita, and once with her sweet baby, Daisy, who'd enchanted everyone by milking every ounce of attention throughout the afternoon.

Peggy had confessed that she'd been a bit worried about bringing a baby to the hospital but had decided that perhaps some of the patients might be missing their own little ones, so it wouldn't do any harm as long as she was well behaved. They both agreed the idea had been a success and that Daisy should come again while the weather was so good.

Kitty had come to adore Peggy, for she was strong

and loving and talked a lot of sense when Kitty was feeling a bit dispirited or impatient with her progress. As for Rita, she'd become a real friend, and despite their very different backgrounds, they'd discovered they had a great deal more in common than just motorbikes.

They were almost childlike in their pleasures, they realised, preferring to watch a film, go for a picnic or eat fish and chips out of newspaper rather than going to dances or flirting with men in uniform. It wasn't that they didn't like men, just that they were wary. They'd both seen friends have their hearts broken when a husband or fiancé didn't make it back, or when things went wrong – and things did go badly wrong, with so many Americans, Canadians and Free French flirting their way through the ranks of girls who were flattered to be noticed, and who saw them as rather exotic and romantic.

Of course both of them would like to meet Mr Right one day, but to Kitty's mind it would have to be a very lucky day for any man to want her now she was crippled. The sight of her stump was enough to put any man off. Dismissing this gloomy thought, she grabbed her crutches and went in search of Doreen, who could always cheer her up.

'Wotcha,' Doreen shouted with a wave as Kitty reached the terrace. 'Come and sit down while I tell you the latest gossip.'

Most unusually, Doreen had discarded the scarlet dressing gown and was dressed in rather sober slacks and a pretty blouse – and she was also alone and in a quiet corner of the terrace.

Kitty put her crutches to one side and hopped into a nearby chair. Doreen could always be relied upon to know the juiciest gossip, and this place was a seething hotbed of it – though she'd quickly learned to take most of it with a pinch of salt.

'Matron's leaving,' said Doreen with relish. 'The Administrator caught her bullying that new kid in bed nine – you know the one: neck brace, one eye probably blinded and a broken leg? Doesn't look as if she'd say boo to a goose?'

At Kitty's nod, she continued in a stage whisper. 'It seems the girl isn't as shy as we thought, 'cos she'd already made a complaint about Matron to the admin officer. He come into the ward to talk to her and caught the old cow 'aving a right go.' She giggled. 'He give her what for and marched her outta there, and I 'eard tell she were seen an hour later, bag and baggage, going off down the drive.'

'Let's hope her replacement is kinder,' said Kitty with a sigh of relief. 'Do you know who it might be?'

Doreen shook her head. 'As long as it ain't the old dragon what runs Cliffehaven General, we should be all right, but who can tell, Kitty? Seems to me one matron is much like another from what I 'eard.'

'Well, it's all right for you, Doreen. You'll be out of here soon. I'm stuck here for weeks yet.' She smiled at her friend. 'I'm going to miss you. You've livened this place up no end, and I'll have no one to play cards with.'

'Gawd 'elp us, Kitty. There's about eighty people in this place and I ain't the only one what knows how to play five card brag.'

'I'm sure you're not, but I bet no one can cheat as well as you,' Kitty teased.

Doreen's green eyes widened in feigned innocence and then she tipped back her head and roared with laughter. 'And 'ere's me thinkin' you hadn't a clue.'

Kitty laughed along with her. 'You forget, Doreen, I have an older brother and I know all the tricks, believe me. You didn't fool me a bit.'

Once they'd stopped giggling, Kitty became serious. 'Where will you go when you leave here?'

'Back to the smoke for a bit to see me mum and the young 'uns, then I'll come south again.' Doreen lit a cigarette. 'They've promised me my old job at the factory, and me landlady wrote back and said she's got a ground-floor room for me as long as I don't leave it for too long. So I'm sorted.'

She eyed Kitty thoughtfully through the cigarette smoke. 'Wot about you?'

Kitty shrugged. 'It's too early to make any plans, and as I haven't got any family to turn to, it means I'll be here until I'm fit enough to cope in the world outside this place.' She gazed out over the lawn to the woodland beyond. 'The doctor said they'd make sure I had a good billet before I was released.'

'What about Peggy? She's a good sort, and I wouldn't mind betting she'd give you a good 'ome if you asked her.'

'She's done more than enough already,' said Kitty firmly. 'She has quite enough on her plate as it is, and I wouldn't dream of burdening her with all the complications my presence would cause.'

'That's a shame,' murmured Doreen. ''Cos if you asked me, I'd've said Peggy Reilly would open her arms and carry you home without so much as a blink. She's a proper diamond, is Peggy, and there ain't too many of them about.'

Kitty decided to change the subject, for she had absolutely no intention of asking anything more from Peggy. 'So, apart from the gossip about Matron, are there any other rumours flying about?'

Doreen looked solemn for once as she stubbed out the cigarette and narrowed her eyes against the sun's glare. 'Well, there was something I overheard yesterday,' she said softly as she leaned closer. 'But from what I could make out, they shouldn't have been talking about it at all.'

Kitty regarded her with some amusement. 'You're being very mysterious,' she said.

'Well, it ain't something I feel easy talking about,' Doreen confessed. She leaned closer still, her voice barely above a whisper. 'But I been thinking and worrying about it all night and I gotta tell someone.' She glanced over her shoulder to make sure no one was in earshot. 'You gotta promise to keep shtum, 'cos I reckon I'm about to break the official secrets thingummy.'

'You've got me worried now,' said Kitty with a frown. 'Come on, Doreen, spill the beans. And I promise that whatever you tell me will go no further.'

With another glance round, she put her lips close to Kitty's ear and began to whisper. 'I couldn't hear too much, 'cos I was on the window seat in the library behind the thick curtain, and they was muttering. But it seems there's been a terrible disaster on some raid across the Channel, and both officers have been ordered back to HQ.'

She paused for breath. 'It was mainly the Canadians involved, and they was to be supported by the navy and the RAF. But there was a complete cock-up with communications, so when Jerry got wind of what was going on, the Canadians and the navy was caught like sitting ducks. Several ships were sunk by U-boats, and thousands of men was killed or badly injured.'

'Oh, dear God,' breathed Kitty. 'Who were these officers you overheard? Can their information be relied upon?'

'I reckon so,' she murmured. 'They was Canadian, and high-ranking.'

Kitty knew immediately who she was talking about, for there were only two senior Canadian officers recuperating here, and both of them were highly respected and eminently reliable. 'Did you hear any more details?'

Doreen shook her head. 'They left the library when someone else came in, and I had a bit of a job getting off the window seat to follow them. By the time I made it out into the 'all, they was gone.'

Her usually lively little face was drawn and her expression thoughtful as she lit another cigarette. 'Less than an hour later, I saw a flash staff car with the Canadian flag flying on the bonnet come and pick 'em up.'

Kitty slumped back into the seat, her thoughts in turmoil, her spirits low. 'If it's true, then it will be a terrible blow for morale – especially after the humiliating withdrawal of the British and Commonwealth troops from El Alamein.'

'Yeah, it ain't good, is it?' murmured Doreen through the cigarette smoke. 'But now Montgomery's in charge over there, I reckon they'll give Rommel a bloody good hiding.'

Kitty nodded, but her thoughts were still churning over what had happened to all those poor men who'd been trapped and killed in the Channel. She could only pray that it was all just a rumour, and that Doreen had misheard and jumped to conclusions. But even as the thought entered her head, she knew it was a false hope, for those officers had not been known to gossip idly, and their swift departure was very telling.

She shivered despite the warmth of the sun. This war had already cost the lives of so many – would there never be an end to it?

*   *   *

Peggy stood at the back gate and waved as Ruby and Ethel went arm-in-arm with Stan down the twitten to the main road. They all looked so happy together, and Peggy had been delighted to see the twinkle in Stan's eyes as Ethel had fussed over him. The poor man had been a widower for too long and it was clear that he was thoroughly enjoying the attention – and Ethel's cooking, for the buttons on Stan's waistcoat had definitely been under a bit of strain.

But Stan wasn't the only one to have benefitted from this new-found friendship, for Ruby and her mother had lost their city pallor and the sharpness in their expressions which had defined the hardships of surviving London's wartime slums. Ethel's hair had been freshly washed and set and she'd taken the time to put on some make-up. Her cotton dress had been carefully ironed and she'd sported a sparkling necklace and earrings.

Ruby's youthfulness shone in her clear skin and eyes, and in the obvious contentment of having her mother by her side, and she'd looked extremely pretty in her sprigged cotton frock and pale pink cardigan.

Peggy smiled as she turned back to the house. It had been a lovely afternoon, and great fun to catch up on the gossip at the factory and the news of Ruby's young Canadian. He still seemed very keen and had written almost every day since he'd left Cliffehaven for some mysterious training camp, and Peggy rather hoped something might come of it.

Ruby deserved some happiness after what she'd been through, and it would be the icing on the cake if that young man proved to be worthy of her.

Cordelia was sitting beneath the umbrella next to the playpen, where Daisy had fallen asleep amongst her soft toys. 'It's no good you having that soppy grin on your face, Peggy Reilly,' she said sternly as she peered over her half-moon glasses. 'Ethel's husband will come home eventually and then there'll be fireworks, you mark my words.'

Peggy knew there was no point in arguing, for Cordelia was very set in her ways, and Peggy had to agree that the situation was far from ideal. She looked at the sleeping Daisy and then gazed around the garden. 'Where's Monty?' she asked with growing suspicion.

Cordelia shrugged. 'I have no idea. He was here a minute ago.'

With visions of her house being turned upside down by the mischievous puppy, Peggy went into the basement. She closed the back door and her spirits sank as she stood and listened to the scuffles and squeaks coming from Ron's bedroom. Monty had managed to open the ferrets' cage again.

But as she hastened to stop them escaping, her feet became entangled in a flying fury of ferrets, and she almost fell over the overexcited puppy chasing after them. She grabbed the door jamb to steady herself as they flew up the concrete steps into the kitchen.

'Monty! Leave!' Peggy yelled as she swiftly followed them. 'Monty, stop that at once! Sit!'

She was just in time to see Monty's wispy tail disappearing into the hall.

'Oh, Lord,' she sighed. 'Here we go again.'

Following the sound of scampering feet, she ran up the stairs to find that Rita had left her bedroom door open and Monty was running in circles around the unmade bed. His excited yips and whines were accompanied by the high-pitched screams and hisses of the trapped ferrets.

She closed the bedroom door to stop them all escaping again and made a grab for the puppy, but Monty was too quick. He managed to evade her clutching fingers, skidding off over the polished floor, yapping furiously at the hissing creatures cowering under the bed.

'Monty,' she scolded. 'They'll bite you – and it will hurt. Come here this instant and do as you're told for once.'

Monty was having none of it, and he kept out of her reach as he darted back and forth with excited yelps.

Peggy could see that Flora and Dora had worked themselves up to attack, and she knew that if they did, Monty would be in terrible trouble. Ferrets could do a lot of damage with their needle-sharp teeth, and once they'd taken hold, their jaws locked and it was the devil's own job to get them open again without losing a finger.

She made another grab for Monty, but he skittered away.

Flora shot out from beneath the bed, teeth bared. She missed the puppy's back leg by inches, as Dora hissed furiously.

'Monty!' shouted Peggy as she grabbed the dressing-table stool and used it like a circus lion tamer to ward off Flora from attacking Monty again.

There must have been something in her voice, for Monty skidded to a halt and turned to look at her.

Peggy kept the chair between her and the hissing ferrets and grabbed the puppy by the scruff. She was just backing away with Monty under her arm when someone's heavy hand banged on the door behind her, and she almost dropped the puppy and the stool.

'Auntie Peg? What's going on in there?'

'The ferrets are loose,' she called back to Anthony. 'I need help.'

The knob turned and the door was carefully opened a few inches before Anthony eased round it. 'Take the puppy out and give him to Suzy,' he ordered quietly. 'I'll deal with those two.'

'You won't be able to do it on your own,' she said. 'They're wound up like clocks and will bite as soon as look at you.'

She handed over the stool and quickly passed a squirming Monty through the narrow gap to a worried-looking Suzy. 'Shut him in somewhere,' she ordered, 'and then come back and give us a hand.'

She turned back into the room, noting for the first time that Rita had left it in a terrible mess, and that the puppy and the ferrets had all left deposits on the floor in their fear and excitement. 'So,' she said to her nephew, 'how are we going to do this?'

Anthony pushed his glasses up his nose and then ran his fingers through his hair. He gave her an uncertain smile. 'I don't really know,' he admitted. 'But it seems to me we have to get them from under the bed before we can trap them.' He glanced round the room, then quickly darted forward and yanked the sheet from the unmade bed.

Suzy eased into the room and closed the door on Monty's piteous howling. 'I've shut him in the bath-room,' she said. 'And I thought this might help.' She held up the bathroom mop.

Anthony stood with the sheet in one hand and the stool in the other, his expression determined as he regarded the two hissing, screaming ferrets. 'Well done, Suzy. Now, Peggy, take the mop and go to the other side of the bed. Use it to prod them towards me and Suzy, and we'll have the sheet to catch them in.'

Peggy didn't think this plan had much chance of working – ferrets were cunning, very fast, and inclined to do the unexpected – but as she didn't have any other suggestions, she clutched the mop and warily approached the bed.

The ferrets hissed defiance and backed off as she tentatively poked the mop beneath the bed. Then, feeling bolder, they tried to attack it.

Peggy jabbed harder and stamped her feet. 'Back. Go back,' she shouted.

They turned and fled straight into the sheet which Suzy and Anthony dropped on top of them.

'Quick,' panted Anthony, 'stand on the corners, make sure they're trapped.'

Peggy shot round the bed to help, and just managed to put her foot on an opening before one of the creatures escaped. She looked down at the squirming ball of fury beneath the sheet. 'Now what?'

'Um.' Anthony had clearly run out of ideas.

'If we quickly gather up the two ends, we can slide the bottom bit under them and make the sheet into a sack,' said Suzy. 'But we'll have to do it together.' She waited for their nods of agreement. 'Right, then. On my count of three. One. Two. Three.'

The sheet slid beneath the fighting, squirming ferrets and knocked them off their feet. Before they could retaliate or attempt to escape, the sheet was tightly knotted like a bag and the animals were securely trapped in a heap at the bottom.

Peggy was hot and a bit out of breath, but there was a certain air of triumph between them of a job well done. 'Thanks, Anthony,' she panted. 'I couldn't have done that on my own.'

'It was a rather different problem to the ones I usually have to solve for the MOD, but I'm glad to have been of help.' He eyed her with concern as he pushed his glasses up his nose again. 'Are you all right, Auntie Peg? You didn't get bitten, did you?'

She swept back the damp curls that were sticking to her forehead. 'I'm fine,' she said briskly. 'But Ron will get the sharp edge of my tongue when he gets back. I've told him time and again to fix that blasted latch on the cage.'

'I'll fix the latch while you make us all a cup of tea,' Anthony replied as he lifted the sack with its squirming, hissing cargo and carried it out of the room.

Peggy glanced round Rita's bedroom then closed the door on the mess. She'd be having words with that young lady, too, she decided as she approached the bathroom door.

Monty was howling as if trapped in hell, his paws scrabbling at the door and no doubt scratching all the paint off.

Peggy opened the door a few inches, reached in and grabbed his scruff. Holding him tightly in her arms, she put the mop back and then went downstairs.

Delighted to be free, Monty licked her face and gave little whines of pleasure, but Peggy was in no mood to pet him, however endearing he might be. She carried him into the kitchen and clipped his lead onto his collar, then secured it firmly beneath the table leg. He was in disgrace.

Monty had definitely inherited Harvey's talent for drama, she noted with some amusement, for he slumped down, nose on paws, his ears and eyebrows twitching in distress, as his soulful brown eyes watched her every move.

'Don't feel sorry for him,' she warned Cordelia, who'd come in from the garden. 'He's let the ferrets loose again and has to learn when he's been naughty.'

Cordelia's bright blue eyes widened in horror. 'You can't possibly leave the poor little mite there until he's forty,' she gasped.

'He's been NAUGHTY,' snapped Peggy, with unusual impatience.

Cordelia sniffed and sat down at the kitchen table. 'Well, there's no need to shout in that rude manner,' she said crossly. 'I'm not deaf.'

Peggy gave a deep sigh of exasperation and slammed the kettle onto the hob just as Harvey came bounding up the steps. Monty perked up immediately, she noticed, and with little whines and yips of pleasure, the puppy happily allowed Harvey to lick him all over.

'Well now,' said Ron as he tramped into the kitchen in his filthy wellingtons and threw his cap on the table. 'There's a fine sight. To be sure, Harvey's a good father.' His beam of delight faded as he realised the puppy was tethered to the table. 'Ach, Peggy, that's not right.'

'You'll leave him tied up, Ron,' said Peggy. 'He's being punished.'

He frowned at her as Monty's paws scrabbled up his legs. 'And who's that banging about in me basement? Honest to God, Peggy, I go out for a few hours and . . .'

'Don't you *dare* complain, Ronan Reilly,' stormed

Peggy. 'That's Anthony down there fixing the catch that I've asked you over and over again to sort out. As for Monty and your blasted ferrets, they've run me ragged and I've had enough.'

Ron looked alarmed. 'Me ferrets? Are they all right?'

'Oh, they're just *fine*,' she retorted with heavy sarcasm as she folded her arms and glared at him. 'Don't mind about *me*, and the mess they've left on Rita's bedroom floor.'

Ron's expression was wary as he slowly retreated towards the stairs. 'Well, I'll just be going down to give Anthony a wee hand, so I will.'

'You'll go and clean up Rita's floor first,' she said flatly.

Ron was still edging towards the cellar steps. 'Ach, Peggy, to be sure I will, but Flora and Dora will be upset, and I need to see . . .'

'Do it, Ron. Now.'

Peggy's glare could have stopped a rampaging bull at ten feet, and Ron knew better than to argue. He reluctantly collected the old newspapers, cleaning rags and dustpan and brush from under the sink and mournfully traipsed out of the kitchen.

'And take those boots off before you go tramping muck into my stair carpet,' Peggy shouted after him.

'Goodness me, Peggy,' muttered Cordelia. 'What you need is a cup of tea and a good sit down while you cool off. I've never seen you in such a temper before.'

'Maybe not,' muttered Peggy as she slumped onto a kitchen chair and lit a cigarette. 'But that man and his animals are enough to try a saint.'

'Well, it is hot,' Cordelia said with a frown, 'but I don't think it's the right time to go out for a can of paint. It's after five and the shops will be shut.'

Her tantrum over, Peggy smiled weakly back at Cordelia as she placed the cup of tea in front of her. There were times when she'd have given a week's ration for peace and quiet and a bit of sanity – but there was as much chance of that in this house as a snowstorm in August.

Harvey had quietened the puppy and now it was snuggled up next to him under the kitchen table, still tethered to the leg. They both looked up as Ron came back but didn't move as he put the soiled paper into the range fire and then washed his hands.

'Is it safe to sit down for a cup of tea now?' Ron asked.

Peggy puffed on her cigarette. 'After you've helped Anthony with the job you should have done weeks ago,' she replied more moderately.

'No need.' Anthony came up from the cellar, swiftly followed by Suzy, who bustled about with cups and saucers. 'It's all fixed, and if the pup manages to get that undone, then you should rename him Houdini.'

Peggy smiled. 'Thanks, Anthony.'

'I'll go and check on Flora and Dora,' rumbled Ron.

'No, wait,' said Anthony. 'Suzy and I have something to tell you.'

Peggy's bad mood was instantly swept away as she saw the glow in Suzy's face and the proprietorial way that Anthony was holding her hand. It was good news, she could tell – and that could only mean one thing.

'Suzy has given me the honour of agreeing to be my wife,' said Anthony with a shy smile.

'Oh, Suzy, Anthony, I couldn't be more thrilled,' said Peggy as she raced across the small kitchen and threw her arms about them. She kissed them both. 'Well done, oh, very well done. Now, let me see the ring.'

Suzy blushed and held out her hand to show off the beautiful solitaire diamond which flashed fire in the sunlight.

'Well done, Anthony,' said Ron with a beaming smile and a heavy-handed thump on the younger man's shoulder. 'You won't go wrong with this wee girl. She'll make a fine wife, so she will.'

'Oh, Anthony,' twittered Cordelia. 'The ring is utterly beautiful.' She looked up into Suzy's radiant face. 'And so is your bride. You're a lucky man.'

Anthony softly kissed Cordelia's cheek and then put his arm round Suzy's shoulders and held her to his side. 'I know I am, Granny Finch. And I'll spend the rest of my life taking good care of her. You can be sure of that.'

'So, when's the wedding?' asked Peggy excitedly.

'We've decided on December,' said Suzy, blushing prettily. 'Then we can spend our honeymoon and first Christmas in the darling little house Anthony bought for us.'

'Oh, how lovely,' sighed Peggy. She blinked away the tears. 'Have you told your family yet, Suzy?'

She shook her head. 'We thought we'd drive up there and tell them this Sunday. We're both off duty and Anthony has been promised the loan of a pool car.'

Peggy turned her attention to Anthony. 'And Doris?' she asked warily. 'How has she taken the news?'

Anthony cleared his throat and a silent look passed between the engaged couple before he replied. 'Father is invited for supper tonight, and as Mother's evacuees are on the night shift, we thought it would be the ideal time to break the news.'

He pushed his glasses up his nose and ran his fingers through his brown hair. 'We're rather hoping that she and Father will have settled things between them by December so they can both attend the wedding and be pleasant to one another.'

'Let us hope so,' murmured Peggy. She looked at Suzy. 'I know you'll want to keep things fairly low key because of the war, but it might be an idea to get Doris involved in some small way.'

'Yes, I'd already thought of that,' the girl replied. 'Because travelling is so difficult, we've decided to get married at the church round the corner from here and have the reception at Havelock Gardens, if Doris agrees. She loves entertaining and is an absolute whizz at organising food and tables and such-like.'

'That sounds like a splendid idea,' said Peggy, 'but just make sure she doesn't try and take over completely, because before you know it, she'll be discussing wedding dresses and bridesmaids.'

Suzy laughed. 'She hasn't met my mother, who is certainly no pushover and more than a match for Doris. Don't worry, Auntie Peg. Everything will turn out just fine.'

'I wish I had something stronger to offer than tea,' said Peggy fretfully to Ron. 'We should be toasting the happy couple.'

Anthony grinned and opened the larder. 'I've come prepared,' he said as he pulled out a bottle of champagne from the marble shelf. 'This is from my father's cellar, and I'm reliably informed it is a very good vintage.'

'Then what are you waiting for, Anthony? To be sure, it'll do no good sitting in that bottle much longer,' said Ron as Peggy scuttled about to find clean glasses.

The champagne cork popped delightfully and the frothing, pale gold liquid was carefully poured into the glasses.

'To the happy couple,' said Peggy.

'Aye, may all your blessings be little ones,' said Ron with a wink.

Suzy blushed scarlet, Harvey barked, Monty yapped, Cordelia twittered like a flustered sparrow, and Peggy was all smiles. The shadows of war had been chased away for a few hours during this happy day – and it seemed that the future was looking much brighter.

Chapter Sixteen

It was just after nine in the morning and very quiet in the smaller of the two physiotherapy rooms, and as Kitty watched the middle-aged doctor carefully bandage her stump and pull on the padded sock, all she could hear was the thud of her heart. This was a hugely important day, for all the exercises she'd done and the pain she'd endured had led to this single defining moment.

She glanced across the room to the nurse who was holding the ugly metal leg with its leather straps and wooden foot, and tried very hard to see it as something she must learn to accept as an intrinsic part of her life from now on. But accept she must – for it was her ticket out of this hospital, and perhaps, if she was very lucky, back into a plane.

'Now, I'm just going to fit the prosthesis,' said Dr Thorne. 'Watch carefully, because you'll have to learn to do it on your own soon.'

As Kitty felt the top of the leg cup her knee joint and watched him carefully adjust it and begin to buckle the leather straps, she experienced a strange emotional mixture of excitement and dread. What if it didn't bear her weight? What if her stump was still too soft to put up with all that rubbing? What if . . .

She had to stop being so negative, she silently berated herself. This was a positive step, a new beginning, and she should damned well face the fact and stop whining.

'How does that feel?' he asked as he set the wooden foot on the floor.

'Odd.' Kitty stared down. It looked so ugly and alien compared to her lightly tanned leg, and she took a wavering breath as she blinked back the sudden tears and forced herself to be brave.

'It will feel odd for a while,' he said quietly, 'but you'll be surprised at how quickly you get used to it.' His rugged face creased into a smile as he patted her shoulder. 'You aren't the first, and unfortunately you won't be the last young woman to have one of these fitted, Kitty. But I can assure you that science in the development of prosthetics has come a long way in the past few years, and this is the Rolls-Royce of legs.'

Kitty shot him a brave little smile. 'It looks more like the landing gear of a Spitfire.'

'Either way, it will help to get you where you're going. Now, let's put on this shoe and then we can get you onto your feet.'

As he knelt before her and fitted the unflattering shoe, she giggled. 'I feel like Cinderella.'

He smiled back at her as he tied the laces. Once this was accomplished, he stood and held out his hands. 'Then, as your rather ancient and grey-haired Prince Charming, I'm inviting you to join me in our first waltz.'

Kitty eagerly gripped his warm, sturdy hands and slowly pulled herself up, keeping her weight firmly on her good leg.

'Now even out your weight,' he said quietly. 'Let your knee joint settle more firmly into the cup.'

Kitty tentatively shifted her weight and winced as her stump was pressed into the cup. It still felt very tender, and she was beginning to have serious doubts as to whether she'd ever be able to manage to walk on it. 'I think the waltz will have to wait,' she breathed.

His grip tightened on her hands as she teetered on the unfamiliar leg. 'Try again, Kitty,' he coaxed. 'I know it must feel quite tender, but the more you use the leg, the tougher your stump will get.'

Kitty warily pressed down again, but the weight on her stump still made her take a sharp breath. 'It hurts,' she gasped. 'I can't do it.'

The kindly doctor eased her back into the chair. 'I'm sure it's a little uncomfortable,' he said, 'but that will pass. As for not being able to do it,' he shook his head and gave her a wry smile. 'I believe you can do anything you set your mind to, Kitty Pargeter. But this is only the first step on your road to recovery. Surely you're not going to give in quite so easily?'

'I never said anything about giving in,' she replied

gruffly. 'But it *does* hurt, and I'm frightened of doing any more damage to myself.'

The doctor took off the leg and the padded sock, then stripped away the dressings over her stump. 'Look, Kitty,' he ordered firmly. 'There's no reddening, no puffiness – nothing at all that could be giving you any pain.' He placed his hand on her arm. 'I think that once you really believe you can do this, then the pain will go. It's all in your mind, Kitty – really it is.'

She looked back at him in wide-eyed disbelief, for the pain had felt real enough, and she wasn't the sort of girl who had hysterics at the slightest little thing.

He replaced the dressing, the sock and the prosthesis. 'It's up to you, Kitty,' he said quietly as he held his hands out to her again. 'Do you want to walk out of here on two feet? Do you want to climb back into a Spitfire or a Typhoon? Or do you want to be hampered by crutches for the rest of your life?'

Kitty glanced across at the silent nurse who'd been watching, and saw the same questions in her eyes. Taking a deep breath, she gritted her teeth and grasped his hands. 'I've never backed away from anything before,' she panted as she stood and placed her weight evenly on both legs. 'And I'm damned if I'm about to do it now.'

'I thought as much,' he murmured, his mouth twitching with a smile. 'So how about trying a little step for me?'

Kitty could feel her stump nestled into the cup, but strangely it didn't seem to be hurting at all – it just felt odd and a bit uncomfortable. She concentrated hard, remembering how Doreen swung from the hip, then put her weight on her good leg and forced her thigh muscles to lift the false leg and place it firmly an inch in front of her.

'There,' she panted. 'Satisfied?'

He nodded. 'Well done, Kitty. But if you really want to impress me, you need to bring the other leg forward to join it.'

Kitty gripped his hand, put all her weight on the false leg, ignored the discomfort, and took a step. 'I did it,' she breathed in awe. 'And it didn't hurt much at all.'

'I think that's enough for now,' he replied.

'But I need to get some practice in,' she protested.

'You'll be back here every few hours to get the practice in,' he said as he eased her back into the chair. 'The training will be intensive over the next few weeks, so you'll need lots of rest in between the sessions.'

He took the crutches from the nurse and handed them to Kitty. 'Now, go and sit in the sun, and I'll see you back here at eleven.'

Kitty had been back to the treatment room twice more during the day, and she was due to return for a shorter session just before supper. That tiny step she'd taken earlier this morning had been just the first, now she was able to grip the parallel bars and proceed, rather like a drunken sailor, some way along them.

But the effort was exhausting, and although she was elated by her progress, she just wanted to sleep away the rest of the day. She was happily dozing in the comfortably cushioned chair beneath the umbrella on the terrace when she was startled awake by Doreen.

''Ere, Kitty. Guess what?' she said as she sat down next to her and clattered her walking stick onto the metal table.

Kitty reluctantly opened one eye. 'I was asleep,' she protested.

Doreen waved away her complaint. 'There's time enough for that when yer old and past it,' she said dismissively. 'You know what I was telling yer about yesterday?'

Kitty gave up on her sleep and reached for her sunglasses. 'What about it? Have you heard something more?'

Doreen shook her head impatiently before leaning forward so she couldn't be overheard. 'There's been things 'appening today,' she said quietly, 'and I reckon it only confirms wot I overheard.'

'What things?' asked Kitty with some alarm.

'There's been over twenty new admissions,' said Doreen, 'and apart from a couple of commandos and a Yank, the rest are all Canadians.'

She glanced towards the two women who were

sitting at a nearby table, and lowered her voice to a whisper. 'I 'ad a word with my mate who's in charge of cleaning the operating theatres, and she said the surgeons have been going full tilt all day. She hears enough to know that they've been dealing with bullet wounds, shrapnel, crush injuries, oil burns, salt water damage, and fire burns.'

'Then it's true,' sighed Kitty with deep sadness.

'It looks like it.' Doreen lit a cigarette. 'And from what I heard, there are more to come before the day's out. The blokes in admin are rushing about trying to get enough beds, and I wouldn't mind betting that people like me will be discharged early to make room.'

'But you've only been using your new leg for a couple of weeks,' Kitty protested. 'You can't possibly leave.'

Doreen smiled and reached for her hand. 'I'm ready enough, gel,' she said. 'It's time I shook off the dust of this place and went 'ome to face the real world. But when I comes back down south I'll visit yer. I promise.'

Kitty felt a deep pang of loss, for Doreen was the only person she'd got to know well here. 'I'm going to really miss you, Doreen. This place won't be the same without you, that's for sure.'

Doreen laughed. 'Gawd 'elp us all,' she spluttered. 'Some might say it'll be an improvement without me flashing me garters and making so much flamin' noise.' She cocked her head and shot a meaningful look at the two women on the next table who were looking at her with withering contempt. 'At least I ain't got me nose stuck up me arse like some I could mention,' she said loudly.

Kitty giggled. 'You are impossible, Doreen.'

Doreen grinned as she stubbed out her cigarette. 'Yeah, but I bet I cheer up more of this lot than those two sour-faced pusses.'

The two women in question moved from their chairs and rather pointedly went to another table at the far end of the terrace, where they put their heads together in an earnest and clearly self-righteous discussion. Both were high-ranking officers in the WRNS, and neither was popular, for it was well known amongst the other patients that they thought themselves far too superior to mix with anyone below their rank and social class.

'Good riddance to bad rubbish,' muttered Doreen. 'They deserve one another.' She looked away from the women and sat up abruptly. 'I don't Adam and Eve it,' she breathed.

'What?' Kitty turned to see what Doreen was on about, but apart from the usual gathering of patients, nurses and visitors, there didn't seem to be anything untoward.

'Ruby!' shouted Doreen as she grabbed her walking stick and waved it about frantically. 'Ruby Clark, over 'ere! It's me! Doreen Larkin.'

Kitty saw a slender, pretty girl with hair the colour of cobnuts turn from the doorway in surprise. She was accompanied by an older woman who could only have been her mother, for they were both short and delicately boned, with the same dark hair and eyes and determined chin.

'Doreen?' asked the girl as she approached. Then her face broke into a beaming smile and she hurried forward to embrace her. 'As I live and breathe. Doreen Larkin. Wot the bloody hell are you doing 'ere?'

'It's a bit of a bugger, but they cut me leg orff, so now I'm stuck with this.' She waggled her false leg about so they could admire it, then grinned at the older woman who was looking a bit unsure of herself. 'Wotcha, Ethel. Long time no see. How come you're 'ere, then? You weren't looking fer me, were ya?'

Ethel gave her a swift hug. 'Na, sorry love, we didn't know you was down this way, or we'd have been round to see yer and no mistake.'

'Sit down then and tell me what's been going on up in the smoke, and why yer here,' ordered Doreen.

'Mum will tell you everything, Doreen,' said Ruby breathlessly. 'There's someone I've got to see, and he'll think I ain't coming if I'm much longer.' Before Doreen could question her further, Ruby was hurrying across the terrace and through the French windows.

'What's going on, Ethel?' Doreen asked. 'Who's she visiting in such an 'urry? It can't be that rotten pig of a husband of hers, 'cos I 'eard he got killed in some accident.'

'I'm Kitty, by the way,' said Kitty, who was feeling distinctly left out of things.

'Sorry, gel,' said Doreen hurriedly. 'This is my mate Kitty, and she's an ATA pilot. Her and me 'ave both had a leg orff as you can see.'

'Nice to meet yer.' Ethel smiled at Kitty and settled into a chair. Digging in her handbag, she took a roll-up from a tobacco tin and lit it. Having expelled a cloud of smoke, she began to relax.

'The flaming bus from Cliffehaven were late,' she grumbled. 'Then it broke down coming up the flaming hill and we 'ad to walk the rest of the way. That's why we're late.'

'But what on earth are you doing down here at all?' asked Doreen.

'It's a long story,' said Ethel, who now had the roll-up firmly wedged in the corner of her lips. 'Ruby come down 'ere after that pig almost killed her,' she said grimly. 'She didn't have it too good for a bit but found a lovely place in the end, with Peggy Reilly.'

'But I know Peggy,' interrupted Kitty, who was utterly fascinated by the ever-lengthening ash on the end of Ethel's cigarette, which wobbled when she talked, but didn't fall. 'She comes to visit me twice a week.'

Ethel nodded. 'That sounds like 'er. A diamond, is Peggy. None better.' She took the cigarette out of her mouth and delicately tapped off the ash.

'Never mind all that,' said Doreen impatiently.

'Why're you here – and who is Ruby all dolled up for?'

Ethel had clearly decided to tell her tale in her own good time. 'After Ray were killed, Ruby come up to Bow and told me I gotta move down 'ere.' She sniffed. 'I were a bit reluctant, like, 'cos I ain't never left London before. But I could see it had done the gel good, so I said I'd give it a go.'

She shot the two girls a grin. 'And I'm glad I did, an' all. We got a lovely bungalow, and good jobs at the machine factory – and I've even made a few friends. There's quite a lot of gels from the East End down 'ere, so I feels quite at 'ome.'

Kitty was finding her accent quite difficult to follow, but she got the gist of it all as the fag ash grew longer and still trembled without falling down Ethel's front.

'So, who's she visiting, Ethel?' asked Doreen rather briskly.

Ethel stubbed out the cigarette. 'It's a young Canadian soldier called Mike Taylor,' she said. 'Seems she met 'im on the train when she were coming down 'ere that first time. He's ever so keen, 'cos he's been writing nearly every day since he left for some training camp.'

She seemed to drift off for a moment as she gazed across the lawn, then pulled her thoughts together. 'Anyway,' she continued, 'he sent Ruby a telegram to say he'd been injured and was about to be trans-ferred 'ere, and he'd really like to see 'er if she 'ad a mind to.' She chuckled. 'She certainly did, 'cos before I knows it, we're in our best togs and on the bus.'

'Was he involved in that raid in the Channel?' asked Kitty.

Ethel shrugged. 'I don't know about no raid. But I expect he'll tell Ruby what happened to 'im.' She looked towards the French windows and smiled. 'Here she is now. You can ask 'er yerself.'

Kitty watched as Ruby set a tray of tea things on the table. She looked much more relaxed, so her young man couldn't have been too badly injured, thank goodness. Kitty introduced herself as Doreen bombarded Ruby with questions.

Like her mother Ethel, Ruby took her time to answer. 'Mike wasn't making much sense,' she said after she'd stirred the tea in the pot and left it to stew. 'They filled him full of drugs, so he were 'alf asleep. But he were ever so pleased to see me,' she added with a sweet blush.

'Did he say anything about how he got his injuries?' asked Kitty before Doreen could butt in.

'Not much. He just said he were on a raid to France, and it all went belly up when they sailed straight into a Jerry convoy.' Her pretty face was shadowed with sadness. 'It were total carnage, 'e said, and although the RAF did their best to fight off the Jerry planes, and the battleships laid down a thick smokescreen, it's reckoned that over sixty percent of the total raiding party were lost.'

Everyone stayed silent as she blinked away her tears and determinedly began to pour the tea into the cups. 'He were one of the lucky ones,' she continued, ''cos he were still waiting to land when the Jerry convoy attacked and the big guns started firing from the beaches, but 'e could still see what was happening to all his mates.' Her voice broke despite her clear determination not to cry. 'He said he'd never forget what he saw, and that it would haunt him for the rest of 'is life.'

'Poor bloke,' murmured Doreen sadly. 'You can't even begin to imagine what 'e's been through, can you?'

'How bad orff is he?' asked Ethel as she softly put her hand on Ruby's knee.

Ruby lifted a determined chin as she passed the teacups round. 'He were shot in the shoulder, back and hip, Mum. Then, when his boat were blown up, he was thrown into the sea and got stuff in 'is eyes. The doctor reckons it were burning oil from the sunk ships and planes.'

Kitty winced at the stark images her words had evoked, but she could also see the concern for her daughter in Ethel's expression.

'He ain't gunna be blind, is he?' asked Ethel sharply.

Ruby shook her head. 'The doctor said the sight in his right eye is fine, and that 'e's hopeful the left one will heal with time.' She gave her mother a wan smile. 'He'll come through, Mum, and I'll be up here every day to visit, so 'e won't be on 'is own.'

'That's a big responsibility,' said Ethel, 'and you gotta think where all this might lead. After all, Rubes, you hardly know the bloke, and 'e might get ideas.'

Ruby rolled her eyes. 'I know 'im well enough, Mum. Blimey, we've been writing to each other fer weeks. Anyway, I want to look after 'im. He's a lovely bloke.'

Ethel folded her arms tightly, a fierce look on her face. 'So wot you gunna do if he don't get his sight back in that eye and 'e's sent home to Canada?'

Ruby shrugged. 'I dunno, Mum. It's too early to make them sort of decisions, but when the time comes, I'll know what to do for the best.'

'Well, I ain't moving to bleedin' Canada,' Ethel said with a sniff.

Ruby sighed. 'I don't remember you being asked if you wanna go ter Canada. Wind yer neck in, Mum, and 'ave a fag, why don't you?'

Ethel looked rather disgruntled as she lit a fag and stuck it into her mouth. 'Gawd,' she muttered. 'This flamin' war's a bugger, and no mistake.'

Peggy had been so busy she hadn't even had time to read the letters that had arrived from Jim. She left the girls to clean the kitchen after tea and went to settle Daisy in her cot, hoping she'd go to sleep quickly, for she was impatient to catch up on Jim's news.

But Daisy wasn't having any of it, for each time Peggy tucked her in, she wrestled her way out of the bedclothes and pulled herself up on the rails. With giggles of delight, Daisy kept this game going for some time before she got bored with it and finally fell asleep.

Peggy breathed a sigh of relief and went back into the almost deserted kitchen. It would be a quiet evening in, for Ron had already left on one of his Dad's Army night manoeuvres, Suzy and Fran were on night duty and the other three girls were catching up with their mending and ironing.

Harvey was stretched out on the rug in front of the low-smouldering fire in the range with little Monty curled between his great paws – the pair of them looking as innocent as a new day – and Cordelia was knitting something that defied description, and would, no doubt, have to be unpicked soon and started again.

Peggy took the letters from the mantelpiece and sat down. There were three in all, which was a rare treat – but the numbers Jim had scrawled in the corner of the envelope showed that one of them was the missing letter between the last two she'd got the week before. It was all a bit frustrating, but then there was a war on, and with so many letters to deliver it was hardly surprising there was the odd slip-up or delay.

She scanned them swiftly, and then saw the words she'd been wanting to read for so long. 'He's coming home on leave,' she said joyfully as she waved the letter about.

'He's got a reprieve?' said Cordelia as she fiddled with her hearing aid. 'Why? What's he done to get himself arrested?'

'No, Cordelia,' Peggy said loudly. 'He hasn't done anything wrong. He's coming home on leave.'

'Oh, that is good news,' sighed Cordelia. 'I've missed his wicked smile and winning ways. When's he coming?'

'He thinks early in September.' Peggy read the scrawled writing again and then held the letters to her heart. 'Oh, Cordelia, I've waited and waited for this. I hope he can be home for more than just a few days.'

'I'm sure he will,' said Cordelia comfortably. 'After all, he's had no home leave since he went away, and even the army must realise that's not good for a family man.'

'I don't think the army gives much attention to such things,' Peggy replied. 'But to have him home for just a little while will be wonderful.'

Cordelia put down her knitting and regarded Peggy over the top of her spectacles. 'It certainly might put you in a better mood,' she said with a wry smile. 'You've been on edge and crotchety for weeks.'

Peggy could feel the shame redden her cheeks. 'I've rather let things get on top of me, haven't I?' she admitted softly.

'It's only natural,' said Cordelia. 'What with every-thing you've had to put up with since your operation, I'm only surprised you haven't crumbled completely.' She looked down at Harvey and Monty. 'That pup's very sweet, but I suspect he's the last straw.'

Peggy shook her head. 'I'm used to chaos, and to Ron's shenanigans – and I certainly would never get rid of Monty. He's part of the family now, and I'm sure that once he gets a bit older he won't be such a nuisance.'

'Hmph.' Cordelia picked up her knitting again. 'That's what you said about Harvey – and he's as bad now as ever he was.'

Harvey and Monty looked up at Peggy with big, soulful eyes as if to reassure her that they were deeply hurt by the accusation and completely innocent of such slander.

Peggy chuckled and returned to her letters, knowing full well that she'd give them both a biscuit before too long. A house wasn't a home without a dog or two by the hearth – and she could forgive them anything now that Jim was coming home.

Jim wrote an eloquent letter, and as Peggy slowly absorbed every precious word, it was as if he was standing beside her and telling her his news in his soft, lilting Irish accent. His new posting was much more comfortable, for instead of being housed in barracks, Jim and the rest of the men in his REME unit had been billeted with local families. It seemed that Jim had fallen on his feet as usual, Peggy noted wryly, for he was living with two elderly spinsters and they were spoiling him rotten.

He was continuing to drive some colonel about, and as he seemed to have plenty of spare time, he'd done some repairs to the spinsters' cottage, chopped wood and managed to snare a few rabbits for the pot. The exact location of this billet was blanked out, but from the description, Peggy could guess it was a small country village with plenty of woods and streams nearby where, no doubt, Jim found it easy to go poaching.

'Like father, like son,' she murmured as she finally tucked the letters back in their envelopes. 'He and Ron are as bad as each other, bless them.' But as she placed the letters in the box she kept for just such a purpose, she was thankful that Jim was safe and being well looked after, and not stuck in some horrid desert fighting Rommel.

'Can you help me with this, dear?' Cordelia asked plaintively. 'I seem to have made a bit of a mistake.'

Peggy regarded the tangle of wool hanging from the knitting needle. It was a complete mess, but as she had nothing much else to do for once, she was happy to try and help untangle it.

With the knitting completely unravelled and started again, Peggy left Cordelia to it, stoked the fire to life and began to make hot cocoa for everyone. It was a treat they all looked forward to, and the girls would be down in a minute. But, as she took the pan of milk from the hob, her pleasant thoughts were disturbed by a knock at the front door.

With an anxious glance at the clock, she abandoned the cocoa and hurried into the hall. It was after ten, and visitors at this time of night usually meant trouble. With rising, almost smothering fear, she opened the front door.

Her heart thudded, and the lump of terror in her throat made it impossible to speak as she saw who was standing on her doorstep. She knew for certain now that something terrible had happened.

Chapter Seventeen

Ron was sitting comfortably in a deckchair with a tin mug of hot cocoa and an unlit pipe, deep below the ground. Neither his family nor his colleagues in the Home Guard knew about this place, and as far as everyone was concerned, he was on night manoeuvres. And yet this secret bunker and huge armament store was only one of hundreds buried along the south coast, and if there was an invasion, the men guarding these bunkers would be the front line of defence.

He cupped the warm metal in his cold hands, for it was damp, gloomy and chill down here, despite the small paraffin stove and the flickering light from the lantern that hung from the concrete ceiling. At the start of the war, each bunker had been manned by eight men, but as the threat of invasion had waned in the past year, the patrols had been cut to two men on each shift, with a radio line of communication to HQ should there be any alerts.

Ron had been recruited at the very beginning of the war by Colonel Gubbins, who'd been ordered by Churchill to form a force of civilian volunteers from the Home Guard. The recruits were mostly men who knew the surrounding countryside well, and within the ranks of this secret force were fishermen, gamekeepers, farmers, foresters, ramblers and wily old poachers like himself. If there was an invasion – which was looking ever more unlikely – then Ron and the other recruits would sabotage the enemy convoys and their fuel and supply dumps, blow up railway lines, roads and bridges, and make the enemy-held aerodromes unusable.

Ron had experience of sabotage from the previous war, for he'd been behind enemy lines on many occasions to clear the way for advancing troops and, to his regret, had learned to kill swiftly and silently. He glanced across at the sheathed knife which was part of his kit. It was wickedly sharp and could kill a man in an instant – but then so could the rifle which leaned against the upturned crate they were using for a table.

He gave a wry smile, for people thought the Home Guard was a bit of a joke, with the old men and callow boys marching down Cliffehaven High Street in their ill-fitting uniforms and playing at soldiering. How surprised they would have been if they'd known about the secret force recruited from those ranks, whose age and experience meant they could still play an important role in defending their country.

He had just finished his cocoa and was contemplating the unopened packet of digestive biscuits, when he heard the retired Rear Admiral returning from his inspection of the ammunition store which lay a mile away through a maze of tunnels. Maurice Price liked to stretch his legs by taking that walk, and after spending the previous day cooped up at Admiralty House in London, he probably needed the exercise.

'Everything all right?' Ron asked rather needlessly, for they'd both know it if something was wrong – the whole place would go up like a giant firework display.

'No deterioration.' Maurice placed his rifle next to Ron's and reached for the flask of hot cocoa. 'The charges, detonators and explosives are well insulated against the damp and cold in the lead-lined trunks. Nothing has been disturbed.'

He poured the hot drink into a tin mug and warmed his hands in front of the little stove. 'I wish we could smoke down here,' he grumbled. 'There's nothing like a pipe to while away the time.'

'I agree,' said Ron as he examined his own, cold pipe with some longing. It was a common complaint amongst the men who had to stay down here, but regulations had to be obeyed. Cigarette and pipe-smoke could drift out of the air vents and be smelled by anyone who happened to be passing – though that was highly unlikely, for they were buried deep in the hills around the Cliffe estate and well camouflaged by brambles, gorse and fallen trees.

Ron reached for the biscuits. 'At least we've plenty of food to keep us going.' He opened the packet and eyed the vast number of crates and boxes of tinned food surrounding them. 'There're enough supplies down here to keep half the town fed for a month.'

Maurice took a biscuit and bit into it with relish. 'Emergency rations, Ron,' he said, 'but I doubt a few biscuits here and there will make much difference.'

They sat in companionable silence as the retired Admiral finished his cocoa and polished off another two biscuits. Ron liked Maurice, and although they weren't class equals, they enjoyed one another's company when they were assigned the same night duty.

Maurice was still a handsome, vigorous man. Despite having retired from the navy some years ago, he was often called to Admiralty House, where his long experience and wise advice was highly respected. He was an old seadog, of a different calibre to Ron, but the pair of them could tell a rollicking good tale to pass away the time.

'I suppose you've heard the rumours?' Maurice asked after a while.

'About the raid on Dieppe?'

Maurice's expression was grim as he nodded. 'The worst kept secret of the war so far – more's the pity. A disaster like that is bad for morale.'

'But with so many people involved, it was bound to get out sooner or later,' said Ron. He regarded the other man solemnly. 'Is that why you've been in London, Maurice?'

He nodded as he stared into the glowing stove. 'It was a waste of time,' he said dolefully. 'Rather like shutting the stable door after the horse has bolted.'

'What really happened, Maurice? Or aren't you allowed to say?'

Maurice tucked his thick woollen scarf more firmly round his neck and ears and pulled on his gloves. 'Most of the rumours are true,' he confessed, 'so I'm probably not speaking out of turn if I tell you it was a total cock-up from beginning to end.'

Ron waited patiently while he collected his thoughts. They both knew that whatever was said down here would not be repeated, and Maurice's continued connection with the top brass meant that he knew a great deal of what went on behind the headlines in the newspapers – not that Ron expected to be told everything, Maurice was far too careful for that, but at least he'd get part of the truth.

'The Russians called for a Second Front after the Germans invaded them back in 1941,' said Maurice thoughtfully. 'A second call was made by the Americans to do the same, but Churchill wasn't keen. There had been several small raids on the French coast which had been quite successful, mostly because of the new Commando Force, but these raids were, in actual fact, only mounted for propaganda purposes and to boost morale.'

Maurice leaned back in his chair and folded his arms. 'In March this year, Admiral Lord Mountbatten succeeded Admiral Keyes as Chief of Combined Operations, and a successful raid on St Nazaire encouraged the Chiefs of Staff Committee to mount a further, much larger attack in early July. Dieppe seemed an ideal target. It's less than seventy miles from the English coast, would allow the attacking force to approach in darkness, and is also within fighter aircraft range.'

Maurice paused as he reached for his unlit pipe, woefully regarded the empty bowl and then chewed on the stem. 'I can't go into the details of the planned attack,' he said, 'suffice it to say enemy defences, radar installations, power stations and so on were to be destroyed, and the forty invasion barges thought to be in the harbour at the time were to be captured and put to our own use.'

'But there was no raid in July, was there?' asked Ron.

Maurice shook his head. 'Operation Rutter was cancelled due to bad weather and a German air attack which sank two of our ships anchored off the Isle of Wight. Some military leaders, including General Montgomery, were delighted that this would probably be the end of any more plans to raid France, for there had been serious misgiving over the wisdom of making a dangerous Channel attack using inexperienced and untried troops.'

'But they went ahead anyway,' muttered Ron.

Maurice gave a deep sigh. 'Churchill was in a difficult position, because he had to appease both the Americans and the Russians, and needed to be seen to be doing something decisive – but a cross-Channel raid was a huge risk. Mountbatten argued that Dieppe was the only choice, for there was no other target that could be reconnoitred by Combined Ops in time to mount another big raid this year.'

Maurice gave up chewing his pipe stem and shoved it in his jacket pocket. 'Operation Jubilee went ahead with a force of around six thousand, nearly five thousand of which were Canadian – the rest were Commandos, Americans and official observers. The Royal Navy assembled two hundred and fifty-two ships and landing craft, and the RAF provided sixty-three squadrons which included light bombers, two bomb-carrying Hurricanes and fifty-six fighters.'

'I can't tell you the finer details, Ron, but our communications were all but non-existent through some almighty cock-up, and there was a fatal delay in getting the landing craft ashore before the sun came up. There was a German convoy hugging the coast of France at the time, and our fleet ran straight into it.'

He dipped his chin, his voice breaking with emotion as he continued his tragic story. 'Our destroyer, HMS *Berkeley*, and thirty-three landing craft were sunk with five hundred and fifty dead or wounded. The RAF lost one hundred and six aircraft, with sixty-two killed, thirty wounded and seventeen posted as missing. And the British Commandos lost two hundred and forty-seven men. But the Canadians bore the brunt of the losses, for nine hundred men were killed, hundreds more were injured, and it's just been confirmed that nearly two thousand were taken prisoner.'

Maurice gave a shuddering sigh. 'All in all, it was a complete and absolute disaster.'

Ron placed his hand on the slumped shoulder and gave it a squeeze of understanding, for he could see the anguish in the other man's face and knew there were no words that could bring him comfort. The tragic loss of so many young lives was a heavy burden to bear, and Ron suspected that his friend felt each and every one of them personally.

Kitty had enjoyed sitting back and listening to Doreen chattering away to her friends from Bow, and although she'd only understood part of what they were saying, she'd felt quite sorry to have to leave them when she'd had to go back to the gym for her final session of the day.

Ethel was quite a character, with an acerbic outer shell that hid a caring and rather worried mother. Ruby was more gentle, but having heard the terrible story behind her coming to Cliffehaven from Ethel, Kitty suspected that there was a core of steel beneath that sweetness.

Kitty had come to the conclusion that they were

born survivors, and regardless of might happen next, they would come through. But she understood Ethel's concern over Ruby's blossoming relationship with Mike Taylor, for sooner or later the girl would have to make some tough decisions.

Kitty had worked hard during that half hour in the gym, and had almost fallen asleep over her supper despite the excited chatter going on around her. The news of the raid was no longer a secret after the sudden influx of so many injured Canadians. Speculation was rife and the gossip-mill was grinding deep and swiftly, for although it was now known that the disaster had happened off the coast of Dieppe, there was precious little further information.

It appeared that all those taking part had been ordered to say nothing, and Kitty could only assume that Mike had been so heavily drugged, he'd been unaware of how careless he'd been to tell Ruby what he did. Doreen seemed to understand this too, and with a tacit agreement between them, neither revealed Mike's version of the full horror of what had happened on the nineteenth of August.

Kitty had waited until it was clear there would be no visitors for her that night, then, as Doreen entertained her usual coterie of admirers, she curled up in bed and was soon fast asleep.

She woke early and stretched luxuriously. She'd had a very good night's sleep and was feeling refreshed and eager for the day. Her first session in the gym was scheduled for nine o'clock, so she had plenty of time to have a bath and eat breakfast.

The major luxury of being able to get about on crutches was to use a proper lavatory instead of a bedpan, and to soak in a hot bath. She needed help in and out of it, but the nurse was happy to leave her in solitary splendour for a while, and she relished these quiet moments to herself.

Having finished her bath, she made sure her stump was dry, massaged and powdered, and then applied the bandage and thick sock. Her underwear was utilitarian and came from RAF stores, and as she pulled on the unflattering knickers and fastened her bra, she grimaced at her reflection in the bathroom mirror. She was far too skinny, and her arms looked like a couple of matchsticks. But the scar on her abdomen was fading to silver and her hair had at last begun to grow. It would soon be time to seek out the hairdresser when she came next.

With this thought, Kitty sat down and eased on a pair of lightweight slacks, and fastened the buttons on the thin cotton blouse she'd bought in London at the beginning of the year. Charlotte had thoughtfully packed all her things from the cottage they'd shared and had organised for them to be flown down to Cliffehaven. Roger had turned up the previous week with her two cases, and once he'd gone back to the aerodrome, she'd cried bitter tears over the lovely shoes that she could no longer wear.

Determinedly pushing this memory away, Kitty slipped her foot into a flat sandal, grabbed her crutches and headed for the dining room and breakfast. She had another long and probably tiring day ahead of her, and she couldn't afford to weaken her resolve by feeling sorry for herself.

The dining room was noisy and crowded as the NAAFI staff served porridge, scrambled dried egg and brown toast. Tea was poured from a huge urn, and there were jugs of milk and orange juice on every table.

Kitty eyed the orange juice with delight. 'Goodness,' she breathed as she sat next to Doreen. 'Where on earth did that come from?'

'Courtesy of the Yanks, evidently,' she replied. 'I just wish they'd give us some decent flamin' bread. This stuff tastes like something scraped off the bottom of a bird cage.'

Kitty poured some of the juice into her glass and took a sip. 'It's made of real oranges,' she said in awe. She regarded Doreen's rather sour expression as her friend chewed on the toast. 'I don't know how you can possibly compare that bread to the scrapings off a bird cage,' she said with a wry smile. 'When was the last time you ate seed pellets and bird droppings?'

Doreen finished chewing and laughed. 'You know what I mean, Kitty. This stuff looks horrible and tastes worse. What I wouldn't do for a decent white bloomer, all warm and crusty straight from the oven,' she added on a sigh.

Kitty's mouth watered at the thought, but she quickly ate her porridge and dipped into the rapidly cooling scrambled egg. 'The dried egg isn't much to write home about either,' she replied as she regarded the yellow, congealed mess on her friend's plate. 'But it's better than nothing. Aren't you going to eat that?'

Doreen shook her head. 'Nah. You 'ave it.'

'Thanks, it would be a shame to see it go to waste, and I'm ravenous this morning.' Kitty scraped it onto her own plate, added a healthy dollop of tomato sauce, and tucked into the unappetising-looking food with relish.

'Gawd, gel,' said Doreen with a grimace. 'I don't know 'ow you do it.'

'If you eat it quickly it isn't so bad,' replied Kitty as she scraped the plate clean.

Doreen rested her elbows on the table and drank her tea as she listened to the gossip going on around her. 'I popped in to see 'ow Ruby's bloke was getting on,' she murmured some minutes later.

'Trust you,' teased Kitty. 'So, did you get to speak to him?'

'Nah, he were out cold.' She shot Kitty a lascivious grin. 'I can see why Ruby's so taken with 'im,' she said, ''cos even covered in bandages, he's a bit of all right. He's got broad shoulders, a lovely brown chest and good strong, muscled arms. I tell you straight, Kitty, I wouldn't mind 'aving a bit of that.'

'You're impossible, Doreen,' Kitty spluttered in her tea. 'Leave him alone. He's spoken for.'

'Yeah, don't I know it, and I ain't one to nick a mate's feller, but cor,' she shivered delightedly, 'he's one 'andsome bit of stuff and no mistake.'

Kitty giggled as she scraped some margarine onto the dry brown wheatmeal toast. 'Did you manage to find out how he's doing while you were ogling him?'

'He's doing well, according to the nurse. She says the bullets have been taken out and the fracture in his arm was a clean break, so it should heal quickly.' She lit a cigarette and stared into the teacup. 'But they are worried about the sight in his left eye. It seems it were more badly damaged than they thought.'

'If it doesn't heal, there's a good chance he'll be discharged from his regiment and sent home,' replied Kitty sadly. 'Poor Ruby. It seems her budding romance is fated.'

Doreen gave a snort of laughter. 'You don't know Ruby,' she said. 'Once she gets something in 'er 'ead there ain't nothing gunna shift it. Mark my words, Kitty – if 'e goes back to Canada she won't be far behind 'im.'

'But what about Ethel?'

'Ethel might moan and groan, but she ain't got

nothing to go back to in London. Her old man's a right brute, and when 'e gets back from the war he'll soon be up to 'is old tricks – bashing 'er about and drinking 'er wages.' Doreen puffed on her cigarette. 'Nah, I reckon she'll go where Ruby goes, and if that's Canada, then good luck to the pair of 'em.'

'I doubt either of them will be going anywhere until the war's over,' said Kitty.

'Yeah, yer right.' Doreen stubbed out her cigarette in the small metal ashtray and turned to Kitty, her face rather solemn for once. 'Speaking of which,' she said. 'I've been given me marching orders.'

'No,' gasped Kitty. 'Oh, no, Doreen, not already?'

Doreen nodded and squeezed her hand. 'Sorry, gel, but I ain't got no choice. They needs me bed.'

Kitty was blinded with tears. 'When are you leaving?'

'In half an hour,' she said as she gave Kitty a swift hug. 'Don't get all soppy on me, Kitty. I 'ate good-byes – and I'm gunna miss you too, and that's a fact.'

'I'll come and see you off,' said Kitty, reaching for her crutches.

'Nah, you stay 'ere and finish that toast. I ain't one for tears and such, but if you comes to wave me orff, then I don't know what I might do.'

She pushed back from the table, leaning heavily on her walking stick, and gave Kitty a sweet smile. 'I'll send you a postcard or two, though me writing's not up to much.' She dug in her trouser pocket and handed Kitty a slip of paper. 'This is the address of me billet down 'ere. I should be back there in a couple of weeks.'

'I'll write and let you know what's happening here,' Kitty promised as she fought back the tears. 'And once I'm up and about on two feet again, we'll have to go out for a celebratory drink or three.'

Doreen smiled although her green eyes were also suspiciously bright. 'Good luck, mate, and I wanna be there when you climb into yer Spitfire again.'

'I'll arrange it, I promise,' said Kitty, 'but it could be a while yet.'

The bright ginger hair bounced around Doreen's face as she shook her head. 'Nah. The Kitty I know won't take long at all to get into 'er stride. You'll be outta here and up in the skies before yer know it.' She rested her hand on Kitty's shoulder. Stay safe, gel,' she murmured, 'and don't let the buggers grind you down.'

Kitty watched as she walked away, head high, waving goodbye to everyone. And then she was gone.

As the door clattered behind her, Kitty eyed the cold toast and greasy margarine with distaste and pushed the plate away. Doreen's departure would leave a huge void. Her vitality and cheerfulness had helped Kitty through those dark first days and she would miss her acutely.

But as the noise in the canteen went on around

her, Kitty knew that life had to go on for both of them, and that their friendship was strong enough to endure this brief separation. They would meet again outside this place, she was certain, so there was no point in moping.

She pushed back from the table, grabbed her crutches and went to the pigeonholes in the hall to see if she had any post. Letters from home were always a real boost, and she was in need of some good news.

There were three comic postcards from Charlotte and a letter excitedly detailing her plans for the wedding, and odd snippets of gossip from the ferry pools. She was now sharing the cottage with a girl called Bunty Brown, who was proving to be extremely irritating with her silly chatter, and frightfully untidy.

Kitty smiled at this, for Charlotte wasn't exactly the most organised of people, and she'd lost count of the times she'd had to hunt for a lost shoe or blouse amongst the piles of clothing she'd left on the floor.

She quickly checked the rest of her mail. There was a saucy seaside postcard from Freddy, who promised to come and see her soon, and another two from Roger telling her to keep her landing gear down and her chin up. Dear Roger. He was such a lovely man, and she counted herself lucky to have him as a friend.

There were two more letters from Charlotte's

mother, who wrote every week to relay village gossip, repeat her invitation for Kitty to come and recuperate at her home, and to keep her up with the plans for the wedding reception. There were more letters from girls in the ATA, another card from Margot Gore, her CO at Hamble Pool, wishing her a speedy recovery and apologies for not coming to visit – and three precious airmails from Argentina.

Kitty longed to tear them open and read them, but caution made her check her watch. She didn't have time and was already in danger of being late to the gym. With deep regret, she stuffed all the post back into the pigeonhole to savour later, and headed down the long corridor towards the physiotherapy wing.

'Pilot Officer Pargeter?'

Kitty paused and turned with a frown towards the unfamiliar voice to find that she had been addressed by the new matron – a short, rotund little woman whose shape rather reminded Kitty of a cottage loaf. 'Yes?'

Matron's smile was soft in her pleasantly rounded face. 'I wonder if you could come with me, dear,' she said.

'I have to be in the gym,' she replied, 'and I'm already late.'

'The doctor will understand,' she murmured as she held open the door to one of the small consulting rooms. 'This is rather important.'

Kitty felt a stab of alarm. 'What's happened?'

'Come along, dear.' Matron gently pressed her hand into Kitty's back. 'There are people waiting to see you.'

The alarm was sharper now and she could feel her heart crashing against her ribs as she approached the open door. 'Who?' she asked fearfully.

Matron pushed the door fully open.

Kitty saw Peggy Reilly and Commander Black waiting there and knew in an instant why they'd come. 'Freddy,' she gasped. 'It's Freddy, isn't it?' The room seemed to sway and the floor tilted beneath her as a terrible darkness claimed her.

As her eyelids fluttered open she looked blearily up into Peggy's concerned face, wondering what she was doing here. And then she remembered. 'Freddy,' she gasped as she sat up on the examination couch and clutched at Peggy's hand. 'Please, please don't tell me he's dead,' she sobbed.

'There's no confirmation of that, Kitty,' said Peggy carefully. 'So please don't imagine the worst.' She dried Kitty's tears with a clean handkerchief.

'Drink some water, dear,' said Matron. 'It will help to clear your head so you can concentrate properly on what Commander Black has to say.'

As Peggy put a comforting arm round her, Kitty clutched the damp handkerchief and drank the cold water, her tearful gaze fixed on Commander Black. Waving the glass away once her head had cleared, she steeled herself to remain calm. 'What's happened to him?' she rasped.

'He was on ops over Dieppe,' he replied. 'His Spitfire was shot down, but there are two confirmed sightings of his parachute opening before the plane crashed.'

'So he made it out,' breathed Kitty. 'Did anyone see him land?'

Commander Black shook his head. 'As you can imagine, there was a lot of activity at the time and the navy was laying down a thick blanket of smoke to cover the raiding fleet. He's been posted as "Missing in Action", and it's hoped that he was taken prisoner. I'm sorry, Kitty, but as yet I have no confirmation of that.'

Kitty had stark, terrifying images of Freddy falling from the skies, of him landing and injuring himself and being left to die in some remote corner no one thought of searching – or being killed by a stray bullet, or trigger-happy Germans. 'How soon will you know?' she asked fearfully.

Commander Black cleared his throat. 'There are already reports coming in of Canadian and naval POWs – the Germans are efficient if nothing else. I hope to hear soon.'

'And if you don't? Will that mean he's . . . he's . . . dead?'

'It could mean a number of things,' he said carefully. 'Freddy is resourceful, and if he survived the landing and hasn't been captured or badly wounded, then I wouldn't put it past him to try and make his way back to England.'

Kitty clung to that hope with every fibre of her being. 'Yes,' she whispered. 'That's exactly what he'd do.'

Peggy held her hand tightly. 'Keep faith in that thought, Kitty,' she urged. 'Don't give up on him now.'

But the doubts were already crowding in. 'How many others have been accounted for?' Kitty asked.

Commander Black's face was lined with weariness and grief. 'The RAF lost one hundred and six aircraft and sixty-two brave young men. There are thirty wounded and seventeen unaccounted for. Freddy is one of the latter.'

'Oh, God,' she groaned in an agony of despair as the hot tears rolled down her face and she remembered the laughter and the riotous game of pirates in the Cliffe mess. 'I can't bear to think of it.' A terrible suspicion made her look up at the Commander through her tears. 'Roger Makepeace was on Freddy's wing. Did he . . .? Was he . . .?'

'He's fine,' he said quickly. 'In fact he wanted to come with me to tell you about Freddy, but I didn't think it was necessary as you have Peggy to lean on.'

Kitty gripped Peggy's hand, warmed by her presence and deeply grateful for her support. 'Have my parents been informed?' she asked tentatively.

'Not yet. I thought it better to wait until I had more information.'

'And his fiancée, Charlotte?'

'I telephoned Hamble and spoke to her CO. She will tell her as soon as she returns to the ferry pool this evening.'

'Poor Charlotte,' she sobbed. 'She was so excited about their wedding – making plans – talking about dresses and cakes and . . . and . . .'

He put a sympathetic hand on her shoulder. 'I'm so sorry I have to be the bearer of such tidings, Kitty, but the moment I have any news of Freddy, I will see you're informed immediately.'

She nodded as he picked up his gold-braided peaked cap and tucked it under his arm. 'Thank you,' she murmured. 'It can't have been easy.'

His smile was wan. 'Unfortunately it's something I've had to learn to do,' he sighed, 'and you're right, it never gets any easier.'

He softly kissed Peggy's cheek. 'I have to get back to Cliffe, but there will be a car and driver waiting for you when you're ready to go home, Peggy.' With that, he nodded to Matron and they both left the room.

As the door closed behind them Kitty sank into Peggy's embrace and clung to her as the fears for Freddy multiplied and her sobs reflected the awful pain that was squeezing her heart. Freddy mustn't be dead. He simply couldn't be, for she would have known, would have felt something – for a light as bright as Freddy couldn't just be snuffed out.

Yet it was as if the light in her world had grown suddenly dim as the doubts and terrors closed in, and she held Peggy even tighter as if, by doing so, she could will that light to shine brighter and give her hope.

Chapter Eighteen

Peggy held fiercely to the slender, sobbing girl and prayed with all her heart that the delightful young man she'd met once and spoken to several times on the telephone had survived. Such a bright and lively force of energy surely couldn't be wiped out so cruelly – could it?

And yet, as she continued to comfort Kitty and blink back her own tears, she knew all too well how swiftly this war could snatch loved ones away. Her two nephews had been on the same minesweeper when it had struck that fatal mine – and they too had been young and vital, with so much more life to live. Frank and Pauline treasured their only surviving son and prayed he would be spared now that he'd been assigned to a safer posting in London, but Peggy knew they still mourned the two who would never come home again.

She looked out of the window to the garden. There were men and women gathered on the broad, sunlit terrace, or playing croquet, hampered by walking sticks, crutches, plaster of Paris and false limbs. But despite these handicaps there was much laughter.

The human spirit was amazing, she thought, for regardless of what people went through, there was a spark of determination to overcome and survive, and to make the best of things. These youngsters like Kitty had risked their lives for their country and were paying the price, just as almost an entire generation of young men had paid with their lives in the first war.

We never learn, she thought sadly. *That war was supposed to be the one to end all wars, but here we are again, and it's the young who are making the sacrifices to keep us safe.*

'I'm sorry, Peggy,' sniffed Kitty as she eased from the embrace. 'I've made your cardigan all damp and creased your lovely frock.'

'Good heavens, that doesn't matter a jot,' she replied warmly. Digging into her handbag, she pulled out another clean handkerchief from the wad she'd shoved in there before leaving the house. 'Here we are, dear,' she said softly. 'You dry your eyes while I pour out the tea.'

Kitty looked puzzled as she eyed the tray on the desk. 'Where did that come from?'

'Matron brought it in a few minutes ago.' She poured out the rather stewed tea and added a generous amount of sugar to both cups before topping up with milk and giving it a good stir. 'Here we are, dear,' she said with a gentle smile. 'There's nothing like a good cuppa to fortify you.'

Kitty put the cup and saucer on the examination

couch and wriggled down until her foot touched the floor. 'I'm getting a bit stiff sitting up there,' she explained as she looked round for her crutches, which had been put on the far side of the room. 'Can you help me into one of those chairs?'

Peggy held onto her arm as she hopped the few steps to the nearest chair and sat down. Then she fetched the crutches and the tea and put them both where Kitty could reach them. She settled into the other chair, feeling rather stiff herself after holding such an awkward position for so long on that examination couch, and it was nice to be able to relax a bit and gather her wits.

'Matron's nice, isn't she?' she said after a long, soothing drink of tea. 'A far cry from the last one.'

'She could only have arrived a few hours ago,' said Kitty. 'I've never seen her before.'

'Well, she came last night on the late train, and the hospital sent a staff car to pick her up,' said Peggy. 'She's from some unpronounceable village in Wales and before she retired from nursing was Matron at the Cardiff General. She's been widowed for many years and has no children to worry about, so when the call went out for a replacement here, she rented her little house out and jumped on the first train.'

Peggy smiled. 'She's a nice little body, with a kind heart. But I suspect she won't stand any nonsense.'

Despite her deep sorrow, Kitty eyed her in astonishment. 'How on earth do you know all that?'

Peggy chuckled. 'I like talking to people, and a friendly smile works wonders.' She watched as Kitty sipped her tea. The colour was coming back into her face, she noted, and she seemed calmer now, and yet Peggy knew her heart must be aching and her thoughts in turmoil.

'I was wondering if you'd like to come home with me for a bit,' she began. 'You see, I have a lovely spare room at the moment, and it would be a shame to let it go to waste.'

Kitty slowly shook her head. 'That's very kind of you, Peggy, but I have to get used to using my new leg, and the training is very intense. It's probably better if I stay here.' She shot Peggy a wan smile. 'Besides, you have quite enough to do without me cluttering up the place.'

'There's always room for one more,' said Peggy determinedly. 'And Rita said that either she or one of the others from the fire station can bring you up here each morning and pick you up in the evening. So you'll still get your treatments, but you'll have the comfort of home every night.'

She could see the girl was wavering and pushed the point. 'Cordelia is cooking her famous fish pie tonight, so you certainly don't want to miss that,' she said. 'And I've made your room all lovely and clean, with fresh sheets and towels, and a vase of roses out of the garden. It's on the same floor as the bathroom, so you'll be able to manage very well.'

There were tears shining in Kitty's eyes. 'But I can't expect you to take me in like that,' she softly protested.

'Why ever not?' Peggy looked at her in astonishment. 'We're friends, aren't we? And friends help one another in times of trouble.' She took Kitty's hand. 'I know I'm not your mother and can only be a very poor substitute, but I'll do my very best for you, Kitty, and my home is your home for as long as you need it.'

The tears were running freely again. 'But I need help to get in and out of the bath, and it will be an awful bother getting me to the hospital and back every day – and I don't know if I can manage stairs yet,' she said all in a rush. 'It's very kind, Peggy, and I do appreciate it, but . . .'

'When I was having my ectopic and the air raid siren was going and Daisy was screaming, I slid down the stairs on my behind,' Peggy interrupted firmly. 'I'm sure you could manage that. As for the bath – there are two nurses in the house as well as me, and I'm sure that between us we can cope with a little sprite like you.'

Kitty covered her face with her hands as she wept. 'You're so kind,' she sobbed. 'So very kind. But I can't ask you to . . .'

'Now, now,' interrupted Peggy as she put her arm round her and held her close. 'We'll have none of that. You're coming home with me, and that's an end to it. I've arranged the government grant with the billeting people, and discussed it with Gwen. She agrees that a good dose of home cooking and a bit of pampering will do you the world of good.'

Kitty sniffed back her tears and regarded Peggy with a frown. 'Who the heck is Gwen?'

'Well, Matron, of course. Didn't I tell you?'

Kitty shook her head and gave a sigh as she mopped her tears and blew her nose. 'You really are the most surprising, kind-hearted and yet determined woman I've ever met,' she said. 'Are you absolutely sure about this, Peggy? Please be honest and tell me if you have even the slightest doubt.'

Peggy handed her the crutches. 'Go and wash your face, then pack up your locker. I've already asked Gwen to get your cases out of storage and they should be in the staff car ready and waiting for you by now.'

Kitty stared at her and then giggled. 'You don't play fair,' she murmured.

'Playing fair doesn't always get you where you want to be,' replied Peggy, 'and once I've set my heart on something I'm like a terrier. Now shoo. I'll meet you out at the front after I've said goodbye to Gwen and fetched the schedule for your physio and your pills.'

Kitty took the crutches and gave Peggy a kiss on her soft cheek before she left the room and headed back to the pigeonholes in the hall. The card from

Freddy was on the top of the pile and fresh tears gathered as she read the scrawl on the back.

See you soon, Sis. Try not to prang the crutches like you do planes.
Freddy XXX

'Yes,' she breathed. 'You'll come back. I just know you will.' With her precious letters and cards tucked safely in her trouser pocket, she went back to the ward.

Nurse Hopkins had already emptied her locker into the small vanity case Charlotte had given her on her last visit. 'I think that's everything, but you'd better check,' she said brightly.

'But how did you know I was leaving?'

The nurse chuckled. 'Peggy Reilly is obviously very persuasive,' she replied. 'Our new matron came in to tell us you were to be an outpatient from today and that you'd be living with Peggy from now on.'

Kitty sank onto the bed, overwhelmed by the speed of everything, and feeling rather disorientated and helpless. 'I don't know that I'm ready,' she said hesitantly. 'It's all happened so quickly and . . .'

'It's all right, Kitty,' soothed the nurse as she sat on the bed beside her and took her hand. 'Things might look bleak at the moment, but Peggy is a kind soul. She'll make you feel at home and be there when you need a shoulder to cry on.'

Kitty nodded. 'I know, but I'm afraid,' she admitted softly. 'Afraid of being stared at – of being different.'

'I understand,' murmured the nurse. 'You feel safe here surrounded by others with similar injuries. But you can't hide here forever, Kitty.'

Kitty knew she was right as she gripped her hand. 'It's the moment of truth, isn't it?'

'It's the moment when you take your first step back into the big wide world out there, certainly,' the nurse agreed. 'It will be daunting at first, I can't pretend otherwise. But with Peggy's love and kindness, you'll do it, Kitty. I just know you will.'

Kitty used the soggy handkerchief again, and then reached for her crutches. 'Thanks, Suzanne. I'm sorry to be so feeble.'

The nurse picked up the little vanity case and smiled. 'Come on then. Let's get you on your way. I understand you have a chauffeur-driven staff car to drive you home in style, so we'd better not keep it waiting.'

Kitty bravely smiled back, but her thoughts were in a jumble. She wasn't going home – it was a boarding house full of strangers, and although Peggy was lovely and Rita was fun, she was dreading having to face everyone and seeing pity in their eyes as she tried to keep her emotions over Freddy in check.

As she waved goodbye to everyone and went out of the ward, she was amazed at how many people knew she was leaving, for there was quite a gathering on the front doorstep.

'I'll see you tomorrow morning at nine o'clock,' said Matron. 'Enjoy the home comforts, dear, and don't worry. Commander Black is fully aware of this arrangement, so you can rest assured you'll get any news of your brother very quickly.'

Peggy was waiting beside the staff car smoking a cigarette as she chatted to the young WAAF driver. 'That's quite a send-off,' she said with a warm smile. 'You're obviously a popular girl.'

Kitty dredged up a smile as Nurse Hopkins packed the vanity case in the boot with the rest of her luggage. 'It feels a bit like the last day at boarding school,' she admitted.

Peggy ground the cigarette beneath her shoe. 'Come along, then. Let's get you settled, and then we can be on our way.'

Kitty gave the nurse a hug and a murmured 'thank you' before letting Peggy help her into the car. She rested back on the soft leather seat and found that she'd been holding her breath. Letting it out in a soft sigh, she told herself she'd taken the first step into the outside world – but she was all too aware of how many steps it would take to gain independence, and couldn't help but be daunted at the thought.

She mentally shook off these gloomy notions and turned to wave to the gathering on the steps as the car pulled smoothly away. Then she settled back and looked out of the window as Peggy chattered to the driver.

The countryside was very beautiful in the August sunshine, and there was a heat haze shimmering on the voluptuous curves of the surrounding hills. The car was following a narrow country lane lined with hedgerows, and as they crested a hill, she could see flocks of gulls following a horse and plough in a distant field. There were hayricks in another field and the tiny figures of farm workers labouring to gather in a harvest of wheat. It was peaceful and quintessentially English, without a hint of the dark clouds of the war being waged across the Channel. Life went on, even though Freddy was missing.

'Not far to go now,' said Peggy a few minutes later. 'Can you see the sea? Doesn't it look lovely?'

Kitty nodded as she glimpsed the sun diamonds sparkling on the water before the car swept down the hill. The road had widened and now she could see the roof of a rather grand house that was hidden by a tall hedge, and soon they were winding their way past rows of terraced houses and over a hump-backed bridge crossing a railway line.

'Our poor old station has taken a bit of a battering,' said Peggy, 'but Stan's got a cosy Nissen hut to sit in when he's not tending his allotment, and it's perfectly adequate for a ticket office and the left luggage.'

Kitty followed Peggy's pointing finger.

'The bus station was blown to bits, and we lost our cinema,' Peggy continued. 'That was where my Jim used to work as a projectionist before he was called up.' She gave a wistful sigh. 'He's a good mechanic and could have earned a much better wage in a garage, but after what he went through in the first war, he said he never wanted to look at an engine again – now he's back doing just that with REME.'

Kitty's thoughts were still occupied with Freddy, and she regarded the High Street with little interest. There was some bomb damage, and several of the larger buildings had sandbags stacked like walls around their doorways. But there were the inevitable queues outside the shops, and it was clear that the Americans were in town, for there were knots of them everywhere she looked.

'I've asked Cynthia to drive us along the seafront so you can get a proper look. It isn't up to much, I'm afraid, not now the army has covered the prom in barbed wire and gun emplacements, and our poor old pier has fallen into the sea. But it doesn't take much imagination to see it how it used to be.'

Kitty's lips twitched in a smile. Peggy had made it her business to find out their driver's name – and she probably knew her life story as well. It made her feel ashamed, for she'd been so centred on Freddy and herself that she'd hardly even noticed the girl, let alone spoken to her.

She looked out of the window at the coils of wire along the edge of the promenade, the damaged shelters with their broken glass and bullet-riddled concrete seats, and at the remains of the forlorn pier with the burnt-out skeleton of a German Stuka dive-bomber sticking out of it. A strong wind would see both of them crumble into the water.

Kitty regarded the small private hotels and guest houses which had either been boarded up for the duration or taken over by the Forces. She saw the vast bomb crater and the solitary and rather poignant remains of the Imperial Hotel which stood right next to the undamaged Grand, and then looked towards the towering chalk cliff that overshadowed the mined beach.

She had a sudden, terrifying image of Freddy heading straight for it and veering off at the last moment, and it made her shudder.

'What's the matter, Kitty?' asked a concerned Peggy.

'I was just remembering Freddy's close call with a white cliff a few weeks ago,' she replied softly. 'He survived to tell the tale then, so I can only pray he's survived this time.'

Peggy grasped her hand as the car began the steep climb away from the seafront. 'I'm told he's a lucky young man – so let's hope his luck has held,' she murmured. Then she brightened. 'Don't turn up into Beach View Close,' she told the driver. 'Go along a bit and we'll take the twitten. It's flatter, and Kitty won't have to cope with so many steps.'

Kitty determinedly pulled her thoughts from Freddy and concentrated on their destination. She could see that the streets going off this main road consisted of tall Victorian terraced houses, and to her left she caught a glimpse of a busy road with shops and a pub. The hill seemed to go on forever between the terraces, but the car drew to a halt about a third of the way up.

'Here we are,' said Peggy excitedly. 'Do you need a hand getting out?'

Kitty shook her head, gathered up her crutches and eased her bottom forward on the leather seat. She placed her foot firmly on the pavement, balanced on the crutches and swung out. They had parked next to the opening of an alleyway running along the back of two rows of houses which seemed to have been bomb-damaged.

'We had a bit of a to-do in an air raid a few months back,' said Peggy lightly. 'Our house suffered a bit of damage, but our poor neighbours are still waiting for theirs to be declared safe.'

She turned to the WAAF driver and smiled as she took the cases. 'Thank you, Cynthia. You drove us home beautifully. Now, you be sure to enjoy those little buns with your friends, and give my love to Cissy.'

'Thanks, Peggy,' the girl replied. 'And good luck, Pilot Officer Pargeter. I hope to see you back in the air before too long, and the next time you land at Cliffe, be sure to look me up.'

'I will, thank you,' replied Kitty who was taken aback and rather mortified by this show of friendliness from someone she'd all but ignored until now.

The girl climbed back into the car, gave them a cheerful wave and drove off.

'I don't know about you, Kitty, but I could do with a cup of tea and no mistake,' said Peggy as she grabbed the cases. 'Will you be all right walking down our twitten? Only it's a bit rough in places, and I don't want you to fall.'

'I'll be fine, she reassured her. 'You lead the way.'

As Peggy slowly went along the rough path, Kitty followed, placing her foot carefully at every step before she moved the crutches. It was a hot day and she could feel the perspiration run down her face and back and soak into her thin blouse. But she was doing it, she thought triumphantly. And it felt good.

'Here we are,' said Peggy as they reached the back gate, and she put the cases down. 'I'd better warn Ron to keep Harvey indoors, or he'll have you over in a trice.' She turned towards the house. 'Cooee! Ron. We're here. Keep the dogs in, will you?'

As the sound of furious barking disturbed the stillness of the late morning, a sturdy man appeared from behind a shed. Dressed in baggy corduroy trousers, thick boots and a faded shirt, he had a thatch of black, unruly hair liberally sprinkled with the same grey that glinted in his rather wild eyebrows. His blue eyes twinkled as he smiled at them both.

'To be sure, there's no need to shout, Peggy me darlin'. They've been shut in me room for over an hour waiting for you to be home, so they have.'

Kitty liked him immediately, and as he opened

the gate and shook her hand, she felt strength, warmth and security in his grip. 'Hello, Ron,' she said in delight. 'Peggy's told me all about you. It's nice to meet you at last.'

He ruffled his hair as he winked. 'Ach, to be sure, young Kitty, you'll not be wanting to believe everything she tells you. Our wee Peggy has a wild imagination, so she has.'

Peggy rolled her eyes at this and then handed him the cases and waited for Kitty to get through the gate. 'He's a rogue and a scallywag, as you'll soon find out,' she muttered to Kitty, 'and suffers from a terrible case of the blarney.'

Kitty caught Ron's eye and giggled. She had no doubt of it.

'Take the cases up to Kitty's room,' ordered Peggy. 'Then come back and help her up the cellar steps.'

The garden was long and quite narrow, and as Kitty slowly made her way past the ugly Anderson shelter and along the path, she paused now and again to admire the flourishing vegetable plot, the fruit cage and tubs of herbs by the back door, and the glorious red roses that clambered up the wall, their scent drifting to her on the warm air. There were deckchairs placed beside a deserted playpen in the shade of a large umbrella, two sheds, and to the right of the back door were a concrete coal bunker and a neatly stacked pile of wood.

'That's the outside lav,' explained Peggy over the

sound of the barking coming from inside the house. 'Ron's just sorted it out after it got flattened in the raid. The other shed is for his tools, but it's where he hides to read his paper so I don't find things for him to do.'

Kitty was smiling as she carefully negotiated the step into what appeared to be a basement scullery. The dog was now howling and the puppy giving little yaps of excitement from behind one of the closed doors.

'Poor things,' she murmured. 'They must hate being locked away.'

'Better that than having you upended,' said Peggy firmly as Ron came down the concrete steps. 'Ron, will you help her up there?'

'I'm sure I can manage,' said Kitty as she eyed the three sturdy steps. 'If I sit on the bottom one, I'll be able to push myself up one at a time.'

'Now, you'll not wanting to be doing that on your first day,' said Ron, and before Kitty could say anything, he'd swept her up into his strong arms.

'I really don't . . .' she protested.

'Ach, you're a wee feather of a thing, so you are,' he rumbled as he carried her up the stairs. 'And this is Cordelia,' he said as he gently deposited her in a kitchen chair. 'She's as deaf as a stone, so ye'll have to shout.'

'I am not deaf, you old rogue,' twittered the little woman as she playfully slapped his arm. 'Hello, Kitty, dear,' she said brightly. 'Welcome to Beach

View. I've put the kettle on and made some spam sandwiches, so I hope you're hungry.'

Kitty was overwhelmed by their warm welcome and the ready tears pricked again. 'You're all so very kind. I really don't deserve it.'

Cordelia frowned. 'Of course I don't mind, dear, but I don't think we have any preserves left. Will a bit of tomato sauce do instead?'

Puzzled, Kitty looked at the others and discovered they were smiling and shaking their heads. 'You'll find you have plenty of odd conversations with Cordelia,' said Peggy as she put the vanity case on the table next to Kitty and placed the crutches nearby. She turned back to Cordelia and explained in loud, clear words what Kitty had really said.

'Oh, dear,' muttered Cordelia as she fiddled with her hearing aid. 'You must think I'm a very silly old woman. I forgot to turn it on after I'd finished the ironing. You see, I love singing along to "Workers' Playtime", but I can't stand the sound of my own voice, so I turn the wireless up and my hearing aid off.'

Kitty grinned but said nothing as she didn't want to confuse her any further.

Cordelia shot her a beaming smile. 'You must call me Grandma Finch. All the other girls do, the naughty, sweet things. Now, drink this tea and eat something. I'm sorry it's only the horrid wheatmeal bread, but we need to put some flesh on those poor little bones, and no mistake.'

'Cordelia, I don't think you should say . . .'

'It's all right, Peggy,' interrupted Kitty. 'She's right, I am far too thin, and those sandwiches look lovely.'

'Then tuck in, Kitty, and make yourself at home. If there's anything you need, you only have to ask.' Peggy sipped her tea and sighed gratefully. 'As Daisy seems to be asleep I think I'll leave her for a few more minutes,' she said as she took a sandwich from the heaped plate. 'It's nice to have a bit of peace and quiet for a change.'

Kitty ate her sandwich and drank her tea as Ron went back down to the cellar to try and quieten the dogs. Cordelia, she noted, was trying very hard not to keep looking at her empty trouser leg, but she could see the pity in her expression and momentarily cringed from it.

Then, realising she would have to get used to such things, she finished her lunch and dug into her vanity case for her ration book and cigarettes. Having handed over the book, she offered a cigarette to Peggy, then she lit them both and sat back to take in the room.

It was small and cramped and fairly dark with all the tape over the window, but although the furniture was well worn and the range was old-fashioned, they shone with the same loving care that had been applied to the linoleum. Pretty gingham curtains fluttered at the open window and masked whatever was under the stone sink, but it was the mantelpiece that held her attention. Below the large portrait of the King and Queen, the mantelpiece was covered with photographs of Peggy's family, and as Kitty had heard all about them, she spent a moment trying to figure out who was who.

The handsome, dark-eyed man in uniform had to be her husband Jim, and of course she recognised Commander Black, so that had to be Anne and Rose Margaret with him. The pretty fair girl must be Cissy who was a driver with the WAAF, and the two grinning boys could only be Bob and Charlie. There was a lovely studio shot of a smiling, almost toothless Daisy, and another of three handsome young men that Kitty suspected must be Peggy's nephews. A third studio portrait showed a radiant blonde girl with a rather studious-looking young man who was smiling shyly at the camera. They had to be Suzy and Anthony who'd just become engaged; and the small black-and-white snapshot of five girls in sunhats and pretty summer dresses could only be Peggy's other lodgers.

With a sigh of longing for her own family, she absorbed the warm, friendly atmosphere of this homely room. It was clear that Peggy and her family weren't well off, but they were rich in love, and now she too had been drawn into the warmth of its glow.

'I expect you're a bit tired after all that excitement,' said Peggy as she folded the newspaper. 'Would you like to go up for a little rest?'

Kitty was tired, achingly so after all that had happened this morning, but she didn't want to leave this lovely room just yet, for these people and this place soothed her and eased her terrors for Freddy. 'I'd like to see Daisy and the dogs first, if that's all right,' she said shyly.

'Well, of course it is. But I warn you, Daisy's teething and isn't her usual sweet self at the moment and Harvey can get very boisterous. It might be an idea to keep your legs under the table, because he's likely to try and sit in your lap.'

'But I thought he was a big lurcher, not a lapdog?'

'He is big, with great trampling feet, but it's something he forgets when he gets overexcited,' said Peggy with a wry smile. She went to the cellar steps. 'Ron, let the dogs out, but keep a grip on Harvey, will you?'

Kitty heard the squeak of a door opening and then the scrabbling of paws on concrete, and seconds later she was bombarded by the lolloping puppy. She reached down and picked him up, holding his squirming little body tightly as she tried to avoid the licking tongue and wet nose. 'Hello, Monty,' she laughed. 'My goodness, you've got some energy.'

'To be sure, he's nothing compared to Harvey,' said Ron as he held tightly to the straining leash. 'Sit down, ye heathen beast, and stop pulling.'

Harvey took absolutely no notice and shoved a large paw on Kitty's thigh as he tried to lick her face and the puppy at the same time.

Kitty looked into bright, intelligent eyes, noting the expressive eyebrows, the floppy ears and wagging tail. He was the canine equivalent of his owner, and Kitty could now understand why Peggy was often at her wits' end.

She patted Harvey's head and ran her fingers over the silky ears as the pup squirmed in her arms and tried to lick him. 'There's no doubt they're father and son,' she murmured. 'And Monty's got enormous feet. He's going to grow just as big.'

'Aye, that's what Peg's afraid of,' muttered Ron as he lifted Harvey's paw from Kitty's leg and pulled him away. 'But to be sure I'll be taking him out and training him soon, so I will.'

'That won't make any difference,' sniffed Cordelia. 'It didn't work on Harvey.'

'Before you two fall out, I'll go and fetch Daisy. It's time she had her lunch, and if she sleeps much more she'll have me up all hours of the night.'

Kitty smiled as she petted the puppy. 'We had lots of dogs in Argentina,' she said clearly to Cordelia. 'I could never resist the puppies. They're so sweet, aren't they?'

The puppy immediately let the side down by weeing all down Kitty's blouse and trousers.

'Oh, dear,' laughed Kitty as Ron grabbed the pup and took him outside. 'It seems I spoke too soon.' She dabbed at the wetness with her handkerchief, remembered the precious letters and cards in her pocket and yanked them out. With a sigh of relief she saw they were unharmed, and quickly put them in her vanity case.

Peggy came into the room with a whining Daisy, noticed the damage to Kitty's clothes immediately and gave a sigh of exasperation. 'I'll help you change once I've seen to Daisy,' she said. 'I'm so sorry, Kitty, but that's the way things are in this house – and you've yet to meet the blasted ferrets.'

Kitty chuckled as she pulled the damp shirt from the waistband of her trousers and dried her midriff. 'You've no idea how wonderful it is to be in a real home again,' she said softly. 'I'm so very glad to be here.'

Chapter Nineteen

Peggy had already changed Daisy's nappy in her bedroom, so she swiftly poured some milk into her bottle and sat down to feed her. 'Are you all right, dear?' she asked Kitty, who was looking rather pale and weary.

'I am a bit tired,' she admitted, 'but I so wanted to see Daisy again. Could I hold her, do you think?'

'Here we are then.' Peggy lugged Daisy from her lap and carefully placed her into Kitty's, well away from the damp patches. 'I swear she's put on weight since this morning,' she sighed. 'You mind she doesn't hurt your bad leg.'

'Of course she won't,' said Kitty softly. 'And it's lovely to hold a baby again. There were always babies back home in Argentina – the gauchos are a virile race,' she added with a smile.

Peggy would have loved to know a bit more about Kitty's life in Argentina, but she had other things on her mind at the moment, so it would have to wait. She satisfied herself that Kitty seemed to be managing Daisy very well, and then turned to Cordelia.

'Have you started that pie yet, dear? Only the

others will be home by six and starving hungry as usual.'

'Ron cleaned and gutted the fish and I've made a lovely sauce from the stock. Fred brought round a few prawns which are a terrific treat,' she replied with a shrug of delight. 'Everything is prepared, and there's only the spuds to boil and mash before it all goes in the oven.'

'Prawns,' sighed Peggy. 'My goodness, I can't remember the last time we had those. Fred the Fish must be feeling very generous.' Dark suspicion rose. 'Either that,' she said sharply, 'or he's got a guilty secret he thinks I might tell Lil.'

Cordelia went rather pink and avoided Peggy's gaze. 'I don't think he mentioned his wife – but then I didn't hear half of what he said, so I couldn't possibly . . .' Her voice tailed off as she finally met Peggy's suspicious eyes.

'What's he been up to?' Peggy folded her arms and tried to look stern but knew she'd failed, for a smile was tweaking her lips. Fred the Fish was a large Cockney who was terrified of his fierce, tiny wife finding out his secrets – and although they were never very serious, they were legion. 'Is it something Lil should know about?'

Cordelia became quite flustered. 'I think Lil has suspicions,' she admitted hesitantly, 'but really, Peggy, I didn't . . .' She gave a deep sigh and her shoulders slumped. 'Oh, dear,' she murmured. 'I've never been able to keep a secret.'

Peggy reached out for her hand and smiled. 'What is it, Cordelia?'

'He said he'd got the prawns from a fisherman friend who goes out after the curfew on the other side of the headland. They're a special treat for Lil to celebrate their wedding anniversary, and he thought we might like a few as Ron had told him we were having fish pie tonight,' she finished in a rush.

Peggy breathed a sigh of relief. 'That was very generous of him,' she said. 'I'll be sure to thank him the next time I go to the shop.'

'Please don't say anything,' pleaded Cordelia. 'Fred made me promise not to tell you, and if Lil finds out he's been dealing on the black market, he swears she'll have his guts for garters.'

'Don't worry,' Peggy reassured her. 'Lil isn't daft and usually knows everything he gets up to long before he confesses to it. But I won't say anything, I promise.'

She turned back to Kitty, who had finished feeding Daisy her milk and was now keeping her amused by making shapes with her fingers. The girl looked exhausted, she realised, and it was time she had a snooze before everyone came home.

'I'll take her now,' she said, gently plucking Daisy from her arms. 'It's time you had a rest, and I won't take any arguments. Stay there, I won't be a minute.'

She carried Daisy down the steps and into the garden where Ron was pottering about and trying to keep the puppy from digging up his winter seed-lings.

'Keep an eye on Daisy for a bit, will you, Ron?' At his nod, she sat Daisy in the playpen and spent a moment or two handing her some toys before she went back indoors to find that Kitty was on her way into the hall. She picked up the vanity case from the table and joined her.

'Is my room up those stairs?' Kitty asked.

Peggy nodded, but the stairs looked suddenly daunting, and she was plagued with grave misgivings about Kitty getting up them. She couldn't lift her and Ron wouldn't always be here – and she didn't like to think of her getting stranded, or worse, taking a tumble trying to do it on her own.

Peggy made a swift decision. 'Perhaps it would be better if you had my room, dear,' she said hastily. 'It's right here off the hall, and it wouldn't take a moment to change things about and bring down the commode.'

'I won't hear of it,' said Kitty firmly as she grabbed the newel post with one hand, thrust her crutches at Peggy and sat on the second stair. Before Peggy could react, she'd put her weight on her hands and foot and swung her bottom up onto the third stair.

'Goodness, you're much stronger than you look,' Peggy said in admiration.

'It comes from riding bad-tempered and very strong polo ponies and keeping them in check.' Kitty went up two more stairs. 'And I was quite the gymnast at school – could climb a rope faster than anyone in my year.'

Peggy clutched the crutches and vanity case as she slowly followed Kitty's progress up the stairs. She was deeply concerned, for despite her undoubted agility and strength, Kitty was doing far too much. 'I do wish you'd let me help,' she said fretfully.

'I can manage, Peggy, really,' she panted. 'And I need to do this on my own, because there won't always be Ron to carry me.' She finally reached the landing, grabbed the bannister and struggled to get her balance on her good leg. 'There,' she said with a triumphant smile. 'And I bet it's much easier and far more fun on the journey down.'

'I think you've done enough for now,' said Peggy swiftly, suspecting the girl was about to slide all the way back down again just to prove a point. 'Here, take these crutches before I drop them, and I'll show you where everything is.'

Kitty was still a little out of breath as she took the crutches and listened while Peggy told her about the need to be careful when lighting the boiler, because it had a nasty blow-back which could singe eyebrows and lashes. She then dutifully admired the lavatory and the airing cupboard and then followed her along the landing, past Cordelia's room and the stairs leading to the next floor, to the door at the end.

'Rita's room is the one at the front behind the stairs,' explained Peggy. 'Suzy and the other girls are on the next floor up. They work different shifts and Jane leaves just before dawn every morning for the dairy, but they're all very quiet, so you shouldn't be disturbed.'

She pushed the door open. 'This was Ruby's room before she moved into the bungalow with her mother. I hope you like it.'

Kitty's face lit up as she took in the pretty counterpane and matching curtains, and the vase of red roses Peggy had placed on the kidney-shaped dressing table. There was a Chinese rug by the bed, clean towels folded on the dressing stool, a small stack of paperback books on the bedside chest of drawers beside the little lamp, and a highly polished wardrobe waiting for her few clothes.

'It's perfect,' breathed Kitty as she rested her head for a moment on Peggy's shoulder. 'I can't begin to tell you how much I appreciate all the hard work you must have done to get this ready for me. Thank you so much, Peggy.'

Peggy carefully placed the vanity case on the dressing table. She was feeling a bit emotional and found she had to clear her throat before she could speak. 'It was no work at all,' she said, lightly dismissing three hours of hard labour in the middle of the night. 'Now, do you need help to get undressed?'

Kitty shook her head. 'Thank you, no. That's one thing I really can do for myself.'

'You settle in then and have a good sleep,' Peggy said gruffly. 'I've put a little bell on the bedside table, so if you need anything just give it a ring, and I'll be up.'

She saw the brightness of tears in the girl's eyes and made a hasty exit before her own emotions got the better of her. 'Goodness me,' she muttered as she ran back down the stairs. 'I'm an absolute wreck after everything that's happened. Lord only knows what that poor little mite is feeling.'

Kitty sank down onto the soft bed and admired the little room. The scent from the roses was struggling a bit from the beeswax polish Peggy had used liberally on the wardrobe and floor, but she'd spoken the truth when she'd told her it was perfect. For although it was a world away from her spacious, sunlit bedroom back in Argentina, it held the promise of peace and tranquillity after a terrible day, and the comfort of solitude after all those weeks in the noisy, crowded hospital.

She sat for a moment thinking about her warm welcome into Peggy's home, and of how very lucky she was to have met her. Then she opened her cases, put her travelling alarm clock on the bedside table, plucked out her nightdress and washbag, and went along the landing to the lavatory and bathroom.

Having carefully attended to her stump, she washed her face and hands, ran a brush through her ragged hair and then paused as she caught sight of her reflection in the bathroom mirror. There were dark shadows beneath her eyes, and the hollows in her face seemed more pronounced as she thought about Freddy and wondered where he could be – and if he'd survived.

She gave a deep, trembling sigh, turned from the mirror, and with her stained clothes bundled under her arm, made her slow way back to her bedroom. Opening the taped-over window, she glanced down into the garden where Ron was carefully watering his vegetable plot and the dogs lay panting in the sun. Then she pulled the sprigged curtain across it so the room was cast in shadow, but she could still smell the lovely sea air and the scent of roses and freshly watered earth.

With her crutches leaning against the bedside cupboard, she sank onto the bed, exhausted mentally and physically. But her thoughts still churned, for although she loved being in this friendly home, she was beginning to doubt the wisdom of trying to live here.

Despite her protests to the contrary, the stairs *were* a problem, even though fierce determination and a fair dollop of grandstanding had seen her manage to get up them earlier. But now she had to admit that the little show of bravado had utterly drained her.

Then there was the fact that Peggy clearly had a great deal on her hands already, and once Jim came home on leave, she would have even less time to see to everyone – let alone help Kitty in and out of the bath.

But this was only part of what worried Kitty, for

there was also her reliance on people – mostly strangers – to get her to the hospital and back every day. Her presence was causing nothing but trouble for everyone, she thought sadly, and although she'd been met with only loving kindness, she suspected it could easily wear thin after a while.

Kitty's spirits were at their lowest ebb as she drew back the downy quilt to reveal crisp cotton sheets and an enticing pillow. Poor Charlotte was probably delivering a plane somewhere, happily thinking about her wedding and unaware of the terrible news that awaited her back at Hamble Pool. Freddy was lost on the other side of the Channel – perhaps in terrible pain, or even dead, and her parents knew nothing as yet.

Then there was Doreen, who was, no doubt, facing the curious, pitying stares and endless questions of her friends and family in London. How was she coping outside the security of the hospital walls? Was her laughter just that bit more brittle, the smile a little more forced – or was her indomitable spirit still unbroken?

And what about Ruby? She could only wait and hope that Mike would pull through and not lose his sight, but then, if things became serious between them, she'd have choices to make that might change her life forever.

The awful consequences of this war had brought not only sorrow, but the profound and terrible fear of the unknown, and Kitty could no longer deal with it. Easing between the sheets, and with the soft quilt tucked comfortingly to her chin, she closed her eyes. She desperately wanted to sleep – to sink into that welcoming nothingness and shut out the world and all its terrors for a while.

Yet her mind refused to be still, and the images of what might have happened to her beloved brother tormented her until the exhaustion finally overwhelmed her, and she could think no more.

The sounds outside her window filtered into the darkness and she slowly emerged from it feeling heavy-limbed and disorientated. The light coming through the curtains was paler now, and the small travelling alarm clock showed it was after five. She'd been asleep for almost four hours but she didn't feel at all rested, so she turned over and snuggled back down beneath the covers.

But, as was always the way, the pressure on her bladder forced her out of bed. Quickly dressing in a fresh pair of trousers and a light sweater, she shoved her foot into the flat sandal and headed for the bathroom. She could hear Rita's voice downstairs and guessed she was calling out to the others through the kitchen window as they sat in the garden. Proof, if ever she needed it, that life went on regardless of what might have happened to Freddy.

She quickly washed her face and hands, ran her fingers through her awful hair and went out to face the stairs. They posed much fewer problems on the downward journey, so she sat at the top, clutched her crutches and slowly bumped from stair to stair until she reached the bottom.

A little out of breath but feeling quite pleased with herself, she leaned on the crutches and was about to cross the hall when Harvey galloped out of the kitchen to greet her. Alarmed that he might jump up and knock her over, she held out her crutch towards him to ward him off. 'Good boy, Harvey,' she said quietly. 'Sit down and be still.'

Harvey sat and cocked his head to one side, his intelligent eyes darting between Kitty and the crutches as his eyebrows wriggled.

'That's a very good boy,' Kitty praised. 'Now I'm just going to go in the kitchen, so you stay there and don't trip me up.'

Harvey gave a questioning whine as she headed away from him, then quietly and calmly, he got to his feet and walked beside her.

Kitty praised him again, but just as they entered the kitchen, she gasped with anxiety. Monty was dashing towards her at full tilt and there was no possible way of avoiding a collision.

Harvey moved swiftly and with one great paw he felled Monty and held him to the floor. As the puppy squirmed and yipped, Harvey caught his scruff in his soft mouth and then sat and waited to see what Kitty would do next.

Kitty was amazed, for the puppy hung from

Harvey's mouth, unharmed and as limp as a wilting willow. 'You are an incredible dog, Harvey,' she breathed. 'Now, if you could just hold onto him for another minute or two while I get into the garden, that would be really helpful.'

Harvey's ears pricked and his eyebrows rose and fell, but Monty remained blissfully content in his mouth.

Kitty hastily bumped down the cellar steps and then negotiated the doorway into the garden to discover Ron, Peggy, Cordelia and Rita were waiting for her with broad smiles. 'Well done,' they said in unison.

'It's Harvey you should thank for my safe journey. If he hadn't grabbed Monty, I'd be in a heap on the kitchen floor.'

She quickly explained what had happened, and they all turned as Harvey made a grand entrance into the garden with Monty still ensnared by the scruff. He carefully placed the puppy on the ground and then barked as if he understood how clever he'd been before he went off to cock his leg and wee luxuriously against the garden wall.

'There, Cordelia,' said a proud and beaming Ron. 'Are ye not willing to admit that Harvey is a well-trained, clever dog?'

'I never said he wasn't clever,' retorted Cordelia from beneath her broad-brimmed and rather battered sunhat. 'In fact, he's too clever by half, which is why he's always in trouble.'

'Are you all right, Kitty?' asked a concerned Peggy

as she dithered about trying to help her into the low deckchair. 'You should have rung your bell and I would have come up to help you.'

Kitty had absolutely no intention of ever ringing that bell. 'I'm fine, really.' She smiled. 'But Harvey certainly is a special dog. He seemed to know instinctively that I was vulnerable and obeyed me instantly.'

Rita grinned. 'He isn't always so obedient,' she warned, 'so I wouldn't take it for granted.' She poured some tea into a cup, added milk and a sprinkling of sugar. 'You must be thirsty after your sleep,' she said, handing it over.

Kitty settled into the deckchair and sipped the refreshing tea before reaching into her trouser pocket for her cigarettes. 'Damn,' she muttered.

'What?' asked Rita. 'Have you forgotten something?'

'I left my cigarettes upstairs. But never mind,' she added hastily. 'I'm probably better off without them.'

Without a word, Rita shot back indoors and less than a minute later was back in the garden with the packet of Players. 'Here you go,' she said cheerfully, 'and I brought your sunglasses as well,' she added as she held them out. 'It's very bright still.'

'Oh, Rita, thank you,' she sighed. 'But you mustn't keep running about after me.'

Rita widened her big brown eyes. 'Why ever not?'

'Because I have to learn to remember such things, and until I do, then I'll either go and fetch them or do without.'

'Stuff and nonsense,' muttered Rita. 'This is your first day at home, and you've got enough to deal with without going up and down the stairs.' She smiled and squeezed Kitty's hand, her tone much softer. 'We want to spoil you a bit, Kitty, so please let us.'

Kitty was afraid of this, but the genuine affection she could see in her friend's eyes kept her silent, and she accepted Rita's offer with a grateful smile. Still, she vowed, if she was going to stay here, then she would jolly well have to learn quickly to walk on her false leg so she wasn't any more bother.

Later that night, Kitty was once more settled into the comfortable bed, her letters and cards scattered over the counterpane. The blackout was in place and the curtains drawn over it, and she rested against the pillows in the soft pool of light coming from the bedside lamp as she thought about her first day at Beach View.

The pleasant interlude in the garden had been followed by the arrival of the other girls. After being introduced and chatting for a while, Kitty had determinedly refused all offers of help and made her own way up the steps to the kitchen. They'd all sat round the kitchen table for supper – or tea, as Peggy called it – and Kitty had felt quite at home as Ron surreptitiously fed scraps to the dogs and the girls told everyone the latest gossip at their workplaces.

Kitty smiled. The fish pie had been an enormous

success and Cordelia had gone quite pink with pleasure at their praise, but Peggy had caught Ron slipping a bit of fish to Harvey and told him straight that if she saw him do it again, she'd clout him one. This started a bit of light-hearted banter which soon ended in laughter, as Kitty suspected most confrontations did in this house.

She thought about her first impressions of her fellow lodgers. Sarah was typical of the girls who'd spent their formative years in the sophisticated world of the expats living in the tropics, and in a way, she rather reminded Kitty of a very pleasant girl from South Africa that she'd once shared a dormitory with.

Jane seemed a little less sophisticated and rather young for her years, but she was delightful company, and it was clear she thoroughly enjoyed working at the dairy and doing the books at the uniform factory.

Kitty had heard the sisters' story from Peggy, and she rather admired their stoicism in the face of such worry over their father and Sarah's fiancé, for she knew there was very little news coming out of the Far East, and absolutely no word from the Japs on the numbers of dead or the POWs.

Kitty turned from these unsettling thoughts to Suzy. She too had the quiet assurance of someone who'd been carefully raised and educated, and as she'd excitedly shared her plans for her wedding and talked about the little house they would move into, Kitty had been sharply reminded of Charlotte and her plans which, by now, would tragically be in tatters.

Kitty steered her attention determinedly back to Fran, the redheaded Irish nurse who seemed to be getting over her brush with a young married American and was looking forward to going dancing at the weekend. Fran was a lively spirit, with her flashing green eyes and tumbling hair, and Kitty rather hoped she'd learned not to wear her heart quite so clearly on her sleeve.

As for Rita, she could be a touch acerbic at times, she'd noticed, especially when Fran teased her, but Kitty wondered if that was because Rita was a bit daunted by the other girl's stunning looks and easy-going manner which could so easily charm everyone around her. On the whole, Kitty realised, Rita was shy and unsure of herself, and the brittle shell she hid behind masked a sweet nature. She'd already proved it by being admirably efficient in working out a fire station roster for the hospital run, and had even persuaded John Hicks, the Fire Chief, to lend one of the station's trucks for the purpose.

Kitty smiled as she remembered the chaos of coming back up to bed. With so many willing hands, and much jostling, it had taken far longer to get up the stairs than it would have if she'd gone up on her bottom. But it had been enormous fun, and she'd been warmed by their enthusiasm and affection as they'd bid her goodnight with hugs and kisses.

And yet it was Harvey who'd really touched her

heart, for he'd followed her every step as the puppy yapped and wriggled in Peggy's arms, and now she could hear him snuffling and snoring outside her door. It seemed she had her own personal shaggy bodyguard.

Kitty reached for her mother's letters, which she'd now read several times and knew almost by heart. Turning off the bedside light, she slid further beneath the covers. With the letters close to her heart she could remember her mother's sweet words, finding comfort in the fact that she and father had yet to learn about Freddy.

'Please God they never have to,' she whispered into the darkness.

Chapter Twenty

Peggy had tried to get Harvey away from Kitty's door but he refused to budge, and she simply couldn't shift him. She knew from past experience – such as trying to get him through the door into the vet's – that when he was determined like that, nothing short of a ten-ton bomb would move him, so she'd left him to it and gone downstairs to find Ron.

'I don't want him getting into the habit of sleeping up there,' she said as she prepared the porridge for the next morning.

'Ach, Peggy, he's doing no harm, and the wee girl will feel safe knowing he's there.'

'Why should she feel at risk?' she asked him in astonishment. 'No one here is out to harm her.'

'Well, she's grieving, so she is, and there's nothing like a dog to comfort you when you're low,' he replied round the stem of his pipe.

'I don't want fleas in my carpet,' she retorted.

'My dog does *not* have fleas,' protested Ron like an injured father. 'He's vermin-free, so he is. I bathed him only three months ago.'

'Then you'd better get some of that special stuff

from the vet and do it again tomorrow,' she said flatly. 'And while you're at it, you can do the ferrets too.'

Ron gave the deep sigh of a beleaguered man. 'To be sure, Peggy, you'd try the patience of a saint.'

She pushed the pot of porridge to the back of the hob and began to lay the table for breakfast. 'If it's a saint I'm trying, then I'm sorry,' she said as she tried not to giggle, 'but if it's you, Ronan Reilly, well, that's quite another thing.'

He stilled her busy hands. 'Leave that,' he said quietly. 'It's time you went to bed and caught up on the sleep you didn't have last night. Go on,' he said as she hesitated. 'I'll finish here and make sure the fire's damped down for the night.'

Peggy kissed his grizzled cheek and gave him a swift hug. 'I do love you, Ron,' she murmured.

'Ach, will ye stop all that daft talk and get yerself to yer bed, Peggy Reilly. You're in need of some beauty sleep before that son of mine comes home.'

If she hadn't been so tired she would have taken umbrage at that, but she said nothing and went upstairs to wash and prepare for bed.

The soft, rather lumpy mattress and downy pillow were sheer heaven, and she sank into them exhausted by the very long, traumatic day and the lack of sleep the night before. Closing her eyes, she expected to nod straight off, but her thoughts were still whirling as she lay there in the darkness listening to Daisy's snuffles.

She was still worried about Kitty, because she could see what an effort it was for her to get anywhere, and with so many steps and stairs to climb, there was a danger she'd become a prisoner in the house. But the girl seemed determined to do things on her own, and she supposed that was right – yet it all seemed a bit too soon, and she was frightened that she'd hurt herself.

All the girls had been marvellous, of course, chattering away as if they'd known her for years, and not at all prying about her missing leg – or indeed, about her missing brother. But she'd caught Cordelia looking at that empty trouser leg a bit too often and had noticed the mournful, pitying look on her face. So when she'd helped her into bed earlier, she'd sat for a while and explained how necessary it was not to show Kitty pity, for the girl needed to be accepted for who she was, not what had happened to her.

Poor Cordelia had shed a few tears as she'd raged against the war and the cruelties it had inflicted on the young, so Peggy had stayed with her until she'd calmed down. This war was getting to all of them, and Kitty's presence in the house only served to emphasise the very real consequences of the bitter conflict that was going on beyond these sheltering walls.

Peggy turned over and nestled her cheek into the pillow. It no longer had the scent of Jim, but she thought she could hear his soft chuckle as he told her not to be such a worry wart and to stop fretting, for it did no one any good and just gave her even more lines on her forehead.

She smiled at that, although if he'd been here and said it, she'd have given him a poke in the ribs. The knowledge that he would soon be lying next to her, his arm lying heavily across her waist, his knees fitting so perfectly into the hollows of her own as he snored in her ear, comforted her. His snoring had once been an irritation, but now she yearned to hear it again, and to feel his long, strong body curved protectively about her own.

She remembered she had yet to tell him about the ectopic pregnancy and the fact she'd had a hysterectomy, and that worried her too, for she had no idea how he would react. 'There you go again, Peggy Reilly,' she murmured into the pillow as sleep began to claim her. 'Worrying over things you can't change. Will you never learn?'

Kitty stirred as she heard light footsteps coming down the stairs, and realised it must be Jane on her way down to breakfast before she left for the dairy and her milk round. She glanced at the clock. It was still very early, so perhaps now would be a good time to use the bathroom and prepare for the day.

As she swung her leg out of bed and reached for her crutches, she could feel the tenderness on her skinny behind from all that stair-climbing. Her arms and stomach muscles were a bit stiff too, but with continued use, that would pass and she'd be the stronger for it. Having gathered up clean clothes and her washbag, she opened the bedroom door.

Harvey sat there with what Kitty could only describe as a grin. His quizzical eyebrows were twitching as he cocked his head and regarded her expectantly.

'Good boy,' she whispered. 'You can go down to your own bed now. But be quiet, because everyone's asleep.'

He wagged his tail and got to his feet, and Kitty expected him to rush off. But as she began to make her way along the landing, he followed her right to the bathroom.

'You can't come in here,' she whispered as she opened the door. 'Go downstairs.'

Harvey sat down with a determined thud and rested his nose on his paws as he regarded her from beneath those ridiculous eyebrows.

'Please yourself,' sighed Kitty. 'But you are *not* coming in.' She eased round the dog with some difficulty and managed to shut the bathroom door behind her. It was all very well having a protector, but there were times when a girl needed some privacy.

She balanced on her good leg and pulled the bathroom chair closer to the bath and then sat down to turn on the taps just enough so the water trickled in and didn't make too much noise. She eyed the door and wondered if she should lock it – but common sense told her that would be very foolish. If she had an accident and needed help, then no one could get to her.

Not that she was planning to do anything of the sort, she thought fiercely as she pulled off her night-dress and began to take the strapping and sock off her stump. This was an experiment, and if she felt the slightest bit unsure about it, she would stop and be satisfied with a good scrub-down with a flannel. She had absolutely no intention of asking anyone to help, for they all had far too much to do already.

Once the water had reached the thin blue line someone had painted round the bath to comply with the rationing orders, she turned off the taps and placed her washbag on the wooden tray that straddled the bath. She leaned on the bath and stood, then before she could think about it too much, she perched her behind on the edge, gripped the sides and swung her good leg over and into the water.

'So far, so good,' she breathed. 'Now for the difficult bit.' She carried on gripping both sides of the bath, dug in with her toes and slowly lowered herself into the water. Her arms were trembling a bit from the effort, but she'd done it. 'Yes,' she whispered triumphantly as she slid beneath the hot water.

'Well done you.'

She sat up quickly and stared at Fran, who was standing in the doorway. 'I didn't hear you knock,' she said rather sharply.

'Well now, that's because I didn't,' said Fran as she closed the door on a fretful Harvey and came to stand by the bath. 'And I'm sorry for the intrusion, but I knew you had to be in here with him outside, so I thought you might be needing a hand.'

'I can manage, thank you,' replied Kitty rather stiffly.

Fran smiled as she tossed back the wayward russet curls. 'Well, I can see that, Kitty, but I'm thinking you might need a wee bit of steadying on the way out of the tub.'

Kitty could see that she meant well, but she was feeling horribly exposed and rather foolish sitting there naked in the rapidly cooling water. 'If I do, I'll let you know,' she replied in softer tones.

The green eyes regarded her with some amusement. 'You know, Kitty, it's great that you're doing so well on your own, but sometimes it takes a wee bit more courage to ask for help.' She tightened the belt on her dressing gown. 'I'll wait outside with Harvey until you're ready for that hand,' she said with a soft smile.

Kitty waited until the door had closed behind her and then slid back into the water with a sigh. She did appreciate all the loving care everyone showered her with, and Fran was only being a caring nurse – but next time she had a bath, she'd be sure to lock the damned door so no one could come barging in without knocking.

The water was cooler now, so she quickly soaped the flannel and gave herself a good scrub before shampooing her hair and rinsing it off under the tap. This proved awkward, but she managed it finally, and now she had the problem of getting out. It was a deep tub.

Having let the water out, she dried the bottom of the bath with her flannel so her foot wouldn't slip. Then she grabbed the sides of the bath, gripped with her toes and hauled herself up. Her arms were trembling as she sat on the side and eased her leg and stump over so she could slide across to the chair. Grabbing a towel, she wrapped it tightly round her torso and sat for a moment to get her breath back.

'I heard you letting the water out. Are you all right in there?' asked Fran from the other side of the door.

'I'm just fine, Fran,' she replied. 'I'm out of the bath and about to dry off, so you don't need to worry.'

'Ach, to be sure, I knew you could do it.'

'That's rather more than I did,' murmured Kitty as she rubbed a towel over her hair. And yet the knowledge that she had gained a modicum of independence this morning made her spirits rise. It was going to be a good day – and might even bring happier news of Freddy.

'She did what? On her own? Oh, Fran, you should have insisted on helping her,' protested Peggy.

'Not at all, Aunty Peg,' Fran replied as she fastened the nurse's cap firmly over the tamed curls which had been ferociously pinned into a tight knot at her nape. 'Kitty needs to do things on her own to test out her capabilities and strength. I think she's bright enough to ask for help should she be needing it, but for now we should all stand back until that time comes.'

Peggy jiggled a grizzling Daisy in her arms. 'But it's such a struggle for her,' she said fretfully. 'And what if she tries to do something like that and has an accident when there's no one here to help?'

'I'm not daft enough to do something like that,' said Kitty from the doorway. She came into the kitchen with her attendant Harvey. 'And please don't worry about me, Peggy. If I can fly planes, I can certainly fly a pair of crutches, and I promise I'll never try to do anything the remotest bit adventurous if the house is deserted.'

Peggy had to believe her, and she certainly looked very well this morning, with good colour in her cheeks and a certain assurance that had been missing the day before. 'Of course you won't, dear,' she replied. 'Now, you sit down and I'll get you some porridge.'

Kitty eased the strap of her shoulder bag from round her neck and hung it over the back of a chair. 'I can do it, Peggy, really. You see to Daisy.'

Peggy watched uncertainly as Kitty went to the stove, scooped some porridge in a bowl, hesitated for a moment, and then abandoned one of her crutches to hop to the table and set the bowl down. She hadn't spilled a drop.

Daisy squirmed and started to yell, making further conversation impossible, so Peggy turned to the sink and filled the tin bowl with warm water for her bath.

'I'll be off then,' said Fran as she fastened the navy cape round her neck. 'We've been very busy in theatre these past couple of days, so I suspect I could be late.'

'Which hospital do you work in?' asked Kitty.

'Cliffehaven General,' she replied. ''Tis just down the road, past the shops, and takes only a few minutes for me and Suzy to get to.'

'Then it would make far more sense if I could have my treatments there,' said Kitty happily. 'I'll . . .'

'I'm sorry, Kitty,' Fran broke in hastily. 'But we don't have the facilities. We're accident and emergency, and general theatre – along with maternity and paediatrics. That's why the Memorial takes all the more serious cases and those which need long-term care and rehabilitation.'

'Oh,' said a deflated Kitty. 'I just thought it would save everyone so much bother if I only had to get down the road.'

'Ach, to be sure, you're no bother,' said Fran with a grin. 'And you're getting the very best care at the Memorial.' She looked at the watch pinned to her starched apron and gasped. 'I've got to go or Matron will be on the warpath. See you later.'

Peggy had listened in to this conversation as she'd bathed and dried Daisy, who was now thankfully quiet again as she chewed on a spoon. 'Don't get downhearted, Kitty,' she said as she wrestled to dress the baby. 'Fran's right. You're getting the very best of care at the Memorial, and before you know it, you'll be racing about like the rest of the girls.' She reddened as she realised how tactless she'd been. 'I mean . . . that's to say . . .'

Kitty laughed. 'Please don't apologise, Peggy, because that's exactly what I intend to do – though "racing" is probably a bit optimistic. Clumping would be a better word, I think.'

Peggy's heart ached at how brave the girl was being, but she said nothing as she finished dressing Daisy and sat her in the high chair. Kitty was clearly a feisty girl who was not only capable of flying Spitfires and Typhoons but who would meet every challenge with steely purpose until she had gained her independence again. Peggy could only silently salute her, and all the other brave young- sters who faced the same challenges with such stalwart resolution.

Kitty had finished the porridge and toast and washed up her dishes and cutlery. It was quite easy to move around in this crowded kitchen with just one crutch, for there was always something close at hand to cling to. Now she was drinking her second cup of tea as Peggy cleaned Daisy's face of the remains of her breakfast, and then set her on the floor to crawl about for a while.

Ron had come up from the basement and taken both the dogs for a walk, Sarah had rushed in, grabbed a bit of toast and headed straight out again for the WTC office on the Cliffe estate, and Cordelia was taking her time over her porridge as she read the newspaper. It was a very normal scene, and Kitty felt relaxed and perfectly at home.

Rita came stomping up the basement steps in her heavy boots. After greeting everyone and giving Daisy a tickle under the chin, she poured herself a cup of tea.

'The van's at the end of the twitten,' she said as she slathered margarine on a slice of toast and added a small dollop of Peggy's blackberry jam. 'I'll be taking you this morning and John Hicks will pick you up at five.' She grinned. 'You should be very honoured, you know, to have the boss chauffeuring you about. I bet he wouldn't do it for any of us.'

'Everyone's being terribly kind,' replied Kitty on a sigh. 'I do hope it's not too much of an inconvenience.'

Rita shook her head, making the dark curls bounce around her face as she chewed on her toast. 'He offered to do it straight away,' she said after she'd swallowed. 'He lost a leg too, you see, when he was with the fleet that went to rescue our boys from the beaches of Dunkirk.'

'Really? Goodness. But doesn't he find that hampers him as a firefighter?'

Rita laughed and took a large slurp of tea. 'Not a bit. He marches about shouting orders and is a right slave-driver when it comes to keeping the engines clean and ready for service.' She regarded Kitty solemnly. 'He might not actually climb ladders and go rushing into burning buildings like he used to, but he's most definitely in charge – and we count ourselves very lucky to have him. He's a good bloke.'

'He married Sally, my first evacuee from London,' said Peggy as she topped up the teapot with hot water. 'She runs a home dressmaking business that's doing very well, and their little boy will soon have a brother or sister to play with.'

Peggy's smile was one of sweet contentment. 'She and John make a lovely couple, and it's heart-warming to see how happy they are together.'

Kitty and Rita grinned at Peggy's customary pleasure in other people's happiness. 'Come on,' said Rita as she pushed back from the table. 'We'd better get going or you'll be late.'

Kitty quickly swallowed her pills with the last of her tea, checked that the small shoulder bag held everything she would need for the day and then grabbed her gas-mask box and crutches. 'You will ring the hospital if you have any news, won't you?' she asked Peggy.

'Of course, dear.' Peggy patted her arm and gave her a soft kiss on the cheek before lifting Daisy out of the way of the crutches. 'Try not to overdo things today,' she murmured.

Kitty grinned, said goodbye to Cordelia and Daisy, and then, using her crutches to steady herself, hopped down the cellar steps and out into the garden.

The sun was shining, a blackbird was singing in a nearby tree, and there was the promise of another beautiful day in the cloudless blue sky. Kitty took a deep lungful of the glorious fresh air and then followed Rita down the path, through the gate and along the twitten to the bright red truck that waited by the kerb.

'Ready for take-off?' asked Rita as she climbed in beside her and slammed the door.

'More than ready,' Kitty replied happily.

'Then let's get this show on the road,' said Rita as she turned the key in the ignition, rammed it into first gear and jammed her foot on the accelerator.

Kitty grabbed the edges of her seat as the truck shot forward with a screech of tyres and they roared up the hill. Rita was clearly the sort of driver who relied solely on her brakes to avoid trouble – but the speed was exhilarating, and Kitty relaxed her grip on the seat and settled back to enjoy the ride.

It had felt strange to be back in the rarified atmosphere of the hospital, even after such a short space of time, and it rather reminded Kitty of school holidays when she'd gone to stay with Charlotte and her family. After the large, echoing rooms, bare floorboards and constant noise of school, it had always taken a while to get used to calm and quiet and lovely deep-piled carpets.

Matron Prior-Jones had greeted her warmly, and after enquiring how she'd settled in at Beach View, had left her to get on with her day. And it had been a successful day, for during her final session in the gym, Kitty had managed to get from one end to the other of the parallel bars on her new leg.

'Can I take the leg home so I can practise?' she asked Dr Thorne as she sat down to rest after this marathon.

He shook his head. 'It's far too soon, Kitty.'

'But I feel so much stronger,' she protested. 'And I'm sure that if . . .'

'Patience is a virtue, Kitty Pargeter,' he said firmly. 'And I'm afraid it's something you will have to learn if you're to succeed with this. You'll damage the scar tissue if you do too much too soon – and perhaps even cause an infection. If you do that, you will set your progress back by days if not weeks.'

Kitty had to concede that he was talking sense, but it was frustrating not to be able to do more now she felt so well and able. 'So how soon will it be before I can take it home?'

He shook his head and gave a weary smile. 'Not until you can walk without the aid of the bars or the crutches. And definitely not before you can walk out of this room and down the corridor onto the terrace, where I will expect you to go from one end to the other without stopping.'

'That far, eh?' she breathed, rather daunted by this challenge. She thought about it for a moment and then grinned back at him. 'What's the quickest time anyone achieved that?' she asked.

'I'm not going to tell you,' he said firmly as he unstrapped the leg and checked her stump for bruising or redness before the nurse reapplied the dressing and sock. 'Because if I do you'll only try and beat the record.'

'That's not fair,' she protested.

'I'm the doctor,' he said mildly, 'and I'll decide what's fair or not.' He smiled down at her as the nurse finished dressing her stump. 'Now get out of here and I'll see you tomorrow morning.'

Feeling rather disgruntled, Kitty thanked the nurse and left the gym. She didn't like to admit it but she was utterly exhausted, and although she felt a warm glow of achievement, she was longing to lie down for a rest.

She checked the time as she passed the clock in the hall. There was half an hour before John Hicks was due to pick her up, so she would find a quiet corner in the library where she could finish her letter-writing. With luck, she could put them with the rest of the post in the box in the hall before they were collected at five.

Everyone who could be out of bed was outside enjoying the sun, so Kitty found a comfortable chair in the deserted library and finished off her letter to her parents. She'd mentioned nothing about Freddy but had described, in full, her arrival at Beach View, and the speedy progress she was making with her new leg.

Her letter to Charlotte had been harder to write, but she tried to keep it hopeful, and added Peggy's telephone number so she could call.

She had just sealed the letter when the door opened and a handsome, dark-haired man came in. 'Kitty Pargeter?' At her nod, he came into the room with the all-too familiar gait of someone who had a false leg. 'Hello. I'm John Hicks. Are you ready for your ride home?'

'Yes, thank you,' she said as she looped the straps of her bag and gas-mask box round her neck and reached for her crutches. 'I just need to put these in with the rest so they don't miss the last post.'

He walked with her into the hall and waited while she checked they all had stamps before dumping them into the box. 'Rita tells me you're from Argentina,' he said as they headed for the front door. 'How does it compare to dear old Cliffehaven?'

'It's very different,' she replied as she stepped out onto the gravel drive. 'But Peggy has made me feel so welcome, it feels very much like home.'

John grinned. 'Yeah, she has that way with her. I know my Sal was very happy when she lived there.' He opened the van door and stood back, his brow raised in a question.

'I can manage, thank you,' she said as she clambered in. 'And thanks for this. I really appreciate it.'

'I had an enormous amount of help when I lost my leg,' he said nonchalantly as he took his place behind the steering wheel. 'So I'm glad to do it.'

He looked across and smiled. 'And I know just how frustrating it can be when people – out of kindness – try to do everything for you and make a fuss. It can be quite a lonely journey to get back on your feet again, for it becomes a bit of a battle, and only those who've gone through it can fully understand what it means to be self-reliant.'

'Yes,' replied Kitty, remembering Fran's offer of help this morning and Peggy's fussing. 'I'm beginning to learn that.'

John turned the ignition and drove the truck sedately down the driveway. 'Peggy only wants to mother you,' he said above the engine noise. 'But if you explain how you feel, she's wise enough to understand and let you find your own way. She's a good woman, and has only your best interests at heart.'

Kitty smiled inwardly at the careful way John was driving, for it was a far cry from the journey up here with Rita. 'Peggy said you're about to be a parent again,' she said as they trundled slowly down the hill towards Cliffehaven.

His face lit up in a smile as he negotiated the hump-backed bridge and drove down the High Street. 'Our little boy is two now, and a bit of a handful, but I'm sure Sal and I can cope with another little one.'

Kitty laughed. 'I don't think you'll have much choice in the matter.'

John proudly told her all about his handsome, very talented baby son as he drove down Camden Road past the fire station, the uniform factory, the hospital and the row of small shops.

'That's the Anchor,' he said, pointing to an ancient pub with leaning walls, sway-backed roof and tiny diamond-paned windows. 'Ron can be found in there most days. He's courting the rather voluptuous and very glamorous landlady, Rosie Braithwaite. Though that is the worst kept secret in Cliffehaven,' he added wryly.

Kitty wasn't really surprised to learn that Ron, despite his age, was courting. There was a twinkle in his eye and a robustness about him which spoke of a lust for life – and clearly a lust for the voluptuous landlady of the Anchor. Harvey was certainly not the only old dog that still had some life in him, she thought with a smile.

'Here we are,' said John as he made a three-point turn and drew up to the kerb. 'Would you like a hand getting down that rough path?'

She shook her head. 'I can manage. But aren't you coming in? I'm sure Peggy would love to see you.'

'Can't, I'm afraid. I have to be on baby-sitting duty while Sal goes for her check-up at the clinic.' He opened the door for her and waited until she was balanced on her crutches. 'Give Peggy my regards and tell her I'll pop in next time.'

Kitty smiled and thanked him, and as she made her slow way over the ruts and potholes, she heard the truck's engine fire back into life and then the sound of it fading as John drove it back down Camden Road to the fire station. It had indeed been a very good day, and all she needed now was the news Freddy was alive to make it even better.

Chapter Twenty-one

There had been no news of Freddy, and as an entire week went past, Kitty was beginning to despair. Martin and Roger had been very thoughtful in the way they'd telephoned each day to reassure her that everything possible was being done to find out what had happened to her brother – but neither of them voiced their deepest fear that the chances of Freddy being found alive had dwindled with each passing hour of silence.

Charlotte had telephoned a couple of times, but she'd been tearful and mostly incoherent, which made Kitty feel depressed and even more helpless. As the first week drifted into the second and there was still no news, Charlotte threw herself into work and didn't phone again. Their letters went back and forth, but they offered little comfort to either of them, for only the news of Freddy's fate could ease the torture of this terrible state of uncertainty.

Following Charlotte's lead, Kitty pushed herself even harder in the gym. She used the weights to strengthen her arms and thighs, and did more and more sit-ups to tone her stomach muscles, and with every exercise she did and every step she took, it was with a prayer for Freddy.

'That's more than enough for one day,' said the retired army instructor as he took charge of the weights and stored them away.

'But I have to keep going,' she replied as she towelled the sweat from her face and chest. 'I haven't finished my twenty lifts.'

'Killing yourself by lifting too many weights and doing endless sit-ups won't get you out of here any quicker,' he said as he folded his arms over his well-defined chest. 'It will merely put you back into a hospital bed.'

Kitty bit down on an angry retort. He didn't understand that it was essential to carry on with this punishing routine, for if she exercised hard enough and prayed long enough, Freddy would come home. A small part of her mind told her it was illogical, but she refused to listen just in case she was right.

She slung the towel over her shoulder and grabbed her crutches. 'I'll see you tomorrow,' she muttered. Letting the door swing shut behind her, she headed for the showers. She had an hour before her next session with the doctor.

Peggy had been at the station for the past hour, handing out sandwiches, hot tea and cigarettes from the WVS mobile canteen to the young servicemen who were on their way to their next posting. Daisy had caused quite a stir among them, she'd noticed, and being the star of the show, she'd beamed and giggled delightfully as she was petted and praised. But Peggy's feet were hurting now, and she was looking forward to getting back to the Town Hall.

Not that her task was over even then, she thought wearily, for all the rubbish had to be cleared away, the canteen and urn scrubbed clean, and the tin mugs washed out thoroughly. She eased from one foot to the other as she stood by the pram and collected the empty mugs, but she didn't stop smiling, for these youngsters were facing far worse than sore feet, and she shouldn't have been stupid enough to wear these silly shoes in the first place.

'Hello, Stan,' she said as the stationmaster appeared through the crush. 'How's things?'

'They're very good, Peggy,' he replied with a beaming smile as he dug his thumbs into his waistcoat pockets and rocked on his heels. 'Ethel and Ruby are coming for tea on Sunday after they've been to visit Mike, and she's promised to make me some of her rock buns.'

Peggy eyed the pot belly beneath that straining waistcoat. 'It looks as if you've had quite a few of those already, Stan,' she teased. 'You want to watch it, or those buttons will go pop.'

He laughed and patted his stomach. 'Ethel's cooking is hard to resist,' he confessed, 'but she did say she likes a big strong man to whisk her about on the dance floor, and we've had no problems so far.' He leaned in a bit closer and lowered his voice. 'We're off to the Lyceum tonight, and I've promised her a fish supper.'

Peggy laughed. 'It's good to know you're happy, Stan. And that's all that really matters these days, isn't it?'

He nodded and his smile was rather smug.

'How is young Mike getting on?' she asked. 'Ruby popped in the other day, but she didn't seem too hopeful about his sight.'

Stan gave a deep sigh, his expression grave. 'They don't think he'll get it back,' he said. 'Ruby's at sixes and sevens about it, because she's fallen hard for that young man, and if he's discharged and sent home it could be months, even years, before they can be together again.'

'Poor Ruby. She's gone through enough without that.'

'Don't worry, Peg. I'll keep a fatherly eye on her, never you mind.'

Before Peggy could ask any more questions, he pulled his watch and whistle from his waistcoat pockets. 'I'd better get this lot on their way.' He put the whistle to his lips and gave it a mighty, ear-splitting blast. 'Train's leaving in one minute,' he shouted. 'All aboard. All aboard.'

As the gathering slowly melted away, Peggy helped the other women to stow everything into the canteen, and then followed along behind with the pram as they trundled it down the hill towards the alleyway that ran alongside the Town Hall.

It was always a bit of a job, for the hill was steep, the mobile canteen was heavy and unwieldy, and the women weren't blessed with a great deal of muscle power. But they got there in the end and wheeled it through the gate to the rear entrance of the Town Hall and parked it in the yard by the kitchen door. There were rumours they were going to receive one of the proper mobile canteens that could be driven everywhere, which the Queen had provided, and if the rumours were true, then it couldn't come soon enough.

Peggy was helped up the steps with the pram by a young Home Guardsman who couldn't have been much older than her Bob. The poor lad had been put on duty for most of the afternoon beside the sandbags that sheltered the Town Hall entrance. Thanking him, she parked the pram in the main hall and fetched him a cup of tea and a biscuit. It was a boring duty, and the boy looked half-starved and totally fed up.

Returning to the hall, she rolled up her sleeves to tackle the mammoth task of washing up, for there were not only the canteen mugs and plates to deal with, but all the ones that had been used that afternoon in the WVS café. Someone hadn't been doing their job, she thought rather crossly, for the café stuff should have been cleared and washed the moment it was finished with.

Willing hands came to help with drying up, and there was quite a lot of muttering going on that Freda Lynley wasn't pulling her weight – that she was a flighty piece and no better than she should be, going out with all those Americans, and that if she wasn't prepared to do the work, then she shouldn't have volunteered in the first place.

Peggy let it all go on around her. She just wanted to finish up here and sit down before she went home. Gossiping was all very well, and she usually enjoyed it, but it slowed them down, and there was still a mountain of things to wash.

She finally dried her hands and took off her apron. She was hot and sweaty after bending over a sink full of boiling water for almost an hour, and now she needed a cup of tea and a sit-down before she made the trek home. Pulling off her headscarf, she ran her fingers through her damp hair and didn't much care that she must look a fright as she took her cup of tea to a nearby table and plumped down into a chair.

She eased off her shoes and wriggled her toes, wondering if she'd get the shoes back on when it was time to leave. Deciding she'd rather walk home barefoot than suffer the agony of those heels again, she relaxed and took a sip of tea. She was just about to light a well-earned fag when she saw her sister Doris making straight for her.

'If you've come to moan about something then you'd better find someone else,' she said as she drew on the cigarette and blew smoke. 'I'm knackered.'

'Margaret! Language like that is not ladylike.'

'It's a word I learned from Ruby,' she replied. 'And it describes exactly how I feel.'

She regarded her sister through the cigarette smoke as Doris brushed the chair with her handkerchief before sitting down rather prissily with her expensive leather handbag on her knees. Dressed in a cotton frock, big hat, white gloves and shoes, she looked as if she was going to a garden party, Peggy thought sourly. 'So what do you want, Doris?'

'You really shouldn't jump to conclusions, Margaret,' said Doris smoothly. 'Perhaps I've merely come to see how you are and to have a chat.'

Peggy snorted smoke. 'And pigs might fly,' she retorted.

'Really, Margaret, you have learned some disgusting habits from your ghastly lodgers. It's frightfully common to swear and snort.'

Peggy was used to this sort of insult from Doris, so she drank her tea and waited. Doris had something to say, and sooner rather than later, she'd reveal her reason for seeking her out.

'I understand you've taken in some girl from the Memorial,' Doris said casually once she'd lit her own cigarette.

Peggy wondered where this was leading, but no doubt Doris would get to the point eventually. 'That's right,' she murmured. 'She's been with me for almost two weeks now and is coming on a treat.'

'How long do you expect her to remain with you?'

The tone was still casual, but there was a steely glint in her eye.

Peggy had noticed the glint, and knew it meant trouble. She shrugged. 'She'll stay with me until she can manage on her own, I suppose. We haven't really talked about it.'

'I see,' said Doris. 'So she could be with you for some months?'

Peggy now had an inkling of what this was about, but she wasn't going to help her sister in any way by supplying too much information. 'It takes a long time to get rehabilitated after losing a leg.'

Doris looked rather ill at ease as she shifted in her chair. 'Susan and Anthony have very kindly asked me to organise their wedding reception,' she began. 'Anthony is such a thoughtful boy,' she sighed. 'He understood that I would want to be an intrinsic part of his special day. But of course I will need a list of the guests so I know how many to cater for.'

'I'm sure Suzy will make up a list once she knows how many of her family will be able to get down here,' said Peggy, stubbing out the cigarette.

Doris fidgeted with her gold lighter. 'But I do have some concerns, you see.' Her gaze slid to somewhere beyond Peggy's shoulder.

'Surely you won't have any difficulty getting all the food, not with Ted being the district manager for the Home and Colonial?'

Doris waved this comment away. 'It's not about

the food,' she said impatiently. She pursed her lips, hesitated and then said in a rush, 'It's about that girl.'

'What girl?' asked Peggy with feigned innocence and the flat, quiet tone that should have warned Doris she was treading on very thin ice.

'The cripple,' she replied with a sniff – and then got into her stride, the words pouring out with her usual complete absence of tact or thought for anyone but herself. 'My son's wedding will be an elegant occasion,' she said, patting her hair. 'And with Susan's parents being so well connected, I am expecting some extremely important guests. I don't want that cripple putting a damper on things by turning up in trousers and clumping about on a wooden leg. So I wondered if you could have a word with Susan. I'm sure the girl wouldn't mind if she didn't receive an invitation. After all, she's merely a transient lodger – and a foreigner at that, I believe – and definitely not one of the family.'

Peggy's fury was incandescent as she pushed back from the table and shoved her feet back into her shoes. 'She's family while she lives in my house – and if you *dare* call her a cripple again, I'll hit you so hard you won't get up for a week.'

Doris must have noticed Peggy's bunched fists, for she looked quite alarmed. 'Well, really,' she gasped. 'I don't think that sort of thing is called for at all.'

'Neither is your attitude,' Peggy snapped. 'That

girl lost her leg in the service of this country, and if Suzy wants her to attend the wedding then attend it she will. And you can just ruddy well lump it.'

With that, Peggy stormed off, leaving her sister open-mouthed and gasping like a trout out of water.

Kitty had worked hard during the day, stopping only for lunch in the canteen and a short gossip with some of the other girls. Her session in the gym had left her feeling energised instead of exhausted, so she had to assume her muscles were getting much stronger. Peggy's good food helped, of course, but it was her own determination that had been the driving force.

She went into the physio room for her final session of the day, greeted the doctor and nurse, then eagerly strapped the leg on. Her progress along the parallel bars and back was slow but steady, and now she could do it just holding onto one bar.

'That's very good,' said the doctor as he let her rest in a chair. 'Now, when you're ready, I'd like you to try to reach the door using just a couple of walking sticks.'

Kitty's pulse was racing as she took the sticks from him. She had waited for this moment for what felt like months, and now she was about to discover whether all those hours in the gym had been worth it.

She shuffled forward in the chair, then, steadied by the sticks, pressed her feet to the floor and stood up. It felt strange without the crutches she'd become so used to, but oddly liberating. She took a step, and then another. Her stump was complaining a bit after all the work she'd put in today, but she chose to ignore it and took two more steps.

'Well done,' chorused the nurse and the doctor.

Kitty's whole focus was concentrated on the door, and how many steps it might take to reach it. She took two more steps, and then another two. But the door was too far away and her stump felt as if it was rubbed raw. She stopped as hot tears blinded her and she had to accept she simply couldn't go another inch.

She felt the wheelchair sliding behind her knees, and the nurse's steadying grip on her arm as she sank down onto the seat. 'I failed,' she said bitterly. 'I couldn't do it – and it's not that far, for goodness' sake.'

'It's a mountain, actually, but one that you've almost conquered,' said the doctor as he pulled a chair up beside her so they could converse eye to eye. 'You haven't failed – far from it. You've just achieved far more than most of my patients on their first trial run.'

This was music to her ears. 'Really? Even Doreen?'

'Even Doreen,' he replied with a gentle smile. 'Now, you rest while I take off this leg and have a look at your stump.'

Kitty's emotions were a strange cocktail of elation and frustration. She'd so wanted to reach that door

– but the knowledge that she'd gone further than Doreen at this stage gave her a tremendous boost.

'The scar tissue is a little red,' murmured the doctor. 'And there is some bruising and swelling.' He looked back at her. 'I'll give you some cream to rub in morning and night, but you won't be using the prosthesis again until I can be certain there's no infection setting in.'

She looked at him in horror. 'But I can't give up now. Not when I'm so nearly there.'

He signalled to the nurse to apply the thick white cream and rewrap her stump. 'Infection is your enemy, Kitty,' he said softly. 'If you don't rest that leg, you could be in serious trouble.'

Kitty tasted the copper of fear and had to swallow the lump in her throat before she could answer. 'How serious?' she whispered.

His expression was grave. 'It could lead to more surgery.'

She stared at him as the words rang in her head and an icy chill ran down her spine. 'You mean I could lose more of my leg?'

He nodded. 'But we're getting ahead of ourselves,' he said more cheerfully as he handed her the tub of cream. 'As long as you rest and let the redness and swelling go down, you should be as right as rain in a few days.'

He placed his hand over her fingers. 'All it takes is patience,' he reminded her.

Kitty knew she didn't have a great supply of that

particular grace, but with the threat of more surgery hanging over her like the sword of Damocles, it was time to learn patience and damned quick. 'So, what happens now?' she asked as she slipped the tub of cream into her trouser pocket.

'I'll arrange for you to be seen in my clinic at the Cliffehaven General each morning until I'm satisfied you're ready to start again. But when you are,' he added sternly, 'you will take it slowly.'

Kitty nodded, fully prepared to do whatever he asked if it meant she could walk on that leg again and avoid surgery.

He crossed the room and picked up a heavy ledger. Running his finger down the columns, he made several notations as he turned the pages. 'You won't need a long appointment, because it's more of a check-up really, so I've squeezed you in at eleven for the next seven days – and that includes this Sunday.'

Seven days. It felt like a lifetime. 'Thank you,' she murmured. 'I'll be there.'

He closed the book and dropped it on his desk with a thud. 'My clinic is to the left of the main doors and is always busy, so don't be late.'

She shook her head, and before she could disgrace herself by bursting into tears, she grabbed her crutches and headed for the door which had seemed so far away only minutes before. She needed to get out of here – to find a quiet corner somewhere and curl up against her misery and bitter disappointment.

'Hello, old thing. Matron said I'd find you here.'

Kitty saw Roger Makepeace's cheerful face and bristling moustache, and burst into tears. As his sturdy arms wrapped round her and his big hand gently pressed her head against his broad chest, she dropped the crutches and clung to him as all the anguish she'd been holding back poured out of her.

'There, there, old thing,' he murmured. 'No need for tears. I've only come to pick you up and take you back to Beach View.'

She made a determined effort to pull her emotions into some kind of order before she leaned back in his embrace and looked up at him. 'There's no news of Freddy? I thought . . . When I saw you, I thought . . .'

'I'm so sorry, Kitty. I should have said straight away that I'm not here because of Freddy.' His brown eyes were full of regret as he kept his arms about her and regarded her affectionately. 'I just thought I'd pop in while I had the chance and give you a lift home. But by the expression on your face when you came out of that room, I'm guessing these tears aren't all about Freddy.'

She nodded and scrabbled in her trouser pocket for a handkerchief. 'It's my leg,' she said brokenly. 'The doctor thinks it might have become infected, and . . . and . . . Oh, Roger, I couldn't bear to lose any more of it,' she sobbed.

He held her close, his big, gentle hand once more cradling her head to his chest. Kitty could hear the steady beat of his heart beneath the Air Force blue uniform jacket, and feel the sturdy strength of his arms as his fingers softly ran through her hair. She felt comforted and secure in his embrace, and her tears gradually came to an end and she was calm again.

'I'm sorry, Roger.' She drew back and put her weight on her good leg, keeping hold of his steadying arms. 'I don't usually let things get on top of me like that. But what with the worry over Freddy and now this – well, it was the last straw.'

'Then I'm glad I came,' he said rather gruffly. 'At times like this we all need to have our friends about us.' He quickly picked up the nearest crutch, and once he was assured that she was properly secure, he fetched the second one.

'Let's go and find a cup of tea – or coffee if they have it here. Then we can sit and talk for a while until you're ready to go back to Beach View.'

'That sounds like a good idea. I don't want to turn up with a tear-streaked face and swollen eyelids because it will only worry Peggy, and I don't think I could stand any fussing just at the moment.'

She looked up and gave him a watery smile. 'We can get coffee in the canteen,' she said. 'The Americans and Canadians refuse to drink our tea, and as it isn't rationed, there's plenty to go round.'

'Jolly good,' he murmured. 'Lead on, then.'

As they headed for the canteen, Kitty realised she wasn't at all fazed by Roger's unexpected appearance, or the fact that this was the first time he was seeing her having to get about on crutches. Even the empty trouser leg that she'd pinned up beneath her stump didn't cause her a moment of silly hurt vanity. Roger was Roger. She'd known him ever since Freddy had joined the RAF, and he was as familiar and unthreatening as a big, cuddly second brother. It was wonderful to see him.

Roger paid for his coffee and Kitty's tea and then carried them out to the terrace, where they found a quiet spot in the dappled shade of the nearby trees.

'I have to say,' he said after he'd tasted the coffee and given it his approval, 'that this is a very fine spot.' He regarded the lawn and the formal flower beds. 'One wouldn't have known this place existed if one hadn't been told about it.'

'They work miracles here,' said Kitty quietly. 'Or at least they try to. The doctors and nurses are so dedicated, and I feel rather ashamed of my outburst earlier. It's my own fault, you see.'

His dark brown eyes regarded her steadily. 'Why don't you tell me about it? A trouble shared and all that.'

So Kitty told him of the long weeks she'd been struggling to get strong enough to learn to walk unaided with the prosthesis, and about the doctor's warning that afternoon. She found it so easy to talk to him that she described the initial difficulties she'd encountered at Beach View, and the battle she'd had trying to stop people from fussing over her.

'But if I lose more of my leg it will mean being

readmitted here and starting all over again,' she finished with a break in her voice.

Roger lit their cigarettes and leaned back in his chair. 'It sounds to me as if you're very down, Kitty,' he said after a while. 'But if you obey the doctor's instructions, I'm sure you'll be up and about again on that leg in no time.'

At the mention of time, Kitty gasped and looked at her watch. 'Arthur will be waiting to take me home,' she said frantically. 'I must go and . . .'

'No need, old thing,' he interrupted. 'I knew about the arrangement with the fire station, so I went there first and told them I would take you home this evening.'

'Oh, Roger,' she sighed in relief. 'I can't believe that I forgot about Arthur.' She giggled. 'He's actually quite difficult to forget, because he's taller and wider than you, with a voice that could give a cannon a good run for its money.'

He smiled at her warmly and patted her hand resting on the arm of the chair. 'That's more like my old Kitty,' he said affectionately. 'I like hearing that naughty giggle of yours.'

Kitty read something in his expression that suddenly made her feel very shy and a bit awkward. She hurriedly finished her cigarette and then drained her cup of tea. 'We'd better get back to Beach View,' she said. 'Peggy will wonder where I've got to.'

'There's no rush,' he said as he sipped his coffee.

'I popped in to see her earlier too, so she knows where you are and so on.'

'It seems you've thought of everything,' she replied with a warm smile. 'But I'm hungry after all the exercise I've had today and ready for my supper.'

'Well, in that case, we'd better get a move on,' he said cheerfully as he picked up his Air Force hat and slipped his cigarettes and lighter into his trouser pocket. 'We don't want you fainting away from starvation, now do we?'

Kitty was thankful he didn't try and help her to her feet, or make a fuss by moving chairs and tables out of her way as she weaved round them and headed back indoors. 'I just have to pick up my handbag and gas mask, and then I'm all yours,' she said as he matched his pace with hers down the long corridor towards the bank of lockers.

'Now there's a thing,' he said with wistful softness.

Kitty didn't quite catch what he'd said, for she'd been busy opening her locker and reaching for her bag. She eyed him with a frown. 'What was that?'

'I'm on your wing, Kitty,' he said hurriedly. 'Now, have you got everything?' At her nod, he beamed down at her. 'Jolly good show. Chocks away.'

Kitty chuckled. 'You really are the limit, Roger,' she teased. 'Do you have to equate *everything* with flying?'

He reddened slightly as he held the front door open for her. 'It comes rather easily when one is surrounded by it all the time,' he replied as they reached the gravel driveway. 'Besides, flying's the only thing I can do well.'

'That isn't true,' she said softly. 'You're the most loyal, kindest man I know, so don't sell yourself short.'

His face went scarlet and he cleared his throat rather purposefully as he opened the car door. 'Just get in, Kitty. And stop teasing a poor chap when he can't defend himself. It's really not cricket.'

Kitty was still smiling as she climbed into his lovely car and settled on the soft leather seat. Dear Roger, he was just so very English. But that was his charm and what made him special, and she thanked her lucky stars that he'd come just at the right moment to bring her out of her doldrums.

The car purred along the country lanes and swept up and down the hills without the familiar groans and twangs of the fire station truck. They talked about the weather and Cliffehaven, and what life was like at Beach View. But the subject of Freddy's fate lay between them, and neither of them seemed willing to be the first to mention him.

It wasn't until they had reached the twitten behind Beach View that Kitty turned to Roger and said, 'He will come home, you know. I'm certain of it.'

'So am I,' he replied firmly as he switched off the engine and quickly climbed out of the car.

Kitty ignored his proffered hand and slid out of the seat. With her handbag and gas-mask box swinging from their straps round her neck, she made her slow and rather unwieldy progress along the narrow alleyway.

'Harvey will be all right,' she said as they reached the gate and heard the dogs barking. 'But Monty's likely to trip me up, so if you could put your fielding skills into play, I'd be very grateful.'

'You seem to forget, Kitty. I was in the first Eleven at Eton and won a blue at Cambridge. Monty will be no trouble at all.'

She didn't like to say that Monty was nothing like a cricket ball – more of a darting, wriggling evasive missile – and Roger wasn't as fast as he once was. She went through the gate and headed up the path just as Peggy opened the back door.

'It's all right, dear,' she called. 'Ron's got both dogs upstairs and Monty's on a lead, so you're safe to come in.'

Kitty stepped over the threshold and saw immediately that Peggy's eyes were bright, and there was a flush of excitement in her cheeks. 'You look like the cat that got the cream,' Kitty laughed. 'Has Jim come home already?'

'Oh, no dear,' she said hastily. 'He's not due for another week or two. I'm just a bit flushed from standing over that oven.' She turned to Roger. 'Could you help Kitty up the stairs, please? The dogs have trampled dirt right the way through and I don't want her getting her nice clean trousers all mucky.'

'There's really no need,' Kitty protested.

But it was too late, for Roger had gathered her up, crutches, handbag, gas-mask box and all, and was holding her tightly to his chest.

Kitty gave in, for it was a rather pleasant experience, even though his moustache was tickling her forehead.

He carried her into the kitchen and gently deposited her on a chair. 'There we are,' he said. 'Safe and sound, and all ready for take-off.'

Kitty smiled at him and was about to say hello to everyone when she realised they were all looking rather furtive. Her smile faltered. 'What's going on?'

'I couldn't possibly say,' twittered Cordelia, and then collapsed into giggles.

Kitty looked at Rita for an explanation, but she dipped her chin so her face was hidden behind her curls. Jane tittered as she and Sarah pretended to read the newspaper, Fran's sole attention was on Monty as she gave him a brush, and the other girls had their backs turned as they helped Ron with something at the sink. She knew it couldn't be anything unpleasant, but there was definitely something going on here.

She looked at Harvey, who gave a single bark as he wagged his tail. 'Well, you're no use, are you?' she laughed. 'Even if you knew what all this is about you couldn't tell me.'

Peggy chuckled as she placed a cup of weak tea in front of Roger, but before Kitty could question

420

her, she heard footsteps crossing the hall. She looked towards the door and was surprised to see it was closed for once. Then, before she had time to question this, the door creaked open, and there – whole and handsome and very much alive – was Freddy.

Chapter Twenty-two

In two strides Freddy was across the room, and before she could speak he'd lifted her out of the chair into a bear hug. 'You've no idea how good it is to see you again, Sis,' he said in her ear. 'But what on *earth* have you done to your hair? It looks as if rats have been chewing it.'

She thumped him hard on the shoulder with her fist and burst into tears. 'I'll give you rats,' she sobbed as she clung to his neck and smothered his face in kisses. 'Where the *hell* have you been?'

He hugged her tightly and swung her back and forth, which made the dogs bark and Peggy gasp in alarm. 'I'll tell you if you'll stop soaking my shirt and slobbering all over my face,' he said gruffly.

She sniffed back her tears and released some of her grip on his neck. 'I thought you were dead,' she breathed as she dangled from his embrace. 'So did Charlotte. Oh, my God, Freddy, have you told Charlotte yet?'

He nodded and set her carefully back onto the chair before sitting opposite her and taking her hands. 'I managed to get through to her before she left Hamble Ferry Pool this morning. She's been given some compassionate leave and is flying down this weekend.'

'You've been back since this morning?' she gasped. 'But why didn't you let me know – or come to the hospital to see me?'

He glanced across at Roger before he spoke. 'I actually got back very late last night,' he confessed. 'But I had to be debriefed, and that took most of today. I asked Roger if he'd do the honours by bringing you back here, but not to give the game away.' He shot her his famous grin. 'And it seems my special surprise worked brilliantly.'

'Oooh,' said Cordelia with a pleasurable shiver. 'Isn't it wonderful when things go right?'

There were appreciative murmurs from the girls and even Peggy was looking misty-eyed as she checked on Daisy, who was watching all this with wide-eyed curiosity from Rita's lap.

Kitty laughed as she looked back at her brother, who was relaxed and basking in the admiration with all the aplomb of someone who was quite used to being the centre of attention. 'You really are the absolute limit,' she sighed as she drank in the sight of him. 'You come swanning in here as if nothing had happened and make yourself right at home when I've been worried silly about you.'

But to have him home and to know that he'd come through his ordeal unscathed made her heart swell with love as she reached out and ruffled his thick mop of hair. 'I'm not the only one who needs a proper haircut,' she teased. 'So come on then, big brother. What have you been up to for two weeks?'

''Tis my way of thinking that a man can only do so much talking before he's in need of liquid refreshment,' said Ron, who had Monty's lead firmly wrapped round his wrist. 'And I believe there's a bottle or three in the larder if someone would like to fetch them.'

'Jolly good show,' said Roger as he got to his feet and rummaged in the large corner larder. 'The mess was a bit short on spirits, but I managed to wangle a couple of bottles of gin and another of whisky.' He placed them on the table with the smile of a proud and happy provider.

'And there's a crate of beer if anyone fancies it,' he added as he drew it out and placed it next to the bottles. 'Wheel out the glasses, Mrs R. It's time for a snifter.'

Kitty heard the girls giggling and saw how Freddy was making a particular fuss of Cordelia, who was blushing and batting her eyelids while she twittered. Nothing changed with Freddy, she thought happily, and his presence had lit up this dark little kitchen and brought laughter and renewed energy.

Roger and Freddy poured the drinks and handed them round. 'To homecomings,' said Freddy as he raised his glass.

'And happy landings,' said Roger with a wink at Kitty.

'To homecomings and happy landings,' they said

in joyful unison as the puppy yapped and Harvey gave a deep bark of approval.

Kitty took only a tiny sip of the gin, for she was on strong medicine and the doctor had warned her that alcohol might have nasty side effects. Once everyone had taken a drink, Kitty's impatience became too much to bear. 'Come on, Freddy,' she urged. 'I've waited long enough now. Spill the beans.'

Freddy took a long drink of whisky and then passed his cigarettes round. 'Well, I was flying over the beach at Dieppe trying to give cover to the poor blighters down below in their landing craft, when I was set upon by two Messerschmitt 109s,' he said almost casually. 'I did everything I could to avoid them and get my shots in first, but they stuck to my tail like glue. Before I knew it I was miles from the bally beach and flying over some sort of town.'

He puffed on his cigarette. 'Roger could see I was in trouble and stuck to my wing. He managed to down one, but then he was attacked by two more, and had to get rid of them. I was on my own again, trying to shoot down that determined 109, but the blighter got me in the tail-feathers.' He paused as if for effect. 'The Spit was on fire, but if I'd bailed out then and let it crash I'd have wiped out half that town.'

The silence was absolute and Kitty found she was holding her breath as he took another long drink of whisky.

'I'm not like my sister,' he said with a teasing grin at Kitty. 'I'm not in the habit of pranging my planes, and my Spit's been with me since the start, so I didn't want to see her go up in flames. The fire was in the tail so my engines weren't affected yet, and I had control, so I flew high and fast to try and put out the bally fire and get well away from that town.'

He gave an almost nonchalant shrug. 'But it didn't work, and I could feel the heat at my back and knew I didn't have long before she blew up. It was time to bail out.'

He stubbed out his cigarette and then looked into the glass of whisky as if he could see the scene in the pale gold liquid. 'The Spit's engines were gone by this time and I no longer had control. She was starting to yaw, and would soon go into a spin as she lost height, so I opened up the canopy and scrambled out. The parachute had just opened nicely and I was floating down when I heard the Spit crash and saw the flames and smoke rise above the trees of a distant wood.'

He drank some more whisky, then swirled the remains in the glass for a moment as if to gather his thoughts. 'Anyway, I was floating down and one of the 109s came back for a recce, saw me dangling there and thought it might be fun to use me as target practice.'

There was a horrified gasp from everyone. 'But that's against the Geneva Convention,' protested Kitty.

Freddy grimaced. 'I don't think the Luftwaffe pilot was familiar with that particular part of the rule book, Sis – and even if he was, he'd chosen to ignore it.'

'So what did you do?' asked a breathless and wide-eyed Cordelia.

He gave her his best boyish, devil-may-care grin. 'I hung from the parachute and shot at him with my pistol,' he said. 'He flew past a couple of times, and then, with a waggle of his wings, went back to the real battle going on further north.'

'Goodness,' twittered Cordelia. 'How terrifying.'

'It was certainly rather exciting,' he admitted, 'but I didn't have much time to think about the 109, because I was about to drop straight into a bally great forest. I couldn't avoid it, unfortunately, and got caught up in the trees. But I cut myself down, buried the chute and made a hasty getaway. I'd seen farm buildings not too far away, and a main road, so it didn't do to hang around.'

'My, my,' breathed an enraptured Peggy.

'If that pilot saw where you went down, he'd have informed someone,' said Ron, who clearly wasn't as impressed by Freddy's gung-ho adventures as the women. 'How long was it before they came looking for you?'

Freddy nodded. 'You're absolutely right, Ron. I'd soon realised they would guess I'd be heading north to link up with our troops, so I turned west. Then two hours later I heard German voices and the crash of people approaching through the trees. Luckily it was just an ordinary patrol and they didn't have dogs, so I shinned up the nearest, tallest tree and watched them go by. I stayed up there until dark and then, with the aid of my trusty compass, went on my way.'

'But it's been two weeks since you crashed,' said Kitty.

He nodded cheerfully. 'Don't I know it? But it took me that long to avoid the numerous patrols and the villages and farms I passed on the way. I didn't dare trust anyone, so made a circuitous route to keep well out of the open countryside.' He grinned ruefully. 'Which isn't easy, because that part of France is open and flat, and mainly farmland. After about ten days I found myself in a tiny fishing village just to the east of Deauville.'

He finished the whisky and waited while Roger topped up his glass. Nodding his thanks to his wingman, he continued. 'I hid in the abandoned ruins of an old house and kept body and soul together by stealing a baton of bread each morning from the nearby *boulangerie*, and eating the cheese I found in the cellar beneath the house. There was some rather fine wine down there too, so it must have been a grand house at one time. But of course I had to be careful with that. Couldn't afford to drink too much and lose my wits after having got so far.'

'Did you steal clothes as well so your uniform wouldn't give you away if you were seen?' asked an awed Rita.

He shook his head and smiled. 'Out of uniform I would have been classed as a spy and probably hauled off by the SS for interrogation. The uniform might have marked me out, but if I was captured, it would be as a POW.'

'But there was no guarantee of that,' said Kitty sharply. 'If they have no qualms about shooting at a pilot as he's parachuting down, then who's to say what they'd do if they caught you?'

'That was the chance I had to take,' he said as he reached for her hand. 'I was alone in occupied territory, and my only goal was to get back to England in one piece.'

'So you must have had to trust someone to help you,' persisted Kitty.

He nodded. 'Eventually, of course, I had no choice. I moved round a bit during the night to recce the place, and watch from several strategic spots to see if there was any Jerry about, and what the mood was in the village. This wasn't part of Vichy France, but it didn't do to assume everyone was anti-Jerry.'

'So how did you escape?' asked an impatient Jane.

'I was just coming to that,' he replied with a cheeky grin. 'There was a German officer who strutted about importantly every morning before returning to his lair in the Post Office where he harried the locals and made himself generally unpopular. He was in charge of six men who were supposed to guard the quay and patrol the town, but once he'd gone to the local bar for his lunch, they knew they wouldn't see him for the rest of the day.'

He grimaced. 'They were a slovenly, sloppy lot and spent most of the time drinking wine and harassing the younger women. It was soon clear that this occupying group was despised by all, so after a couple more days, I decided to approach one of the older fishermen.'

'That was risky,' murmured Kitty.

Freddy shook his head. 'I'd been watching him for two days and realised he was my best hope. He was an old curmudgeon who spat every time he saw a German and scowled if they spoke to him, or got in his way as he unloaded his day's catch.'

The smile lit up his face again. 'It turned out he was a lovely old chap, name of Pierre, of course, and his little wife, Yvette, cooked me the most amazing fish stew I've ever tasted.'

'Are you sure they didn't have a daughter you managed to charm along the way?' asked Kitty dryly. 'It would explain why you took so long to get home.'

He put his hand over his heart and looked sorrowful. 'Now, Kitty, that's not very charitable, is it?'

'I know you too well, Freddy Pargeter,' she replied with a grin.

'Well, in this particular case you've got it very wrong,' he said firmly. 'I saw neither hide nor hair or heaving bosom all the while I was in France, so

I'll thank you not to blacken my reputation in front of these lovely people.'

Kitty laughed. 'Get on with it then. I'm starving, and it's way past supper time.'

'We had to wait until the patrol had drunk their fill of wine and were sleeping it off in the bar. So it was gone midnight when we pushed the boat out and rowed until we were sure the engine couldn't be heard from shore.'

He grinned at Ron. 'You would have liked Pierre,' he said. 'He was a real old sea dog, tough as nails and as strong as a man half his age. He'd been fishing in the Channel all his life and knew it like the back of his hand – even the mined areas.'

Ron smiled back. 'Aye, they're a tough breed, those men from Normandy, and there's been many a time they've drunk me under the table, so they have. I don't speak a word of their lingo, mind you, but that never seemed to matter.'

Freddy nodded, drank some whisky and lit another cigarette. 'My French isn't up to much either,' he admitted. 'But I could understand enough to have a fairly decent conversation with him on the way over.'

He fell silent for a moment, his smile fading into solemnity. 'He's the third generation of fishermen in his family, and had hoped his sons and grandson would take over. But all three had been captured and shot by the SS for being part of the underground movement in the area which had caused a good deal of sabotage. He hated the Germans,' he said softly. 'Hated the very sight and sound of them, and so he was only too pleased to be able to do something for me.'

There was a profound silence in the room, the mood suddenly sombre.

Freddy broke the silence with a chuckle. 'When we landed in a tiny shingle cove just below Beachy Head, Pierre whispered, '*Vive l'Angleterre, bonne chance*,' before he rowed back out into the Channel again.'

'To be sure, I'm amazed that our coastal defences are so poor that you could sail in and out again with anyone shooting at you,' said Ron.

'We saw plenty of shipping, believe me. But luck seemed to be on our side, and somehow we made it without being spotted. Yet it was a very tiny bay, and it posed the devil's own job to get out of it, because there was no path and I was faced with a very steep cliff to climb.'

He winked at Kitty. 'All those years of climbing mountains and trekking across the pampas paid off that night, because I shinned up that thing without breaking sweat.'

'Honestly, Freddy,' she sighed with affectionate exasperation, 'a bit of humility wouldn't go amiss at this point.'

He shot her a rueful smile. 'As it happens, I wasn't all that clever,' he admitted, 'because, as I put my head up over the top of the cliff, I came face to face with a group of trigger-happy members of the Home Guard.' He chuckled. 'They all got terribly excited and wouldn't believe that I wasn't a German spy.'

'Serves you right for being so cocky,' teased Kitty.

He ignored the gentle jibe and continued his story. 'They took me to their commanding officer who, after an enormous amount of cajoling from me, eventually rang Cliffe. After a lot of back-slapping and cups of stewed tea, they took me to a nearby airfield, where I got a lift in a Tiffy back to Cliffe.' He grinned and held out his hands. 'And that is the end of my adventures in France.'

'Jolly good, old chap,' said Roger as he put a heavy hand on Freddy's shoulder. 'Glad to have you back on board.'

'You're not going back to flying again, are you?' protested a horrified Kitty.

'Actually no,' Freddy admitted dolefully. 'I've been stood down. Commander Black wants me flying a desk for a while, and I'll be helping to train the new recruits that are pouring out of the schools and colleges.'

'Thank goodness for that,' breathed Kitty. 'You've done more than enough, and you were jolly lucky not to have been killed.'

He gave a soft chuckle. 'You know I've always led a charmed life, Sis. But flying a desk simply isn't my style, and Commander Black knows that.' He grinned at Roger. 'I can't let this old b . . . this old chap go on missions without me. We're a team, and with him on my wing, I know we'll come through.'

He grabbed Roger, and they did the bashful man-hug, slapping of shoulders thing which, to Kitty's mind, looked horribly awkward, and really rather silly.

'The pair of you need your heads testing,' she giggled. 'Honestly, you're no better than children at times.'

'Right,' Peggy broke in. 'The shepherd's pie's nearly ready so we need to clear the table.'

Roger shifted the crate and the girls began to lay the table.

Freddy's expression grew serious. 'It's good to see you out of that hospital, Kitts,' he murmured. 'Roger told me how you came to be here, and I'm sorry I caused you so much distress.' He ruffled her hair. 'So, how are you getting on?'

She quietly told him about her achievements, and then admitted she'd probably done too much and was now in danger of getting an infection in her stump. 'But I've learned my lesson,' she assured him. 'I'm going to rest and be patient, and then take things at a much slower pace from now on.'

She took his hand and held it to her cheek. 'I'm just so thankful that you're back, Freddy,' she murmured. 'Please, please don't do anything foolish. I couldn't bear it if something happened to you.'

'Don't worry about me, Kitty Cat,' he replied affectionately. 'I'm not planning on being a hero for a while yet. How about we make a bargain? I'll be patient, just as long as you are – and then we'll see where we go from there.'

'If it will keep you grounded, then it's a deal.'

Peggy watched the brother and sister as they quietly talked, and felt quite tearful. It was clear Freddy had been through the mill, even though she suspected he'd made light of it by turning it into a sort of Boys' Own adventure. But it was also clear that Kitty and her brother had a deep affection for one another, and she was glad, for they were far from home and fighting a war that seemed endless and cruel.

She finished dishing out the enormous shepherd's pie, relieved that she'd managed to get enough minced meat to make it a good one. Meat was rationed by cost not weight all the time it was available, so she'd managed to get three whole pounds of mince thanks to Alf the butcher, who'd put it by for her. Potatoes weren't rationed either, so there was a good thick topping, and she'd added a small knob of butter so it had gone all golden in the oven.

As chairs were pulled up to the table and the dogs banished to the rug in front of the range, Peggy smiled with contentment. Everyone was here and they were talking nineteen to the dozen as they ate the delicious food. It was quite like old times, but the best thing of all was that Jim would be home soon, and then her joy would be complete.

She listened to the happy chatter and saw how the two handsome young pilots had enlivened the evening. It was lovely to see how at home they were, but her heart was heavy at the thought that soon they would be returning to Cliffe and risking their lives again.

Her gaze drifted from one smiling face to another as she finished feeding Daisy and lifted her out of the high chair. And then she caught the expression on Roger's face as he watched Kitty, who was in animated conversation with Freddy. *That boy's in love with her*, she realised suddenly, *but Kitty seemed oblivious to the fact. Oh, dear*, she thought with an inward sigh. *Life just gets more and more complicated. I do so hope it won't all end in tears.*

Chapter Twenty-three

Kitty woke early the next morning. Finding the ever-vigilant Harvey had once again spent the night outside her door, she gave him a quick stroke behind the ears then went into the bathroom. Sitting on the chair, she carefully examined her thigh and felt a twinge of alarm as she noted the redness and swelling in the scar tissue. Deciding it probably wouldn't do it much good to be soaked in a hot bath, she had a strip wash with a flannel and soap, and then smeared the doctor's cream over her stump and wrapped it back in the dressings and sock.

Having dressed and packed everything she might need for the rest of the day into her shoulder bag, she picked up her gas-mask box and carefully slid down the stairs. With Harvey following every step of the way, she went into the kitchen to find Ron finishing his breakfast, and Peggy already bathing Daisy in the sink.

'You're both up early,' she said as she poured out a cup of tea.

'This one wakes at the crack of dawn,' replied Peggy as she lifted Daisy out of the water and wrapped her in a towel. 'And once she starts grizzling, there's no peace.' She smiled at Kitty as she sat and dried the baby, who was wriggling and trying to reach for Harvey. 'I bet you had the best night's sleep now you know Freddy's safe,' she said.

'Yes, I did.' Kitty put two slices of bread on the hotplate and kept a close eye on them so they didn't burn while she boiled an egg. 'I've told him not to say anything to our parents when he next writes. Having come through unscathed, there's little point in worrying them needlessly.'

'To be sure, you're looking well this morning, despite the late night,' said Ron as he finished his mouthful of toast. 'Now, I'll be taking these two for their walk, and then I have other things to do.' His expression became very solemn for a moment. 'I'll be seeing you both later,' he said gruffly, then clipped the lead onto Monty's collar.

Kitty patted Harvey, who then willingly followed Ron and Monty down the steps and out into the garden. It would have been lovely to go tramping the hills, she thought enviously as she watched them leave – but such pleasures were beyond her now, and she had to accept the fact.

'I don't know what's up with Ron this morning,' said Peggy as she dressed Daisy in a clean nappy, rubber pants and a cotton vest. 'He's usually a bit of a live wire first thing, but today he hardly had a word to say.'

'He's probably got a hangover,' said Kitty. 'I

noticed that Roger was very heavy-handed with the whisky measures last night.'

'Roger seems to be an extremely nice young man,' said Peggy casually as she popped Daisy in her high chair and tied the bib round her neck. 'Have you known him long?'

Kitty turned the toast and spooned the egg out of the water. 'Ever since he and Freddy joined the RAF,' she replied. 'He's a bit like a second brother really, and can always make me laugh. But I worry about the pair of them. They're far too gung-ho for my liking, and one day they'll run out of luck and come a cropper.'

She picked up the browned slices and dropped them onto the plate next to her boiled egg before reaching across to put it on the table.

'Does Roger have anyone special waiting for him back at home?' asked Peggy as she dipped a bread finger into Daisy's boiled egg and fed her. 'He obviously comes from a good family and must be considered quite a catch.'

Kitty laughed. 'Roger's family owns most of Wiltshire, and he always has some woman hanging on his arm, but so far he's managed to avoid anything too serious. I think he's having far too much fun to get tied down just yet.'

She opened the waxed packet of National Margarine and spread some on her toast. Taking a bite, she grimaced at the greasy and unpleasant fishy flavour. 'Yuck. This truly is awful stuff.'

'Yes, isn't it? And they have the cheek to advertise the fact that it contains marine oils, which are supposed to be good for us, and then charge nine-pence a pound for it because it's got "Special" written on the label.' Peggy sighed. 'Oh, for the days of proper butter – all golden and melting into soft, white, crusty bread.'

'Don't, Peggy,' giggled Kitty. 'The thought just makes this taste even worse.' She followed Daisy's lead and dipped the toast into her egg in the hope it would make it taste better. It did a bit, and with a pinch of salt it was quite palatable.

'So, who's taking you to the hospital this morning?'

Kitty realised with a jolt that with all the excite-ment over Freddy's surprise appearance, she'd said nothing about the new arrangements. 'There's been a change of plan,' she said hastily, and then went on to explain, leaving out the bit about possible further surgery.

'Oh, my dear,' breathed a worried Peggy. 'I do hope it's not too serious.'

'It's just a precaution, I'm sure I'll be fine,' she assured her lightly. 'And at least I won't have to ask people to give up their precious time ferrying me about for a while. I can easily make my own way down there.'

'Oh, no, you won't,' said Peggy firmly. 'It's further than you think; and I won't have you struggling all that way on your own.' As she saw Kitty was about to protest, she silenced her with a wave of her hand. 'And I'll take no argument from you, young lady,' she said quite sternly. 'Rita and the lads from the fire station will see you there and back as planned.'

Kitty knew Peggy well enough now not to argue when she used that tone, so she ate her breakfast and drank her tea. 'I'll telephone the fire station in a minute, if I may,' she said once she'd finished the egg and toast. 'I don't have to be at the clinic until eleven, and it will mean changing things about in their roster.'

She gave a deep sigh. 'Honestly, Peggy, it's asking too much of everyone – and they've all been so good to me.'

'I'll telephone John right now,' said Peggy. 'Finish feeding Daisy for me, will you?'

As Peggy hurried out into the hall, Kitty handed Daisy an eggy soldier of bread and giggled as the baby grabbed it and smeared it over her face before eventually finding her mouth. 'You like that, don't you?' Kitty said. 'Well, there's plenty more, but eggs are for eating, not wearing, Daisy, and you're making a terrible mess.'

Daisy chortled and dribbled egg and toast down her bib as she slapped her hands on the tray of her high chair in delight.

Peggy came back into the kitchen just as the final bit of egg and bread disappeared into Daisy's greedy mouth. 'It's all sorted,' she said. 'You'll be picked up at ten-thirty.'

Kitty was profoundly grateful for all the help and

kindness she'd been shown since coming to Beach View, but having been self-reliant for so long, she did wish she wasn't quite so dependent on everyone. 'I'll be glad when I'm back on two legs again,' she said wistfully.

'And you will be soon enough if you take things slowly and do as you're told,' said Peggy with an understanding smile. 'I can only guess how frustrating it must be for you to have this setback, but for now, just try and be patient.'

'Yes, I know,' Kitty admitted softly. She poured a second cup of tea, her thoughts already on her plans for the day ahead. 'After the clinic, I'd like to do a bit of washing, if that's all right, and then I've got letters to write. But if I can help you with anything round the house, please ask me.'

Peggy smiled as she wiped Daisy's face clean and plucked her out of the high chair. 'I can't think of anything I need at the moment,' she said, 'but if I do find something, then you'll be the first to know.'

Kitty knew she would do no such thing, so she started to clear the table of the used crockery and, despite Peggy's soft protest, rolled up the sleeves of her blouse and started on the washing-up.

Cordelia came into the kitchen looking very smart in a cotton frock sprigged with red roses, white sandals and a matching cardigan. She abandoned her handbag, straw hat and walking stick and plumped down at the table with the newspapers which had just been delivered.

'Good morning,' she said brightly. 'Didn't we have fun last night? Those young men certainly livened things up, and Freddy's story was utterly thrilling. Will they be coming for another visit soon?'

'Freddy might pop in now he's been grounded,' said Kitty over her shoulder as she washed the dishes. 'But they're both very busy, so I doubt we'll see much of either of them.'

'To be sure, and that's a shame,' said Fran as she came into the kitchen in her dressing gown. She pushed back the tousled curls from her face and grinned. 'I wouldn't mind seeing that Roger again.'

'Good grief, Fran, is no man safe with you?' sighed Rita as she followed her in and reached for the teapot.

'Sit down and eat your breakfast,' said Peggy firmly to both of them. 'Where's Sarah and Suzy? If they're not careful, they'll be late for work.'

They came in shortly after, and soon there was a clatter of knives on plates and a chink of china to accompany the lively chatter. Sarah left for her long walk over the hills to the Cliffe estate and her WTC office, and a few minutes later, Suzy was on her way to the hospital.

Rita sat for a few more moments to finish her cup of tea and then, with a cheery goodbye to everyone, ran down the cellar steps and headed for the fire station. Kitty realised she would soon learn about the hospital appointments from her work colleagues, but she was glad Peggy hadn't said anything to the others, for she really didn't want to have to explain it all over again.

Fran finished her breakfast and Peggy spent a moment having a murmured word with her while she washed her plate and bowl. She turned from the sink with a broad smile. 'Kitty, to be sure you can't be going about with that hair. And as it seems you'll not be off to the Memorial this morning, I'm going to give it a good trim and see if I can make something out of that bird's nest.'

Kitty was rather startled by this and she ran her fingers protectively over her ragged hair. 'I'm not sure,' she murmured.

'It's all right,' said Peggy. 'Fran's good with the scissors, and she'll soon have you looking much tidier.'

'Well, if you think so,' Kitty said reluctantly. 'But don't take too much off, Fran, it's short enough already.'

'I'll just be fetching me beauty bag and I'll be right back,' she said brightly.

Kitty looked at Peggy with a knowing smile. 'This was your idea, wasn't it?'

'I thought it was time you were spoiled a bit,' she admitted, 'and Fran is very good, so you'll be in safe hands.'

Kitty could only nod and wait for Fran, but she wasn't at all sure she really needed all this fuss with the doctor's appointment looming.

Fran came back carrying a rolled-up towel and a

small vanity case, which she set on the table. She draped the towel over Kitty's shoulders and then squeezed her arm reassuringly. 'I'll just be giving it a wee bit of a trim and tidy up. Don't worry, Kitty, I've been cutting my family's hair for years, and I've had no complaints yet.'

'We've been trying to persuade Ron to let her sort out his hair and eyebrows, but of course he's having none of it,' said Peggy as she opened the bottle of Virol and fed Daisy her daily spoonful of the malt extract.

'Ach, to be sure, I'll catch him one day,' said Fran as she opened the little case to reveal comb, brush and scissors, and a collection of nail files, tweezers, hand lotions and small pots of nail varnish. 'I could also do your nails, if you'd like,' she murmured. 'There's nothing like a manicure to make you feel pampered and special.'

Kitty was still feeling uneasy, for she'd never had a manicure in her life and wasn't particularly worried what her hair looked like as long as it was neat and tidy and regulation length. But before she could do anything about it, Fran had begun to comb and snip.

'There we are,' Fran said cheerfully half an hour later. 'And if I say so meself, that's a vast improvement, so it is.' She plucked the hand mirror from her beauty case so Kitty could see for herself.

Kitty was astounded at how feminine and pretty she looked, for Fran had layered her hair into soft, short waves that framed her face and curled neatly into her nape. 'Goodness,' she breathed. 'You should do this for a living, Fran. It's really lovely, and you've made me look much better.'

Fran beamed with pleasure and began to delve into the case again. 'Now for your nails,' she said enthusiastically. 'They look as if they've been neglected for far too long. What *do* you do to them?'

'Keep them clean and short,' Kitty replied hesitantly. 'I don't know, Fran. I've never really been one for fussing about my nails.'

'Then it's time you did,' she said as she reached purposefully for Kitty's hand. 'And I'm going to do your toes as well. You can't be wearing that sandal with naked toenails.'

Kitty looked to Peggy for support, but she just nodded and smiled and carried on playing with Daisy who was now crawling about on the floor. 'Well, all right,' she said reluctantly, 'but don't go painting them red. That would be too much.'

'Will you do my nails when you've finished there?' asked Cordelia. 'Only I'm going out for lunch with my pensioners' group and Phoebe Harris is always showing off her latest manicure.'

'Of course I will, Grandma Finch,' murmured Fran as she smoothed cream into Kitty's hands and massaged her fingers. 'Why don't you have a look in my box and choose a colour? The pale pink is very nice, or I could use the clear one.'

'I want the red,' said Cordelia determinedly. 'I'm

feeling adventurous this morning, and it will go with the flowers in my dress.'

Ron was experiencing the worst hours of his life, and as he sat with Rosie in her small sitting room above the bar, he couldn't keep his mind on anything but Harvey.

'To be sure, I never should have done it, Rosie,' he muttered fretfully. 'That poor wee boy trusted me, so he did. And I swear to God he knew what was coming when I had to virtually haul him off the pavement and carry him into the vet's.'

Rosie was sitting next to him on the couch with Monty spread luxuriously between their laps. 'You did the right thing,' she soothed. 'Monty's sweet, but you really can't risk having any more puppies dumped on your doorstep.'

'Aye, I know,' he said with a deep sigh. 'But I've betrayed Harvey's trust. 'Tis a terrible thing to do to my best friend.'

Rosie rested her head on his shoulder and held his hand. 'I'm sure he'll forgive you,' she murmured.

'Aye, he will that,' he muttered. 'Harvey's a loyal wee dog, so he is. But it doesn't make me feel any better about it.' He could smell her perfume and feel her soft cheek nuzzle his own, and under any other circumstance, he would have been soothed. But his whole mind was taken up with Harvey as he imagined him lying on the operating table, out cold and utterly helpless as the vet cut and snipped and stitched.

Rosie ran a comforting hand over his bristled chin before she kissed his cheek. 'When are you due to pick him up?' she asked softly.

He looked at the clock on the mantel, surprised that only an hour had passed since he'd left Harvey. It had felt like a lifetime. 'Not until five,' he said mournfully, and then gave another deep sigh. 'I hope he's all right, because if anything happened to him I'd never forgive meself.'

'I think you need something to take your mind off Harvey for a while,' she said purposefully. 'Come on, it's no good moping about here.'

She tipped Monty rather unceremoniously onto the floor as she got up from the couch and pulled on Ron's arm. 'Let's take Monty for a walk along the seafront. We're both going to be stuck indoors over lunchtime, so it will do us good to get some fresh air and sunshine. And if it's open, we'll have a cup of coffee at the little café before we come back.'

Ron did his best to look enthusiastic, but all he could think about was the way Harvey had looked at him so soulfully with those great amber eyes as he'd left him with the vet. He wasn't a praying man, for his faith had been killed along with most of his regiment in the stinking, rat-infested trenches of the Somme, but today he begged silently for Harvey's safe return.

The morning had sped past as Fran conducted her beauty treatments in the kitchen, and Kitty was now admiring her gleaming, pale pink nails. There was no doubt about it, she thought, she certainly felt pampered, and could now understand why her mother paid regular trips to the Spanish beautician's tiny shop in the nearby town.

Fran bustled about, and after she'd packed her things away and swept up the hair from the floor, she got a promise from Peggy that she would let her do her hair and nails before Jim came home on leave.

Peggy returned from the garden where she'd just finished putting the nappies on the line. 'Your lift's here,' she said to Kitty. 'He's in the garden talking to Daisy.'

Kitty hung her handbag and gas-mask box round her neck and gathered up her crutches. Not wanting to keep the fireman waiting, she quickly said goodbye to Peggy and then bumped down the steps and over the threshold.

But it wasn't a fireman who waited in the garden, and she felt a little stab of pleasure. 'Roger? What on earth are you doing here?'

He'd been squatting by Daisy's playpen and keeping her amused with her toys. Now he stood and looked at Kitty in admiration. 'I say, you do look smashing this morning,' he said quietly as he took in her new hairstyle.

It was lovely to see him, but his flattery was a bit embarrassing, and not at all what she was used to from him. 'What's going on, Roger?'

He suddenly looked a little unsure of himself, and he eyed her bashfully from beneath the peak of his uniform cap. 'I hope you don't mind, Kitty, but I've got some leave and so I spoke to John at the fire station and said I'd do the clinic run for the next few days.'

'That's really sweet of you, Roger, and I'm touched by your thoughtfulness. But surely you've got better things to do than run about after me?'

He shook his head. 'I'd like to do this, Kitty. And I thought we could go for a picnic afterwards,' he added in a rush. 'I got one of the NAAFI girls to pack up a basket and it's in the car.' His voice tailed off as she remained silent.

Kitty regarded him affectionately and wondered why the thought of spending time with him on this summer day felt so right – and why she'd experienced that little unexpected tingle of pleasure when she'd seen him waiting for her. 'That's a lovely idea,' she said softly. 'It's been ages since I had a picnic.'

'Jolly good,' he said in his usual bluff way. 'Come along then. Your carriage awaits.'

Kitty went down the path on her crutches, but before she started along the alley, she looked back at the basement door.

Peggy was standing there with an enormous grin on her face. 'Have fun, Kitty,' she called, 'and don't feel you have to rush back.'

Kitty giggled and made her way down the alley on her crutches. Peggy was incorrigible, but if she thought she could see signs of romance, then she was sorely mistaken. Roger was just being nice to his best friend's sister.

The drive down Camden Road took a matter of minutes, and soon Roger had parked by the ramp near the front steps. He opened the door and waited for her to get to her feet. 'I'll come in with you and wait outside, if you don't mind,' he said as she slowly went up the ramp.

'There's no need,' she protested. 'I shall be perfectly all right.'

'I have no doubt of it, old thing. But I'll feel better if I'm close by.'

She paused and looked up at him. 'You mean if it's bad news?' At his reluctant nod, she carried on into the large, echoing vestibule and headed for the clinic. 'Don't let's get ahead of ourselves, Roger,' she said determinedly. 'It's early days yet.'

Peggy was quietly humming to herself as she gathered up Kitty's washing and carried it downstairs. There was nothing like a bit of romance in the air to liven up the day, and it looked as if Roger was pulling out all the stops.

She smiled at Cordelia who was still immersed in the morning papers. 'Your nails look very glamorous,' she said as she paused on her way to the scullery.

'I know what you're up to, Peggy Reilly,' she replied as she regarded her over her half-moon reading glasses. 'But I'd be careful if I were you.

That poor little girl has enough to contend with, without having her heart broken.'

'Oh, I don't think Roger has any intention of doing that,' Peggy replied happily. 'He's obviously head-over-heels in love with her.'

'That's as maybe,' said Cordelia. 'But he's also a Spitfire pilot, and in these uncertain times it doesn't do to fall in love and make plans.'

'Oh, Cordelia,' Peggy sighed as she slumped into the nearby chair with the washing still in her arms. 'That's the very reason why it's so important to fall in love, don't you see? No one knows what the future might hold, but if we don't keep our hopes and dreams, then it will all be for nothing.'

'But Kitty isn't in love with him,' said Cordelia.

'I think she is,' replied Peggy firmly. 'She just doesn't know it yet.'

'You really are an old romantic, aren't you?' Cordelia's smile was gentle and affectionate. 'My goodness,' she murmured, 'if you had your way, you'd be marrying off all our girls – and then where would we be?'

Peggy laughed and pushed back from her chair. 'I'd be sitting down with my feet up and bemoaning an empty house – and you would be bored stiff because you had no one to complain about. Now, I really must get on, or the day will be over.'

She had just finished pegging out the washing when Cordelia called down from the kitchen window that her lift to the club had arrived.

Peggy ran back up the stairs, checked Cordelia had everything, and then watched as a very dapper elderly gentleman with a rose in his jacket lapel solicitously helped her down the steps and saw her safely into the little car.

Cordelia smiled and waved regally as she was driven away, and Peggy's heart was warmed. For all her scoffing at romance, Cordelia Finch still enjoyed the company of a good-looking man.

Daisy was now asleep in her pram beneath the umbrella in the back garden, so Peggy scrubbed the scullery sink until it gleamed and then polished the copper boiler. Ron's mess was beyond her, so she shut the door on his room and went to tidy and dust the kitchen before she washed the floor and started on the hall.

The girls were all very good at doing their own washing, keeping their rooms clean and their linen regularly changed, but the floor tiles needed a good scrub and the landing carpet hadn't seen the vacuum cleaner for days. She worked happily, her thoughts skittering from Kitty and Roger to Suzy and Anthony, before finally settling on Jim's homecoming.

It would be nice to clear out the abandoned dining room before he arrived so they weren't quite so cramped at mealtimes. In the mood for a good day of housework, she opened the dining room door, and her spirits fell. There would be no cleaning today, she realised, for there was a lot of furniture to be moved out first, and those big, heavy curtains needed to be taken down and given a jolly good beating to clear out the dust and cobwebs.

Closing the door, she carried the bucket of dirty water and the mop back into the scullery and emptied the bucket into Ron's water butt, then went back into the kitchen to make a well-earned cup of tea and some lunch.

She had just settled down to her sandwich and tea in the garden when she heard the squeak of the garden gate. Looking up, she smiled in delight. 'Hello, Ruby, love. This is a nice surprise.'

'I 'ope it ain't inconvenient,' Ruby said. 'But me Mum's at work, and I thought it were the best time to come and 'ave a quiet chat.'

'You're welcome any time, Ruby,' said Peggy, noticing how fretful the girl was. 'Come and sit down and share my sandwich. There's plenty of tea in the pot. I'll just get you a cup.'

'No need,' Ruby said hastily. 'I know where every-thing is.' She left her bag and gas-mask box between the newly refurbished deckchairs and was soon back from the kitchen with a cup and saucer.

Peggy poured the tea as Ruby settled into the other deckchair and adjusted her sunglasses. 'I must say, Ruby,' she murmured, 'you're looking very well, and that's a pretty dress. Is it new?'

'Me mum made it from an old dress she found in the Town Hall.' Her smile was fleeting as she tucked the rich brown hair behind her ears and smoothed her fingers over the sprigged cotton frock. 'And if I looks better, it's because the sun's given me a bit of colour in me face,' she continued somewhat distractedly.

Peggy waited for her to sip some tea, knowing that this visit had a purpose and suspecting that Ruby had things on her mind she couldn't – or perhaps was reluctant to – discuss with Ethel.

'Mike's up and about again,' she said after she'd refused the offer of half of Peggy's tomato sandwich. 'But he ain't gunna get the sight back in his eye. He's ever so depressed, Auntie Peg, and I dunno what to do or say to cheer 'im up.'

'I should think that just by visiting him every day you must make him feel better about things.' Peggy laid a consoling hand on the girl's slender brown arm. 'After all, you're a pretty girl, and he must be proud to have you by his side.'

Ruby's head drooped. 'He told me he don't want me to see him no more,' she said with a hitch in her voice. 'He said I was to forget about 'im.' She looked at Peggy with tears in her eyes as she gripped her hand. 'But I can't, Auntie Peg. Really I can't. I loves 'im, you see, and it don't make no difference if he's blind in one eye.'

Peggy returned the grip. 'Maybe not to you,' she said softly, 'but it clearly matters very much to him. He's a young, strong, fit man who's feeling very lost at the moment, because he simply doesn't know what the future holds. Give him time, Ruby. He doesn't really mean to send you away. He's just confused and, I suspect, rather frightened.'

Ruby took a trembling breath, clearly trying to keep the tears in check. 'But 'e were ever so unkind this morning,' she said. 'Told me to stop me fussing and go and find someone else to annoy 'cos he were fed up with me coming in all the time.'

'Oh, Ruby, he's hurting, love.'

'Yeah,' she sniffed, 'but so am I, and 'e don't seem to care. I run out of that hospital crying like a baby, and then I 'ad to walk most of the way home 'cos I missed the blooming bus,' she sobbed.

Peggy dug a handkerchief from her apron pocket and put her arm round the slender shoulders until the storm of tears began to ebb. Life was unfair, and now both these young people were hurting so badly that they were in danger of losing something very special. And yet Peggy felt helpless, for what words could she say to make things better between them? How to make them both see this terrible twist of fate didn't have to be the end of such promise?

'I dunno wot to do,' said Ruby eventually. 'Me mum says I should forget about 'im and get on with me life, 'cos it weren't ever supposed to be – and that I went through enough with Ray, without saddling meself with a blind man.'

Peggy felt a sharp stab of annoyance. Ethel should mind her tongue – even if she did only have Ruby's best interests at heart – for her words had been unnecessarily cruel and very unhelpful.

Ruby looked at Peggy, her eyes bright with fresh

tears. 'But I can't leave him, Auntie Peg. He needs me now more than ever.'

'Ruby, love,' said Peggy hesitantly. 'You have to think very carefully about this. Are you staying with him because you'd feel disloyal if you left? Or are you staying because you really love him and can see a future with him regardless of his injuries?'

Ruby's expression softened. 'It's 'cos I loves him, Auntie Peg.'

'Have you spoken to the doctor or one of the nurses that are looking after Mike?'

Ruby nodded as she mangled Peggy's handkerchief. 'Sister Bennett says it's quite usual for blokes like Mike to be nasty to those they loves 'cos they don't want to be a burden. She said I gotta ignore what 'e says, and just keep visiting.'

'That sounds like good advice, Ruby.' Peggy watched the girl dry her eyes and then sip her cooling tea. 'Is there some reason you're wary of taking it?'

'Yeah,' she admitted softly. 'Wot if he *really* don't want me no more? Or, wot if he does and 'e's sent back to Canada? I can't go with 'im, can I?'

This was the problem Peggy had foreseen long ago, but she said nothing as she lit a cigarette.

Ruby was making a heroic effort to remain calm, but her voice was unsteady as she continued. 'When he first got injured, he were hoping that if his eye weren't right, the army would give him an admin job over here. Now he won't even talk about the possibility, 'cos he reckons he ain't worth nothing and the army won't want him no more.'

'Oh, Ruby,' sighed Peggy. 'The poor boy has a great many changes to deal with, and I'm afraid you're just going to have to be patient and supportive. From what I know about him, he's always been fit and strong and used to being in charge of his destiny. He was a Mountie before the war, remember? And the loss of sight, even in one eye, will be devastating to him and his career.'

'I know,' sniffed Ruby as the tears began to roll once more down her cheeks. 'But 'e keeps pushing me away, and I'm beginning to think he really don't love me no more.'

This was going round in circles, and Peggy realised it was time for some straight talking. 'Then sit down and talk to him, quietly and calmly, and ask him straight out how he feels. Tell him how hurt you are by his pushing you away, and make it clear to him that his injury makes absolutely no difference to how you feel.'

Peggy sighed and smoothed her hand over Ruby's shining hair. 'I'm certain from all you've said that you'll both find a way to overcome this. But it won't be easy, Ruby. A man's pride is at stake, and he doesn't want you to see him as anything less than perfect.'

Ruby shot her a watery smile. 'Ain't no one perfect in my book,' she said. 'Not even Mike. Men are right idiots, aren't they?'

Peggy laughed. 'They certainly can be, but we women are willing to gloss over that when we're in love with them.' She picked up the teapot. 'Let's have a fresh cuppa while you relax and think things through. Life is never black and white, Ruby, and you're only just learning that falling in love can bring far more complications than we could ever dream about.'

She smiled down at her. 'But if your heart is true, then you'll find a way.'

Chapter Twenty-four

Kitty's thigh was still a bit sore from the penicillin injection Dr Thorne had given her to help fight any infection that might be lurking, but he'd been cheerful and optimistic, and she'd left the clinic feeling a little more hopeful.

Roger was his usual teasing self once he knew she was feeling easier about things, and he'd driven out of town and up and over the hills to a tiny village where a rough chalk track wound its way from the narrow lane to the brow of the hill.

'There we are,' he said as he parked to the side of the track. 'How about that for a view?'

'Quite magnificent.' Kitty got out of the car and looked round. 'This was an inspired idea, Roger,' she sighed. 'It's as if you read my mind.'

'I thought you might like to be out in the open after being cooped up between four walls,' he said solemnly as he took off his uniform jacket and tie, and unfastened the top button of his shirt.

'It's exactly what I need,' said Kitty, breathing in the soft, salty air.

Roger spread out a large tartan blanket across the

grass. 'Good. Now you sit down and I'll unpack the car.'

She watched as he brought out the hamper and a bright yellow parasol, then fussed about her with numerous cushions and made sure the parasol was tilted just right so the sun didn't glare in her eyes. She smiled with amusement as he continued to unload everything, for there were linen napkins, proper cutlery and even china plates, as well as a neat little case containing a spirit stove, kettle, silver teapot and milk jug.

'Where on earth did you find that?' she asked.

'It belongs to Father, really,' he confessed. 'He uses it when he goes shooting or spends the day at the races, but he doesn't mind me borrowing it. I did consider bringing the wind-up gramophone,' he continued as he handed her a straw sunhat with ribbons fluttering from the crown. 'But I thought that was rather over-egging the pudding.'

'It would be rather,' she replied lightly. 'You should keep the gramophone for when you're courting some wide-eyed beauty who is more susceptible than me to your undoubted charms,' she teased.

He gave a dramatic sigh and tried to look as if he'd been wounded to the very core. 'You mean you're not susceptible to my charms?'

'Don't be daft,' she teased. 'I know you too well, Roger Makepeace, and I'm not about to fall for any of your old flannel. Anyway, I'm hardly the romantic heroine, am I? Not with this bally stump getting in the way.'

'It's a lovely stump,' he said gallantly. 'And you remind me of Cleopatra lying there amongst the cushions.'

'Then let's hope there are no asps about,' she giggled. 'I understand this is the ideal weather for adders.'

He smiled at her boyishly. 'If I spot one, I'll fight it off with my trusty knife and fork,' he said, waving the cutlery menacingly towards the grass.

Kitty roared with laughter. 'You are a tonic, Roger.'

'Jolly good,' he said bashfully as he went rather red and fumbled about in the hamper. 'I hope you're hungry, Kitty, because there are Scotch eggs, a cheese and onion flan, some salad, tomato sandwiches – with real butter on the bread – and a trifle.'

'It all looks wonderful,' she replied, her mouth watering. 'You are clever, Roger. Do you always have such grand picnics?'

'I just thought you deserved a treat,' he replied airily. 'Now, sit back and enjoy the view while I get the spirit stove going to make us some proper tea.'

Kitty found that it wasn't very comfortable sitting on the ground, for her stump made her unbalanced. Not wanting to spoil things for Roger, who'd clearly planned this picnic with infinite care, she discreetly wriggled about, and with strategically placed cushions, finally found a way to really enjoy the experience.

She looked out over the great sweep of land that ended in the chalk cliffs to the east of Cliffehaven, and watched the gulls hovering over the dazzling water in the Channel. She could hear skylarks, and the soft breath of warm wind rustling the trees, and could smell baked earth and the honey-sweet perfume of the bright yellow gorse and fluffy white cow parsley. It was utterly beautiful, and she gave a deep sigh of contentment.

'It's a far cry from the vivid colours of the Argentine pampas, I know,' said Roger as he knelt by the spirit stove and waited for the little kettle to boil. 'But there's nothing lovelier than the English countryside on a summer's day.'

'It's perfect,' she said as she watched seabirds glide against the blue sky. 'I've been indoors far too much over the past months, and I was only thinking this morning how much I would love to come up here.' She reached across and lightly touched his hand. 'Thanks, Roger. You couldn't have given me a better treat.'

He cleared his throat and busied himself with the small silver teapot. 'No need for thanks, old thing,' he said gruffly. 'Glad to do it.'

Kitty smiled and returned to the panorama spread before her. Spoiled only by several gun emplacements, the grassy hills and valleys dipped and rolled high above the sea. To the west she could see the sun glinting on the many windows in Cliffehaven town; to the north was the Cliffe estate and a scattering of farmhouses and thatched cottages between wide fields where the land army girls toiled to bring in the harvest. To the east, and far in the distance, she could see the jagged line of chalk cliffs which defined this whole coastline.

'You wouldn't think there was a war on, would you?' she said as he handed her a cup of tea. 'It's so peaceful.'

'We're lucky to have days like this,' he said, stretching out his long legs and leaning back on his elbows. 'It seems a lifetime ago since I last had a picnic with a pretty girl in the sunshine.'

'Flattery will get you nowhere,' she teased. 'Now pass me a sandwich. I'm starving.' She munched happily on the lovely buttery tomato sandwich and then reached for another. 'You'd better have something before I eat all of these,' she warned. 'You know me and my appetite.'

'I do indeed,' he replied with a grin. 'That's why I made sure there was plenty for both of us. I've never known someone so slight put food away like you do.'

She giggled and finished the second sandwich, then reached for a Scotch egg, which she suspected had spam round a bit of soggy powdered egg, which was usually how Peggy did them. But biting into the breadcrumb coating, she tasted real sausage meat and real hard-boiled egg. 'Oh, my goodness,' she murmured. 'What a treat. You boys are certainly well fed if this is an example of RAF food.'

He patted his stomach and shot her a rueful smile. 'Rather too good at times,' he admitted as he took another sandwich. 'But the amount of energy we use on an op is quite amazing, considering we're sitting in a cockpit all the time. Everyone's famished when they get back, but I suppose it's because of all that adrenaline sloshing about.'

Kitty finished the Scotch egg, and then cut a thin slice of the cheese and onion tart, helped herself to salad and munched thoughtfully as she adjusted the brim of her sunhat and looked out over the sea. 'You must all be exhausted,' she said. 'It's bad enough flying with the ATA virtually non-stop, but at least we're unlikely to get shot at – unless it's by a trigger-happy ack-ack gunner who's supposed to be on our side.'

'I can't deny that we're all stretched to the limit,' he said solemnly as he finished his slice of cheese and onion tart. 'But we sleep when we can, play hard and get on with it.' He looked across at her and winked. 'We're the boys in blue – Churchill's few – and we'll keep going until this war's over.'

'What about Freddy? Will he go back to flying, do you think?'

He nodded as he reached for a Scotch egg. 'Inevitable, old thing. Without flying, he feels half a man. It's the same for us all.' He looked at her. 'Surely you can understand that, Kitty?'

'Oh, yes,' she said with a sigh as she finished her salad. 'I can't wait to get back into the air.'

'So you can't really blame Freddy for wanting the same.' He finished the Scotch egg in three bites and then grinned. 'Come on, it's time for trifle. We're getting far too serious for such a lovely afternoon.'

He spooned out the trifle into china bowls, hunted out spoons, and they tucked in. 'Jolly good show,' he murmured appreciatively. 'This is absolutely spiffing, with real cream and proper custard. I'll have to find a way to show my appreciation to the cook.'

Kitty was too busy scraping the last of the delicious trifle from the bottom of her bowl to answer him. Licking the spoon clean, she leaned back into the cushions, tipped her sunhat over her eyes and gave a little sigh of contentment. 'That was marvellous, but now I'm so full, all I want to do is go to sleep.'

'Go ahead, old thing. I'll keep watch for adders, never fear.'

She watched him through half-closed lids as he packed away the remains of the food and placed the hamper in the shade of the umbrella, which he'd managed to stick firmly into the rock-hard ground.

He was the nicest, kindest man, she thought as she regarded him sleepily. And, she realised with a jolt of surprise, really rather handsome, with his long-lashed brown eyes, firm chin and flamboyant moustache. His lips were well shaped too, and she wondered suddenly what it would be like if he kissed her.

Horrified she should think such a thing, she flung her arm over her face to hide the deep blush that burned from her throat up. The sun and rich food had to be playing tricks on her mind. Really, she thought crossly, what a thing to think of a friend. He'd be as mortified as she was if he'd had even a hint of what had just passed through her sun-addled mind.

She couldn't sleep now, so she sat up and prodded the cushions about to give her something to do.

'Cigarette?' he asked as he held out the silver case.

She didn't dare look him in the eye for fear he might see something of her rampant thoughts. 'Thanks,' she replied. 'Is there any more of that tea?'

He poured her a cup and set it beside her, then sat with his arms propped on his knees as he smoked his cigarette and stared out towards the Channel.

The silence was companionable, but Kitty still felt a bit unnerved by her earlier thoughts, so she was glad to just smoke her cigarette, look at the dazzling view, and say nothing.

'You know, Kitty, I admire you,' he said finally as he crushed the cigarette butt beneath his heel. 'Not only for the way you're handling this present situation, but for your energy and perseverance. There are very few women brave enough to be a part of the ATA, and,' he paused as his lips twitched, 'even fewer who can eat as much and never get fat.'

Kitty burst out laughing. 'You rotten . . .' She hit him with a cushion.

He sat up sharply, and before she knew what was happening he'd flung her to the ground and was lying on top of her.

'Roger, get off,' she protested. 'What *do* you think you're doing?'

'Keep still,' he rasped.

'Don't you dare . . .' Then she heard the unmistakable sound of a 109 coming from the east, and the answering rattle of anti-aircraft guns from all the cliff-top emplacements.

She froze beneath him as the powerful fighter plane roared overhead with a salvo of gunfire. They were horribly exposed up here in the open, with a bright yellow umbrella marking the spot. But worst of all, Roger had to be in full sight of the Jerry pilot.

She clung to him as if by pressing him to her, they could melt into the ground and be out of sight. But she was finding it hard to breathe, for Roger was very heavy, and she was beginning to get a sharp pain in her chest.

As suddenly as it had appeared, the 109 was gone and the guns fell silent.

Kitty and Roger waited tensely to see if it would come back, and when it didn't, Roger finally lifted his weight from her chest and looked down at her with deep concern. 'That was a very close shave,' he said softly. 'Are you all right, Kitty?'

She nodded, mesmerised by his eyes and the nearness of that well-defined mouth. 'I'm fine, really,' she murmured.

He didn't roll away from her as she'd expected, and there was a tender look in his eyes as he gazed at her. 'Oh, Kitty,' he breathed.

She felt dreamy and floating as she returned his gaze, but when he hesitantly brushed his lips against the corner of her mouth, she felt as if she'd been hit by a thunderbolt.

But this was Roger, her shocked mind was telling her. Roger her friend, and he shouldn't be kissing her – and she shouldn't be enjoying it so much.

But as, with the utmost tenderness, he captured her lips, she felt any resistance melt away and she became languid and pliant in his embrace, giving herself up to the intoxicating sensations he was stirring within her. She had never imagined a kiss could be like this, had never before experienced such a profound desire to be loved and held and cherished. She opened her lips to his soft, searching tongue, and with a groan of desire she was lost.

Peggy was all in a dither as she kept glancing at the clock. 'The picnic must be going well,' she said joyfully to Cordelia. 'It's nearly five o'clock and there's still no sign of them.'

'I'd advise you not to jump to conclusions, dear,' said Cordelia as she grated the cheese and prepared the sauce to go over the fresh vegetables from the garden. 'And if she comes home all glowing and ruffled, don't badger the girl with questions. Let her tell you in her own good time.'

'I'll know the state of play the minute she comes through that door,' said Peggy firmly as she threaded the green beans and sliced them. 'And of course I won't badger her, Cordelia. I'm not that tactless.'

'If you say so dear,' she replied with a knowing smile. 'But young love is a tender thing, and the slightest bit of poking and prying might bruise it.'

Peggy felt rather put out by this little lecture, so she changed the subject. 'How did your lunch party go?'

'It was very nice, thank you.' She abandoned the cheese and grater and folded her arms, but there was an unmistakable twinkle in her eye. 'And before you ask, Peggy Reilly, his name is Bertram Grantley-Adams. He's a retired solicitor who was widowed three years ago and he came to Cliffehaven just before the war. He lives in a very nice house just down the road from your sister Doris, has a touch of arthritis in his hips, and his hobbies are golf, bridge and more golf.'

'He seemed very attentive,' said Peggy, a bit peeved by having the wind taken out of her sails.

'He's like that with everyone,' said Cordelia dismissively. 'So don't even think about trying to matchmake again. Men my age are only looking for a nurse to see them through their last years, and I have far better things to do with my time.'

Daisy gave a yell and began to bawl because she'd pulled herself up and hit her head on the underside of the kitchen table. Peggy rescued her and gave her a cuddle. Once the tears had gone, she put her back on the floor and returned to her conversation with Cordelia.

'I never suggested you were courting,' she said defensively. 'I just asked about your lunch. But it seems to me you rather enjoyed Bertram's company, regardless of what you just said.'

'Oh I did,' Cordelia twittered. 'There might be snow on the roof, Peggy, but there's still enough fire in this old heart to enjoy a bit of mild flirtation.' She returned serenely to her grated cheese.

Peggy shook her head and grinned. Cordelia's zest for life rarely deserted her, and it was lovely to know that she'd enjoyed her lunch party.

Roger slowly drew away from Kitty, his expression regretful. 'It's time I took you home, my dearest, sweetest girl,' he murmured.

'Do you have to? Can't we stay for just a while longer?'

'We'd better not,' he said gruffly. 'A chap can get too carried away, and I seem to have rather overstepped the mark already by kissing you.'

She smiled up at him and traced his lips with the tip of her finger. 'I have no objections, Roger,' she murmured. 'In fact, I wouldn't mind you kissing me again, if you don't mind.'

He kissed her thoroughly and then crushed her to him. 'Oh, Kitty,' he breathed. 'You have absolutely no idea how long I've been waiting for this moment.'

'And I had absolutely no inkling of how much I would enjoy it,' she said against his shirt. She giggled. 'Why didn't you say something earlier?'

'I was going to, but then you had your accident, and Freddy went missing, and I thought you had enough on your plate without me stepping on your toes with my great size twelves,' he said ruefully.

He drew back from their embrace and looked earnestly into her eyes. 'Do you think you could possibly love me just a little, Kitty? I know I'm a bit bluff and hearty, and probably not the sort of chap you might think of as suitable, but I do adore you.'

Kitty was still overwhelmed by all that had happened this afternoon, and she knew that Roger deserved an honest answer. 'I need time to get over the shock,' she said, making light of her words with a smile. She reached out her hand and cupped his smooth cheek. 'But I've never been kissed like that before, and never felt the way you make me feel. When you put your arms round me, it was as if I was always meant to be there.'

'So you think you could love me?' he asked earnestly.

'I think I've always loved you,' she admitted, 'but I just didn't realise until today. It's going to take a bit of adjusting to get used to it all.'

He cupped her face in his hands, his voice raw with emotion. 'I swear to you, Kitty, that I will love and cherish you until I draw my last breath. My sweet, sweet girl.'

Kitty melted back into his arms as his tender kiss confirmed how right they were together and how this was meant to be.

It was quite a long time later that he drew the car in to the kerb by the alleyway. 'Do you want me to come in with you?' he asked as he opened her door.

She shook her head and smiled up at him. 'Peggy will be waiting like a hawk to pounce on us the minute we walk through that garden gate. It's probably best if I go in on my own.'

'If you're sure?' he murmured with a frown.

She lightly kissed his cheek. 'I'll see you tomorrow morning. Sweet dreams, Roger.'

He gave her a swift hug and then stood at the end of the alleyway until she'd reached the gate. Blowing her a kiss, he was almost skipping with delight as he returned to the car and drove away.

Kitty knew her face was radiant and that it would take only a second for Peggy to know what she'd been up to during the afternoon, but she found that it didn't matter. She could have shouted her news from the rooftops for the world to hear, she was so happy.

'Hello, dear,' said Peggy from the top of the basement steps. 'Did you have a lovely picnic?'

Kitty leaned on her crutches and took each step slowly and carefully until she'd reached the kitchen. 'I had a wonderful picnic,' she replied and smiled at Cordelia as she sat down. 'And before you both ask, Roger is utterly wonderful, and I feel as spoiled and pampered as a princess.'

'Oooh,' said Cordelia with a little shiver of pleasure. 'So Peggy was right all along. I'm so pleased for you, dear.'

Peggy laughed. 'I'm very rarely wrong,' she said, 'and I knew that sooner or later you'd realise he was far more than just a friend. I'm so happy for you both, Kitty. Roger seems to be a very dear man.'

'Yes, he is,' Kitty replied with a soft sigh of contentment.

'I'm sure Freddy will be absolutely delighted,' said Peggy. She poured the cheese sauce over the vegetables and put the large stone dish in the oven.

Kitty grinned. 'He'll probably roar with laughter at the thought of his best friend getting gooey-eyed over his sister, and then the pair of them will probably get sozzled in the mess bar.'

Daisy came drunkenly towards her, gripping the table leg before she grabbed hold of Kitty's knee and laughed up at her.

Kitty picked her up and gave her a cuddle. Then she plucked one of Daisy's rag books off the table to keep her amused while she told Peggy and Cordelia where they'd gone for their picnic, what they'd eaten, and how they'd been the victims of a surprise attack by the 109. The more intimate details were carefully left out, but she could see they'd filled in the gaps on their own.

'So I won't be needing any supper,' she said as she put a wriggling, restless Daisy back on the floor. 'But I do need to wash and rest for a bit. It's been rather an exciting day.'

'What did the doctor say about your leg?' asked Peggy.

'He was optimistic that I'd be back at the Memorial and reunited with my prosthesis by the end of the week.' She smiled at both of them, and before they could question her further, she left the kitchen.

Ron had been clock-watching all day, and once he'd helped Rosie clean the bar and prepare for the evening rush, he couldn't stand the waiting any longer. He left Monty with Rosie at the Anchor and strode purposefully down Camden Road, his thoughts focussed entirely on Harvey.

The vet's surgery was on the other side of the High Street and overlooked the northern entrance to Havelock Gardens. It was a big Victorian house set back from the quiet, leafy street, and was next door to the doctor's surgery where Peggy's one-time evacuee, Julie Harris, had worked as a midwife.

Ron stomped over the gravel driveway, heading for the side door into the surgery, and as he stepped into the waiting room, he realised there were already a number of people waiting with their dogs, cats, budgerigars and other assorted pets.

'I've come to collect Harvey,' he shouted above the barking, yipping and caterwauling to the vet's elderly mother who helped out behind the reception desk.

'Oh, yes. My son needs to speak to you about Harvey,' she said as she looked at the notes she'd scrawled on a pad. 'If you'd like to sit and wait, he shouldn't be long.'

Ron felt a sharp pang of fear, and cold sweat beaded his forehead. 'Why does he need to speak to me?' he rasped. 'What's happened?'

'I really have no idea,' she said distractedly above the racket. 'Go and sit down, Ron. He'll see you as soon as he can.'

Ron slumped down into the nearest chair, his heart thudding as his mind whirled with all the dreadful possibilities. He fidgeted for a while and then began to pace back and forth, unable to contain the rising terror that something had happened to Harvey, and it had been his fault.

Jack Barham stuck his head round the door. 'Ron, come in.'

Ron stepped into the small examination room, and before Jack could close the door, he bombarded the younger man with questions.

'He's absolutely fine, although he's still a bit groggy from the anaesthetic and feeling rather sorry for himself,' said Jack hurriedly. 'The reason I need to talk to you, Ron, is because I've discovered he's got a bit of a heart murmur.'

'His heart?' Ron had to lean on the examination table as his legs went weak. 'But he's strong and as fit as a dog can be. To be sure, it was only this morning he was dashing about in the hills with his wee pup, so he was.'

Jack nodded and smiled. 'I have no doubt of it, Ron. There's nothing like a puppy in the house to liven up an older dog. But there is a definite murmur, and he'll need regular check-ups from now on.'

'I can't believe it,' muttered Ron. 'There's been no sign of him getting out of breath or being tired.'

'It's a minor murmur, Ron, so don't imagine he's about to keel over,' Jack replied reassuringly. 'I've given him a thorough examination and everything else is in good working order, so you really have very little to worry about.' He flicked through his notes. 'How old is Harvey now?'

'Six,' muttered Ron.

Jack smiled. 'Then he's got several very good years ahead of him. Just carry on as before, but bring him in twice a year so I can give him the once-over.'

He regarded Ron with understanding. 'You left it very late to get Harvey neutered,' he said, 'so it would be best if you brought Monty in next week to get him done too. Prevention is better than having unwanted puppies, and you have enough to cope with already.'

'Aye,' sighed Ron. 'You're right, Jack. To be sure, he'll be in when Harvey has his stitches out.'

'Good, I'll see them both next Tuesday at nine o'clock.' Jack noted this down in his appointment book and then opened a door to the rear of the building. Ron followed him past rows of cat baskets and several bird cages until they finally came to the large dog enclosures.

Harvey was sitting mournfully by the wire, his eyes and ears drooping with self-pity as he pawed at the broad cardboard frill round his neck.

'He has to keep that on until I've taken out the stitches,' Jack explained. 'I don't want him licking at the wound and pulling them out before it's healed.' He unlocked the gate and held it open.

'Ach, ye poor wee man, what did I do to you, eh?' murmured Ron as he stroked Harvey's back.

Harvey looked at him accusingly, his tail tucked tightly beneath him as his head hung low and he pawed at the hated, shaming cuff round his neck. Then he got to his feet, walked past Ron and the vet and stalked along the narrow corridor until he reached the back door. Sitting down with a thump, he turned to look at Ron in disgust before scraping his paw down the door.

'I'm thinking he's not pleased with either of us,' muttered Ron as he handed over the money for Harvey's operation.

'He'll feel better once he's home and had some food,' said Jack cheerfully as he pocketed the money and headed back to his examination room.

Ron had never felt so guilty in his life as he tramped down to the back door and opened it. Harvey looked heartily defeated and ashamed with that thing round his neck, and it was clear that he blamed Ron for every ounce of that shame and hardship.

Harvey sniffed the air and stepped daintily outside like a maiden aunt on her way to church. He cocked his leg against the wall and then stalked off down the path.

Ron stumped after him, noting how Harvey hung his head in embarrassment as they reached the busy pavements of Camden Road and people stared and pointed and tittered.

A stupid terrier on a lead darted towards them and yapped at Harvey, who, most unusually, barked back ferociously until its owner yanked it out of the way with a sharp word to Ron about keeping his vicious animal under control.

Harvey didn't hang about to listen to the short, sharp exchange, but broke into a lolloping gallop as if he'd had enough trouble for one day and just wanted to hide in the sanctuary of Beach View's kitchen.

Ron left the woman in mid-rant and hurried after him, passing the Anchor on the way. He'd pick Monty up from the pub later, for he'd said nothing to anyone back home about the operation, and that damned ruff would, to be sure, take quite some explaining.

Chapter Twenty-five

Harvey had been petted and praised and thoroughly spoilt by everyone, and Peggy had even given him a spoonful of her minced meat ration to go with his dog biscuits as a special treat.

'I knew something was up when you were so grumpy this morning,' she said to Ron as she fed Daisy some of the vegetable and cheese bake.

'Aye, well, I didn't want to say anything in front of him,' he muttered. 'It was best he didn't know where he was going after his walk.'

Peggy chuckled. 'You are a soft old thing, Ronan Reilly. I know Harvey's an intelligent dog, but I honestly don't believe he understands everything we say.'

Ron didn't look entirely convinced but he said nothing and continued to eat his supper.

'Where's Kitty?' asked Rita. 'Isn't she coming down to tea?'

Peggy grinned with delight. 'She's upstairs resting after a rather exciting day.' Having got everyone's attention – and ignoring Cordelia's glare of warning to say nothing – she went on to tell the girls about Roger and the picnic. 'I suspect she's dreaming about him right now,' she finished with a happy sigh.

'And here's me thinking she had more sense,' muttered Rita.

'Sense doesn't come into it, dear,' Cordelia said dryly. 'Peggy seems to think the whole world should be in love at the moment.'

'To be sure, if it was,' rumbled Ron, 'we wouldn't be in the middle of yet another war. I'm glad the wee girl has something to be happy about. She's had more than enough sadness to contend with.'

'Thanks, Ron,' said Kitty from the doorway. She grinned at Peggy. 'I knew you couldn't keep it to yourself for long.' Then she saw Harvey, who was lying on the rug looking very sorry for himself. 'What's happened?' she asked sharply as she stroked him and regarded the strange ruff round his neck. 'Has he been in a fight?'

Ron explained and Kitty gave a sigh of relief. 'Poor old Harvey. It isn't fair, is it?'

Harvey gave a whimper just to underline the fact that he'd been tortured and made to look a complete fool. Then he rolled awkwardly onto his back so she could see his terrible scar while she scratched his belly.

'Ach, to be sure he'll play the wounded soldier to the hilt,' said Fran with a giggle. 'But you really can't blame him. It must be a terrible burden to his pride to be wearing that ruff.'

Kitty sat at the table and poured herself a cup of

tea while the others finished their evening meal. It had been some time since the picnic lunch, and the smell of that melted cheese made her mouth water, so when Peggy placed a bowl of it in front of her, she tucked in with gusto.

The meal continued as usual with plenty of chatter and a lot of questions from the girls about Roger. It seemed they wanted to know everything about him, and Kitty was starting to feel a bit beleaguered by the time the meal was over.

Then the table was cleared and after the dishes had been washed, Ron and the girls drifted off. Ron went to fetch Monty and have a well-earned pint at the pub while Harvey sulked and dozed on the rug. Suzy was meeting Anthony for a drink at the Three Ferrets in the next village, and Sarah and Jane were going to the pictures, whilst Fran had to get to the hospital for her night shift in theatre.

'It's still warm outside,' said Rita quietly to Kitty. 'Why don't we sit out there and enjoy the last of the summer while you tell me all about you and Roger?'

Kitty nodded, pleased that her friend understood her need to talk quietly about what had happened today. She went out into the garden twilight, settled into one of the deckchairs, and lit a cigarette. The sky was tinged with orange and pink as the sun dipped behind the roofs, and Kitty knew that tomorrow would be another lovely day, and that she and Roger would be together again.

The silence was shattered by the sound of Mosquitoes, Spitfires and Hurricanes roaring towards the Channel, and although Kitty couldn't see them, she could tell there were at least two squadrons. The bombing raids over Germany were obviously continuing, but at least Freddy and Roger weren't up there tonight.

Rita appeared with two cups of tea on a tray, and a couple of blankets over her arm. 'It's nearly September,' she said by way of explanation, 'and the nights are getting colder.'

She settled into the other chair, took a sip of tea, then gave Kitty's elbow a soft nudge. 'So come on then, Kitty,' she coaxed. 'What happened to the girl who didn't want to fall in love in the middle of the war, and who was determined not to be tied down?'

Kitty grinned ruefully. 'She got kissed,' she replied and then giggled. 'Oh, Rita, I'm all at sixes and sevens. Who would have thought it?'

'And with a man you've known for years,' Rita said with a wry smile. 'Didn't you realise he was in love with you? It was obvious to everyone else last night.'

'So Peggy said.' Kitty fell silent, her thoughts and emotions in turmoil. 'Am I doing the right thing, Rita?' she blurted out suddenly. 'Only I swore I wouldn't get entangled with anyone until this war was over. And Roger's a Spitfire pilot, for heaven's sake, which has to be just about the most dangerous job there is.'

'I'm not really the person to advise you,' said Rita. 'I've only had one tiny romance and he just wanted what I wasn't prepared to give him. Fran's American was just the same and he turned out to be married with three kids.'

'Roger's not like that,' said Kitty firmly. 'Oh, he's had women chasing after him and he certainly appeared to enjoy the chase – but I believe he's sincere when he says he loves me and only me.'

'It strikes me you have no choice but to accept the fact and see how things go.' Rita shot Kitty a warm smile. 'After all, you can't live your life worrying about things that might not happen.'

Kitty nodded. 'But I couldn't bear it if something *did* happen to him, Rita, and now I shall be on tenterhooks every time he's on ops.'

'Well, that's understandable,' said Rita. 'Especially after Freddy's escapade – but as I just said, don't tempt fate by always looking on the dark side.'

Kitty gave a sharp sigh of frustration. 'But these are dark days, Rita. And to cap it all, there's the palaver over my leg. It could be weeks before I can get about independently, and I can't possibly expect Roger to run about after me all the time.'

'Did he complain about it today?' asked Rita with the ghost of a smile.

'Well no,' Kitty admitted.

'And hasn't he arranged to take you to the clinic every morning while he's on leave?' At Kitty's nod, she laughed. 'I don't think you have to worry about Roger. He knew you before the accident and has accepted what's happened. He wouldn't have declared himself this afternoon if he'd had even the slightest doubts. Just enjoy being in love, Kitty, and forget about everything else.'

Kitty smoked the last of her cigarette and then stubbed it out rather forcefully in the glass ashtray. 'I don't know that I can,' she confessed. 'Roger's leave will soon be over, and I've got a lot of work to do if I'm going to be independent again. Then, if they'll have me, I'm going back to the ATA. Our time together will be so limited, but while we're apart we'll be worried sick about each other. That's no way to conduct a serious romance, Rita.'

'I've never heard so much nonsense in my life,' said Peggy as she came into the garden and plonked into a nearby chair. 'There are times when I could shake you, Kitty Pargeter.'

Kitty was startled by Peggy's fierceness. 'But how can we possibly concentrate on each other when there are so many other things going on?' she protested. 'Roger and I could have got carried away in the moment, and as I've never been in love before, how do I know it isn't infatuation, or that I was in need of someone to love me because of this bally leg and he happened to be there at the right time and place?'

She blinked away the tears. 'I don't want to be leading him up the garden path, Peggy.'

'Ah,' said Peggy knowingly. 'Now we're getting to the truth of the matter.'

Kitty frowned. 'What do you mean?'

'You're frightened that this all seems to have happened so suddenly,' Peggy replied. 'But if you think back, Kitty, you'll realise you've loved that young man for much longer than one sunny afternoon up in the hills of Cliffehaven.'

'Well, yes,' she replied hesitantly. 'I suppose I have. But we're caught up in this war, and it's all too easy to rush into things. I don't want either of us to make the mistake of thinking we're in love when it could only be the need to have someone close to cling to. It's all very well being misty-eyed, but we could both come to regret the things we said today – and that would simply be too awful.'

'We all go into a relationship starry-eyed and full of hope,' said Peggy, 'but of course there are doubts and some disappointments. There have to be; otherwise you wouldn't be living real life. I've never believed that a happy marriage can be conducted without arguments and tears – it's the making-up that matters, for it's the glue that keeps you together.'

'I wasn't thinking about *marrying* Roger,' Kitty protested. 'Good grief, Peggy, I'm still getting used to the idea that we've crossed the line from friendship to something far more serious.'

Peggy sighed. 'You've obviously given this a great deal of thought, Kitty, and I admire you for that. But with the way things are at the moment, I think you should grab this chance of happiness while you can. None of us knows what tomorrow might bring.'

'That's all very well, Peggy, but I'm not about to rush headlong into anything – and I rather hope that Roger feels the same.'

Peggy nodded and quietly smoked her cigarette for a while. 'What you have to remember is that Roger has loved you for a long time, Kitty. This isn't new to him at all, and I wouldn't mind betting that he's already thinking ahead and making plans.'

'Well, it's all new to me, and I need time to get used to the idea,' Kitty replied stubbornly.

Peggy ignored her and looked dreamily into the rapidly dimming light. 'Jim and I tied the knot when he was home on leave during the last war. We had one night's honeymoon in a lovely little hotel down on the seafront, and then he was on the train to France and I was back living with Mum and Dad here at Beach View.'

She shot the girls a wan smile. 'I spent my first months as a bride fretting over what was happening to him. I'd heard such terrible stories, you see, and seen too many brides become widows almost before the confetti had been swept away.' She gave a sigh of contentment. 'But I was lucky. He came back with his father and brother, and although it's been stormy at times, our marriage is strong and lasting.'

'But how could you bear all that anxiety – the not knowing?' asked Kitty.

'I kept faith that he'd come home, even though I was steeling myself every time the postman came to the door. When you love someone and share the most intimate moments, then you become a part of them. It was better to have had those few precious hours as his wife, than to send him back to the trenches with just a wave and a kiss from some impersonal station platform.'

She smiled at both girls. 'We might have married in haste, but neither of us regrets a minute of it.'

Kitty sat there deep in thought, her heart in direct conflict with her head. What she'd felt today had been overwhelming, and although her common sense told her she should be wary of making any hasty decisions, her heart ached at the thought of not being a part of Roger's life. Perhaps she *was* being over-cautious – something she'd never been before – and she should accept that she was most definitely in love and start to enjoy the experience instead of fretting about things that might never happen.

Her thoughts were shattered by the sound of the sirens beginning to moan all through the town.

Rita immediately dragged Kitty out of the deck-chair and handed her the crutches. 'Go straight into the shelter while I help Peggy,' she ordered before she raced indoors.

Kitty began to make her way down the garden path and was overtaken by Rita, who was loaded up with pillows and blankets, and Harvey, who preferred the shelter to the sound of the sirens.

His cardboard ruff was too wide for the doorway, and he scrabbled frantically about until Rita squashed it so he could get inside. He tried to shoot beneath the bench, but again the ruff hindered him, so he wriggled his backside under it as far as it would go, and then lay there shivering and howling piteously as the sirens reached their ear-splitting, full-blooded wail.

Kitty sat on the bench and tried to soothe him as Rita rushed back into the house for the box of essentials. But Harvey was not to be soothed as long as those sirens were going, so Kitty lit the lamp and stacked the pillows and blankets more neatly.

'Well, this is a fine how do you do,' muttered Cordelia crossly as she entered the Anderson shelter and plumped down. 'I was right in the middle of listening to the "Play for the Week". It was a jolly good story and now I'll never know the ending.'

'I'm sure they'll try and air it again,' soothed Kitty.

'What do you mean? It's not raining, and my hair is perfectly dry.' She tutted and pulled her cardigan over her narrow chest. 'I don't know what the world's coming to, I really don't.'

Peggy came in, carrying a sleeping Daisy, swiftly followed by Rita, who slammed the door on the sound of approaching bombers.

It was cramped, damp and smelly in the poorly lit shelter and Harvey's cardboard ruff was in everyone's way as it stuck out into the narrow passage between the benches. Rita and Peggy had to squeeze past him, and then it was a bit of a job to get Cordelia round him so they could settle her into her deckchair with her pillows.

Once this was achieved and Daisy had been settled in the canvas cot, Rita adjusted the flame in the lamp so it was a mere glimmer, and Peggy lit the gas in the small camping stove so they could boil water and have tea to chase away the chill. Blankets were handed round and the box of essentials provided them with biscuits to go with the tea.

Harvey stopped whining and shivering the moment the sirens stopped screeching, and he settled down contentedly as the first of the enemy bombers could be heard crossing the Channel.

With a blanket over her knees, and her overcoat collar warding off the cold on her neck, Kitty wrapped her hands round the tin mug and shuffled to the far end of the bench to make room for Rita. 'I suppose this means you'll be back on duty again tonight?' she asked above the roar of fast-approaching bombers.

'It looks like it,' Rita shouted back. 'But as long as they don't drop anything on Cliffehaven, I should be back into my bed fairly sharpish.'

Kitty propped her crutches against the door and listened to the ever-increasing drone of the bombers and their fighter escorts. Cliffe and Wayfaring Down would be on alert and scrambling to get their planes in the air before the bombers dropped their deadly cargo on the runways and hangars. Would Roger be amongst them even though he was on leave – and was Freddy already defying orders and climbing eagerly into his Spitfire to do battle?

She closed her eyes and tried to quell the awful fear

that chilled her far more profoundly than this dark, dank shelter. Now she had two much-loved men to worry about, this was how it would be until the war was over, she realised. So she'd better buck up her ideas and bally well learn how to deal with it.

The all-clear went two hours later. Rita roused Cordelia from her deep sleep, while Peggy carried Daisy back indoors and settled her in her cot. Once Rita had telephoned the fire station, they drank Peggy's warming cocoa and then went to bed, leaving Harvey lying disconsolately on the rug in front of the damped-down fire. It seemed that his vigil at Kitty's door was at an end.

Kitty lay awake for a long while after the other girls had got in, and she listened as the household settled for the night and the old timbers creaked and sighed. She curled beneath the covers, her thoughts full of Roger and the sights, sounds and scents of their magical afternoon. And as her mind played over the years she'd known him, she could now see that she'd always been drawn to him, and that what had happened today had been inevitable.

With this happy thought, she fell into a deep, contented sleep.

Kitty slept rather later than usual, and it was almost nine o'clock by the time she was washed, dressed and ready for her day. Her stump was looking much better this morning, her freshly washed hair framed her face in soft waves, and her reflection in the bathroom mirror told her she was bright-eyed and positively radiant.

She went into the kitchen only to discover the other girls had already left for work, and Fran was having a lie-in after a long night in the hospital theatre. Cordelia was reading her newspaper as usual, and looked up briefly as she passed to wish her a cheerful good morning.

'I'm glad to see you've made up your mind about you and Roger,' said Peggy, wielding a metal spatula between two sizzling frying pans.

Kitty laughed. 'How on earth do you know that?'

'It's in your eyes and in your smile,' she replied with a knowing grin. 'And in the fact you had a really good night's sleep. Now, eat your breakfast.' She slid a glistening fried egg onto a slice of toast and added a patty of golden fried potato. 'That should set you up for the day,' she said as she put the plate in front of her.

'It's a good thing our hens are laying so well,' said Ron. 'Most people are lucky to get one egg a week.' He fed Harvey a sliver of eggy toast which went down in a single gulp. 'Ach, to be sure, the auld fella's on the mend, so he is,' he declared, patting the brindled head.

Monty put his paws on Ron's knee, and he was similarly rewarded. Then he made the mistake of getting over-confident and tried to nibble at Harvey's hated ruff.

Harvey growled deep in his throat and Monty decided retreat was in order, so went to find something to chew instead. He found one of Daisy's rubber ducks and set about destroying it with his needle-sharp teeth as Daisy clapped and gurgled in encouragement.

'Um, well now, Peggy,' Ron dithered. 'How would you feel if Monty went to live with Rosie?'

Peggy sat down with a thump and stared at him. 'But I've got used to having him around the place now.' She picked up the wriggling puppy and kissed his soft head. 'He's become part of the family.'

'Aye, I know. But Rosie gets lonely in the pub, and he'd be good company for when I'm not there.'

Peggy put the squirming Monty back on the floor and he scampered about until he found one of Peggy's slippers to chew. 'Well, I suppose it would be all right,' she said hesitantly as she quickly rescued her slipper. 'Rosie would certainly look after him better than I can with so much else to do.'

'That's settled then,' said Ron as he grabbed the pup and clipped on his lead.

Peggy gasped in horror. 'You're not taking him today, are you?'

Ron shook his head. 'He's due to go to the vet next week to be neutered, and once he's fighting fit again, he'll move into the Anchor.'

'But he's still so very young,' said Peggy dolefully.

'He's old enough, and it's the ideal solution,' he replied. 'Monty will grow to be as big as Harvey, and he'll be Rosie's companion and guard dog. Me and Harvey will get to see him every day, and to be sure, he'll only be round the corner.'

'That's all very well,' said Peggy, 'but I'm going to miss him, and so is Daisy.'

'Ach, Peggy, you'll still have Harvey to watch over you, and I'm sure Rosie would love you to call in and visit with Daisy. She was only saying the other day that she missed seeing our wee wain.'

Peggy gave a sigh of acceptance. 'Then I hope Rosie knows what she's letting herself in for. Monty chews everything in sight and still isn't fully house-trained.'

'He'll be trained to a treat by next week. You'll see.' With that, Ron stomped down the steps with Monty on his lead and Harvey at his heels, and was soon tramping along the alleyway for his daily walk on the hills.

'Well, that was a bit of a surprise,' said Peggy as she lifted Daisy out of her high chair and let her crawl about the floor. 'But I can't say I'm too sorry, Kitty. Monty's very sweet, but I have enough to do without him getting under my feet all the time.'

Kitty nodded as she finished her lovely breakfast. 'I think you both made the right decision,' she said. 'Puppies are adorable, but they take a lot of looking after. It isn't as if you're living on a farm where he can run free all the time.'

'Hello, there. Anyone at home?'

'Roger,' breathed Kitty in delight. 'We're in the

kitchen,' she called back as she hastily patted her hair and tested for any stray crumbs around her lips.

He came up the steps with a beaming smile, his gaze immediately finding her. 'Good morning, my dearest girl,' he said. 'You're looking as marvellous as ever.'

'Hello, Roger,' she replied almost shyly. They held one another's gaze until Cordelia cleared her throat to remind them they were not alone.

'I do apologise, Peggy, Cordelia,' said a rather flustered Roger. 'Jolly bad manners, what? And how are you both this beautiful morning?'

'We're both very well, thank you,' said Peggy, trying not to giggle.

Cordelia had no such inhibitions and twittered like an agitated robin. 'My word,' she managed. 'You do look chipper this morning. I wonder what could have brought that on?'

He grinned broadly and smoothed his moustache. 'I couldn't possibly imagine. Now, if you'll excuse us, we need to get to the clinic.'

He held out his hand to Kitty, and she felt the same charge of electricity run through her that she'd experienced when he'd kissed her. 'We're a bit early,' she said as she reached for her things.

'I'll carry those,' he said, sweeping up her handbag and gas-mask box. 'I thought I'd take you on a short tour of Cliffehaven first. The sea is looking particularly lovely this morning.'

'Will you be bringing Kitty back for her tea?' asked Peggy.

He looked down at Kitty with such adoration in his expression that she felt quite weak. 'I do have something planned for this evening, if that's all right with you, Kitty,' he said softly.

'Of course it's all right with Kitty,' said Peggy with a chuckle. 'Now, shoo, and have a wonderful day.'

They left Beach View, and once they were settled into the car, Roger reached for her hand across the broad leather seat, his expression solemn. 'No second thoughts after yesterday?'

'None whatsoever,' she fibbed. 'But if you don't kiss me in the next second, I'll start to doubt you meant all those . . .'

His lips smothered her words and as he crushed her to him, the last, tiny, lingering niggles of doubt fled and she was lost.

Later that night when she was once again snug in her bed at Beach View, Kitty closed her eyes and remembered every single moment of her wonderful day. Roger had shown her Cliffehaven and she'd been surprised at how big it was. Then he'd parked down by the seafront for just long enough to drink coffee from the little kiosk at the end of the promenade before taking her to the clinic.

The doctor was delighted with her progress, and

so she'd left the hospital in high spirits to be whisked away in the car to a tiny hamlet set deep in a valley several miles away.

The church was ancient, with a square Norman tower and heavily studded oak door that creaked quite alarmingly when it was opened. The interior had been gloomy and chill after the heat outside, but the smells of incense, candlewax and ancient stone were familiar and comforting.

The little houses that fronted the narrow village lane were thatched, their diamond-paned windows looking out over lovingly tended cottage gardens where beans and peas jostled for space amid the ox-eye daisies and colourful lupins. Roses were rampant round every door and hung from every eave, making the slow drive down the lane a fragrant pleasure.

Apart from the houses, there was a village infant school and a sixteenth-century coaching inn called the Lamb. The pub also proved to be dark inside, but as their eyes adjusted after the bright sun, Kitty could see the heavily beamed ceiling, and the inglenook fireplace where two old men were ensconced contentedly on the benches either side of the unlit fire, with a pint of beer and their smoking pipes.

She sighed dreamily as she thought about the garden behind the inn where they'd eaten their lunch. They'd had a magnificent view of rolling hills and broad green paddocks where horses cropped peacefully or stood sleepily in the shade of trees as skylarks sang high in the cloudless sky.

There were roses clambering over the ancient, leaning walls of the inn, and the scent had been quite heavenly as they'd eaten thick hunks of cheese and bread slathered in real butter and the landlady's homemade chutney. This had been washed down with good strong ale, and when Roger had gone in to get a second drink and pay, the landlady had smiled knowingly at him and told him they could stay in the garden as long as they liked after she'd locked the door.

So they had, and they'd spent the rest of the afternoon talking about everything and nothing. She learned more about his life as the eldest son and heir to his father's vast estate, and she'd told him about her life in Argentina. And although they had come from different worlds and an ocean apart, they discovered they had a great deal in common, for they thought about things in the same way, and had the same sense of humour – liked the same films and music, and of course shared a passion for flying.

Kitty rolled over and sank her head into the soft pillow as she grew drowsy and ready for sleep. Their evening had been spent in a restaurant which was hidden down the narrow, cobbled back street of a large nearby town. The food had been excellent despite the restrictions, and after lingering over their coffee, Roger had driven her home.

Her eyelids were heavy now and sleep was softly enfolding her as she remembered his many kisses during their lovely day, and the sweet promise of something deep and lasting beginning to blossom between them.

Chapter Twenty-six

'Well, you're a sly old thing,' teased Charlotte as the four of them sat around a table in the Anchor four days later. 'You kept that to yourself, didn't you?'

'I'll say she did,' said Freddy. 'And Roger's just as bad. I never thought I'd see the day he'd get pinned down by some girl, but to find out he was moon-faced over my sister – well, it was a terrible shock.' His eyes glinted with fun. 'I thought Roger had taste.'

Kitty jabbed him hard in the ribs with her elbow. 'And I thought Charlotte had more sense than to get embroiled with someone like you,' she shot back.

'You asked for that, Freddy,' said Charlotte as she dug her elbow into the other side of his ribcage.

Freddy roared with laughter. 'We're doomed, Roger, you know that, don't you? These two are already in cahoots, and it can only get worse.' He drained his pint glass. 'Drink up, old man,' he said cheerfully. 'My round.'

'It's lovely to see you again, Charlotte,' said Kitty as the two men went to the bar. 'How are your wedding plans coming along?'

'We've decided to put things forward to the twentieth of September,' she replied. 'After what happened to Freddy, we realised we didn't want to wait. Mother's frightfully put out, of course, but at least she'll still have some flowers in the garden to decorate the house.'

'When was all this decided?' Kitty felt a bit put out that neither of them had thought to tell her about the new arrangements.

'Only this morning,' said Charlotte, with a consoling hand on Kitty's arm, 'otherwise I would have told you before today. But Freddy and I have been discussing it over the telephone ever since he got back from France.' She shuddered. 'I so very nearly lost him, Kitty, and I can't tell you how relieved I am that he's behind a desk for a while.'

Kitty nodded and looked across at where Freddy and Roger were deep in conversation with Ron and the very perky Rosie Braithwaite. 'It's not going to be easy for any of us,' she murmured. 'Roger's leave is up at six this evening, and then he's straight back on ops.'

Charlotte gave her a hug. 'I think it's wonderful you and he have got together,' she sighed. 'I'm just amazed I never noticed that he was so enamoured, because usually I can spot a blossoming romance a mile off.'

Kitty giggled. 'Not half as surprised as me – and anyway, you were too taken up with Freddy to notice anything.'

'I know,' sighed Charlotte as she gazed across the room at Freddy. 'But how could I resist? He's so utterly wonderful, isn't he?'

Kitty gazed at Roger. 'Yes, he is.' And then they looked at each other and collapsed into giggles.

They eventually sobered enough to have a fairly sensible conversation about the wedding plans. Leave had been arranged for Freddy and Roger, and they were going to pick Kitty up and drive to Berkshire the day before the ceremony. Roger was to be Freddy's best man and they would stay in the village pub, whilst Kitty would be with Charlotte and her parents. There was to be a supper for Charlotte's girlfriends, most of whom Kitty knew from her school holidays, but it wouldn't go on too late because Charlotte needed to have a good night's sleep before her wedding day.

The ceremony would be held in the village church at eleven, and after the reception luncheon Roger would drive Kitty back and go on duty again, while Freddy and Charlotte had a few blissful days of honeymoon in the Cotswolds.

'I've found the most gorgeous dress for you,' Charlotte whispered. 'It's a nineteen-twenties evening gown I found in one of my mother's many wardrobes, and is made from the most heavenly turquoise blue silk. Mother's dressmaker will come in on the afternoon you arrive and do any alterations that might be needed.'

Kitty was glad it wasn't pink, but she was

beginning to have serious doubts about the entire occasion.

Charlotte didn't seem to notice Kitty's unease, for she grinned with delight. 'I just know you'll look so stunning, Roger will simply *have* to get down on one knee and propose.'

Kitty regarded her friend with affection. Charlotte's excitement over her wedding had clearly addled her brain. 'Well, I don't know about that,' she replied cautiously. 'It's still very early days, Charlotte, and just because you've got wedding fever doesn't mean we all have to catch it.'

'Oh, but it would be so romantic if he did,' Charlotte sighed.

Kitty took a sip of the rather flat lemonade as all the doubts and fears multiplied. Roger's parents would be there, and she'd yet to meet them, which was daunting enough, but with only seventeen days to go, she simply wouldn't be able to achieve her own goal of following Charlotte up the aisle on two feet. Regardless of how lovely the dress was, she would be a nervous wreck and probably look and feel ridiculous.

'You know, Charlotte,' she said quietly, 'I really think you should ask someone else to be your bridesmaid.'

'Why?' Charlotte looked astonished.

'Because having me clumping along on crutches will spoil the effect of everything.' She silenced Charlotte's protest. 'And besides, I don't know that

I'm brave enough yet to cope with everyone staring at me.'

Charlotte's pretty face was very solemn. 'Kitty, we promised years ago that when we got married we'd be each other's bridesmaids, and that's how it's going to be. You will walk down that aisle behind me looking gorgeous, crutches or no crutches, and I will *not* have you backing out now.'

'But I'll stick out like a sore thumb amongst all your glamorous friends,' Kitty said softly. 'And I couldn't bear it if they stared and started whispering.'

Charlotte folded her arms tightly. 'Do you know what, Kitty Pargeter, you've become paranoid,' she said rather crossly. 'Is everyone staring at you now? Are they whispering and pointing? Have you experienced any of that during these past few days when Roger was taking you out and about?'

Kitty frowned. Was she being paranoid? She took a quick glance round the bar and realised no one was taking the slightest interest in her. 'Not that I noticed,' she admitted. 'But then I was too taken up with Roger to care much about what anyone else was doing.'

'There you are then,' said Charlotte. She took Kitty's hand and her expression softened. 'It's all in your head, Kitts,' she murmured. 'And I'm not going to let you break your promise. I want you as my bridesmaid, and I won't take any argument.'

Kitty realised Charlotte was absolutely right and that she had indeed been on the point of paranoia.

'I'm sorry, Charlotte,' she said with a sigh. 'I was just having a moment of blind panic at the thought of meeting Roger's parents and of doing something daft like falling over or dropping a crutch in the middle of the ceremony. Of course I'll do it.'

'Good. I knew it was just a fit of the collywobbles and that you wouldn't let me down. Besides, you'll have the doting Roger to lean on, so you'll never feel stranded.'

Kitty smiled at this. Darling Roger would sense it if she felt nervous or the focus of attention, and stick to her like glue. Yet the ordeal of meeting his parents was quite another thing and she dreaded it. Roger had assured her they knew all about her amputation, but how did they really feel about their son and heir getting involved with someone who not only had half a leg missing, but who was from a completely different social class?

Charlotte edged a bit closer along the wooden seat. 'Stop daydreaming, Kitts, because I've got a juicy bit of gossip to tell you.'

Snapped from her dark thoughts, Kitty tried to concentrate as Charlotte leaned closer and whispered in her ear.

'The girl I'm sharing our cottage with at the Hamble Pool has turned out to be a lesbian. I caught her in bed with Freda from the machine shop.'

Kitty stared at Charlotte in horrified amazement. 'Not Ferocious Freda who talks with a really deep voice, smokes cheroots and terrifies all the male mechanics?' At Charlotte's nod, they collapsed once more into a fit of helpless laughter.

'I can see neither of you have changed much,' said Freddy dryly as he and Roger returned to the table with their fresh drinks. 'Good grief,' he sighed. 'This reminds me of when I used to take you both out to tea after school sports day. You never stopped giggling then – and you're still at it.'

They looked at the two men's puzzled faces, which only made them giggle even harder.

Peggy was singing away to herself as she finished the ironing. There were two sets of wedding bells in the air – three if Kitty and Roger decided to tie the knot – and Jim would be home next weekend. Life was wonderful, and she felt she could take on Hitler, rationing, air raids and long cold nights in the Anderson shelter single-handedly.

'Freddy and Charlotte make a handsome couple, don't they?' said Cordelia as she folded the tea towels and put them in a drawer. 'It was very kind of them to pop in and say hello, but it's a shame they're getting married so far away. It would have been lovely to see her in her gown.'

'Yes,' agreed Peggy. 'She's a lucky girl to have the sort of mother who keeps everything she ever wore. So many girls today are getting married in their uniform, and although they're smartly turned out, they're hardly what one would call bridal.'

'Well, I for one won't be waltzing down the aisle

in my striped dress and starched apron and cap,' said Suzy as she came into the kitchen to do her own ironing. 'Mother's having her wedding dress altered, and I'm going home next weekend for a fitting.'

'Is Anthony going with you?' asked Peggy, stepping away from the ironing board and putting the flat irons on the hob to get hot.

'Not likely,' Suzy replied with a giggle. 'I'm going to have a lovely weekend with my parents and meet up with some of my friends. Anthony would be bored rigid with all our talk of clothes and wedding arrangements.'

Peggy warmed the teapot. 'How are you getting on with those?' she asked casually.

Suzy eyed her knowingly. 'You mean, how am I getting on with Doris and *her* arrangements?' She spread a linen skirt over the ironing board. 'Doris seems to think this wedding will be the social occasion of the year and is determined to pull out all the stops. Poor old Ted has been roped in to find tinned salmon and champagne, and dried fruit and icing sugar for the cake. *And* she's made out a guest list as long as my arm.'

'I thought you and Anthony only wanted a small gathering?'

'We do.' She picked up the iron and smoothed it over the skirt with rather unnecessary vigour. 'Which is why we've refused, point blank, to send invitations to most of Doris's guests. Anthony and I don't know them from Adam, and she's only inviting them because she thinks they'll add kudos to the occasion. Frankly, we're beginning to consider running off to a registry office one weekend and doing the deed on the quiet.'

'Oh, don't do that,' protested Peggy. 'It would cause huge hurt and terrible ructions all round.'

'I know,' said Suzy. 'But she really is the limit, Auntie Peg. Her latest beef is about my choice of friends and bridesmaid. She's made such a song and dance about it you'd think I wanted Eva Braun to follow me up the aisle.'

'I don't think Hitler's mistress is available that weekend,' said Peggy with a wry smile. 'So who are you having instead?'

Suzy giggled as she continued ironing the skirt. 'I've asked Fran, which of course didn't go down terribly well. But we've been friends ever since we were in nursing college and, regardless of what Doris may think, she'll be perfect.'

She looked up from her ironing. 'And of course everyone else in the house will be invited. You're my second family, after all, and my wedding wouldn't be complete without you.'

Peggy remembered the tasteless altercation she'd had with Doris a few weeks back. 'Is it just Fran she's objecting to?' she asked carefully.

Suzy slammed the iron down on the hob for it to reheat. 'No,' she said flatly. 'She's also been quite horrid about Kitty.' She folded her arms tightly about her slender waist. 'But I put her straight on that one.

I told her that if she didn't like seeing Kitty on her crutches or false leg, then she could forget about holding the reception at her house and that she wouldn't be welcome at the wedding.'

'Golly,' breathed Peggy in admiration of her bravery. 'What did she say to that?'

'She went white, then red – then a sort of deep magenta.' Suzy chuckled. 'When Anthony backed me up, she became frightfully grand and gracious and said that of course it was our wedding, and we could invite whoever we wanted.'

'You do realise that Kitty might not still be here at Christmas time,' said Peggy as she lit a cigarette and sat down. 'There are over three months to go yet, and she's champing at the bit to get back to her aeroplanes.'

'I know,' said Suzy. 'But it's the principle of the thing, isn't it? She's become a friend, just like the other girls, and if she is here, then I want her to be a part of my special day.'

'I've always said that weddings cause nothing but trouble,' said Cordelia, who'd been sitting quietly listening to all this. 'Relatives one hasn't spoken to for years take umbrage at not being invited, others fall out over age-old differences, women buy the most ridiculous hats to try and outdo one another, and the best man usually causes trouble by flirting with the bridesmaids.'

'That won't happen with our best man,' said Suzy. 'He's a rather studious boffin whose mind is usually occupied with some incomprehensible mathematical equation. I doubt he'll even notice Fran, let alone flirt with anyone.'

Peggy thought he sounded very boring. 'Poor Fran. I suspect she was rather hoping for someone who might sweep her off her feet.'

'He's more likely to *tread* on her feet,' giggled Suzy. 'Because I don't think he can tell a foxtrot from a piece of string.'

Wanting to spend their few precious hours alone, Freddy and Charlotte had gone off in their borrowed car to explore the countryside and find somewhere to eat later. Rosie had locked the Anchor and told Kitty and Roger that they could stay for as long as they wanted, so when she'd gone upstairs with Ron and the dogs, they'd taken their drinks out into the small paved back garden.

It wasn't as fragrant or pretty as the one behind the Lamb, and the only view they had was of the surrounding houses. But it was peaceful and private and the perfect place to make the most of the very few hours they had together before Roger's return to the airfield.

As the Town Hall clock struck five Roger clasped her hands. 'I'll telephone every day if at all possible,' he said earnestly. 'And come and see you the moment I have a couple of hours off duty.'

'But I want you to rest between ops,' she replied, 'not rush about after me.'

'Seeing you will be all I'll need to feel whole and invigorated again,' he insisted as he softly kissed her. 'I do wish I didn't have to go,' he murmured against her lips. 'These past few days have been so marvellous, and the thought of not seeing you every day is torture.'

Kitty melted into his embrace as he tenderly gathered her to him. She would miss him too. Miss his kisses and his smiles, his silly sayings and his wonderful ability to make every hour they'd had together special.

'Come on, old thing,' he said eventually. 'We'd better get going, or I'll be late on parade.'

They went back into the pub, put their dirty glasses on the bar and let themselves out through the side door where a short alleyway led to Camden Road. Roger's car was parked at the kerb and he handed her in as if she was royalty before he drove back to Beach View.

There were people walking along the pavement, but Kitty didn't care, and as Roger brought the car to a halt, she threw her arms round his neck and kissed him. 'Fly safe, Roger, and remember that I love you,' she whispered tearfully.

'Now I know I have you to return to I'll take the greatest care, my darling,' he murmured before he held her to his heart and kissed her sweetly and deeply.

Kitty emerged from that breathless embrace and reluctantly opened the door. 'Stay there,' she said softly as he made to climb out of the car. 'I hate prolonged goodbyes, and if we go on like this you'll never get back to the airfield on time.'

'This isn't goodbye,' he replied. 'Merely au revoir. I'll be back to see you as soon as I can.'

She smiled through her tears and nodded as she hung the straps of her handbag and gas-mask box round her neck. Grasping her crutches, she set off down the alley, aware that he was watching her every step. When she reached the gate to Beach View she couldn't resist looking back one last time.

Roger was standing by the car, his expression unreadable in the shadow of his peaked cap as he blew her a kiss.

She returned his kiss and then, before she disgraced herself by bursting into silly tears, she turned away and headed down the garden path to Beach View's back door.

Almost a week had passed since Roger's return to duty, and Peggy had been relieved to find that he'd kept his word and telephoned every day. Kitty seemed to have drawn strength from those daily talks and was back into the routine at the Memorial, working hard to conquer the prosthesis. Rita and the lads from the fire station still ferried her back and forth, so Kitty and Peggy had used some of the precious white flour to make some cakes for them all to show their appreciation.

Despite everything she had to do, Peggy found

the week had dragged all too slowly towards Saturday and Jim's expected homecoming. Needing to keep busy, she had finally collared Ron into helping her move out the unwanted furniture from the dining room, and they'd shifted things about in the boys' basement bedroom to store the chairs, cupboards and tin trunks. Then she'd got him to bring the heavy curtains down so she could shake out the dust before she washed them.

Once the room was cleared, the chimney swept and the ugly boarding taken away from the windows, she'd refused further help and set to with a will to get it presentable before Jim came home. The floor was polished to a gleam, upholstery was beaten to get rid of the dust, the dining table was waxed and a new bulb was screwed into the central light fitting.

Once she was satisfied, she then turned her attention to their bedroom, the hall and the kitchen. She was a veritable whirlwind as she polished and scrubbed, washed and dusted – but it still felt as if Saturday would never come.

By Thursday afternoon Cordelia had had enough. 'You'll wear yourself out and be good for nothing by the time Jim comes home,' she said. 'For goodness' sake, Peggy, be still. You're making me feel quite giddy with all that rushing about.'

'But I want it to be perfect,' said Peggy as she washed the kitchen curtains in the sink. 'He's been away for so long, and I don't want him to think I've let things slide.'

'You silly girl,' said Cordelia fondly. 'He won't care about clean curtains or a scrubbed floor. He'll only have eyes for you and little Daisy.'

Peggy rinsed the curtains and squeezed out the water. 'I do realise that,' she admitted, 'but I've needed to keep busy this past week, or I'd have gone mad.'

'To be sure, we've all been driven mad with your cleaning and tidying,' grumbled Ron. 'Sit down, woman, for goodness' sake, and give us all a rest.'

Peggy eyed him with affection. 'It's no use you being so grumpy,' she said. 'It was your idea for Monty to go to Rosie's.'

'Aye, well, I didn't expect her to take him so soon. I thought he'd stay here until his stitches were out.'

'Is he happy with Rosie?' she asked.

'Oh, aye, spoiled rotten. A proper little prince, so he is.'

Peggy picked up the bowl containing the wet curtains. 'Well then, you can't really complain, can you?' Not waiting for his reply, she went down the steps and into the garden to hang out the curtains.

The bed linen was already dry and ready for ironing, as was her best summer dress. She took them off the line and stood for a moment to hug her happiness to herself and imagine how Jim's homecoming would be. She'd be dressed in her lovely frock and best white sandals, with her hair all done and her nails polished. Daisy would be adorable in the sweet little cotton dress and bonnet that she'd finished embroidering last night, and Jim would open his arms to them both and hold them tightly.

Her thoughts drifted to the night when they would finally be alone in their great big bed and Jim would reach for her and . . .

'Peggy, I'm ready to do your hair and nails,' called Fran from the kitchen window. 'If we don't get a wee bit of a move on, I won't have time to do a really good job before I have to be on shift.'

Peggy's pleasant reverie was broken and she returned to the house, safe in the knowledge that her dreams of Jim would soon be fulfilled.

'If you're about to turn this place into a beauty parlour, Harvey and I are off,' muttered Ron as he sourly regarded the hair rollers, the brush and comb and all the beauty paraphernalia that Fran was taking out of her vanity case.

'Ach, Ron. You'll be sitting for a minute while I trim you up,' Fran replied determinedly.

'I'll not be trimmed,' he said with a frown.

'Aye, ye will.' Fran threw a towel round his shoulders and pressed him back into the kitchen chair. 'To be sure, Uncle Ron, you're looking more like a shaggy dog than Harvey ever did,' and she began to snip at his hair.

Cordelia giggled and Peggy couldn't help but smile, for Ron was a picture of misery as he sat there with Harvey's head on his knee while Fran clipped and combed.

'To be sure 'tis a lot of fuss about nothing,' he grumbled.

'You'll like it when I've finished,' said Fran purposefully. 'And I'm sure Rosie will appreciate you looking a bit smarter.'

Peggy could see Ron was thinking about that possibility and had already begun to perk up. Fran certainly knew how to get her way with him. Yet, as she regarded the saggy, faded corduroy trousers, the string holding them up and the ragged shirt, she had to accept that Ron would never be dapper.

'You be minding what ye're doing, girl,' he rumbled as Fran carefully began to trim his bushy eyebrows.

'Aye, I'll be minding,' she said with a smile, 'but if you'd prefer, I could always pull them out with me tweezers.'

'You'll do no such thing,' he snarled. 'Let me out of this kitchen before ye torture me further.'

Fran had him captured in the chair, her scissors poised close to his eyelids as she continued to snip and comb. 'Nearly done, then you can go and have a shave.'

'I had a shave only last week,' he protested.

Fran giggled and stood back. 'There, all trim and shipshape, so y'are. A shave, clean shirt, some decent trousers and shoes, and you could almost pass as handsome.'

'I'll give you handsome, you cheeky wee girl,' he

muttered with a twinkle in his eye as she took the towel from his shoulders. 'Let's get out of here, Harvey, before she takes those scissors to *your* eyebrows.'

The three women laughed and settled down to a pleasant couple of hours of titivating while Daisy crawled about the kitchen floor playing with her brightly coloured building bricks in her nappy and rather grubby vest.

Fran began by doing Peggy's nails, and while the polish was drying, she combed setting lotion in her clean hair and began to pin it up in rollers. 'This set will last for four days, so you've no fear of spoiling it before Saturday,' she said. 'Now, I'll just be giving you a nice face pack.'

'I don't know about that,' said Peggy as she dubiously regarded the pale green paste that Fran was mixing in a bowl. 'What if it brings me out in a rash?'

'To be sure it'll do no such t'ing,' Fran said firmly.

Peggy fidgeted in her chair and reached for a cigarette. 'Well, I hope not. I don't want Jim coming home to a wife covered in spots.'

'Now there's to be no more talking, Auntie Peg. This has to dry and set, and if you move so much as a muscle, you'll spoil the effect.'

Peggy sat still as the cool green paste was slathered onto her face. It did feel nice, she thought, but lord only knew what she must look like. She caught Cordelia's amused expression and had to fight hard not to break into giggles. This had to be the daftest thing she'd ever done.

'There we are,' said Fran. 'Now I'll be putting this cucumber over your eyes so they'll be all bright and sparkling, and those dark shadows will be all gone.'

'Cucumber?' Peggy managed, barely moving her lips. 'You can't waste good cucumber . . .'

'Hush now,' soothed Fran. 'To be sure 'tis only the wee bits off the end that are always sour anyway. We'll not be wasting anything.'

Peggy felt a complete fool sitting there with the goo hardening to concrete on her face and the cucumber freezing her eyelids. She slipped the cigarette between her lips and took a deep drag. 'How long am I supposed to stay like this?'

'For about half an hour,' said Fran. 'It will make your skin lovely and soft and iron out any creases, so it will.'

Peggy rather took exception to the notion that her face might be creased, but she said nothing, for the girl was only trying to be helpful.

'I must say,' said Cordelia with a hitch in her voice. 'You do look very odd, Peggy. But at least you're sitting down for once, which can only be a good thing after all the haring about you've done this week.'

A rap on the front door startled them all. 'Can you go, Fran? And for goodness' sake, whoever it is, don't bring them in here.'

Peggy heard Fran's footsteps crossing the hall floor and the rattle of the letter box as she opened the door. There was a murmur of voices and then the door closed again and Fran returned. 'Who was it?'

'Peggy, it was something for you.'

She knew from her tone that something was wrong, and a chill swept through her as she ripped off the cucumber. Her gaze fell immediately on the brown envelope in Fran's hand. 'A telegram?' she whispered.

'Aye, it is,' said Fran solemnly. 'Do you want me to read it for you, Auntie Peg?'

She shook her head and reached for the telegram. Her fingers were clumsy as she ripped open the envelope, and her breath was shallow as she steeled herself to read the cruel words that danced before her from the single page.

'ALL LEAVE CANCELLED UNTIL FURTHER NOTICE * LETTER FOLLOWS * JIMX'

Peggy let the telegram flutter to the floor as she burst into tears and ran for the sanctuary of her bedroom.

Kitty sat down wearily after her fourth session in the physio room. 'I'm completely exhausted,' she admitted as she unbuckled the leg and rubbed her aching thigh muscles.

Dr Thorne smiled down at her. 'I'm not surprised,' he said. 'You've been working hard today and achieved a great deal.' He knelt to examine her stump. 'That's looking absolutely fine,' he said, 'so I think you can have another go at reaching the door tomorrow.'

'I could try now,' she said eagerly.

He shook his head. 'Remember what I said about taking things slowly, Kitty? Tomorrow morning first thing will be much better. You'll be rested and feeling stronger than now, which will give you a much better chance of achieving your goal.'

She knew he was right, but her impatient nature meant it was hard to accept. 'There are ten days left until I'm to be a bridesmaid at my friend's wedding,' she said as she pulled the thickly padded sock over her stump. 'Do you think I'll be able to walk with sticks by then?'

'I think you'd be pushing yourself too hard,' he said solemnly. 'It's one thing to get from here to the door, but it will be quite another to walk up an aisle and stand for half an hour or more before you have to walk back. Then there's all the standing about while the photographs are taken and people mingle.' His expression was kindly regretful. 'I think you'll enjoy the day far more if you stick to your trusty crutches.'

Kitty gave a deep sigh of disappointment. 'When you put it like that, I can see how hopeless it was to even consider it.' Then she made an effort to look on the bright side of things. 'Still, at least I won't have that horrid shoe poking out from beneath my dress.'

'That's the spirit.' He handed her the crutches. 'I'll see you tomorrow, Kitty.'

She went out of the room and along the corridor towards the front door, and saw Rita was already waiting to take her home. 'Hello, you're early – or am I late?'

'I'm a bit early because I need to get back to Beach View as quickly as possible.'

'Why?' Kitty asked sharply. 'What's happened?'

'Jim's leave has been cancelled and poor Auntie Peg is in a terrible state.'

'Oh, no,' gasped Kitty. 'Poor Peggy. What a cruel thing to do at the very last minute.'

'That's the flaming army for you,' snapped Rita as they went out onto the driveway.

'Is there someone with Peggy?' Kitty asked as she clambered into the fire station van.

'Fran's had to go to work and the others aren't back yet. I phoned Ron at the Anchor to tell him what's happened, so he'll be there by now to take over from Grandma Finch. She's as upset as Peggy and really not much use.'

Rita slammed the door, fired up the engine and sent the van roaring down the driveway with such force, gravel was spattered everywhere.

Kitty could understand Peggy's bitter disappointment, for she'd been so happy and busy with her cleaning and her plans for Jim's homecoming. 'We must do something to try and cheer her up,' she said as they hurtled round a bend.

Rita nodded. 'We must all muck in and do the tea, then I thought we should take her to the Anchor for a drink. Fran and Suzy are on duty tonight, but I'm sure Jane wouldn't mind staying in to babysit Daisy.'

'What about Grandma Finch? Won't she look after Daisy so Jane can come with us?'

Rita shook her head as she concentrated on the narrow country lane. 'Grandma Finch is as upset as Auntie Peg and she likes nothing better than a sweet sherry at the Anchor, so it will be a treat. She loves being in a crowded bar so she can sit and watch everyone and join in the sing-songs.'

Kitty smiled at this. 'I didn't realise Cordelia enjoyed such things,' she said. 'She's such a quiet little woman, and at times she can be quite prim.'

Rita smiled fondly. 'That's what she'd like you to think, but Cordelia is still very young at heart and enjoys a night out just as much as anyone.' She chuckled. 'She's as out of tune as the old piano, and I can remember at least two occasions when Ron has had to virtually carry her home after she's had two large sherries.'

Kitty grabbed her seat as Rita took a bend too fast and had to screech to a slithering, heart-pounding stop to avoid an oncoming tractor. 'I look forward to that drink,' she said. 'If we ever make it that far.'

Rita grinned. 'Don't tell me you're losing your nerve, Kitty Pargeter. What's forty miles an hour compared to the speed you do in a Spit?'

'I don't attempt to fly a Spit down narrow country lanes – let alone an old van with unreliable brakes,' she said dryly.

'You're getting soft in your old age,' teased Rita as the tractor rumbled past. Then she rammed her foot on the accelerator and they hurtled towards home.

Peggy had emerged from her room briefly to tearfully telephone Martin to ask him to warn Cissy that her father wouldn't be coming home after all. Having returned to her bed, she soon came to realise she couldn't hide in her bedroom all night with so many things to do and so many people to care for. So she'd washed the remains of the face pack off and brushed out her hair in an effort to feel a bit more cheerful.

Yet it felt as if a heavy weight rested on her heart as the sweet, loving girls bustled about her kitchen to prepare the evening meal that she'd planned for Saturday night. There were lovely thick, meaty sausages from Alf the butcher, a pile of mashed potato and fresh green beans from the garden, all smothered in lashings of Jim's favourite thick gravy. For afters, she'd planned to make a sponge pudding with some of her illicit white flour, and use the last of the golden syrup to pour over it.

However, there would be no syrup sponge and no Jim this weekend, and the weight grew heavier in her heart as her tears began to blind her.

'Please don't cry, Auntie Peg,' said Rita as she gave Peggy's shoulder a comforting squeeze. 'He'll come home, really he will – just a bit later than we all expected, that's all.'

Peggy blew her nose and dredged up a smile. 'I'm more cross than anything,' she admitted gruffly. 'How could the army cancel his leave at the last minute like that? And with no hint of how long it will be before it's reinstated. It's unfair on everyone.'

'Ach, to be sure, Peggy girl, the army does as it pleases,' said Ron, who'd come straight home from the Anchor following Rita's urgent telephone call. 'Now dry your eyes and eat some of this delicious food the girls have cooked.'

Peggy regarded the heaped plate in front of her and didn't feel in the least bit hungry. But as she was about to push the plate away she saw how everyone was watching her, so she dug her fork into the potato and took a mouthful. 'It's lovely, girls, thank you,' she murmured.

'Make sure you eat every last bit, Auntie Peg,' said Rita, who was feeding Daisy. 'You're going to need to keep up your strength, because we're all going to the Anchor after tea, and you don't want to be drinking on an empty stomach.'

Peggy didn't want to go to the pub. In fact all she really wanted to do was go to bed and curl up with her misery. 'You all go,' she said. 'I have to look after Daisy.'

'I'm doing that,' said Jane. 'So you've got no excuses – and it would be a shame not to show off your lovely new hairstyle. Fran's done a smashing job on it, don't you think?'

Peggy nodded. She knew when to give in gracefully, and so she ate the meal she should have been sharing with Jim. Yet she found she had to force every last tasteless morsel down.

Once the meal was finally over, she lit a cigarette to go with her cup of tea and watched as the girls cleared the table and washed the dishes. They were such lovely girls, and so thoughtful in the way they were trying so hard to cheer her up. And although the last thing she wanted to do tonight was sit in a smoky pub and be deafened by Cordelia's singing, she'd begun to think that a couple of gins might be just the thing she needed to help her sleep tonight.

'I'll just go and get changed,' she said as she battled her tears and stubbed out the cigarette.

Closing her bedroom door behind her, she sank onto the bed and stared at her reflection in the dressing-table mirror. She'd waited so long for Jim to come home, and now she would have to find the strength to carry on and continue waiting. But if she was going to the Anchor, then she needed to do something to hide her swollen eyelids and pale face.

With a deep sigh of longing for what might have been, she ran her hand over the counterpane, and then opened the wardrobe door to regard the scant few clothes that hung there. Deciding on a blue and white linen dress that had been one of Doris's cast-offs, she found her blue pumps and dug out a hand-knitted white cardigan she'd only finished the previous week. The nights were drawing in now it was September and it could get quite cold, so she took her overcoat off its hanger and placed it on the bed.

Determined not to let her emotions get the better of her, she dressed and put on her face. Adding a defiant slash of red lipstick, she felt ready to face everyone again. The uncaring, mean army wasn't going to beat her down. Not this time. Not ever.

With a deep breath for courage she opened the bedroom door to find that everyone but Ron was in the hall. Harvey came to lick her hand, then shot off back into the kitchen.

'You look lovely, Auntie Peg,' said Rita as she helped Cordelia on with her overcoat. 'And that lipstick tells me you're feeling more like your old self again,' she added with an impish grin.

Peggy replied with a wan smile and tried to look enthusiastic about the outing.

'Come along Ron,' called Cordelia. 'Look lively. The first drinks are on you, so make sure you dig out your wallet.'

'Ach, will ye be still, woman?' he grumbled without rancor as Harvey made a beeline for Peggy.

Ron stomped past Jane, who was holding Daisy

in her arms, and came into the hall wearing his one smart jacket, fairly decent shirt and a pair of sharply pressed trousers. 'I'm a pensioner and me shrapnel's playing up like the very divil tonight, so 'tis sympathy I should be getting, not unreasonable demands.'

'You're not the only pensioner around here, Ronan Reilly,' Cordelia retorted. 'And your blessed shrapnel has little to do with anything. So stop moaning and open your wallet for once. The moths must be gasping for air.'

Peggy smiled at their gentle banter as she regarded Ron's appearance with some pleasure. He'd clearly made an effort to smarten himself up and, she noticed with surprise, he'd also had a shave and put brilliantine in his hair. This was a minor miracle, and no doubt had something to do with Rosie.

Then she caught sight of Kitty, who was standing by the telephone and looking very reluctant to leave. She was about to say something, but Jane had obviously noticed too, for she came to Kitty's side and put a consoling hand on her arm.

'Don't worry, Kitty,' Jane said. 'If Roger telephones I'll let him know where you are and why.'

Harvey clearly thought it was all terribly exciting to have a family outing and ran round in circles getting under everyone's feet, until he was sharply ordered by Ron to keep still and behave.

Once Ron had seen Cordelia safely down the front steps, the girls hovered by Kitty as she slowly negotiated her way to the pavement.

Peggy pulled on her overcoat, kissed Daisy good-night and gave Jane a hug. 'Thank you, dear,' she said. 'Now, Daisy likes to splash a bit in her bath at bedtime. She should settle, but if she doesn't, I've made up a bottle of formula. Her nightclothes are . . .'

'Will ye stop talking, woman, and hurry up?' shouted Ron from the pavement. 'A man could die of thirst the length of time you take to say goodbye.'

'Don't worry, Auntie Peggy,' soothed Jane. 'I've lived here long enough to know the routine. Go and have some fun, and I'll see you when you get back.'

Peggy kissed them both again and reluctantly went down the steps to where everyone was waiting. She linked arms with Rita and Sarah, and they kept their pace to that of Cordelia and Kitty as they set off for the Anchor.

It was almost midnight by the time Peggy managed to escape once more to her room. She checked on Daisy, who was snuffling contentedly in her cot, and then kicked off her high-heeled pumps and stripped off her clothes.

Leaving them on the floor in a heap, she pulled on her old, faded nightdress, turned off the nightlight and clambered into the big, empty bed. There was no more need to keep up the happy façade that she'd struggled to maintain all through the evening.

No more need to hold back the tears or keep her emotions under tight control.

Peggy buried her face in the downy pillow, finally able to give in to the bitter, heart-wrenching disappointment. And she let it flow out of her in a great tide of stormy tears.

Chapter Twenty-seven

Nine days had passed since Peggy had received that devastating telegram, and although she'd tried very hard to mask her emotions, Kitty and the other girls were all too aware of how much she was quietly suffering. So when Jim's letter had arrived assuring her that his week's leave would definitely begin on the eighteenth of October, they'd all breathed a sigh of relief.

Kitty leaned back in the comfortable leather seat and regarded Roger's handsome profile as he drove the car through the Berkshire countryside. He was such a dear man, and she did love him so, for he knew how nervous she was about the coming weekend and had taken great pains to make her feel more comfortable about it.

'Are we there yet?' asked Freddy, who was sprawled across the back seat, surrounded by the litter of discarded newspapers.

Kitty laughed. 'You sound like a bored and impatient child,' she teased. 'If you bothered to look out of the window, you'd see we are just coming into the village.'

'Look lively, old chap,' said Roger as they coasted

along the narrow village street and slowed down to negotiate the rather grand driveway where a tiny gatehouse sat to one side. 'Can't have the future in-laws thinking you're a ragamuffin.'

Kitty heard Freddy scuffling about in the back as he pulled on his tweed jacket, straightened his tie and smoothed the creases out of his twill trousers. But she was more interested in seeing the house again, and the beautiful gardens spreading across almost two acres of land.

The imposing Georgian house came into view as the car swept round the final bend. It had originally been a rectory, but with so many rooms to maintain on a tiny stipend, the last incumbent had moved his wife and child to a small cottage on the other side of the church, and the house had been sold.

Cecilia and David Bingham had moved in after their marriage in 1919, and Charlotte had been born in the blue bedroom which overlooked the rose garden at the back of the house. It was the only house Kitty had been in that had a lift, but it had been put in when Cecilia's elderly mother had become too frail to manage the stairs.

Kitty loved this house, for it had become a second home during her school days, and she gazed with deep affection at the three neat rows of long, elegant windows which surrounded the central stone portico and looked out over the bowling-green-smooth expanse of freshly cut lawn and still colourful flower beds.

The sturdy roof huddled over the top windows where the naked, twisted branches of an ancient wisteria clung to the walls of mellow brick. In the spring they would be smothered with heavily scented purple clusters of blossom, but now the only colour came from the few surviving roses by the front door.

'That's the hedge Charlotte and I used to make our camps in,' she said as she pointed to the right. 'And that's the tree we used to climb,' she added sadly. 'I wonder what happened to the tree house David had built for us.'

'Charlotte said it had become rotten and dangerous, so they had it taken down,' said Freddy, who was at last taking some interest in things.

'It looks as if we have a welcoming committee,' said Roger as he drove onto the gravel turning circle and passed the central fountain where a stone merman was forever pouring water from a stone jug.

The front door was open, and Charlotte and her parents waited on the top step. Kitty sat forward eagerly, and then saw they weren't alone. 'They aren't your parents, are they?' she asked Roger.

'Well yes, actually, they are,' he replied with a frown. 'But I didn't know they'd be here, I promise.' His frown deepened. 'There must have been a change of plan.'

'Sorry, Kitts,' drawled Freddy. 'I forgot to tell you. Cecilia asked them to stay here rather than the dreary hotel they'd booked into.'

'Really, Freddy,' Kitty snapped. 'You are the absolute limit.'

Roger waved to the people on the doorstep and
brought the car to a halt. 'I honestly can't think why
you're so nervous about meeting the parents.
They're really looking forward to meeting you, you
know.'

Kitty didn't know anything of the sort, but there
was no time to discuss it, for Charlotte had come
flying down the steps to open the door and give her
a hug.

'Welcome, welcome,' she said excitedly. 'Your room's
all ready, Daddy's had the mechanic in to service
the lift, and we're going to have such fun, Kitts. All
the girls are coming tonight, and Daddy has promised us champagne.'

Kitty hugged her back and then clambered out of
the car to find herself amid a whirlwind of greetings.
Freddy picked up Charlotte and spun her round
until she was laughing uproariously and begging
him to put her down; Roger shook David Bingham's
hand, kissed Cecilia's cheek and then greeted his
parents; David Bingham did the back-slapping thing
with both Roger and Freddy; and then Cecilia,
looking as cool and elegantly beautiful as always,
was kissing Kitty's cheek.

'Welcome home, my dear,' she murmured. 'I can't
tell you how pleased we all are to have you here
for such a special occasion.' She stepped back from
the embrace and carefully avoided looking at Kitty's

empty trouser leg as David came to give her a hearty hug which almost knocked her off balance.

'Good to see you, Kitts,' he boomed. 'I see you're up and about and as ravishing as ever despite the old crutches. Looking forward to tomorrow?'

Kitty grinned. She liked Charlotte's father very much, for he was a straightforward sort of man, and utterly genuine. 'I certainly am,' she replied.

Roger took her hand as David went off to chat with Freddy. 'Darling, I'd like to introduce you to my parents,' he said. 'Don't worry,' he added in a stage whisper. 'They don't bite.' He turned to the slim blonde woman in her late forties, who was dressed in a beautifully cut lavender tweed two-piece. 'Mother, this is my darling Kitty.'

'How do you do, Lady Makepeace,' stammered a very nervous Kitty as they shook hands.

'Oh, my dear, please don't be so formal,' Lady Makepeace said with a warm smile. 'You must call me Beatrice – and this is my husband, Edward.'

Lord Edward Makepeace was tall and broad and also dressed in tweeds, but his were brown, and the plus fours revealed thick knee-length socks and shining brown brogues. As Kitty's hand was swamped by his huge, rather rough fingers, she looked up into a face weathered and lined from the elements and saw twinkling blue eyes looking down at her from beneath rather fearsome eyebrows that even Ron would have envied.

'Jolly good show,' he said. 'Glad to meet you at

last, don't y'know. Roger's been banging on about you, and I can see why.' He turned to Beatrice. 'She's a little smasher, eh what, Bea?'

As Beatrice nodded agreement, Kitty had to stifle a giggle. Edward sounded so like Roger it was uncanny.

'Come along, everyone,' called David. 'It's still warm enough to have our drinks outside, so they're laid out in the rose garden. Follow me.'

Kitty was feeling much more relaxed now the dreaded meeting had proved so pleasant, and she was about to follow Roger and the others into the house when she felt a light hand on her arm.

'Could we just have a tiny moment before we join the fray?' Beatrice asked.

Kitty was suddenly nervous again, for Beatrice was blocking her way.

Beatrice must have realised how anxious Kitty was, for she smiled. 'Edward and I have been longing to meet you,' she said warmly. 'Roger is so obviously in love with you, and we're both delighted that at last our darling boy has found someone special who makes him so happy.'

'So you don't mind about my leg?' she asked warily. 'Or the fact that my family are working people?'

Beatrice laughed uproariously. 'Silly girl,' she spluttered. 'Of course we don't mind any of that old-fashioned nonsense – in fact we're very proud of you, and admire the courage you've shown during what must have been a terrifying experience.'

'Thank you,' murmured Kitty. 'You're very kind.'

Beatrice smiled. 'Then I hope you feel easier about things now,' she said. 'I remember how ghastly it was when I met Edward's parents for the first time. I was a nervous wreck, believe me.'

She leaned a little closer, her delicate perfume drifting between them. 'His mother was the most frightful old trout and horribly disapproving. You see, I wasn't exactly from the top drawer either.'

Kitty looked at her in surprise. 'Really?'

Beatrice nodded delightedly. 'My father started out as a labourer but he had far grander ideas, and by the time he was forty, he had his own construction company. He designed and built some of the most gracious houses you will see in London and the Home Counties. But to Edward's mother he was still "trade" and it was therefore beneath her dignity to acknowledge him, even after our wedding.'

'She sounds perfectly horrid,' Kitty shuddered.

'Oh, she was,' said Beatrice, 'but as we lived in Wiltshire and she was in London, I didn't have to see her more than once a year.'

Kitty smiled, for she rather liked Beatrice.

'That's better,' she said as she placed her warm, soft hand on Kitty's arm. 'Now we're friends, let's go and do justice to David's super champagne before the sun takes off the chill.'

The next three hours sped by as they drank champagne in the garden and chatted about the wedding, the honeymoon and the planned dinner party for the girls that evening. It was agreed by all that if this glorious weather held out for tomorrow, and the Luftwaffe didn't decide to raid them, it would be perfect.

After Charlotte had run down to visit her grand-mother, who lived in the gatehouse with an elderly housekeeper, they sat in the shade of a large umbrella and ate a light lunch of delicious ham and salad, followed by cheese and coffee. The ham had come from Edward Makepeace's pig farm, and the cheese, butter and lovely white bread were the products of the vast estate's numerous and varied farms, mills and village businesses.

Once lunch was over the dishes were cleared away by the two women who'd come in from the village to help out over the weekend. There had once been housemaids, gardeners and handymen, but of course the war had changed things quite radically, and now Cecilia was running the house almost single-handedly.

One of the women returned half an hour later and tapped Cecilia on the shoulder. 'The dressmaker's here, Mum,' she said. 'I've put her in the front sitting room.'

'Thank you, Edna, but please don't call me Mum. It's ma'am, and it rhymes with ham.' She must have noted the sour look on the woman's face, for she hurried on. 'Would you give her a cup of tea while she waits? The girls won't be long, I'm sure.'

'Yes, Mum,' she replied before stomping off back into the house.

Charlotte pushed back her chair. 'Now Mrs Fowler's here, it's time to try on that dress, and I can't wait to see how you look in it.'

Kitty followed her in through the French windows and along the passage to David's large, book-lined study. The shimmering blue dress hung from a padded hanger that had been hooked onto the picture rail.

'I'll just pop in to say hello to Mrs Fowler while you get changed. You won't be disturbed until you're ready, so don't worry.'

As Charlotte closed the door behind her, Kitty went across the room and felt the weight and smoothness of the beautiful dress. The colour was quite extraordinary, reminding her of the ocean in the way the rich silk changed from turquoise to blue and green as she removed it from the hanger and draped it over the desk.

Eager now to try it on, she set her crutches to one side and stripped off her blouse and ugly brassiere. Sitting in a chair, she pulled off her trousers and kicked off her sandal. Reaching for the dress, she reverently slipped it over her head and felt its sensuous, silky coolness ripple over her skin as she let it slide down her body.

She had to fiddle a bit to get all the tiny covered buttons done up at the side, but at last they were done, and as she stood, the dress slithered over her thighs and pooled on the carpet in delicate, watery folds. She grabbed her crutches and, wary of tripping on the hem, carefully turned to look in the long mirror that had been brought in especially.

The colour was wonderful, for it enhanced her sun-browned skin and golden hair, and made her eyes an even deeper blue. The silk skimmed her body from the delicate shoulder straps and brought an elegance and sophistication to her boyish figure that she'd never before possessed. But the crutches completely marred the effect, and she could have wept with frustration.

Charlotte tapped on the door and came straight in. 'Oh, Kitty, you look absolutely wonderful,' she breathed. 'And the dress fits perfectly, although the hem will have to be taken up.'

'I look awful,' said Kitty, almost in tears. 'The dress is quite the most beautiful thing I've ever worn, but these damned crutches ruin everything.'

'Then we'll have to do something about them,' said Charlotte determinedly. She opened the door. 'You can come in now, Mrs Fowler.'

The plump little woman bustled in and shot Kitty a warm smile as she placed her sewing box on the desk. 'Hello, dear,' she said brightly. 'My, my, don't you look a treat?'

'As you can see, the hem will have to be taken up,' said Charlotte. 'But more importantly, we need you to help us come up with some idea of how we can make those crutches a sight more attractive.'

'Right y'are,' said the homely little woman as she regarded Kitty from head to toe with a nod of approval before she eyed the crutches with a frown. 'I'll think on it while I pin up the hem.'

Charlotte and Kitty were giggling in delight as they returned to the garden almost an hour later. The problem had been solved, and it had been so simple they couldn't believe they hadn't thought of it straight away. But it had meant Charlotte racing down to her grandmother's again to borrow her old crutches.

'Hello,' said Roger. 'Something's afoot, I see. What have you two been up to?'

'It's a secret,' said Kitty as she kissed his sun-warmed cheek. 'You'll find out tomorrow.' She caught Charlotte's eye and winked as she picked up the glass of champagne. No one had noticed the different crutches.

As the sun lost its warmth and started to disappear behind the trees, everyone began to move indoors. 'We'd better be off, Freddy,' said Roger. 'The landlord at the Ox will think we aren't coming and we won't get dinner.'

'I rang him earlier to warn him you might be late,' said David. 'He's still expecting you, and I've taken the liberty of booking me and Edward in for dinner as well, if that's all right. The girls won't want us hanging about, and I suspect we wouldn't enjoy an evening of chatter and giggling anyway.'

'We'd be delighted to have your company, sir,' said Freddy. 'And I agree. There's nothing worse than having to listen to twittering women when they're overexcited and full of champagne.' He gave a cheeky wink to his sister.

'Get out of here,' said Kitty as she playfully swiped at his arm.

She turned from Freddy and looked up at Roger. 'I'll see you tomorrow,' she murmured. 'Please don't let Freddy drink too much. It would be simply awful if he was suffering from a hangover at the altar.'

All too aware of their interested audience, he kissed her lightly on the lips. 'I'll keep an eye on him, never fear. Sweet dreams, darling girl, and I'll see you tomorrow.'

As Charlotte accompanied Freddy to the car, Roger kissed his mother goodbye and then strolled after them.

'I think it's time we all had our baths and took a little snooze so we're fresh for this evening,' said Cecilia once Charlotte returned. 'Dinner's at eight, but our guests will be arriving at seven so we can have a glass of champagne to really get in the party mood.' She looked across at Kitty. 'Did you remember to bring an evening dress, dear?'

Dinner had always been a formal occasion in this house, and Kitty had packed accordingly. 'I certainly did,' she replied. 'It's my trusty cream silk that has travelled all over the country with me ever since I joined the ATA. And my friend Sarah has lent me the most beautiful Indian silk shawl to go with it, so I'll be quite presentable.'

'Jolly good show,' boomed Edward Makepeace. 'Now I'm off for forty winks. Can't let the chaps down by falling asleep over dinner, eh what?' He turned in the doorway. 'What time are we off, David?'

'Ten minutes before the girls arrive,' he replied with a wink at Cecilia. 'But don't worry about wearing black tie, it's only the Ox.'

The evening had been a tremendous success, for Kitty and Charlotte's childhood friends had been as welcoming and accepting as they'd always been, so Kitty had been able to relax and thoroughly enjoy the party.

There were ten for dinner, and although each one of them looked beautiful, Charlotte had outshone them all in her grandmother's diamonds and a black velvet gown. Beatrice had turned out to be quite the raconteur, for she'd kept everyone in stitches with her vivid and rather risqué tales of country life and all its pitfalls and colourful characters.

Now Kitty was in her bedroom, and the glorious dress was hanging in the wardrobe all pressed and ready for tomorrow. She was feeling a little light-headed and rather tired after the long, lovely day, and was glad that Cecilia had called a halt at half past ten. She turned off the light and drew the curtains and blackout right back from the open window so she could see the moon and listen to the owls hooting in the trees while she lay in the comfortable bed.

Her eyelids were drooping with weariness and she was on the very edge of sleep when there was a light tap on the door. 'Only me,' whispered Charlotte. 'Are you awake?'

'I am now,' she replied with a yawn. 'What's the matter?'

'I'm too excited to sleep,' Charlotte murmured as she closed the door. 'Can I come in with you for a bit?' Without waiting for a reply, she slipped into the other side of the big double bed.

'Your feet are cold,' Kitty complained.

'Sorry.' Charlotte giggled. 'It's quite like old times, isn't it? Remember how we used to talk all night and then couldn't get up in the morning?'

Kitty grinned as they lay facing one another in the shaft of moonlight that came in through the window. It was as if they were thirteen again. 'We'd better not talk for too long,' she whispered. 'You have a rather important day tomorrow.'

'I know,' Charlotte giggled. 'Isn't it exciting?'

Charlotte must have left the bed after Kitty had fallen asleep, for there was no sign of her when Cecilia came into Kitty's room with a breakfast tray at seven.

'Take your time, Kitty, dear,' she said as she settled the tray on the bed. 'There's plenty of hot water for everyone, and the hairdresser won't be here for another hour, so I've booked you in for nine.'

'Thank you.' Kitty sipped the reviving tea. 'How's Charlotte this morning?'

Cecilia smiled. 'Radiant, happy, excited. All the things a bride should be on her wedding morning. And who could blame her? Freddy is the most marvellous young man and we're delighted to have him for a son.' She opened the door. 'Lily will be running her salon in the pink bedroom. Now I'll leave you to it, dear,' she said rather distractedly. 'I've lots to do.'

Kitty ate her breakfast, her thoughts on her parents who were no doubt longing to be here to witness this special day in their son's life. And then, not wishing to be sad on such a day, she climbed out of bed and went through into the small bathroom.

Lily was a lively little girl who talked non-stop as she worked, but Kitty was delighted with her hair, so the tip she gave was a bit more generous than she'd planned.

Looking in on Charlotte who was in a flurry of excitement, she gave her a hug and sent her to Lily. 'I'll see you downstairs when you're dressed,' she said as she headed back to her own room.

Kitty saw the crutches immediately and guessed that Cecilia must have brought them up after Mrs Fowler had delivered them. She tested them out and found them to be perfect. With a smile of happy contentment, she sat on the dressing stool for a while to smoke a cigarette and think about how Roger would react to the new, sophisticated Kitty that walked behind the bride.

She stubbed out the cigarette and checked the time, then began carefully applying her make-up. Washing her hands of any residue in case it marked the dress, she returned to the bedroom, and with a shiver of pleasure, felt the silk whisper over her skin. She had a bit of a tussle again to get the little buttons done up and then admired the effect in the cheval mirror. To complete the outfit, there was a 1920s headband of peacock blue that sparkled in the sunlight, and a flat silver sandal which she'd borrowed from Suzy.

As she looked once again in the mirror to check that everything was as perfect as she could get it, she heard footsteps going past her door and a murmur of voices. It was time to go downstairs. With a tingle of excitement, Kitty picked up her newly refurbished crutches and headed out to the small lift that would take her down to the elegant hall.

It rattled and clanged a bit and was rather claustrophobic, but it delivered her safely, and she went into the drawing room to find that David Bingham and Roger's parents were already there. Beatrice looked extremely elegant in a silk two-piece suit of pale grey, and a broad-brimmed white hat with a matching grey ribbon round the crown. She wore pearls in her ears and round her neck, and her shoes were two-tone grey and white high-heeled pumps. Both men were in morning suits, and had already got stuck into the whisky.

'I say, you do look smashing,' said Roger's father. 'You see, Bea. I told you she'd look smashing, didn't I?'

Beatrice rolled her eyes beneath the broad-brimmed hat. 'Yes, dear. So you did – and you were right as always.' She blew a kiss to Kitty. 'You look simply wonderful, and I adore the crutches – what a clever idea.'

'That was Mrs Fowler.' Kitty sat down and handed them over to be admired. The silk cut from the hem had been turned into ribbons which she'd wound neatly round the crutches and finished off with circlets of the tiniest, sweetest dark blue silk roses at the bottom.

David Bingham handed her a glass of champagne. 'Well done, Kitty. You look a real treat. Now I'd better go up and see if that daughter of mine has finished primping and preening. Time is getting on.'

'I do love weddings, don't you?' sighed Beatrice.

Kitty saw the wistfulness in her expression and was madly trying to think of a reply that wouldn't turn the subject to her and Roger when she was saved by the appearance of Cecilia.

'They'll be down in a minute,' she said with breathless excitement as she checked the tilt of her lovely cream hat and ran nervous fingers down the cream silk dress and jacket.

Their glasses were topped up and Beatrice carried Kitty's as they all trooped into the hall to await the entrance of the bride.

'We're coming down,' called Charlotte from beyond the curve of the staircase. 'Are you ready?'

As they assured her they were, Charlotte appeared at the top of the stairs on her father's arm and waited with almost childlike excitement for their reaction.

There were gasps of admiration, for she looked utterly beautiful in the vintage cream silk wedding gown which narrowly skimmed her figure and fell gracefully to her feet in a flowing train. Her dark hair had been carefully brushed into generous Victory rolls, and the antique diamond tiara glittered with fire every time she moved. The gossamer lace veil floated around her as she slowly came down the stairs carrying a bouquet of trailing cream roses and fronds of fern, and the pearls at her neck and in her ears were a perfect match for the stunning dress.

Cecilia and Beatrice were trying very hard not to cry and smudge their make-up, and both men seemed to find it hard to actually speak. Kitty was emotional too, and she took Charlotte's hand and gave it a little squeeze. 'You look wonderful,' she breathed.

'So do you,' she replied with an affectionate smile. 'It's all a far cry from our uniforms, isn't it?'

'It's time we were going,' said David as the church clock struck twelve. 'You're suitably late, Charlotte, but any longer and it will be unkind to poor Freddy.' He ushered everyone out of the door and into the waiting cars which had been festooned with white ribbons and bunches of lucky purple heather.

Once everyone was settled, the cars moved off at a stately crawl down the long drive and into the village street, where everyone had come out to see the bride. The cars pulled to a halt outside the church, which was only yards away from the entrance to the Binghams' driveway, and the chauffeurs jumped out to open doors and offer assistance as the villagers applauded and shouted their good wishes.

Kitty waited with Charlotte and her father until everyone, including the hovering verger, had disappeared inside and the doors were closed.

'Are you ready, Charlotte?' asked David.

'I've been ready for this day since the moment I met him,' she replied softly.

He kissed her forehead and tenderly drew the beautiful veil over her face. 'Come on then, precious girl. Let's get you married.'

Kitty had to blink back her tears as she followed them along the short path, for Charlotte's happiness had affected her deeply. Then the doors were opened and the sound of organ music floated out to them, and they were drawn inside.

Freddy and Roger were waiting at the altar, both strikingly handsome in their dress uniforms, and as Charlotte drifted in a haze of silk and lace towards him, Freddy couldn't resist taking a peek.

Neither could Roger, and as his eyes met Kitty's she felt the love radiating from him and suddenly it was as if she was the bride.

The music stopped and the ceremony began. Charlotte passed Kitty the bouquet, and she had a moment of difficulty before she could hold it securely and maintain her balance.

As the service continued and hymns were sung, she began to tire, but she kept determinedly still, her gaze fixed to Roger's broad back as he handed Freddy the rings and the happy couple recited their vows. Freddy lovingly drew the veil from Charlotte's radiant face and kissed her, and then Kitty returned the bouquet and they were moving towards the vestry where they would sign the register.

Kitty was exhausted and her leg was trembling from the effort of having stood for so long, so she was hugely relieved when Roger came to place a steady hand beneath her elbow. 'Take your time, darling,' he murmured. 'There's no rush, and I can see you're struggling a bit.'

She didn't have the energy to reply as she was fully concentrated on getting into the vestry. He seemed to understand, for the moment they reached the small, cold room, he drew a chair forward so she could sit and rest.

'You do look utterly beautiful today,' he murmured as photographs were taken of the happy couple signing the register. 'I couldn't concentrate on the service much, because I simply couldn't take my eyes off you.'

'I felt exactly the same,' she confessed shyly.

The register was signed, more photographs were taken and then the wonderful music accompanied them all down the aisle. As Kitty walked beside Roger she realised how deeply she loved him, and how life without him would be intolerable. She looked up at him as they reached the doorway and knew he felt the same way, and they shared a secret, loving smile that held promise and hope for the future.

The weather was surprisingly kind and Cecilia had managed somehow to provide a real feast, so the only thing to mar the reception was the roar of several squadrons of Spitfires and Hurricanes as they flew overhead. Grandmother Elizabeth sat in her bath chair like an empress and held court, while the rest of the guests mingled throughout the house and garden as the champagne flowed. Roger gave a wonderfully funny speech, Freddy replied with an equally amusing one, and then it was time to see the bride and groom off on their honeymoon.

Kitty had managed to get through the long afternoon on sheer determination, but as everyone stood on the steps and watched the car go down the drive to the rattling accompaniment of the tin cans and horseshoes trailing behind it she knew she'd overdone things.

Roger, bless him, understood, and within half an

hour they'd said their goodbyes and set off for Cliffehaven.

Kitty rested her head on his shoulder and sleepily watched the road ahead, glad for the peace and quiet. 'It was a wonderful day, wasn't it?' she sighed. 'And I've never seen Charlotte looking so beautiful.'

'I only had eyes for you,' he replied softly as he swiftly planted a kiss on the top of her head.

Kitty nestled into his side, feeling as snug and contented as a cat. 'Cecilia said I could keep the dress,' she murmured, 'so once I've got two legs again, perhaps we could go somewhere smart so I can show it off.'

Roger chuckled. 'Two legs or one, it makes no difference to me, my darling, and of course I'll take you somewhere smart.' He was silent for a while. 'So what was it Charlotte whispered to you that made you giggle and blush just before they left for their honeymoon?'

Kitty smiled, for Charlotte had whispered, 'You're next, Kitty. You and Roger are just perfect together.'

But that was between her and Charlotte – a delicious moment in a wonderful, emotional day. 'It was just a bit of girlish nonsense,' she replied, still with a smile in her voice. 'Nothing for you to worry about, Roger.'

She must have fallen asleep for the rest of the journey, because suddenly they were approaching Cliffehaven. 'Oh, I feel better for that,' she said as she sat up and straightened her blouse.

'I'm glad,' he replied as he drove off the road and

up the narrow chalk track that led into the hills. 'You were obviously exhausted, even though you kept going quite wonderfully throughout the day.'

He parked the car and reached for the flask of coffee Cecilia had given him.

'Why are we up here?' Kitty asked. 'I thought you had to be on duty this evening?'

'Not until later,' he replied as he handed her the coffee cup. 'I haven't been able to talk to you properly all day, and I thought it would be rather nice to come to our picnic spot for a while before I took you back to Beach View.'

Kitty sipped the scalding hot coffee and gazed at the glorious view. 'Roger,' she began hesitantly, 'there's something I'd like to ask of you.' She glanced at him quickly, saw his frown, and hurried on to reveal the plan that had been forming in her mind over the past two weeks.

When she finally stopped talking, he gathered her to him and held her tight. 'I'll see what I can do,' he said. 'But I can't promise anything, you understand that, don't you?' At her nod, he tipped up her chin and kissed her.

Then, before she could get her breath back, he took her hands and looked deeply into her eyes. 'Kitty, will you marry me?'

Kitty stared at him in shock. 'Are you sure?' she breathed.

'I've never been so sure of anything in my life,' he said solemnly. 'And with the way things are, I don't want us to spend another day apart.' His grip tightened on her hands. 'I know this isn't at all romantic, and that I should be down on one knee, but after today, I've come to realise that I simply cannot live without you.'

'Oh, Roger, of course I'll marry you,' she managed through her tears of joy.

It was quite a long while later that he slipped his grandmother's beautiful diamond engagement ring onto her finger.

Chapter Twenty-eight

The first week in October had come and gone, and Peggy was in a complete fluster of excitement, for not only would Jim be home on leave next weekend, but today was Kitty's wedding day.

The house was in chaos, for all the girls were off duty and they were dashing about having baths and running back and forth into each other's rooms in their underwear. Fran had been a real treasure, for she'd spent most of the morning doing everyone's hair. Cordelia was in a twitter, Harvey was galloping about like a mad thing, and Ron had taken himself off to his basement bedroom to get away from it all.

As Peggy pulled a fresh towel from the upstairs airing cupboard, she could hear Charlotte and Kitty happily chattering away with the raucous Doreen, who'd arrived the night before. She smiled, for it was simply wonderful to have the house so alive again, and to know that Kitty's future now shone like a bright new star. The girl had come a long way since they'd first met at the Memorial.

Peggy took advantage of the deserted bathroom, and less than fifteen minutes later, she was in her bedroom struggling to get her corset on. She smiled as she remembered how Jim had once laughed as he'd watched her, and told her he liked her wobbly bits. 'There'll be no wobbly bits today,' she said to Daisy, who was watching her in wide-eyed wonder from the cot.

Once she'd done her make-up, she slipped on the smart navy dress that had been carefully washed and pressed, and then stepped into her two-tone navy and white heels. Her hat was looking a bit tired, she thought as she anchored it with a pin, but it would have to do. She was just screwing on her second earring when she was startled by Doreen's foghorn yell from the other side of the door.

'Oi, Peggy!' shouted Doreen. 'Martin's 'ere! Wotcha want me to do with 'im?'

'Good grief,' Peggy muttered as she hurried out to rescue him. 'Hello, Martin,' she said fondly. 'My goodness, don't you look smart?'

He kissed her cheek and grinned. 'Only the best will do if I'm to give the bride away.' He looked at his watch. 'Is she ready yet, do you think?'

'I shouldn't think so for a minute. You're very early, and it's mayhem up there,' she said happily. 'Go and find Ron, he's lurking somewhere. There's whisky in the kitchen, courtesy of Charlotte's father. I'm going up to help Kitty get dressed, so I'll call you when she's ready to come down.'

Peggy finished doing up all the tiny buttons that ran down the back of the wedding dress, and Kitty stood in the middle of the untidy bedroom and gazed in amazement at her reflection in the mirror.

The romantic and beautiful white lace gown that her mother had sent from Argentina was just about the most perfect thing she'd ever seen – and she knew she would never look as lovely as she did today. The neckline was scooped, the sleeves were long and flared like small flutes over her fingers, and the bodice was closely boned to give her a good bust-line, and then swooped over her slender hips to flare around her feet.

Kitty eyed the boot that Doreen had painted white to go with her flat pump and felt a great surge of victory. It had been her dream to walk down the aisle unaided by crutches, and today that dream would come true, for she needed only a walking stick now, and that had been covered with tightly wound white ribbon and finished off with a big bow.

'Oh, Kitty, you do look so lovely,' sighed Peggy with a hitch in her voice. 'Roger's a very lucky man.'

'I'm the lucky one,' she replied softly. 'I never thought . . . Especially after my accident, I didn't dare to dream – and then . . .' She hastily blinked back her tears and reached for the veil that her mother had also sent from home. 'Would you mind, Peggy?'

Peggy sniffed back her own tears and fixed the gossamer veil to the delicate tiara of diamonds that had been lent by Roger's mother for the occasion. She fluffed it out so it drifted over Kitty's shoulders. 'There,' she breathed. 'Perfect.'

Kitty put her arms round Peggy and held her close. 'Thank you for everything, dearest Peggy,' she murmured. 'You will never know just how much you've done for me, or how very thankful I am that you came into my life.'

'Don't you dare set me off crying,' Peggy said gruffly as they finally drew apart. 'It's been a privilege and a pleasure to have you here, darling,' she continued. 'And I'm so proud of you today, I could burst.' She blew her nose and reached for the door handle. 'I'll get everyone downstairs and tell Martin to come up.'

Kitty stood in the silent room and regarded her reflection as the sound of running footsteps and excited voices passed her door and continued on down the stairs. She knew now how Charlotte had felt at this moment, and although she was excited and a little nervous, she had absolutely no doubt that she and Roger were meant to be together.

The soft tap on the door broke through her happy reverie and she greeted the very handsome Martin Black. 'Thank you so much for agreeing to do this for me,' she said.

'It's a pleasure,' he replied as his admiring gaze swept over her. 'And, may I say, you look absolutely stunning. Roger is a very lucky chap.'

Kitty picked up the posy Doreen had made from the most perfect pink and white silk roses, grasped her walking stick and took his arm.

'Oi!' yelled Doreen from downstairs. 'Wot you doin' up there, gel? We're all waiting.'

Kitty giggled and Martin smiled. 'We'd better not keep her waiting,' he said. 'These old walls might withstand Hitler's bombs, but Doreen's voice is quite a different matter.'

He escorted her along the short landing to the top of the stairs and she blushed as everyone applauded and told her what a beautiful bride she made and how utterly gorgeous her dress was.

She looked down at them all in admiration. Ron was in a suit and spruced up to the nines with the glamorous Rosie on one arm, and the equally glamorous Charlotte on the other. Doreen was wearing red which came as no surprise, and there was a band of scarlet and gold sequins in her ginger hair just to finish off the startling effect.

Fran was almost as spectacular in green, while Suzy, Jane and Sarah had opted for different shades of blue, and Rita was amazingly pretty and very feminine in pink and white. Cordelia was looking chipper in yellow, her straw hat already drooping from the weight of the silk roses that tumbled all over it, and Peggy looked very elegant in her navy blue as she carried Daisy, who was dressed in pink. Even Harvey had joined in the celebrations, for someone had tied a scarlet bow to his collar, even though he would not be attending the wedding.

Kitty gripped Martin's steadying arm and slowly and carefully negotiated the stairs, which still posed a bit of a problem with her prosthesis but were manageable now. As she reached the hall she was surrounded momentarily by everyone, and then they parted like the Red Sea and followed her and Martin down the steps to the line of gleaming black cars with Air Force pennants fluttering on their bonnets.

'Nervous?' Martin asked as the car drew to a halt outside the Air Force chapel which had been built at Cliffe airfield in 1915.

She smiled back at him as they waited in the car for everyone to disappear inside the plain little wooden building. 'Not a bit,' she replied.

'Then we'd better not keep him waiting any longer.' He squeezed her hand.

Kitty felt light-headed as Charlotte carefully adjusted her veil so it fell over her face and drifted to her shoulders. 'This is it,' she breathed. 'Wish me luck.'

'You don't need it,' said Charlotte as she kissed her softly.

Martin gave a nod to the two young airmen and they opened the doors with a flourish. As Kitty gripped his arm and entered the chapel she heard the sweet sound of the organ playing Handel's *Water Music*, but all her attention was focussed on Roger, who stood beside her brother at the altar. And when he turned to look at her and she saw the adoration in his gaze, she felt quite weak and had to grip Martin's arm a little tighter.

'You look simply breathtaking,' he whispered as she came to stand beside him.

'It's because I'm so happy,' she whispered back before the Air Force padre began to speak.

They gazed into one another's eyes as they solemnly took their vows, and then Roger lifted the veil and kissed her so passionately that everyone in the congregation giggled and tittered. They both blushed scarlet, but the padre was smiling as he asked them to sign the register and have it witnessed by Charlotte and Freddy.

As they turned back to the congregation a great fanfare of trumpets filled the chapel with glorious music, and Kitty held tightly to Roger's arm as they greeted their guests on the way to the door.

'Attenshun! Form archway!' shouted the sergeant who was standing outside.

The two ranks of flying officers raised their ceremonial swords, and the two ranks of firemen from Cliffehaven saluted. Kitty grinned with delight to see John Hicks and all the lovely people who'd carted her back and forth to the Memorial every day, and Martin acknowledged each and every one of them with a salute as they stepped through the archway.

As their guests poured from the chapel there was a great deal of hugging and kissing and admiring words, and after a while, Kitty was swept up into Roger's strong arms and kissed thoroughly before he carried her to the large officers' mess where the reception was to be held.

* * *

It was now three in the afternoon and things were getting loud and a bit out of hand as the dancing began. Kitty watched the fun and noticed that Rita was being whirled round the tiny dance floor by a very dashing young pilot, and they both seemed to be oblivious to everyone else. 'Who's Rita dancing with?' she asked Roger.

'That's Matthew Campion. Jolly good chap. Excellent pilot.'

'Is he single?'

Roger laughed. 'He certainly is. But why should that bother you now you're a married lady?'

'Rita looks quite smitten, and I don't want her to find out he has a wife and three children waiting for him at home,' she replied.

Roger laughed. 'You're getting as bad as Peggy Reilly,' he teased. 'Come on, Mrs Makepeace, it's time we sneaked away and prepared for the next part of our special day. Do you have everything you need?' At her nod they shared a conspiratorial smile and then left the mess.

Freddy shouted for silence several times before he got it. 'If you could all please go outside and form a fairly orderly gathering, the bride and groom are preparing to leave for their honeymoon,' he announced.

Peggy linked arms with Doreen and made sure the rest of her girls were nearby before she ushered them all outside. There was lots of chatter and giggling as they stood about beside the cold and windy runway, and Peggy was rather glad she'd left Daisy in the mess with the NAAFI girls.

'Oh, my Gawd, will yer look at that?' breathed Doreen.

There was a stunned silence among the wedding guests as Kitty emerged from the hangar in her thick trousers, leather flying jacket, helmet and boots. She carried her parachute pack over her shoulder and stood there and waved as Roger joined her in his flying gear.

Peggy could hardly see through her tears as she watched the brave little girl slowly climb the ladder into the Oxford and settle into the pilot's seat. 'Will she be safe?' she asked no one in particular.

'She's been practising ever since our wedding,' said Freddy. 'Roger wangled it with Martin to let her retrain in the Ox Box, and she got her licence endorsed yesterday.'

'Gawd, she's brave,' Doreen sobbed as her mascara ran down her face. 'But she said she'd do it – and 'ere she is.'

Peggy had come well prepared, for she always cried at weddings, and she handed handkerchiefs out to Doreen, Charlotte and Cordelia before she mopped at her own tears.

'It's a bugger, ain't it?' shouted Doreen as the Oxford's engines roared into life and the plane slowly approached the runway. 'Yer put yer make-up on and then yer cry it all off again.'

*　　*　　*

Kitty sat at the controls and regarded the runway ahead of them before she turned to smile at her new husband. 'Are you ready to go to the Lake District, Mr Makepeace?'

'More than ready, Mrs Makepeace.'

She kissed him. 'Then let's start our honeymoon.'

She raced the Oxford down the runway, and as they lifted into the air and circled the airfield to say farewell to all those wonderful people down below, Kitty knew that she was not only in control of the plane, but in control of her life – and that with Roger by her side, she could achieve anything.

Where the Heart Lies

Ellie Dean

Can love survive in a time of war?

February 1941. Julie Harris is working in London's East End as a midwife when a bombing raid destroys her family and the house she grew up in. All she has left is her motherless baby nephew William.

Determined to uphold her promise to her sister to keep William safe until his father, Bill, returns from the war, she accepts a post as a midwife in Cliffehaven on the south coast of England. Here they are taken under the wing of the Reilly family at the Beach View boarding house.

But all too soon Julie learns that Bill is 'missing in action' and William falls dangerously ill. As she begins the long vigil by William's bedside, she fears she will lose the little boy she has grown to love as her own . . .

arrow books